KU-649-599

crimemasterworks

Stanley Ellin

The Eighth Circle

ORION

First published in the USA in 1958

This edition published in 2004 by Orion Books
an imprint of The Orion Publishing Group
Orion House, 5 Upper St Martin's Lane, London, WC2H 9EA

ISBN 0 75285 331 7

Typeset by SetSystems Ltd,
Saffron Walden, Essex

Printed and bound in Great Britain by
Clays Ltd, St Ives plc

To my Mother and Father

—so in the eighth circle are the liars, flatterers, and sellers of office, the fortune tellers, hypocrites, and thieves, the pimps and grafters, and all such scum.

The Inferno

Contents

Part One
Conmy

1

'Truly, truly,' Frank Conmy once said to him, 'this is the dirty, beautiful, golden age of the filing cabinet.'

They were at Frank's apartment in the St Stephen that night, a clear, cold night, moonless but star-studded. Thirty storeys below in Central Park sea lions barked zanily at the sky, and tigers snarled at the siren of an ambulance careening along Fifth Avenue . . .

'The soul is no longer a moth,' Frank said later that evening, swashing a bucketful of cognac around in the balloon glass that might have grown root and stem from his hand. 'No longer does it flutter high and free, gladly destroying itself at the end in the flame of the unknown. It is a dead bug pinned on a board. It is a collection of facts placed between the covers of a cardboard folder and locked into a filing cabinet. But the sweetest merchandise there is, if you know how to put it together, and what to do with it afterward.'

Which, as Murray had to admit, was undeniable. If you learned anything from Frank Conmy it was how to get the facts, and how to put them down on paper, or microfilm, or recording tape, so that the customer could pick up and hold in his hand exactly what he had paid for.

But that was long ago, long before the Lundeen case was a matter of record. That case kicked a lot of nice theory and brandy philosophy into a cocked hat. If Frank had been around when it broke, things might have been different, but he wasn't, having died the year before, fighting to the end against high blood pressure and hypertension and damfool doctors with their damfool injunctions against liquor and cigars and good red meat. So the case was all Murray's. And all trouble.

Taking the long view, the trouble can be spotted in the way Lundeen's folder tells everything and nothing. On the one hand, it tells more about Lundeen and the people he was mixed up with than they ever dreamed would go down on any record. On the other hand, it omits some strangely interesting items. It does not, for example, tell about the curious pet kept by a Special Assistant District Attorney of New York County named Felix LoScalzo. Or that a prominent bookie named George Wykoff found Château d'Yquem too sweet for his palate at the dinner table. Or that Murray's father, a poor grocer and worse poet, once addressed a poem to William Jennings Bryan which began:

> *Let us heal greedy myopia,*
> *And look forward to Utopia*

None of these things are in the record, and yet, as Murray came to see, they are very much part of it. Frank would have slapped his forehead and bellowed at the idea, but Frank had always been a great one for the essentials alone, and the essentials were always what the customer was paying for, no more and no less.

'*Who, what, when, where!*' Frank used to say. 'Get the facts, get them right, and get them down on the record. That's what I've built this agency on. That's what we live on here, while five hundred other pisspot outfits licensed in this state are starving to death!'

The first time Murray ever walked into the waiting room of the office he had heard Frank's voice raised in that declamation behind the door, and had almost walked out. But then his hand had encountered the loose change in his pocket – the reminder that his worldly wealth added up to eighty-five cents – and he had stayed, until the receptionist, a woman with the chilling smile of a volunteer social worker, ushered him into the *sanctum sanctorum*.

Nothing has been changed in the office over the years; it was the same then as it is now. Three sides of the room were intricately carved oak panels; the fourth side was a solid bank of metal filing cabinets. The rug underfoot had a deep, soft pile; all the furniture in the room had the patina that fine wood gets from age and proper care. And looking at Frank Conmy, Murray had the feeling that the same patina overlay the old man himself. Frank was close to seventy at the time, with the solid dewlaps and ruddy-cheeked, white moustached look of a retired chairman of the board. But the eyes narrowly scanning Murray were sharp and alive.

'What did you want to see me about?' There was an immense walnut humidor on the desk before Frank. He pushed the humidor toward Murray and opened its lid with a pudgy, beautifully manicured hand.

'A job,' Murray said. 'I thought you might be able to fix me up with one.'

The hand hesitated on the lid of the humidor and then gently closed it. 'What gave you that idea?'

'Somebody from your office – a fellow named Collins – was talking to me last week. He said he was quitting, and you might have an empty spot.'

'And what made Jack Collins think you were qualified to work here?'

'Well, I'm with a law firm – Cunliffe, Mead, and Appel – and he's been around there a few times on jobs for you. We got to know each other that way, and I guess he figured I could swing the deal.'

'Maybe he did. But I'm sorry to say, Mr—?'

'Kirk. Murray Kirk.'

'I'm sorry to say, Mr Kirk, that Jack is now somewhere on

his way out to the Coast on a deal of his own, and not in a position to talk up for you. However, if he ever does get in touch with me, and there is an opening—'

'I know,' Murray said. 'Don't call us; we'll call you.'

'Oh, come, you're being unreasonable, Mr Kirk. You're letting your temper show.' Frank Conmy smiled with venomous sweetness, a thin drawing back of the lips that flashed a set of teeth too perfect to be his own. 'Don't you think someone in your spot should have sense enough to sit on his temper?'

Murray got up from his chair. 'Not unless he's being paid a salary for it. Meanwhile, since I'm not on the payroll—'

'Sit down,' Frank Conmy said, and Murray sat down. In the long minute that followed he came to understand pretty clearly what a man can feel while a bilious income-tax collector sizes him up and down wondering what to make of him. He was given that treatment until his stomach started to crawl.

'Are you still working for Cunliffe?' Frank asked suddenly.

'No. I quit this morning.'

'What did you do while you were there? What kind of duties did you have?'

'Technically, I was a law clerk. Actually, I did a little of everything. Interviewed the cheaper clients, handled a few briefs, did legwork, dusted the office. Oh, yes, once a month I had to go to Altman's to buy some detachable collars for Mr Cunliffe.'

'How long did this go on?'

'About a year.'

'And before that?'

Murray thought that over. 'How long before?'

'As far back as you want to go. But tell it fast, Mr Kirk; you're living on borrowed time.'

'All right,' Murray said. 'Raised on the West Side around 116th and Broadway, where my father ran a grocery. Went to City College and then into the army. When I got out of the army I went to St John's Law on the GI Bill. Passed the Bar, and got a job with Cunliffe, Mead, and Appel. And here I am.'

'Why?' Frank asked. 'What made you quit the job with Cunliffe?'

'Money.'

'How much money?'

'They were paying me forty a week,' Murray said. 'Before taxes.'

Frank snorted. 'And you lived on that?'

'In a manner of speaking.'

'And if I offered you fifty a week, it would be a big break, wouldn't it?'

'No,' Murray said, 'it wouldn't. But I'll take it to start with.'

'I thought you would,' said Frank Conmy.

Not long before his death Frank talked about that day.

'I remember it well,' he said. 'Jack Collins had told me you might be stopping by. "Watch for a fellow with a choir-boy face, and a suit with a high shine on it, and a hungry look in his eye," he told me, "and grab him if you can." I knew you the minute you started speaking your piece, because nobody on this green footstool ever had a hungrier look in his eye than you did. I could have bought you, body and soul, for a five-dollar bill.'

'You old son of a bitch. And you let me sweat it out like that?'

'I did.' Frank sighed wistfully. 'God forgive me for saying it, Murray, but what other fun is left for a man who can't get on top of a woman any more than to kick the young ones who can right square in the belly? However, that's not the point of it. What I'm trying to teach you is that a hungry look is the biggest asset a man can show me. That's just what I was buying when I took you on for sixty a week.'

'Fifty.'

'Sixty,' said Frank equably, 'and let's not argue about it. You know how any kind of arguing sets my blood to fizzing like seltzer water.'

*

It had been fifty a week to start, and a hard fifty at that. Frank Conmy's office had two doors. Murray had entered through one; he was led out through the other into the suite of rooms beyond: the investigators' room, the stenographers' room, the storeroom, the photography lab. From Frank's manner of introduction he gathered that the most important person behind the scenes was Mrs Knapp, who served simultaneously as his personal secretary, supervisor of the stenographers' pool, and assistant keeper of the keys. A small, trim woman with a dazzling, blue-tinted coiffure, she must have been extremely pretty thirty years before. The shadow of the good looks remained, but now they seemed as formidable as the lines of a pocket battleship.

While she filled out various employment forces for Murray she talked away at machine-gun tempo, laying down the law.

'Mr Conmy is very strict about certain things, Mr Kirk. You are not to loiter around the stenographers' room, nor to have anything to do with the girls. You understand exactly what I mean by that, don't you?'

'I do.'

'Now, the confidential files are in Mr Conmy's office, and I want to make it clear that they are not your concern at all. If you need material from them, or wish to return material to them, you will come to me, and I will take care of it. And you are not to leave anything from the files on your desk when you leave the office. Make sure they are all in my hands even if you are just leaving for a lunch period. Is that clear?'

'It is.'

'Any time you enter or leave the office you will sign the roster here – this one on my desk – in the proper column, and note the time. If you wish to make yourself available for extra duties after your regular work you will also sign the Availability column and write down where you may be reached. And please don't sign for availability unless you really mean it. It's a nuisance to go hunting around for a man at the last minute.'

'What's the advantage in signing for availability at all?' Murray asked.

'You'll be paid overtime for such duties. And oh, yes, Mr Conmy prefers that you don't go around talking about your work to anyone on the outside. It's customary for our people to simply say that they work for a research organization, if the matter comes up among strangers.'

'And among friends?'

'You'll have to use your common sense for that, Mr Kirk. Yes, sign here – and here. Do you have any questions?'

'No,' Murray said. And then he couldn't resist saying, 'It's not much like the movies, is it?'

Mrs Knapp looked at him shrewdly. 'No, it isn't, Mr Kirk. We don't supply booze, blondes, or bullets. As a matter of fact, no one here is licensed to carry firearms except Mr Conmy himself, and I very much doubt if Mr Conmy knows one end of a gun from the other. Get it into your head, Mr Kirk, that we are a legitimate business firm, authorized by the New York State Director of Licences to perform certain lawful services. And you, young man, are as much bound by the laws of this state as the next person. I trust you'll always keep this in mind.'

'I always will.'

'Good. Now, you'll start on the executive files. Just follow me. There's an empty place at Mr Manfredi's desk, and Mr Manfredi here will explain what the executive files are. This is Mr Kirk, Mr Manfredi. I'll leave him in your charge.'

There were a dozen desks in the big room, half of them occupied. Their occupants watched Mrs Knapp's departure in silence, eyed their new confrère incuriously, and went back to work. Manfredi, thin, long-beaked, and as sad-looking as a captive crane, turned to Murray.

'And what got *you* into this trap, my friend?'

'There was a fellow worked here – Jack Collins. Did you know him?'

'You're sitting in his chair right now. He and I are like that, only he got this bug to open his own agency in LA.'

'Anyhow, he let me know how much he was making here. It sounded good.'

'Probably did. But Jack was a real hatchet on the job, worked mostly on bonus cases. It takes a long time to get to that. I mean, just in case you figure you struck oil here.'

'Well,' Murray said, 'when it comes down to that, time is all I've got to invest.'

'Fair enough,' said Manfredi. 'Now I'll show you what you're investing it in.'

The executive file was a stack of autobiographical résumés, some typed, many mimeographed, a few printed.

'This is the angle,' Manfredi explained. 'When a white-collar character wants a job with some big outfit around town he doesn't show his face there. He just mails off one of these things with his life history on it, and then prays. Then the company ships the stuff to us, and we make a check of everything in it. You know how to backtrack a lead? I mean, check off all this dope on schools and jobs and so on?'

'I did some for the place I worked at before this.'

'Good. Then every place where you can okay it, you put down OK and your initials, and where you find the guy is lying you mark down NG and your initials. If there's something you can't clear up one way or the other, you leave a blank. Leave too many blanks or get caught faking reports, and you're out of a job.

'There's some other touches, too. For one thing we've already got a file on a lot of these characters; there's nothing like this young executive type for floating around. For another thing – and this you don't go around talking about – you keep our files up to date with everything you pick up from these résumés as you go along. Everything we get on these guys goes into the freezer.

'The other job you've got with this stuff is a pain. Every morning they'll dump a lot of newspapers here. You've got to comb them double-quick, and dig out anything that can go into the files. The big ones like the *Times* are good for marriages, deaths, job promotions and such. The tabloids feed the dirt. You look through them for any scandals where the guy might be the executive type, and where you can come up with something good you just dump it into the file. And that's about the whole deal.'

Murray said, 'It sounds like a nice day's work.'

'Oh, you'll get used to it. Anyhow, it keeps you off your feet, which is something. And it's a helluva lot better than writs and subpoenas. You've never been baptized, have you?'

'In what way?'

'That's what they call it around here the first time a woman spits in your eye because you hand her a writ. There's something about a legal paper that just makes a woman's mouth fill up, and then, brother, you're in for it. You'll find yourself ducking like an expert after a while.'

Murray looked at him and saw that he meant it.

'Is that what most of the job is like?' Murray asked. 'This stuff and legal papers?'

'Hell, no. This is a big operation, friend. All you know about it so far is the tail end. You stick it out for a while, and you'll find out what the rest of the deal is like.'

Murray found out. He worked the executive file, he served legal papers and was baptized, he went on cases with Bruno Manfredi, and there came a time when he went on cases alone. Along the way he made the discovery that if you're paid well enough for lifting a rock you don't get too queasy at the sight of whatever is crawling underneath it.

Out of this he got not only money, but through some slow, mysterious, unplanned process Frank Conmy's friendship as well. There was, Murray came to see, a terrible loneliness in Frank, the loneliness of a man who has kept his guard up so long that he has frozen rigid in that position. But then as brisk talks about agency business turned to amiable conversations the thaw set in. The first time Murray was ever in the apartment at the St Stephen was on his thirtieth birthday, when Frank invited him up to celebrate at a party for two. It was a tremendously successful party, running through eight hours of monologue by

Frank – part lecture, part reminiscence, and largely pornographic – and a quart of Grand Armagnac which left Murray praying for a swift death to end the retching vertigo that seized him at the dawn's early light.

After that night there were many others when they dined together and drank together, and occasionally went on the town together. Frank had a weird catholicity of taste, and through him Murray learned that grand opera could be a rousing experience, that Western movies served better than Nembutal for inducing sleep, that horse races could be enlivened by betting more on them than you could afford to lose, and that any stage production was worth seeing if it had been written by Sean O'Casey or by Rodgers and Hammerstein. Altogether, what you might call a heady draught of the local brew, strongly flavoured by Frank Conmy's talk and Frank Conmy's brandy.

There were mild reverberations in the office, of course. Murray was shaving at the mirror of the men's room one afternoon when one of the investigators – a sour character named McNally – walked in. McNally studied himself briefly in the mirror and then turned to Murray. 'Tell me, dearie,' he said in a loud falsetto for the benefit of everyone else in the room, 'if I had those looks, do you think the old man would go for me, too?'

The trouble was that Murray knew what was rankling in McNally, and couldn't altogether blame the man for it. So when he put down his razor and swung, it was half-heartedly and ineffectually. McNally swung back, both punches missed, and the two men clutched each other and clumsily wrestled around like a pair of inept preliminary fighters until Bruno Manfredi pulled them apart.

Later, Bruno shook his head at Murray. 'Jesus, to fall for a stupid crack like that. You've got to laugh off that kind of stuff. Otherwise, you'll get people figuring it's on the level.'

'What do you figure?'

'Who, me? I figure it the way it is. The old man never had any family or anything, so you're the one he picked on to be sonny boy. And don't let it bother you any, pal. It's like money in the bank.'

It didn't bother Murray, because he knew when he finally browbeat Frank into giving him a partnership that he was worth it. He was top man in the agency by then; he handled only the big cases. He had sold Frank the idea of starting the payroll-guard service, which proved immediately profitable. He had convinced Frank that expensive publicity can pay off, and had hired the public-relations outfit which made it pay off in radio and TV guest appearances for Frank, and through gossip columns where the Conmy name could become familiar to fat cats in trouble.

The partnership lasted two years. The day after it was ended by Frank's death Murray learned with considerable gratification but small surprise that he had been willed his partner's entire share of the agency.

So there it was. He had walked into the office ten years before with eighty-five cents as his worldly wealth. Now – almost on the anniversary of that day – he followed the scanty funeral cortege in his own Cadillac, and on the way back from the services he stopped at the St Stephen to sign on the dotted line as the new tenant of Frank's apartment.

He took possession that evening. At midnight, he drank a final toast to the departed spirit from the familiar balloon glass, and then smashed the glass in the fireplace. It was a self-conscious gesture made on maudlin impulse, but it was well intended. He had liked Frank, and wanted to say farewell in a way that Frank himself might have approved. He thought – he really believed at that moment – that he was saying farewell to Frank.

But there were times after that – bad nights now and then – when he found himself alone in the apartment wondering about it. Then oddly irrelevant thoughts would move through his mind in a disorderly procession. Like a pointless parade they would circle around and around, going nowhere. Thoughts of his father, who had sold groceries at a loss and written bad poetry, or of the wall of filing cabinets in the office with the double locks on them, or of Frank, or even of the people locked away in the compartments of the St Stephen below him. Too many people. Too many thoughts.

And all of them, like the scattered pieces of jigsaw puzzle, waiting for the Lundeen case to come along and start putting the picture together.

2

Although his name is not to be found on any record at all, it was Otto Helmke who put the first piece into place.

Helmke was a waspish, dried-out little householder in the Ridgewood district, the doting father of a remarkably *zoftik* young daughter, and the fractious neighbour of Police Officer Everett Walsh. The feud between Helmke and Walsh had gone on for years, dating back to some hair-splitting argument over property lines. It culminated the night that Helmke walked into his garage and caught his daughter and the oldest Walsh boy hotly tangled together in the rear of the family car.

Helmke took his revenge in two ways: he belted the boy off the premises with a rake handle, and then in the small hours he sat down at his kitchen table to write a letter. Its opening paragraph simply raised the question of how anyone supposedly living on a policeman's salary could live the way Everett Walsh did. Its contents then went on to describe with astonishing accuracy every detail of Walsh's financial life, with emphasis on the two new cars in Walsh's garage, an expensive refurnishing of the Walsh home, and a twenty-four-foot cabin cruiser named the *Peggy W.* moored in Sheepshead Bay. It was a letter which Helmke had dreamed of writing many times before, and he read it through now with pleasure. Then he signed it 'A Worried Citizen' and addressed it to 'The District Attorney, New York City'. It was his mistaken impression that there was just one district attorney in the city, but, as it happened, it was not a mistake that mattered.

Countrymen west of the Hudson, where they know about such things, have observed that seed, even if tossed recklessly in the air, will take root if it lands on fertile ground. The fertile ground in this case was a Special Grand Jury recently set up to investigate corruption among New York's Finest. Helmke's letter landed before this grand jury, and then, after close investigation by two bright young men from the District Attorney's office, so did Walsh.

What Walsh had to say was graphically summed up by the first tabloid headlines to deal with it as COP BLOWS WHISTLE ON PALS. One pal called to the spotlight before the grand jury turned out to be a bookie on a phenomenal scale. George Wykoff, who operated a city-wide betting ring from an estate on Staten Island, the most remote and pastoral of New York's five boroughs.

If Walsh had blown a whistle, Wykoff blew the kind of trumpet that Joshua must have sounded before Jericho, and at its blast the walls of the Police Department came tumbling down with a crash. Three hundred men, ranging in rank from patrolmen to deputy inspectors, were caught in the wreckage. Most of them crawled free by hastily resigning or retiring from the force. Twenty of them, however, trapped by conflicting testimony before the grand jury, were indicted for perjury and held for trial. Arnold Lundeen was one of the luckless twenty.

So Otto Helmke, whose name is not to be found on any record, cast his bread upon the waters, and it came back increased three-hundredfold. A fair return, you might say, and still he was not happy about it. He lost appetite, snapped continually at his stolid wife and chastened daughter, and brooded behind his newspaper for hours on end.

It is always hard for a man to know that he is the agent of Divine Providence and yet remain anonymous.

Part Two
Conmy and Kirk

1

At noon on Thanksgiving Day, Murray was in the bathtub, immersed both in *Gulliver's Travels* and in water so hot that it was an exquisite agony to wiggle a toe in it. When the phone rang he tried to close his ears to it, then finally heaved himself from the tub and went into the bedroom, dripping as he went.

'What the hell, Marge,' he said into the phone.

The girl at the switchboard said: 'I'm sorry, Mr Kirk. I know you didn't want any calls put through today, but this gentleman's been at it since nine o'clock, and I finally had to tell him I'd see if you were in. Are you?'

'Who's the gentleman?'

'It's a Mr Ralph Harlingen. He said you'd know him from the Rector Street office.'

The name was a familiar one, because the Harlingen office was an old client. It was one of those overgrown law firms around Wall Street where ten senior partners and twenty juniors politely argued corporation cases for lush fees. Conmy-Kirk had handled its executive files for a long time.

But Ralph Harlingen was one of the lowliest juniors there, very small fry, indeed, and his only distinction, as far as Murray knew, came from the fact that his father was head man of the outfit. Murray had met him a few times at the Harlingen office, a big, rangy man with crewcut hair showing some grey at the temples, and a manner uncomfortably youthful for his years.

They had talked about Ivy League football, a subject about which Harlingen was evidently as passionate as Murray was indifferent, and that was it. It was hard to imagine what he could be calling about.

On the phone Harlingen was voluble with apologies, then quickly came to the point.

'You have no idea, fella,' he said, 'but right now you're the one indispensable man. Look, did you ever hear of somebody named Arnold Lundeen? Does that ring a little bell somewhere?'

'No.'

'Oh,' said Harlingen. 'Well, anyhow, he's a client of mine, one of the cops indicted in that Wykoff mess. And I don't have to tell you this case has nothing to do with Rector Street, fella. I've left the old shop, and I'm on my own now. How does that sound to you?'

Murray shifted his feet out of the pool of water collecting on the rug beneath him. 'Fine,' he said. 'Fine. It's a big step.'

'Right. And what you and I have to do now is put our heads together over the case. The thing is that Mrs Harlingen and I are leaving tomorrow to spend the rest of the weekend with her people in Philadelphia, so I'd like to see you today. Tonight, possibly. We're having open house, and there'll be a lot of folks here, but we can fit business into it somehow. And the drinks are the best. Positively ambrosial.'

'Fine,' said Murray. 'I'll be there, Mr Harlingen.'

'Ralph, fella. Ralph.'

'Sure,' Murray said. 'Thanks a lot, Ralph.'

Good old Ralph.

Murray put down the phone, then lifted it and dialled the Conmy-Kirk number. The office was closed for business Sundays and holidays, but one of the men was always supposed to be there on stand-by duty. In this case it was Lou Strauss, an old-timer.

'Do me a favour, Lou,' Murray said. 'Check that master index in Mrs Knapp's desk and see if we have files listed for two names. That's Ralph Harlingen and Arnold Lundeen.'

'Is that the Harlingen who called up here this morning? I told him he could get you at the hotel.'

'He did. Check him and Lundeen.'

Murray waited briefly, and then Strauss picked up the phone.

'Harlingen's name is down here, Murray, so there's a file on him, all right. But nothing on the other character.'

'I figured not. Anyhow, leave a note for Mrs Knapp to have Harlingen's file on my desk when I get in tomorrow. Were there any other calls?'

'Only Mrs Knapp,' said Strauss. 'She wanted to make sure I was on the job. Thank God I was.'

At ten o'clock Murray drove to the Harlingen apartment and found it in one of the gigantic new glass and aluminium boxes that tower, terrace to terrace, over the grimy banks of the East River. The apartment itself was a Swedish rhapsody of foam rubber, sleek furniture, and long, low couches on which people perched in a row like birds on a telephone wire. Good, uninhibited talkers, their voices filled the place with a nervous clamour.

Murray, taken in hand by Mrs Harlingen, an intense and wiry blonde, worked free of her and idly drifted from group to group until he finally found himself pinned down by a young man in a black corduroy jacket with a velveteen collar.

'The *most* unforgettable character, for God's sake,' the young man said bitterly. 'How do you like that? The *most* unforgettable character!'

'Who?' asked Murray pacifically.

'Not *who*,' said the young man. 'It's the *most* that's wrong. Don't you see? Unforgettable doesn't take the superlative degree. You can't have a partly unforgettable thing, can you? If something is unforgettable, it's always there in your memory, isn't it?'

'I guess it is.'

'What do you mean, guess?' the young man said belligerently. 'Either you know or you don't. It's your kind of guessing that's destroying the purity of the language while we stand here.'

A tall girl with black bangs jostled Murray with her elbow. 'Don't mind Donald,' she said. 'He's hipped on the subject.'

The young man stared at her incredulously. 'Hipped,' he said, 'oh, my God, hipped!' and stalked off in outrage.

The girl watched him go, then turned apologetically to Murray. 'It's not altogether his fault,' she said. 'He's really awfully bright, but he went to Oxford on a Fulbright, and it's sort of an obsession. What do you do?'

'Research.'

'Oh? In what media?'

'No media,' Murray said. 'Just facts and figures.'

The girl's eyebrows went up. 'That sounds perfectly stupefying,' she said, and it was clear that he had lost her.

At the buffet he poured himself a finger of Courvoisier. The man next to him, stout, red-faced, and with a tonsure of white hair fringing a splendidly gleaming scalp, followed suit, but kept the bottle tilted until the glass was almost brimming. They touched glasses solemnly and drank, and the stout man snorted with pleasure.

'Know why I'm here?' he demanded.

'Because you're in media,' Murray told him.

'Hell, no. I wouldn't know media from a hole in the ground. I'm in banking; handle investments for the Commercial Trust downtown. Name's Walters.'

'All right, I give up,' Murray said. 'Why are you here?'

'Because,' Walters said triumphantly, 'I'm the downstairs neighbour. Way these places are built you can hear a pin drop, and sometimes with these shindigs going on I thought the ceiling was coming down on my head. I'm a peaceable man, don't like any fuss between neighbours, as who does? So I just made a deal with friend Harlingen. He can have a crowd up here any time he wants, and in return I'm free to join in and drink up my troubles in his liquor. And he serves the best, son. I must be five hundred bucks ahead of the game already.'

' "Good fences make good neighbours," ' said Murray.

'What's that mean?'

'It's from a poem,' Murray said, 'by Robert Frost.'

Walters blinked. 'Is he here?'

'I wouldn't be surprised,' said Murray.

He was alone, nursing the last of his drink, when a child appeared before him. She bore the sallow-complexioned, nail-bitten, pony-tailed earmarks of adolescence, but her mouth was a bright, sticky smear of lipstick, and her shoulders sagged in a world-weary droop. She looked like a bony question mark.

'Hello,' said the child. 'I'm Megan Harlingen. Daddy's told me all about you.'

'Delighted,' said Murray. 'And where have you been all along?'

'Oh, out to the movies. It's a form of escape for me. I mean, literally. I can't understand these parties, can you? They're so full of people getting potted and being pretentious.'

Murray hastily set down his drink. 'I don't know,' he said cautiously. 'They look like nice enough people to me.'

'Then you don't know them at all,' Megan said firmly. 'Actually, they're all full of emotional conflicts. Just *writhing* with them. Practically everybody here is in analysis, you know. Have you ever been in analysis?'

'Not yet,' said Murray. 'Have you?'

'Only for a little while, and it was deadly, deadly, deadly. Then when Grandfather raised a stink about it, they let me stop going. Of course, Grandfather's a sort of religious fanatic; he would be dreadfully anti-Freudian. You know what he told me once? He said that if heathen witch doctors went to hell, so did psychiatrists! Isn't that the everlasting end?'

'I wouldn't be too hard on him,' Murray said. 'He's probably just a little old-fashioned.'

'A *little*? You should have heard what he said about newfangled ideas when Daddy left the old office and set up practice for himself. The *scene* they had. And the things Grandfather had to say about people who go to work for criminals! You could hear every word of it right in my bedroom even with the door shut.

'Of course, Daddy's been unspeakably heroic about the whole thing. I mean, taking criminal cases and all. He's the first one in the family to ever do it, and it's all so new. I suppose that's why he's asked you to help him, isn't it?'

'M-m-m, I doubt it. Usually, my job is just to help on details.'

'What kind of details? You know, I think it's absolutely heroic being a private detective. You *are* a real private detective, aren't you?'

'I am.'

'I mean, because you don't really look like one. But do you have adventures?'

'What kind of adventures?'

'Oh, you know what I mean. Don't you ever watch TV or anything?'

'Only Kukla, Fran and Ollie,' said Murray.

'Well, no wonder,' Megan said in relief. 'Now you come along with me, and I'll show you.'

She guided him to a bedroom strewn with feminine things in wild disorder, pushed him into an armchair facing a television set, and, after a brief search among the channels, located Private-Eye Brannigan battering his way through the Case of the Missing Finger. Then she briskly swept the bed clear of books and garments and settled there tailor-fashion, chewing away at the ragged edges of her nails, her eyes fixed raptly on the screen.

The darkness of the room, the patter of television dialogue, were treacherous temptations. Murray closed his eyes for a second, found he couldn't open them, and came to with a start only when Private-Eye Brannigan had cleared up his case with a salvo of pistol shots. The blare of three successive commercials finished the wakening process, and then the eleven-o'clock newscaster appeared, looking, if anything, even more steel-eyed than Private-Eye Brannigan.

'What's the news from all parts tonight?' he demanded. 'Well, the holiday traffic toll continues to rise. The latest local casualty was sixty-year-old Charles Pirozy, a Westchester resident, who was wantonly struck down and killed by a hit-and-run driver at Madison Avenue and Sixtieth Street one hour ago. Drivers, we urge you—'

Megan hastily arose and turned off the set. 'Happy Thanksgiving,' she said. 'Ugh.'

'It didn't bother you when Private-Eye Brannigan was shooting them down right and left,' Murray pointed out with malice.

'That's different,' protested Megan. 'Anyhow—'

The lights of the room suddenly went on, and they both turned to blink at the figure in the doorway. It was Harlingen.

'Oh, there you are,' he said, and then he groaned. 'God, Megan, this room is the foulest mess. How can you stand having anyone see it like this?'

She glowered at him. 'It isn't a mess. Anyhow, Dr Langstein said it was perfectly normal for somebody my age to be sloppy. You heard him say it.'

'I only wish he had to live in this room for a while, that's what I wish,' said Harlingen. 'Now get that goo off your face and go to sleep.'

At the doorway Murray turned. 'Good night, Megan,' he said, and saw the smeared lips start to tremble, the drooping shoulders droop more than ever. 'Hey,' he said, but Megan wheeled sharply around, turning her back to him.

'Kids,' said Harlingen darkly as he pulled the door shut. 'Fourteen years old, act four, and expect to be treated like forty.' He led the way to a small room sparsely furnished as a study, and dropped into a chair behind a littered desk. 'No, you won't find much worth while there,' he said, as Murray squatted to study the contents of the low bookshelves along the wall. 'Most of it's jurisprudence – I took them along when I left the office –

and those small ones are poetry by my wife. Privately printed, of course. She doesn't write very good poetry, really, but she finds it a wonderful means of expressing herself.'

'I know,' said Murray. 'She was telling me about it.'

'She was? Then you probably had a chance to see for yourself the kind of person she is. *Muy simpática*. And very outgoing. Very dynamic. As a matter of fact, she was the main force in getting me to strike out for myself.'

'You mean, practising criminal law?'

'That's right. And I've been very lucky in finding a client like Lundeen right off. You know, usually when you open shop like this you can go round in circles for a long time trying to dig up a client, but here I am, just getting started, and with a case ready for action.' Harlingen picked up a pencil and tapped its point in a nervous rhythm on the desk. 'The trouble is,' he said plaintively, 'that the case itself poses so damn many problems. I mean, there's a lot of investigation to be done, a lot of legwork. And when you're without a staff of any sort there's just no way to cope. That's where you come in.'

'Whoa,' said Murray. 'I'm not in yet.'

Harlingen looked startled. 'But I thought—'

'I know. But from my angle – from Conmy-Kirk's angle – there are things about this kind of case I don't like.'

'Ah, look. It's a plain and simple indictment for perjury in the first. If I gave the impression—'

'Just how plain and simple?'

'Well, Lundeen's a patrolman, a plain clothes man attached to the Vice Squad. Some time ago he arrested a man named Schrade, Eddie Schrade, for bookmaking. Then, when the Wykoff scandal broke, Schrade was called before the grand jury where he said his arrest was a fake; he was just a stand-in for the real culprit, an Ira Miller, one of Wykoff's big shots.'

'It takes two witnesses to make a perjury case.'

'Miller's the other one. He told the grand jury he had paid Lundeen a thousand dollars to arrest Schrade in his place, and when Lundeen wouldn't recant *his* testimony he was indicted.

Of course, Miller and Schrade are the sort of hoodlums who'd swear their own mother into the electric chair. The whole thing smells of frame-up a mile away.'

'Maybe yes,' said Murray. 'Maybe no.'

Harlingen flushed. 'Look,' he said earnestly, 'this might sound a little top-heavy, it might sound like something you've heard before, but I count myself a pretty good judge of human nature. And before I agreed to take Lundeen as a client I made it a point to have a long, long talk with him. Not just about the case, mind you. What I really wanted to do was to get deep down inside, to sort of poke and prod around and see the man underneath. And what I saw was all right. I wouldn't have touched the case if I didn't think so.'

'Oh, Jesus,' Murray said. 'Do you think that's what I'm worried about: whether your man is a deserving case or not?'

'From what you said—'

'I didn't say anything about that. You ought to know, Mr Harlingen, that an outfit like mine doesn't give a dawn about a client's character. For that matter, neither do most of the lawyers I know. We'd all be out of business tomorrow, if we did.' Murray shook his head. 'That isn't the point at all. What I'm getting at is that your case is tied right in with this Wykoff business, and I don't like it. Wykoff's testified that he's been paying one million dollars a year in graft to the police for the past ten years. What does it mean, now that he's blown the lid off the deal? It means that the whole department is as sick and surly as a bagful of rattlesnakes, and it's not a bag I want to stick my hand into. Conmy-Kirk has always gotten along with the police on a nice, quiet, live-and-let-live basis. We'll string along with the policy now.'

'But it's *my* case,' argued Harlingen. 'If there's any trouble, I'm the one to take the responsibility.'

'Maybe, but the axe would still fall on us. In this state, Mr Harlingen, an agency is hedged all round by a lot of nasty little statutes. If the police wanted to be literal about them, Conmy-Kirk would be in a fine mess.'

'Oh, great,' said Harlingen. 'That's great.' He held the pencil up to his eye and sighted along it. 'What you're telling me, then, is that if Lundeen wants his chance in court he'd damn well better go to some big law office where they have the staff to handle it personally. That's what it comes down to, isn't it?'

'No, it isn't. There's a couple of other agencies – Inter-American, Fleischer – pretty good outfits that might do just the job you want. Or,' said Murray in sudden enlightenment, 'have you already tried them?'

The pencil cracked apart in Harlingen's hand. 'Sure, I tried them. Not that I didn't have you in mind as the logical first choice, but, what the hell, Lundeen isn't a rich man, and it was a case of trying to shop cheap at the outset. It didn't matter. Every one of them is cold on this thing. The kind of work some of them offered to do wouldn't even scratch the surface.'

'I see,' said Murray. It was embarrassing to watch Harlingen's naked distress.

'And I can't turn the case over to somebody else,' Harlingen said. 'I just can't see myself doing that.'

'Why not? There are law offices that would be glad to handle it. You could work along with one of them for the experience.'

'At my age?' Harlingen leaned forward toward Murray and spoke with slow intensity. 'Do you know how old I am? I'm forty-five, man. Forty-five years old.'

'What about it? You've still got a long time to go.'

'Go where?' Harlingen demanded. 'Ah, you don't understand. You don't understand at all. Don't you see that now that I found the guts to walk out on a job as oldest office boy in town I *can't* crawl back into another one like it? That's what's at stake here. It's not just a matter of handling a case on my own. I know I can do a decent job on any case, if I have the chance. But I have to – well, it's terribly important for me to get the chance. That's the thing.'

'For you, yes,' said Murray wearily. 'But I have to think of my agency's interests.'

'That's definite?'

'Yes.'

Harlingen hefted the broken pieces of pencil in his palm. Then he suddenly asked, 'You wouldn't mind if I got in touch with you again about this, I suppose?'

'I'm in the office every afternoon,' Murray said.

2

Cold November rain suddenly spattered against the window, and Mrs Knapp rose from her chair, flicked on the overhead light, and drew the window curtains together. Murray waited until she sat down beside the desk again and picked up her pad. He flicked a finger at the Harlingen file before him.

'So eight years ago he sent this résumé and job application to Conway Industrial, asking for a place in their legal department. And he was turned down. We know that, because we happen to handle Conway, but there's more to it than meets the eye. I'll bet my money against anybody's marbles that there's a load of his applications stuck away in files all over town. And all of them turned down the same way.'

'It's possible.'

'It is, it is. The first few times, his old man must have put the quietus on things whenever he was asked for references. Then, all of a sudden, our boy finds that he's over the forty-year mark. I leave it to you what chances anybody over forty has of getting a job with Conway. Or with any outfit like it.'

Mrs Knapp's lip curled. 'If you're asking me to feel sorry for someone who had a good thing with the J. D. Harlingen office, and who deliberately—'

'Uh-uh. *Cherchez la femme.* Also, *cherchez* the psychiatrist. Mrs Harlingen is untangling her complexes by writing lousy poetry and having it printed up in nice expensive books. She and that professor of theirs must have convinced Harlingen that criminal law is just what he needs for his aching soul.'

'What about it?'

'Ah, but they overlooked one small point. If you foul up a poem, nobody goes to jail. It's a little different with a perjury indictment.'

'That's the client's concern,' said Mrs Knapp. 'If we're not working on the case, there's no reason for us to get upset about it.'

'Take my word for it, I am not upset.'

'Well, if not about this, then about something else. You've been awfully edgy about a lot of things lately, Mr Kirk. I've been thinking that a vacation might be called for.'

'It might. A tall, willowy, blonde vacation. Cool-eyed but hot-blooded. Stupid but sinuous.'

'Strange,' observed Mrs Knapp, 'how all men's minds run in the same channel.'

'Do they? I guess they do. Tell me, Mrs Knapp, when you first came to work here, did Frank Conmy by any chance make a pass at you?'

'The question is out of order, Mr Kirk. And we have a full day's work to clear up.'

'Did he?'

Mrs Knapp smiled. 'He did. That was during Prohibition, so I had him take me over to a very nice speakeasy on East Thirty-ninth Street for a drink after work. He met my husband there. Mr Knapp was the bartender.'

Murray slid down in his chair, closed his eyes, and folded his hands comfortably over his belt buckle. 'That's a terribly depressing story,' he said. 'Let's get on with the day's work instead.'

It was a routine Friday – out-of-town reports to collate, assignments to arrange, all punctuated by incessant phone calls – but a vague restlessness in him made it seem endless. At four o'clock he drew open the window curtains and stood looking down at what could be seen of New York five storeys below. Umbrellas, the first sprinkling of packages done up in Christmas wrappings, the first Santa Claus of the season, a scarecrow with the inevitable hand bell and tripod. He was calculating the chances of tossing a quarter into the collection pot from fifty feet above it, when the receptionist walked in and called him to attention.

'It's a young lady, Mr Kirk. She says it's about an Arnold Lundeen.'

Murray pocketed the quarter. 'What would you say she was, Miss Whiteside? Wife, sister, or friend of the family?'

'Engaged to him, I guess.' Miss Whiteside had the hauteur of a tearoom hostess, a passion for confession magazines, and a fine eye for detail. 'She's wearing a ring. One of those half-carat bargain things.'

'Anything else?'

'Well,' said Miss Whiteside, 'she's awfully pretty.'

Her eye had not deceived her. The girl was more than pretty; she was astonishingly beautiful. Ebony-dark hair, long-lashed blue eyes, camellia skin – or, Murray wondered, was gardenia supposed to be the word for it. Whatever it was, it was incredible that a cop, a dumb, dishonest New York cop, should ever have come into the possession of anything like this.

She sat down, placed a small overnight bag beside the chair, and opened her coat. It was a bulky tweed, the kind that Frank Conmy used to snarl at as Madison Avenue dowdy. 'Whenever I see a fine-looking woman wearing stuff like that,' he had complained, 'I always find myself wondering what the hell she's ashamed of.'

'I'm Ruth Vincent,' the girl said; 'Arnold Lundeen's fiancée.' She sat primly on the edge of the chair, her hands clasped in her lap like an illustration of decorous good posture. 'Mr Harlingen called me this morning before he left town. He told me all about talking to you last night, but he said that maybe if I spoke to you personally – I mean, explained things from Arnold's point of view – you might change your mind. That's why I'm here.'

'I see.' Murray carefully arranged two pieces of paper on the desk, edge to edge. 'How is it that Lundeen isn't here himself? Something wrong with him?'

'No, but he's working today, and I'm not. An army friend of his got him a job in a diner, but it's way out on Long Island, near East Hampton, so he stays out there during the week.'

'That sounds pretty inconvenient for all concerned, doesn't it?'

Ruth Vincent said in a tight voice: 'It's not easy for a policeman under suspension to get a job anywhere, Mr Kirk. He takes what he can get.'

'True enough. And what do you work at, Miss Vincent? Modelling?' He gestured at the overnight bag, and the girl glanced down at it.

'Oh, that. No, it's full of notes and papers I've been putting together, at the library. I'm a teacher.'

'A teacher?'

'Yes,' Ruth Vincent said flatly.

'I'm sorry, I didn't mean—'

'I know. It was meant to be flattering, except that it isn't.'

'It should be.'

'Why? Are you flattered any time a woman walks into this strangely sedate office, sees the handsome, Brooks Brothers type of executive behind its desk, and says in that same tone, "A detective?"?'

'I don't know,' Murray said. 'It's never happened.'

'I doubt that. Meanwhile, Mr Kirk, take my word for it that I'm in the English Department at the Homestead School, a very highly regarded private school which, I've been told, hires its teachers for their ability. Don't mind if that sounds stuffy. It's a little something I memorized a long time ago.'

'*Mea culpa*,' said Murray cheerfully. '*Mea maxima culpa.* Miss Vincent, by any chance is there a kid named Megan Harlingen in your school?'

'Why, yes. She's Mr Harlingen's daughter.'

'I know. Is that how you met Harlingen? How he happened to get Lundeen's case?'

'In a way. Arnold's first lawyer was someone from his political club, a John McCadden. When it became clear that McCadden was half-hearted about the case, when he got around to suggesting that Arnold plead guilty, that maybe a deal with the District Attorney could be made on that basis, we knew we had to find someone else.'

'But why Harlingen?'

'Why? For one thing, he's been a lawyer for twenty years, Mr Kirk. More than that, he's been as much a friend to us from the start as a lawyer. You find yourself counting your friends very carefully at a time like this, believe me.'

'I'm not denying that. I'm not even denying that Ralph Harlingen is a nice guy with a great big heart shaped like a valentine. Count him as a friend, if you want to.'

'I have every reason to. And I don't see what you're driving at.'

Murray dug his fingers into the nape of his neck. 'What I'm driving at is that he's not the man to handle this case.'

The colour rose in the girl's face. 'That fascinates me. I mean, the ethics of it. How anyone in your position—'

'Lady, people in my position make up their ethics from day to day, so don't let it bother you for a minute. The fact is that as a lawyer Harlingen isn't in the same league as Johnny McCadden. Didn't it ever strike you that McCadden knew what he was doing when he told your boy friend to take a guilty plea? That it might mean an easier sentence on a sure conviction?'

The girl stared at him. 'I see,' she said hoarsely, and cleared her throat with an effort. 'Then there's no doubt about Arnold's being convicted. About his being found guilty.'

'I didn't say that.'

She shook her head slowly. 'Oh, please, don't start backing away now, Mr Kirk. You've been doing fine so far.'

'All right,' said Murray angrily, 'if you want to play it that way, let's do it. I know McCadden, because I've done work for the Hirsch and McCadden office, and when they want to soft-pedal a case they've got good reasons for it. And I know that ten of these Wykoff cases have been tried already, and the DA's had a field day with them. And I know cops. Is there anything more you'd like me to say?'

'Yes,' the girl answered, and her voice trembled. 'Now tell me what you know about cops. What makes you God Almighty to pass judgement on anybody who happens to wear a badge? I want to know.'

'No, you don't. What you want me to tell you is that Lundeen had nothing to do with the Wykoff mob. That he never took graft in his life. That when all this passes away like a bad dream, he'll be standing there with a halo on his head, right in the middle of this best of all possible worlds. All right, consider it said.'

'But you don't believe it?'

'Not for one little second. In my book your boy friend is as guilty as they come.'

'In your book! Without evidence!'

'Evidence!' Murray cried. 'What do you think McCadden was worrying about when he gave you his opinion? Everything he turned up on the case must have told him Lundeen was a loser! And it wasn't McCadden's fault; he's a good man with a good staff. The same thing would happen whoever worked on the case! It would happen if I worked on it for Harlingen!'

'Then why don't you?'

He looked at her, not comprehending at first, and she looked back at him, stonily beautiful, rigidly defiant, only the hands knotting together in her lap giving her away.

'You mean,' he said, 'take Lundeen's money to help hang him?'

'Why not?' she whispered, hating him with her eyes. 'From what you've told me, you ought to enjoy doing it!'

He would. That was the realization that exploded in him, the knowledge that he would. He could feel the savour of it in his mouth, the sweet pleasure of handing her Lundeen's head on a silver platter. And he wouldn't have to fake the job. It would be an honest job all the way. Lundeen would get full value for every dollar.

Granted, it would be like walking a tightrope. It might mean tangling with the DA's office against all Frank's canny advice, or with the politicos around Wykoff, or with the Police Department, for that matter. But it could be done. Frank had once gone down to Trinidad on a case, had set the whole colonial administration on its tail to pull a client clear of a murder charge, no less, and had lived to gloat over it. Lundeen's case was a joke compared to that kind of deal. And the joke was on Lundeen.

'All right,' Murray said, 'I'll work for you on those terms. I cut, and the chips fall where they will.'

The girl's head moved in a numb gesture. 'That's all we want.'

'Maybe.' He pressed the buzzer under the desk for Mrs Knapp. 'How long do I have? When's the trial?'

'January sixteenth. About six weeks.'

'It's not much. It'll take time getting started, and I need Lundeen for that. When can you have him here?'

She seemed dazed by the sudden quick tempo of events. 'I don't know. Oh, of course, Sunday. He always comes home Sundays. But I suppose you won't be here then.'

'I won't, but it doesn't matter. One of my men'll be here, and he'll set up a tape recorder for you. Or is Lundeen likely to get tongue-tied around a recorder?'

'I'm sure he won't.'

'Good. Then all he has to do is talk his head off into it. I mean, get the whole story down, including names, addresses, times, places – the works. I don't care how much he rambles on, or how many times he stops to think things over. He's the one who's paying for the tape, anyhow. You can tell him that for me.'

Mrs Knapp's head appeared inside the door, and Murray beckoned her in. She came to attention at the desk, the good soldier, her pad and pencil at the ready.

'Mrs Knapp, this young lady is Arnold Lundeen's fiancée, and we've just been having quite a talk about his case. It looks like we'll be handling it, after all.'

Mrs Knapp was a good soldier, but she was also human. Her eyes moved to the girl, then back to the pad again, and her lips twisted in a curious grimace.

Murray said coldly: 'I'd like you to open a file in his name, and draw up the usual contract for our services. Oh, yes. He's being taped Sunday, so have one of the girls make a transcript of the tape first thing Monday morning. And book an appointment with Ralph Harlingen early next week. Here, if possible.'

'Right. Is that all, Mr Kirk?'

'That's all.'

When she had gone, the girl said, 'You're very efficient here, aren't you?' It was not a compliment; there was almost a distaste in the way she said it.

'That's what we get paid for,' Murray answered flatly. 'By the way, did Lundeen get a bill of particulars on this indictment?'

'Yes. McCadden got it for him.'

'Then tell him to bring it along Sunday and leave it for me. I suppose you'll be phoning him now about all this, anyhow.'

'Yes,' said the girl, 'I will.'

He waited until he heard the elevator door close behind her in the outer hall, and then he went to the window. The rain had stopped, the street below was filling with the first rush of homeward-bound office workers, the Santa Claus and his paraphernalia were no longer there. Then the girl appeared outside the building. She stood there hesitant a moment, her hand holding her coat collar together, and finally she moved off with the crowd down the street. Even at that distance Murray could see the men turning to watch her as she passed.

They would, he thought, suddenly hating them for it. *They would.*

3

FILE: AL391
TAPE RECORDING: AL391–01
RECORDED: 27 *November*
TRANSCRIPT: 28 *November*
BY: *Dolores-May Mulqueen*

My name is Arnold Lundeen, and my regular address is 500 Bleecker Street. That is in the Greenwich Village section. But I used to work out of the Third Division, Manhattan West, which is around midtown Manhattan from Fifth Avenue to the Hudson River. I was on the Vice Squad, Shield 32C720.

This whole thing started last May 3. I met my buddy in the precinct house in the morning, because that's the way we handled it, two of us in a team so we could cover each other. His name is Benny Floyd – Benjamin Floyd – but I don't know his address. Just somewhere out in Queens, around where they have all those used-car lots.

Anyhow, that morning we worked Seventh Avenue from the precinct house up to Central Park, pretty near, and then we cut over to Eighth Avenue and headed back downtown that way. We were mainly on the lookout for bookies, because the ones who operate out in the open have to show themselves around this time. That is, between when you can pick up a scratch sheet in the morning and about one o'clock in the afternoon, which is just before post time at the New York tracks.

Most of the time coming down Eighth Avenue Benny and I worked opposite sides of the street, keeping each other under surveillance. Now and then we got together to pass the time of the day. Around twelve o'clock we had a hot dog at a stand near Madison Square Garden, and so far everything was all quiet. I remember saying something to Benny about working a different territory, because it almost looked like some hustler had spotted us moving down the avenue and had gone ahead to tip off the bookies and numbers men. I don't remember what he said exactly, but anyhow we just kept along Eighth, and it was around Forty-fifth Street that I finally spotted this guy. He was operating right out where you could get a good look at him.

There's some kind of shop there that sells all kinds of theatre equipment, because that's around where the theatres are, and then next to it is one of those joints sells sexy books and practical jokes – they have a window full of that stuff – and in between them is a hallway leading up to the apartments in the building. And there was this character standing a little bit back in the hall, a scratch sheet sticking out of his pocket. He was wide open. All he needed was a cash register in front of him to ring up the bets.

I laid back a little, watching him, and after he booked three bets I moved right in on him. As soon as I said he was under arrest he put up a terrific squawk about what the hell was this, he was just standing there minding his own business, and all that kind of birdseed. He didn't pipe down until I dug in his pockets and came up with the roll of money he was collecting for bets, and with six bet tickets. I took that and the scratch sheet and a couple of pencils he had stashed away – you have to have all that for evidence to back up the charge in court – and then he quietened down some, but he was still nasty. Oh yes, his name was – is – Eddie Schrade, and he lives at 3501 Stillwell Avenue. That's way to hell and gone out in Brooklyn, right in the middle of Coney Island.

He said to me: 'I got friends. I'm in with plenty big people around here. They'll have your ears for this, you so-and-so flatfoot.'

So I told him it would be all right with me to hear who his friends were if he wanted to tell me. Then I could take them right along where he was going, and it would save me trouble some other time.

Then he started whining. He said: 'You got my dough; why not let it go at that. Why pick on me? I'm only a first-timer. I'm brand new. I just wanted to make a dollar.'

Meanwhile Benny came from across the street. I told him what was what, and we talked some about whether we should walk down to the precinct house or maybe ride it, because we were so far uptown.

Right away when this Schrade character heard us talking about it he started to hop up and down and make speeches.

'You got no right to walk me to death!' he yelled. 'What are you trying to do, make a parade out of it so you can be heroes? I got a right to ride in. I'm an American citizen. I stand on my constitutional rights!'

Up to then I was thinking myself maybe we ought to ride in, but with the way he was yelling, and then some people piling up around the door so they could see what was happening, I got peeved.

I said to him: 'Enough out of you, friend. You'll walk on your constitutional feet the way I tell you,' and that's how we brought him in, walking all the way. We booked him at the precinct, and then we took him over to Magistrate's Court. He didn't have bail money on him, but they released him on his fingerprints, and later when the case was called up he just took a guilty plea. You'd figure with all the fuss he made he'd show up with some big-time lawyer handling the case, but, no, he didn't let out a peep. Just said guilty and shelled out fifty for the fine.

I didn't think twice about this whole thing – not even when the Wykoff business busted wide open in the papers a couple of weeks later – because to me it was just another arrest. As far as when Wykoff started shooting off his mouth it didn't mean a thing to me because I was clean. It's God's honest truth I never took a penny of pay-off money since I got into the Department. I never rigged up any stand-in arrests. I never set up any stiff arrests, no matter how much the heat was on.

Sure, there are guys on the squad – I'm not naming any names – but as soon as the Inspector says to them: 'What's this? You don't have any score on bookies lately. Did they all move out of the neighbourhood?' they rig up deals with a couple of small-time bookies to take arrests, so that the score looks okay and the heat is off.

I never played that angle or any other, so I naturally figured the Wykoff blast went right over me. Then in September – that was September 15 – I was called down to the DA's office. I knew it was that cruddy LoScalzo right away, because one of the guys that came for me was this leg man of LoScalzo's, Myron Kramer.

Anyway, they sat me down in like a corridor outside the office along with some other men from the squad, and we just stayed there for an hour, wondering what it was all about. They didn't let us talk or smoke. We just sat there sweating it out.

Then LoScalzo came walking out of his office with this fellow I didn't know at the time, and he says to him: 'Point him out. Take your time and make sure. Then point him out to me.'

This fellow puts on a big act of looking us over, and then all of a sudden he comes up to me and puts the finger on me. I didn't know till later that he was that Ira Miller bastard. I didn't even know what it was all about.

That was all that happened right then, but when I went back on duty I was plenty worried. I talked to the Inspector, and he just said, 'If you're clean you got nothing to worry about.' But what the hell, with this Wykoff business and all I figured maybe I was being put on the spot. That's when I went to Johnny

McCadden, who I knew from my political club, and he was the one took care of things after the grand jury called me up. Johnny's all right – I don't have a thing in the world against him – but later on when he started to sound like LoScalzo had reached him, I had to change over.

What I want to say is – and I don't give a goddam who knows it – the whole trouble is this LoScalzo. He runs that grand jury, and he runs it the way he wants. They sit there and look at him like he was a little tin god, and you don't stand a chance.

Take the way he worked me over before the grand jury. Did I know Miller? Did I ever deal with Miller? What happened when I arrested Eddie Schrade? He kept throwing the ball so fast that half the time all you could do was stand at the plate and watch it go by. I brought along a copy of that bill of particulars, Mr Kirk, so when you read the minutes of my grand jury hearing you'll see for yourself how it was.

If I could have figured what Miller told them I could have done better. But I didn't know Miller, so how could I guess what they were getting at? All I knew when I got out of there was that they were going to throw me to the wolves. It didn't surprise me any when I was indicted. If LoScalzo told that bunch to take a running jump out of the window, they wouldn't even wait to open the window when they jumped. He's just using that investigation to build himself up for DA or governor or what the hell. Johnny McCadden knows that. Everybody on the cops knows that. It's no secret.

That's how it all happened, and everything important is right in here. Maybe I left out some small things, but I can fill you in any time you want, Mr Kirk. I hope you can use this to help Ralph Harlingen on the case. Thanks. I'm signing off now.

Murray shuffled the pages of the transcript into their proper order, reread them – slowly this time – and laid them aside. The recorder was on the desk, the tape ready in it. He leaned forward, switched on the machine, and held the earphones to one ear.

'*My name is Arnold Lundeen*,' said the machine, '*and my regular address—*'

Murray snapped the switch off, and the sound went dead with a yelp. He put the earphones down and sat there contemplating them with a frown. Lundeen's voice was no surprise; it pretty well fit the man's narrative style. A hard New York voice, slovenly in enunciation, a little truculent in tone. Anyone reading the transcript had that voice subconsciously in his ears.

What didn't fit was Ruth Vincent. Her milieu was the Homestead School, and beyond it something like Westpoint or New Canaan or even the saner part of the world that the Harlingens frequented. The idea pulled him up short. The girl and Harlingen. On the one hand – on the other hand—

On the one hand, Harlingen might just have been man enough to snatch at dark-haired, blue-eyed opportunity when it hovered so tantalizingly close. On the other hand, the irony of any such situation would be too rich, too perfect, to be plausible. The girl, using Lundeen's case as a front for an affair with his lawyer, would be a sort of Francesca da Rimini in reverse, and while she certainly looked the part it was doubtful that she would ever play it. It was nonsense even to think of her in those terms.

Or was it?

Murray took a deep breath and picked up the bill of particulars Lundeen had left for him. This consisted of a few typed pages, badly soiled, and heavily scored with pencilled notations along the margins. It was no surprise that it was so brief, although Lundeen's testimony in full would probably have added up to quite a pile of paper. Public prosecutors have a violent dislike for revealing grand jury testimony. Murray, flattening the first page before him, had the feeling that the court must have twisted LoScalzo's arm before he gave up even this much.

FOR THE DISTRICT ATTORNEY: Felix LoScalzo
FOR THE GRAND JURY: Thomas L. Price, foreman
TESTIMONY OF: Patrolman Arnold Lundeen, 32C720 (sworn)
REFERENCE: page 1281

Q (by Mr LoScalzo) You say you are familiar with the duties of a plain clothes man attached to the Vice Squad?

A (by Patrolman Lundeen) That is right.

Q Then please tell this jury what those duties are.

A You mean, what the job is, or how we work on it?

Q You seem to be a normally intelligent man, officer. You're not usually this slow on the trigger, are you?

A All I—

Q Just tell me what you think your duties are.

A Well, we function against vice, gambling, and violations of the ABC. That is the Alcoholic Beverage Control.

Q Thank you. Now let's hear how you work on a case.

A What kind of case? There's all different kinds.

Q Any kind of case. Just a case in general. No, wait. Is it your impression, officer, that I'm trying to trick you into something? That can't be done, if you're telling the truth.

A Yes, sir. I am telling the truth.

Q All right. Go ahead and keep telling it.

A Well, the way we work is to patrol an area, and when we see a suspect we keep him under observation until we catch him with the goods.

Q And then?

A Well, then we arrest him and seize the evidence. After we book him at the precinct house we take him to court.

Q And that's it?

A Yes, sir. My record—

Q Never mind your record, officer; it's been duly entered. What interests me right now is the way you've been using that editorial 'we'. I take it that this includes you as well as all the other men on your squad?

A   Sure.

Q   That wasn't intended to be funny. It was intended to point up that while I asked you how *you* worked on a case, you answered with some glittering generalities about your squad in phrases drawn from the departmental instruction book. Are you – you, personally – always so careful to follow departmental instructions?

A   I guess so.

Q   You guess so. Do your instructions allow you to consort with known criminals?

A   Well, there might be some assignment—

Q   I am not talking about special assignments.

A   In that case, no, sir.

Q   Good. Do your instructions allow you to make a deal with any suspect, so that you will be paid to arrest someone in his place?

A   Of course not. You know that, Mr LoScalzo.

Q   I know it, yes. But do you?

A   If you're saying—

Q   Let me finish. Have you ever made any such deal? Have you ever taken money – graft is the word for it, officer – to arrest someone in a suspect's place?

A   No, I have not.

Reference: page 1289

Q   (by Mr LoScalzo): So that is your story of the Schrade arrest?

A   (by Patrolman Lundeen): Yes, sir.

Q   You say you arrested him at Forty-fifth and Eighth?

A   Yes, sir.

Q   Do you know that section well?

A   Pretty well.

Q   Did you ever hear of the Songster Corporation? It is right around the corner from there.

A   No, sir.

Q   Do you know the owner of that company? His name is Ira Miller.

A   No, sir. I've heard of him, but I don't know him.

Q   Did you know that the Eddie Schrade you arrested was an employee of that company, and a long-time associate of Ira Miller?

A   No, sir.

Q   Do you know that Ira Miller is a notorious bookie, an associate of George Wykoff, and that he uses the Songster Corporation only as a front?

A   Well, I told you, Mr LoScalzo. I know about Ira Miller now, but I didn't know then.

Q   When?

A   When I arrested Schrade. I didn't know about Miller then.

Q   You didn't? How do you know who he is now?

A   I – do I have to answer that?

Q   You do.

A   Well, I asked around.

Mr Price (jury): Mr LoScalzo, could you ask the witness to speak a little louder, please? Some of us back here cannot hear him.

Q   Officer, let's have that answer again, and make it a little louder this time.

A   I said, I asked around.

Q   You mean to sit there and tell me under oath that you had to ask around, as you put it, to find out who the biggest bookie in your district was? Who did you ask?

A   Just some people.

Q   What people? Please speak louder. I can hardly hear you myself.

A   Just people. I don't remember who.

Q   People in the Police Department, by any chance?

A   I don't remember.

Q   I see you don't. And these mysterious people told you who Miller was?

A   Yes.

Q But when you arrested Schrade you didn't know anything about Miller?

A That is right.

Q There's an old saying, officer, that a plain clothes man can't be in a district for more than a day without knowing who operates all the rackets in it. Do you agree with that?

A It's just a saying.

Q Then you don't agree with that?

A I don't know. I just know I never heard of Ira Miller until after I was in your office that day.

Q That was – wait, I want to check this. That was September 15?

A Yes.

Q And you say this under oath?

A Yes, sir. I do.

4

Murray had wondered if the girl would show up at the meeting. He was curiously pleased – after Harlingen had shaken hands with Bruno Manfredi and Lou Strauss – that she had not.

The trouble was, he reflected, that Harlingen's presence in the office somehow threw everything else in it into sharp and shabby relief. It was nothing you could blame the man for; he was obviously not working at being well bred. But there was no escaping the way that fine old Harvard Law School aura invited every kind of ass-backward comparison. The Old Massah talking over crops behind the plantation house. The Knight in Armour hobnobbing with the varlets, laying out tomorrow's strategy. The White Knight himself. But with a lot of spirit now that Conmy-Kirk was around to guard him against the bites of sharks.

Harlingen was in fine fettle. He held out a folded newspaper to Murray and tapped it with the back of his hand. 'I suppose you saw that,' he said. 'That item about Appeals reversing the verdict on one of the Wykoff convictions. Is that a slap at LoScalzo or isn't it? I ask you.'

'I saw it,' Murray said. 'Matter of fact, Mr Harlingen, I thought it was a pretty nice compliment to him.'

'A compliment?'

'Sure. Appeals was bawling out the judge and jury because LoScalzo got a conviction out of them without even making a case. I'd say that's roses for him, not scallions.'

'It is,' Lou Strauss said with admiration; 'it is. You know, I saw him in court a couple of times, back when he was defending some of the biggest bums in the country, and he was a real hatchet. A loud talker maybe, but always on top of the case. It looks like whatever he learned on that side of the fence he knows how to use double now.'

Harlingen seemed baffled by this. 'But Appeals is clearly condemning his Star Chamber methods. If he—'

'If he what?' cut in Bruno Manfredi. 'Look, *his* methods are working fine. What I want to know is, what's *our* methods? We're all primed on this Lundeen – I mean, Lou and me. Now what are we supposed to do about him?'

'Ah,' said Harlingen. He carefully placed his fingertips together. 'That's the question.'

'Right,' said Lou Strauss.

Harlingen looked suspiciously at Strauss, who smiled at him with a cherub's smile. 'Well,' Harlingen said, 'Lundeen's defence hinges on proving that Miller framed him. That an honest arrest was made, but now, for some reason, Miller and Schrade want it to look like a stand-in arrest.'

'Wait a minute,' said Bruno. 'I thought Lundeen claimed he never ever knew this Miller.'

'That's right.'

'Then why would Miller want to frame *him* out of all the cops in New York? You want to knife a guy, you do it to somebody who crossed you up, maybe, somebody you got it in for. But you'd sure as hell know each other.'

Harlingen said a little irritably: 'And there's where you come in, isn't it? I mean, it's my impression that an agency is supposed to dig up just this sort of information. Miller's motive, for example.'

'Jesus,' said Bruno, 'this isn't the movies, Mr Harlingen. How can you figure Miller framed Lundeen, if Lundeen himself don't know why he'd want to do it?'

Murray took a grim pleasure in watching Harlingen stir uneasily in his chair. 'I think it's a perfectly logical assumption,' said Harlingen, 'but if we by-pass that question for the time being—'

The phone clicked, and Murray lifted it. 'It's a call for Mr Harlingen,' said Miss Whiteside's voice. 'Should I connect you, or tell her to call later, or what?'

If it's 'her', thought Murray, it's Ruth Vincent looking for a communiqué. 'No, he'll take it now,' he said, and handed the phone to Harlingen.

There was a shrill clatter in the earpiece, and Harlingen's face darkened. 'For God's sake, Megan,' he said, 'you know you're not supposed to bother me when I'm busy. If this isn't important—'

The clatter in the receiver grew sharply insistent.

'Yes,' said Harlingen. 'I do remember. Of course I remember. Yes, I'll tell him.'

He slammed the phone down, and Murray winced at the impact that must have had on Miss Whiteside's eardrums.

'Believe it or not,' Harlingen told him, 'that was my daughter. She wanted to remind me to apologize for her. That is, for the way she acted that night. She instructed me to do it when I saw you, and I forgot all about it. Although God knows why I should bother you with it.'

'No bother,' Murray said; 'she's a nice kid.' Then he glanced sidelong at Harlingen. 'Funny that she knew where to find you, though. Or do you keep her in touch right along?'

Harlingen laughed. 'No, but, of course, we don't try to shut her out. We've always felt that it's better to take her into our confidence than build a whole world of mystery around her. She's high-strung enough without that.'

'I've got four kids,' Bruno suddenly remarked to the wall. 'If any of them stuck a nose into my business I'd slap his high-strung ears off. They don't even know what business I'm in.'

'It's a fact,' said Strauss. 'All kids are blabbermouths. It comes natural to them, like making noise.'

'Lou,' Murray said gently, 'before we get started on child guidance can we finish talking about the case? All we know so far is that we have three leads: Miller, Schrade, and this buddy of Lundeen's, Benny Floyd. How about concentrating on them?'

'I've already talked to Floyd,' said Harlingen. 'He backs up Lundeen's story of the arrest all the way.'

'Fine. Have you lined him up as a witness?'

'Well, yes. But he's very shaky about it. Very much upset.'

'He's high-strung,' said Bruno.

'The fact is,' said Harlingen stiffly, 'he's afraid of reprisals. I'm not saying he has cause for it, but he may be a shaky witness when LoScalzo starts working on him. That's what worries me.'

'All right,' said Murray, 'we'll brace him up. Make a date with him for some afternoon this week when he's off duty, and the three of us will walk right through the whole arrest. We'll check every inch of his testimony that way, and if there are weak spots we'll clear them up before he gets on the stand.'

'Now look,' Harlingen protested, 'I don't want to prepare his testimony for him. It's just—'

'You won't be preparing it, Mr Harlingen. You'll be looking for holes in it. You'll be refreshing his memory. Or would you rather wait until LoScalzo does that for you?'

'Well, viewing it in that light—'

'Sure,' said Murray. 'Now, the next thing is Schrade's and Miller's police records. All we know so far is that Schrade claims to be a first-time loser, but if we can show he's lying about this it weakens his credibility when he testifies. And Miller must have some kind of record, if he's as big a bookie as they say. When you get him on the stand it's worth something to smear him with a bad record. You have to keep selling the jury the idea that Miller and Schrade are born thieves and liars. You've got to hammer at that.'

'Well, as a pair of known bookmakers—'

'That won't mean a thing offhand, not unless you can put together a jury of twelve old maids out of the Ladies' Aid. And nobody's giving you the chance to do that. You'll be working with a blue-ribbon jury, Mr Harlingen; good, solid, substantial citizens who head for their bookies as soon as they get a tip on some horse. They won't rate Miller and Schrade as criminals. Just as hard-luck cases.'

'Fine,' said Harlingen wryly. 'Put a policeman up against a bookie, and the bookie automatically draws the sympathy.'

'Yes, but that's where Lou here comes in.' Murray turned to Strauss. 'You've got that line to the clerk in Records, Lou. Start working on him right away. Get everything they have down against Schrade and Miller. Some of the stuff might be under different names, but the fingerprints'll show it up.'

'And the pay-off?' asked Strauss.

'Keep it reasonable. What the hell, we don't want to tear up the records or erase anything on them. We just want to look at them. Maybe make a couple of photostats.'

'Even so, it might come high right now, Murray. With this Wykoff thing so hot there's maybe a boom going on with those records.'

'Then use your head and let Lundeen worry. He's contracted for all expenses, anyhow.'

Harlingen had been following this with an increasingly worried expression. 'I don't know,' he said. 'I mean, using sub rosa methods . like this to get the information. After all—'

Murray shrugged. 'If you don't want us to bother about it—'

'I didn't say that. It's just that I – well, frankly, I did have hopes of going to court without getting involved in this kind of thing. Not that it matters too much if it's in a good cause, I suppose. Or is that the devil's argument?'

'I'm afraid you'll have to answer that for yourself, Mr Harlingen.'

'Of course, of course. I realize that.' Harlingen sat meditatively chewing his lip. 'Well, let's by-pass that for the time being. What else is there to work on?'

'Lining up Miller and Schrade in person. We want to locate them, and we want to see what they're up to right now.'

Harlingen looked doubtful. 'It's my guess that they'll be behaving themselves for a long time to come.'

'It's likely, but it's not a sure bet. Anyhow, we'll leave that to

Bruno. He'll look them up and tail them a little, and that might give us some ideas.'

'And after that?'

'After that we play it by ear.' Murray stood up and Harlingen followed suit. 'Meanwhile, I'm counting on you to get in touch with that Benny Floyd so we can go over the arrest with him.'

'I'll do that,' said Harlingen. He put on his coat, picked up his hat, and shook hands all round. Murray watched him almost to the door, and then said, 'Oh, one thing, Mr Harlingen.'

'Yes?'

'It's about those police records. You haven't said whether you wanted us to get them or not.'

Harlingen stood there weighted down by indecision, his hand restlessly twisting the doorknob back and forth. 'Well,' he said at last, 'I can't see letting a man go hang for want of evidence when it's there for the asking. Handle it any way you think is best, Kirk. I'll leave it to you.'

When the door had closed behind him, Bruno gave Murray a long and meaningful look. 'Now you tell me,' he demanded.

'Tell you what?'

'Don't play dumb with me, Murray. Since when do we con a lawyer into okaying how we operate? Or all that stuff about Records. What's it his business how we pay off Records? And the way you were sitting there watching him with that cat-who-ate-the-canary smile, that was a picture. Come to think of it, there was a lot going on I didn't get. How about letting me in on it before I stick my neck on the block?'

'What block?'

'You know what I mean. If I'm supposed to go around tailing a couple of state's witnesses in a front-page mess like this, there's a fifty-fifty chance there'll be a dick from the DA's office tailing *me*. I don't mind being in the middle of the sandwich, but I sure as hell want to know what I'm doing there. I'd hate to look as stupid as that Harlingen if somebody catches up with me.'

'I don't know about the stupid,' Lou Strauss protested. 'To me he's an unusual type. A purist. You know – clean-cut. He reminds me of this polo player from Long Island we worked for on that divorce a couple of years back. Remember? I was on that case with Mernagh. So when the house dick kicks open the door, there's me and Mernagh and him and this polo player all jumping into the room together, and there's this dame stark naked – a beautiful piece – trying to untangle from the chauffeur.

'And what does the polo player do? A big strapping fellow – you wouldn't even think a horse could hold him – and he starts to bang his hands on the wall and cry great big tears like a baby. "I don't believe it!" he yells. "I loved you! I married you because I loved you! I don't believe it!" Right in front of everybody he's carrying on like this for a floozie who's been handing it out free to every guy in town. And you know why? Because he was a purist, too. There's some people got such clean minds they just can't see how it really is around them. That's the way this guy Harlingen looks to me.'

'Sure,' Murray said, 'that's the way they educated him. He went to Harvard Law just like his pappy and grandpappy did, and it's quite a place. All they turn out there are corporation lawyers who can tell anybody big enough how to get away with an income-tax swindle. Only, Harlingen wasn't any good at the job, so now he moved down among us riffraff where he'll be appreciated. Look at the way Lou appreciates him already.'

Strauss turned red. 'I only said he was an unusual type. Green, maybe, but wholesome. What's wrong with that?'

'Who cares what's wrong with it?' Bruno asked in exasperation, 'I put a question to Murray, and I want an answer. What's all this game with Harlingen? What're we working on him? That's all I want to hear about.'

'We're taking our turn educating him,' Murray said.

'What's that mean?'

'We're teaching baby to walk. If he doesn't like this first step, he'll like it even less when Lou gets those police records for him.'

'Aha,' said Strauss. 'You mean he bothers you. But why?'

'Never mind that,' Bruno said impatiently. 'What makes you so sure about those records, Murray? How do you know what's in them?'

'Because I'm not turning the case upside down the way Harlingen's doing. I say Miller's telling the truth, and Lundeen is lying. Look at it that way, and it's easy to figure.'

'How?'

'Ah, use your head, Bruno. Why would a bookie pay a thousand dollars to duck a fifty-dollar fine for a misdemeanour? See if you can think up a reason.'

Bruno reflected on this. 'Oho!' he said at last.

'You can say it again, sweetheart. Because he's got a police record he's worried about, that's why. And with Miller it isn't a criminal record, because Johnny McCadden would have dug that up and known he had some sort of case. It's just a plain record of misdemeanours. Four or five of them, I figure, because the sixth one would have tagged him a habitual criminal which is a different kettle of fish altogether.

'Miller knew that. He knew that once he got that habitual criminal label hung on him he was in trouble every time he turned around. *That's* what was worth a thousand dollars to him. And that's all we'll ever turn up here – Miller's motive for paying the graft.'

Strauss said: 'Say, wouldn't it be better then to do something about those records? Get rid of them, maybe?'

'It's too late for that, even if we wanted to. LoScalzo knows all about them already. And besides, we don't want to. Everything we turn up goes to Harlingen and Lundeen just the way it is.'

'All right, you sold me,' Bruno said. 'So why do I have to tail Miller and Schrade? If the case is a stiff, why shouldn't anybody work up a sweat over it?'

'Well, there's a thin chance that one or the other of them is consorting with known criminals, or some stupid thing like that.

If we can tag them with it, it's a score for Harlingen, and we're earning our pay. Anyhow, work on it for a couple of days, and we'll see.'

Bruno said: 'All right, but don't short-change me, Murray. After I find them it'll be one man on two. I want somebody helping me out on it.'

'You'll have him.'

'Who?'

'Me,' said Murray. 'You can count me in.'

He knew, even as he said it, that it was unpremeditated, it was as much a surprise to him as to Bruno. And he couldn't understand why he had said it, any more than he could understand why he knew he had to go through with it. The office was his place, and the St Stephen was his place; the cold, wet winter streets were meant to be walked by the hired hands he paid to do it. For him to walk them on a case that turned around on itself like a dog with its tail between its teeth, a case that was just a cruel joke on itself, didn't make sense. Where, as Frank Conmy would have said, is the profit? Where's the pleasure? And if there's no profit or pleasure, what's the compulsion working on you?

The question, undigested and acid, lay on his mind that night, making sleep impossible. He shifted from one position to another in the bed, the blanket always too heavy, the pillow too hot, too soft, too lumpy under his head. Finally, he sat bolt upright, turned on the bed light, and looked at his watch. Three-thirty. He picked up the phone, held it while he decided on a suitable opening remark, and then dialled.

The voice that answered him was blurred and languorous with sleep. 'Yay-us?' it said, and then trailed off into something between a yawn and a sigh.

'Didi,' said Murray, 'the world is waiting for the sunrise. Are you waiting for it all by your own self, perhaps?'

'I guess I am. Murray, are you feeling all right? You sound all sorts of queer to me. Are you drunk?'

'No,' he said, 'but it's an idea. I'm sorry I bothered you, Didi. I'll call you some other time during the week.'

'Any time, honey. Any time at all.'

He hung up when he heard her phone click. He lit a cigarette, then rolled over on his back and studied the shadows on the ceiling.

Blow, blow, thou winter wind, he thought. She was quite a girl, was Didi. When he had worked on her divorce suit a few years ago she had been Mrs Alfred Donaldson of Amarillo, Texas, whose husband had discovered the fleshpots of New York with a whoop and a cry. Then she had been a lanky, sunburned girl, her hair tortured into a cast-iron permanent wave, her slightly too-large teeth showing in an eternally hopeful, hesitant smile. Now she was smoothly rounded, the complexion was ivory, the hair was a sleek golden casque, the capped teeth were flawless to behold, and the little smile was all-knowing.

Quite a girl. She was the one who had taken him one night to the West Side saloon where a mad Welsh bard was holding court. She was completely, undyingly in love with the bard, she explained, and since he was combining an erratic lecture tour of America with a sterling effort to drink himself to death she was making it her life's work to save him from himself.

It had been a wild night altogether, the bard roaring fantastic obscenities, pawing at Didi until in the ensuing wrestling match he emerged triumphant with her brassière, and then drinking himself into a puking collapse. Another woman might have left before the final round, but Didi remained to the bitter end, watching starry-eyed as the sodden remains were hauled away.

Murray had borrowed a book of the man's poetry from her that night. Back at the St Stephen he read pages at random, walking the floor barefooted, feeling his first incredulity at the splendour of the lines turn to a voluptuous pleasure in them and then finally become an anger at the gifted hulk who had written them, just for being a hulk. It was impossible, he found, to dissociate the work from the man, once you had met the man.

The bard had died, Didi had wept and moved on to a young

Accidentalist painter, but the book of poetry was still somewhere in the apartment. Murray got out of bed and padded around the bookshelves until he found it. He opened it, and then felt such a qualm of revulsion that he almost flung it from him.

The bottle of cognac was in a cabinet nearby. He used that, instead.

5

Harlingen called Friday morning to say that he had arranged the meeting with Benny Floyd.

'It's at twelve o'clock noon in the Madison Square Garden arcade,' he said apologetically. 'I know it's short notice, but Floyd wasn't keen about going through with this in the first place, and I didn't want to give him time to change his mind.'

'That's all right. Did he have anything interesting to say when you talked to him?'

'No. Oh, when I said something about getting in touch with Lundeen so that he could come along with us Floyd made quite a fuss. I imagine that he feels the best policy is not to be seen publicly with Lundeen right now.'

'You can't blame him for that,' Murray said. 'All right, I'll see you at twelve.'

It was a fifteen-minute walk cross-town to the Garden. When Murray entered the arcade he found Harlingen and Floyd already there, coat collars up against the dankness of the place, feet stamping against the numbing chill of the concrete floor. Floyd turned out to be one of the new breed of policeman, the kind who look too young and callow to be carrying a badge. He was a tall, skinny boy with pale eyes, and with a habit of now and then suddenly shooting out his jaw as if to drag an oversized Adam's apple up from under his collar. Not a bad witness,

Murray reflected, if he could face cross-examination without tripping over his tongue. He was something any jury would immediately recognize, the gawky kid with the makeshift fishing pole right off the cover of a family magazine.

Harlingen made the introduction, and the three of them moved out to the street.

'I'll lay it on the line for you,' Murray said to Floyd. 'Schrade was arrested six months ago, so naturally you won't be able to remember everything about it. That means that LoScalzo can really put you through the grinder when you testify. You know. Every time you have to say, "I can't remember," or you have to stop and think things over, he gives the jury that great big look to point up what a faker you are. But, what the hell, I'm not telling you anything new. You must have testified before.'

'I never testified for the defence,' Floyd said unhappily.

'It comes to the same thing. Just sound as if you know what you're talking about, and don't get rattled. That's why I want to run through this thing now, so that you'll have it all straight in your mind.' Murray pulled out the transcript of Lundeen's tape and studied it briefly. 'First of all, when you and Lundeen were around here that day how were you working things?'

'Well, we were heading downtown. He was over here, and I was across the street. We were keeping each other under surveillance.'

'All right. Now, how does Mr Harlingen here compare to Lundeen in height?'

Floyd eyed Harlingen up and down. 'About the same, I guess.'

'Then he'll be Lundeen, and you and I'll cross over and keep him under surveillance.'

They moved along like this for two blocks, Murray watching Harlingen's pearl-grey fedora bob up and down over the roofs of the cars that filled the avenue. Then Floyd suddenly stopped, and Murray observed that Harlingen's hat stopped simultaneously.

'Now I went across the street, and we ate in that place right where Mr Harlingen is standing,' Floyd said. 'That hot-dog joint.'

'Would the guy who runs it know you?' Murray asked.

Floyd looked doubtful. 'I don't think he knows anything. He's just about bright enough to make change. He don't even speak English.'

'All right, let's take a look.'

They joined Harlingen in front of the stand, which was glassed in against the weather, its counter stained and dirty, its floor a litter of used paper cups and cigarette butts.

'I have an idea,' Murray told Harlingen. 'I don't know if it's worth anything, but it's an idea. Anyhow, it's cold enough for a cup of coffee.'

He led the way in, and the three of them lined up at the counter. The man behind the counter was small and swarthy, with a badly pockmarked face, but with the beautifully kept hair and the well-trimmed moustache of a dandy. Young, Murray estimated; about twenty-two or twenty-three. The thin, tired-looking girl who was his assistant was probably his wife.

The coffee came in paper cups, a dollop of milk and sugar in each, a wooden paddle shaped like a tongue depressor laid on the counter beside the cup. Murray idly stirred his coffee and watched the counter-man run a foul-smelling rag the length of the counter. When the man was opposite him Murray smiled, and the man smiled back, a bright, meaningless smile.

Murray leaned forward and pointed at Floyd. '*Tú conoces a éste hombre?*' he asked.

The man's smile remained as fixed, as bright, as meaningless as ever. 'I know him,' he said in Spanish. 'He is of the police.'

'That is true. And he has a friend who is also of the police. Do you know that one, too?'

'Why should I? I am not a man who cares for the horses or the *bolita*. What would I have to do with the police?'

'I do not know; I do not care. I speak only of this policeman's friend, who is in trouble. This other man and I are lawyers who wish to help him.'

'Then help him, and God go with you.' The man made a brushing motion with his hands and turned away, and Murray saw Harlingen and Floyd following every gesture with blank incomprehension. He reached out and tapped the man's arm, and the man turned the bright smile to him again.

'Is the whole world your enemy?' Murray asked.

'I did not say it was. I do not say you are. Where did you learn to speak the language like that? That is not the way they teach it in the schools here.'

'I learned it from friends I lived with many years ago. Friends to me, benefactors to my father. Julio and Marta Gutiérrez. Perhaps you know them?'

'No, but what matter? It is sufficient that you knew them, and that they were friends. As for me, I knew that policeman who is now in trouble, although he was no friend. A strange man. A very strange man.'

'In what way?'

'Oh, that is something that would take a big brain to understand. For myself, I see him as a man as handsome and arrogant as a cock on a dung heap, but with no real happiness in him. That is a sort of sickness, is it not? It seems to me that sooner or later someone like that comes to trouble.'

'Then it does not surprise you to learn that he is in trouble now?'

'I will not lie to you. It did not surprise me when I first heard it, and that was when he was removed from the police. It is the kind of thing idle people talk about while they are drinking their coffee here.'

Murray nodded. 'I see. And did you also know this Ira Miller?'

'I knew about him. He was an important man in this vicinity. Why not, when he was the one to whom the idlers gave all their money every day?'

'There is another – George Wykoff – of even greater import-ance than Miller. Was he also spoken about here?'

The man hesitated. 'Who am I to say?'

'You are a citizen. It is a matter of duty.'

'You are wrong. I am nothing. I am less than nothing.' The man held up a hand against Murray's protest, cutting it short. 'Please, this does not matter to me greatly, because, if God is good, my children will be a little more than I am, and my grandchildren will be everything I am not. That is a good idea, I think. Come back some time, and speak to my grandchildren in English, and perhaps they will understand this talk about citizens. It is something that must he said in English. Your people up here do not believe it can have a meaning in another language.'

Murray shook his head. 'Your quarrel is not with me.'

'My quarrel is with nobody. I will prove that by giving you more coffee. Yours is already cold. There is no charge for this; it is my pleasure.'

'You are kind.' Murray waited as the fresh coffee was put before him, a dark and bitter brew, and drank it slowly. Then he drew a card from his wallet and handed it to the man. 'Now I ask a small favour.'

'Which is—?'

'Which is to give anyone concerned with this affair of the policeman my address. And this,' he said, putting a five-dollar bill on the counter where Harlingen could see it, 'is for the children you spoke about. They will have a good father and grandfather, I think.'

He led the way out, the fixed smile following him, he knew, to the very door. Outside, Floyd said with envy: 'I wish to hell I could jabber Spanish like that. With all these monkeys flooding into town everybody'll have to talk like that in a couple of years.' There was the light of professional interest in his eye. 'He was saying something about the numbers game, wasn't he? The *bolita*. What was that about?'

'Nothing,' Murray said. 'He told me he stays away from the rackets. I don't think he's lying about it, either.'

'Well, what did you find out?' Harlingen demanded.

'I wasn't trying to find out anything from him,' Murray said impatiently. 'Look, I want to get together with Wykoff. There are questions about Miller's operations, his pay-offs, things like that which Wykoff could clear up in no time. And the only way we'll ever get together is for him to come to me. That's what I want our friend in there to do – shake the grapevine a little and stir up some interest. Then we'll see.'

'I don't know,' Harlingen said. 'Wykoff's been co-operating' with the DA's office since they nabbed him. Why would he take any interest in Lundeen's troubles?'

'Because a man like Wykoff wants to know what cards everybody is holding. Anyhow, I'm not saying it'll work. It's just something we have to take a chance on. Meanwhile,' he said to Floyd, 'let's get back to the arrest. What did you and Lundeen do after you ate? Keep moving downtown the same way?'

Floyd rubbed a hand slowly over his face, his brow furrowed with concentration. 'Well, no,' he said at last. 'Not exactly.'

'What does that mean?' Harlingen asked.

'Well,' Floyd said, 'there's a couple of hotels across the way, and I went over to check them – you know, go through the lobbies. Arnie wasn't along with me then.'

'How long was it before you got together again?' Murray asked.

'Oh, not long.'

'How long? Ten minutes?'

'Maybe a little more than that.'

'Twenty minutes?'

'It could be. That's about what it was, I guess.'

Harlingen looked aghast. 'You mean that just before Lundeen arrested Schrade he was off some place where you weren't even in touch with him!'

'Jesus, Mr Harlingen, I knew where to get in touch with him if I had to.'

'Where?' Harlingen demanded.

'Why don't you ask Arnie about it?' Floyd pleaded. 'Why do I have to go talking about it?'

'Because,' said Harlingen, his voice heavy with sardonic emphasis, 'you'll have to go talking about it when you're in the witness chair. Where was he for that twenty minutes?'

'Ah, what the hell,' said Floyd. 'Any time we were around Forty-eighth Street he used to take off for one of those flea-bag boarding houses down the block here. The dame who runs it is a real piece, Helene something-or-other. She's nuts about Arnie. All he had to do was ring the bell, and she had her pants off for him. That's all there was to it that day.'

'That's all!' Harlingen said in outrage. 'When Miller might have an interest in that woman? When he might be hitting at Lundeen out of plain jealousy? Damn it, why would you and Lundeen even try to keep anything as important as this hushed up?'

Floyd said doggedly: 'Because of Arnie's girl, that's why! Jesus, I've been on double dates with Arnie and Ruth, and she doesn't even like it if he tries to hold hands with her. She's against all that kind of stuff. How do you think she'd feel if she found out?'

Harlingen took off his hat, drew a handkerchief from his coat pocket, and patted it over the red weal on his forehead left by the hat. He was an angry and bewildered man, and Murray, watching him, felt sorry for him.

It wasn't hard to understand his train of thought. Lundeen had been caught holding out on him; Lundeen could not be completely trusted any more. Yet Lundeen had apparently acted out of chivalry; he was willing to martyr himself to keep Ruth Vincent's respect. That was something Harlingen could appreciate and condone. But, to go a logical step further, what kind of man could claim Ruth Vincent and still go tomcatting behind her back? Altogether it made a nice set of wheels within wheels. Anyone sticking a hand among them stood an interesting chance of winding up with no hands at all.

Murray said abruptly: 'There's no use standing here like this. The smart thing to do is talk to this Helene. If she has anything to do with Miller it might come out that way.'

'I was just thinking of that,' Harlingen said. 'If I approached her in the right way—'

'I'll take care of it,' Murray said. 'You have to finish checking the arrest with Floyd, anyhow. He might remember some other things if he works at it a little.' He turned to Floyd, who stood sullenly hunched into his coat, his hands thrust deep into his pockets, a sorry Judas wondering how he has come to this plight. 'Where do I find this dame?'

'It's that first brownstone down the block there, right after the warehouse. You just ask for Helene.'

The neon sign in the window of the house flickered wildly: OOMS FOR ENT, it said. A man answered the doorbell, a gnome-like little man with a few strands of white hair combed across his head, a waxen pallor, and a pair of enormous, fan-like ears. He squinted suspiciously at Murray.

'You looking for a room?' he said. His voice was as thin and quavering as a note badly played on the E-string of a violin.

'No, I'm looking for the owner. Is she in?'

The man wheezed and coughed. From his expression the sounds were probably intended to be a laugh.

'You mean Helene, she's been lying about it. She's my wife, but I'm the owner. I'm the only owner around here. Every stick and stone here, it's in my name.'

'That's fine,' Murray said, 'but she's the one I want. Is she in?'

'She's in.' The man thumbed Murray inside, and carefully closed the door behind him. Then he led the way along a dark corridor which reeked of cabbage and disinfectant to a kitchen at its far end.

The kitchen was obviously the centre of household life here. A stack of dirty dishes was piled high in the sink, a battered collection of movie-fan magazines littered the cupboard shelves, there was a huge television set in one corner, and at the table in the middle of the room a woman was undergoing some process of beautification. Wrapped in a bath sheet which outlined plump breasts and which afforded a fine view of sleek, naked legs exposed almost to the thigh, she sat forward holding dripping-wet red hair over a bowl of murky fluid.

'Now what?' she said, and peered through the tangle of hair at Murray. Then she slung the hair back to her shoulders and smiled up at him, a surprisingly young girl with wise, cat-green eyes and a childishly pretty face. 'Hey,' she said, 'you're cute.'

The old man seemed indifferent to this. He went up behind her, took a wad of absorbent cotton from the table, dipped it into the fluid, and suddenly dug it into her scalp. She yelped and grabbed at his wrist, and he slapped her hand away.

'See that?' he said to Murray, hefting the weight of hair. 'Costs eight bucks to do in one of them beauty parlours. Costs me one buck if I do it for her right here. Takes a fool woman not to know how much seven bucks is worth in your pocket.' He applied the cotton vigorously, and the girl yelped again.

'Take it easy,' she said. She looked coyly at Murray. 'I'm really a natural redhead, but sometimes it needs touching up, and he does it real good.'

The old man wheezed loudly. 'Ought to open up a regular beauty parlour all my own. Make a million dollars easy.'

'Go on,' the girl told him, 'you got a million already.' She reached for a cigarette on the table and lit it, the bath sheet slowly, inexorably slipping downward. The old man, dabbing steadily away with the cotton, saw it, glanced slyly at Murray, and then did nothing about it.

'Slut,' he said. 'You won't get a penny of that money. Not a cent.'

'Bow-wow,' the girl jeered.

'Not a cent. Give it to my poor old sister, that's what. Treated her bad all my life, and it's time for a change.'

'Not with my money,' the girl said.

'Give her the house, too. Been in the family a hundred years. Ought to stay in the family.'

The girl reached out behind her and caught his wrist, and this time he could not shake her off. 'Daddy-o,' she said gently, 'remember me? I'm the family now.'

'You're a slut.'

'I'm all the family you got now, daddy, and don't you forget that. And don't talk so much. You're blowing down my neck.' She released his arm and he went back to work, clucking and muttering to himself. 'Never mind him,' she told Murray; 'he don't know what it's all about. You got any business here, I'll take care of it.'

'I've got business,' Murray said. He took one of the cigarettes from her pack and lit it, watching her closely. 'I'm handling a law case for somebody named Arnold Lundeen. You know him?'

'Know him! Are you kidding?'

'No.'

'Mister, Arnie's my boy friend. As soon as daddy here kicks off he and I are getting married. You mean, you're handling his case, and you don't know that?'

The flame of the match he was holding suddenly stung Murray's fingers. He dropped the match, and then with great care ground it out under his heel.

'No,' he said, 'I don't. But you can see why he didn't want to talk about you. I guess he'd do anything to keep you from getting involved in this mess.'

The girl's eyes shone. 'That's Arnie, all right. Isn't he the sweetest man thing you ever met up with? I even told him I'd stand right up in court for him, but he said that was O-U-T, out. But anything I can do to help, mister, you can count on me, all right.'

'You mean,' Murray said, 'you'd be a witness for him in court?'

'Sure I would. Why not?'

It was wondrous to contemplate. It would be a three-ring circus for everybody concerned. If she didn't testify, there were twenty great big unexplained minutes in Arnold Lundeen's life that would hang him; if she did, Ruth Vincent was in for the shock of her life right there in open court. But was the courtroom the place to strip Lundeen naked for Ruth's benefit? With the wheels within wheels spinning fast now, it was something to be thought out very carefully.

'What's on your mind?' the girl said. 'Do I look funny to you or something?'

'You look fine to me. Say, do you know this Ira Miller, this bookie who's supposed to have paid off Lundeen?'

'No, I don't, and that's all right with me. I wouldn't waste my spit on his kind.'

The old man tossed the cotton on the table and then thrust the girl's head over the bowl. 'Bookies,' he said. 'They're all bums. Cops are different. You're smart, you get close to cops. Then you got no violations in your house. Save plenty of good money that way. Just got to be smart, that's all.'

'Ah, shut up,' the girl said. She twisted around to see Murray. 'Look, next time you talk to Arnie, mister – hey, what's your name, anyhow?'

Murray handed her his card, and she took a long time to read it, her lips silently framing each syllable. 'What's this investigations stuff? I thought you were his lawyer.'

'I'm working with his lawyer.'

'Oh. Well, anyhow, Murray, when you see Arnie you tell him to keep on writing me, even if I ca— even if I don't write back. You tell him I got all his letters saved up, and I read them all the time for kicks. You do that, huh?'

'And have him jump on me for bothering you with this? You know how he is, Helene; he'd worry himself sick about it. He'd be sore as a boil.'

The girl thought that over happily. 'He would, too, the doll. He can be real worrisome sometimes.'

'You see? Best thing right now is to keep it to ourselves. Don't tell him anything about it. When we need you in court I'll get in touch with you.'

He went out through the dark corridor unaccompanied. At the curb before the house a truck was parked, its trailer bundled high with Christmas trees, the first he had seen coming into the city this season. The air all around the truck was permeated with the spicy scent of resin and green, and he stopped to take a long breath of it.

It was a good, clean smell.

6

Didi barged into his apartment the next day at noon, magnificent in mink.

She said: 'Sweetie, if you're going with me, you simply cannot sit there all day over breakfast or whatever it is. Now be a lamb and get all shaved and prettied up, and I'll have a cup of coffee meanwhile. How can they always make such wonderful coffee here, and no matter what I do with mine it's practically obscene. And a piece of toast, please. No, wait a second, what are those things under the napkin?'

'Bagels,' said Murray. 'Want one? And where am I supposed to be going with you?'

'No, they look like plastic doughnuts. And today is Alex's opening, of course. It's the preview.' Alex was the Accidentalist painter. 'Oh, Murray, don't tell me you didn't get my invitation. I know you'd be lying.'

'All right then, I got it,' Murray said equably. 'Say, come to think of it, I did get a card from some gallery during the week. Was that about Alex?'

'Of course it was. And I wrote a perfectly beautiful note on the back of it that you never even read. Sweetie, why do I have anything to do with you when you can be such a gargantuan stinker?'

'Because I appreciate you. And I think you look like the Empress of All the Russias in that coat. What is it, another love token from Alfred?'

Didi raised her eyes to heaven at the thought of the unlamented Mr Donaldson. 'It is. Isn't it just scandalous how that man keeps courting me all around town lately?'

'Ever think of remarrying him?'

'Why? So I can go back to being little old Dorothy who waits around the house until he gets tired of chasing the fancy ladies? He hasn't changed any, sweetie. He's just interested because I'm one of the field now. He never could resist playing the field.' She carefully dripped a spoonful of marmalade on her toast. 'But don't you fret about that any. All you have to do is get dressed up and come along before I get a ticket for double parking.'

'Sorry I can't oblige. I'm all tied up with work this afternoon.'

'Murray, you're just saying that to get out of it. You know if it was any other kind of painter, you'd be glad to go. And nobody works Saturdays any more, do they?'

'Wait and see. Ten minutes from now I'll be holding down that phone on a highly important case. I'll meet you there later, if you want.'

'That won't do. Murray, you have got to be right along with me when I walk into that place. I mean, you've *got* to.'

'I do?'

'Yes, you do.'

He laughed. 'But why?'

'It's not funny,' she wailed. 'You know the kind of people that'll be there. They'll talk and talk, and I won't understand a thing they're saying. All about Jackson Pollock and tonality and linear rhythm and God knows what else. But if you're there, I can talk to you and not look like a total idiot. You're very comforting to have around at times, honey.'

'So are you. But what about Alex? He'll be there, won't he?'

'Yes, but when he's in company he's just like the rest of them. It's different when we're alone. He doesn't want to talk about painting then.'

'I suppose not,' said Murray, and then happened on a pleasant notion. 'Look, I really do have some business to clear up, but I'd just as soon do it in person. If you drive me over and stand by, I'll rush things along and go the rest of the way with you. Is that a deal?'

'I don't know. It can be awful tiresome sitting out in the car and waiting for you to remember I'm there.'

'You won't be waiting outside; you'll come right in and meet these people,' Murray said. 'I want to show you off to them.'

Not only were all the Harlingens there, gathered in the living room, he discovered, but Ruth Vincent was there as well. She sat straight-backed in her chair, pale and beautiful and remote, and the sight of her hit him like a finger driven hard into his diaphragm. As Harlingen made hostly small talk, putting everyone on a first-name basis, he watched her, seeing the colour tinge her cheeks, the small pulse flicker at the hollow of her throat, knowing that even in his waking dreams she had never been lovelier than this. When she suddenly turned her face away from him he realized that he had been unabashedly staring, and didn't care. Let her know, he thought. Let her pile the furniture of her conscience against the door and think she was safely barricaded behind it. He had enough on Lundeen already to blow apart her tie to the man whenever the time was right.

Dinah Harlingen said brightly: 'Ruth's been rehearsing Megan for a little play they're going to do at school. One of those old moralities about Goodman Willing and Goodwife Ready, and so quaint and charming. Isn't it, dear?'

Megan plopped down on a hassock, locked her hands over her head, and slowly pulled back until her face was turned toward the ceiling. 'No,' she said in a sepulchral voice, 'it is deadly, deadly, deadly.'

'Megan,' said her father, 'don't be difficult. And stop twisting your head like that.'

Megan pulled her head back to normal. 'I am not being difficult. Why does something have to be good just because it's

73

old? When Grandfather talks like that he's so stuffy. But everybody else talks like that, and it's terribly heroic and adult. You listen to them sometime, and see for yourself.'

'Well, you recite some of it for us, honey,' said Didi. She sank back in the couch and threw her coat open, prepared to be the good audience. 'Anything's got to do with theatre I just eat it up.'

'Thanks a lot,' Megan said loftily, 'but no thanks. Anyhow, Goodwife Wanton is the only real part in the whole thing, and Evvie Tremayne's got it. And,' she said pointedly in Ruth Vincent's direction, 'she only got it because she's over-developed.'

'She got it because she took an interest in the play,' Ruth said. 'You know that as well as I do, Megan.'

'And it is perfectly charming,' said Dinah Harlingen nervously. 'At least, what I heard of it. The background music is all done on a single woodwind recorder, too. So medieval. Who is that little boy who plays it, Megan? He looks like a miniature faun.'

'That's William Hollister Three,' said Megan. 'And he's a total neurotic.'

'He is not,' said Ruth. 'And I wish you and everyone else in the Thespians would stop calling him Three, Megan.'

'If he doesn't want people to call him that he should stop putting it down on all his papers,' Megan said. 'He's going to be a total neurotic, too. He said so himself. He said learning to play the recorder is enough to make anybody a total neurotic. No matter what you do with it, it sounds sick.'

'You know, Ruth,' Dinah Harlingen said, 'perhaps this play wasn't the wisest choice after all. If the children—'

Harlingen stood up abruptly. 'Drinks, anyone? Didi? Ruth? Murray? No, well I suppose it is pretty early to start lubricating. So if you'll excuse us now, Murray and I have important things to talk over. We won't be long.'

Behind the closed door of his study he said to Murray: 'I wish Dinah wouldn't interfere like that. Ruth's got her hands full with that gang of demons as it is, and don't think every word said here won't get back to them. Not that I entirely disagree with Dinah, mind you. That is, on the pearls before swine basis. Giving those kids pre-Elizabethan drama is sheer waste. Tennessee Williams is their speed.'

Murray laughed. 'Goodwife Wanton and William Hollister Three on the recorder sound tempting, though. I'd like to see them in action.'

'Don't say that in front of Dinah, or you will. She happens to be chairman of the ticket committee. Say, your friend is a remarkably attractive woman, isn't she? Do I know her from somewhere? She seems vaguely familiar.'

'If you hang around the Stork or 21 you've probably seen her there. She's done a couple of bits on TV, too. Earl Wilson wrote her up last year.'

'I can see why he would. Yes, it was probably 21. Dinah and I are there now and then.' Harlingen sat down, found a pencil, and toyed with it while they talked about nothing consequential. Then he abruptly asked: 'Well, did you have any luck with our friend Helene? Did she have anything to do with Miller?'

'No. Nothing at all.'

'Are you sure? I could have sworn—'

'Dead sure. Her business was strictly with Lundeen.'

'But how could you verify that? How do we know she isn't keeping Miller her secret? Just talking to her wouldn't settle the matter, would it?'

'It would in this case. You'll have to take my word for it that she wasn't Miller's motive, that he didn't frame Lundeen out of jealousy, or anything like that.'

'Well, exactly what did you find out from her?'

Murray smiled. 'I'll have to pass on that one. Any information not related to the case is for Lundeen alone. It'll be in the file, waiting for him.'

'Yes,' said Harlingen, 'I can't argue with that.' He tossed the pencil on the desk, then watched dispiritedly as it rolled off at an angle to the edge, teetered there, and fell to the floor. 'I don't know. I just don't know. Is there any chance that the time he spent with that woman might be overlooked during the trial?'

'There's a chance, but I wouldn't bet on it.'

'God almighty,' said Harlingen. 'And if she does testify, can you see what it means? An officer on duty taking time off to go to a whorehouse?'

'It isn't exactly a whorehouse.'

'That makes it even worse. Anyhow, it means that no matter what happens at the trial Lundeen and Floyd will have to go before the commissioner afterward for dereliction of duty and a dozen other things. That's what Floyd's been terrified about.'

'Too bad about him,' Murray said. 'He should have thought of that before he started to cover up for Lundeen. He and Lundeen both turned my stomach. They want to play by their own rules, and when they're caught at it they yell their heads off. All right, let them yell. Your job is to defend Lundeen in court, not to hold his hand and tell him what an unfortunate case he is.'

'Yes,' Harlingen said thoughtfully, 'I know what you mean. That's been your attitude from the start, hasn't it, Murray?'

'I've never made any secret of it. I took the case with that understanding. Why?' Murray asked flatly, and he had the electric feeling of holding the image of Lundeen in his hand, waiting for the signal to close his fist and crush it to a pulp. 'Do you have any objections? Is this where I get off?'

'No, Ruth's told me all about your talk with her. About your attitude toward the case. I don't agree with it, but it doesn't matter as long as you're willing to work with me the way you have been working. What I don't understand though, is that – well, it's hard to put into words – that contempt, I suppose you'd call it, for someone who's been knocked down by circumstances and is looking for help. Not that Lundeen is crying for help the way you put it, mind you. He's accepted me as his lawyer and friend, because I convinced him he should. And it wasn't easy. He's a man with a great deal of pride, and, I'm afraid, with the same innate suspicions of the human race that you seem to have.'

'I'm not under discussion,' Murray said. 'All I want to know is whether you have the same holy faith in him even after finding out about this woman and the way he tried to cover up about her.'

'He was doing that for Ruth's sake. You'd have to know his feeling about Ruth to appreciate that, Murray. He venerates that girl. He acts as if she were some sort of sacred treasure put into his keeping, and he can't get used to the idea that he's worthy of it. It's amazing, really. You don't see much of that attitude nowadays. It's that kind of thing that lets a man risk a jail sentence, rather than allow an affair with a passing tramp to become public property.'

'But the tramp comes in handy, doesn't she?' Murray said. 'As long as she's around, Ruth is safe from a fate worse than death. Let's not forget that.'

'That's a cheap way of looking at it.'

'It's calling a spade a spade, mister. What the hell else is this whole fine attitude built on except a tramp off somewhere to take care of the manly impulses while milady keeps her drawers buttoned up tight? Not that this particular tramp needs any worrying about. She can take care of herself and Lundeen and anybody else who comes her way. But if there's any pity required, I'll give mine to her, not to Lundeen.'

Harlingen said angrily: 'How did we get into this in the first place? Do you want to drop the case? Is that what this is all about?'

'No, not as long as I'm wanted.'

'All right then. Let's get down to facts and skip theorizing.' Harlingen leaned back in his chair, clasped his hands on his head, and turned his face up to the ceiling. 'Now, about this woman, I don't know. What I'd like to do is let it go for the time being. Maybe Lundeen will come to me about it himself; maybe something'll turn up that'll help us get around it. Meanwhile, we'll roll it up and put it on the shelf.'

'What about Floyd?' Murray asked. 'Won't he be talking to Lundeen about it?'

'Well, I told him not to discuss it with anybody until I spoke to you. I'll call him up tonight and make sure he keeps mum even with Lundeen.'

'That's sound policy,' Murray said. 'As far as my end goes, I'm getting together with Strauss and Manfredi first thing Monday. Manfredi hasn't gotten anything worth while on Miller so far, but he'll be working on him over the weekend, and that's a good time for things to happen. I'll keep in touch with you, anyhow.'

'And that about ties it up, doesn't it?' Harlingen said. He came forward in his chair with a jolt, and flexed his shoulders pleasurably. 'Now, how about that drink I owe you? Say, if you don't have to rush away—'

'We'll take a rain check on that,' Murray said. 'We've got an important appointment with genius.'

Didi arranged herself behind the wheel of the car in stony silence, and drove three blocks without saying a word. That, as Murray knew, was something of a wonder in itself.

'Are you sore about something?' he asked.

'No.'

'What does that mean?'

'It means no, that's what it means. And please stop trying to sit on my lap. If you're cold you can just turn on the heater. That's what it's there for.'

'I am trying to turn on the heater,' he said. 'It doesn't seem to work.'

'*That* heater.'

'No, you're not sore,' Murray observed placidly. 'Just a little more than wrought, and a little less than overwrought.'

'How nice people like that,' said Didi in a choked voice, 'can raise such a wretched little brat and not be tempted to strangle her in her sleep, I for one do not know. Of all the insufferable—'

'Megan?' said Murray. 'Why, I wasn't gone long enough for her to kick you on the shins.'

'She did not kick me on the shins, sweetie,' Didi said between her teeth. 'You just listen to this. She sat there after you were gone – she just sat there and *glared* at me. It was like waking up and finding something from Mars on the foot of your bed. And then when that Dinah woman stopped talking for one second to catch her breath, this *thing* said in that deep, fake, throbbing voice of hers: "I think it's vulgar to wear mink so early in the day." *She* thinks it's vulgar! Of course, when she goes off to that idiot school of hers in the morning she just throws on an old Persian lamb! Who the hell does she think she is at her age?'

'That's the point,' Murray said. 'At her age she thinks she's Marilyn Monroe. Or you. Jesus, you aren't going to let a kid get under your skin with some stupid remark she picked up somewhere, are you?'

'Picked up where?'

'Oh, God,' sighed Murray, 'how do I know where? From somebody who can't afford a mink coat and wishes she could, I suppose.'

'Well, I don't have to suppose. That child is getting her notions from that schoolteacher of hers. That frozen beauty. The one who stopped you dead in your tracks when you walked into that room.'

Murray shrugged. 'I cannot tell a lie. I have a fatal weakness for a pretty ankle.'

'Oh, she's got more than a pretty ankle, pet. She's got a pretty everything else, right up to the last pretty hair on her head. And don't you make a doubtful face as if you don't know that. Any time I see a man make a face like that when I'm talking about a good-looking female I can see through him like glass.'

'Didi,' Murray asked, 'are you being bitchy?'

She looked at him wide-eyed. 'Me?'

'Yes, you.'

She shook her head solemnly. 'Now, that hurts,' she said. 'It truly does. Here I am, thinking only of your good—'

'What a question!'

'—thinking only of your good, and you can say something like that. Murray, you listen to me. I know that kind of girl. She might look as good as whipped-cream cake, but when you get real close you can tell it's all sugar and cardboard like those fake ones in the store window. You trust my womanly instincts, pet, and stay away from that kind. In their hearts they've just got no use for any man. I mean that, Murray.'

'Who the hell cares what you mean?' he said. 'Will you please watch where you're driving!'

'Ho!' said Didi. 'Now who's a little more than wrought?'

7

Time was not the essence when Bruno Manfredi prepared to make a report. Long ago he had cultivated a ritual of preparation – much like that of a nurse laying out the instruments for an operation – in answer to Frank Conmy's bristling impatience during conferences. Frank would sit there gnawing his moustache, fingers drumming on the desk, face mottling with pent-up fury, while Bruno would solemnly open his leather envelope, extract the pages of written report from it, place them next to the envelope, grope through the envelope for any photographs and photostatic prints, arrange them next to the report, repeat the process for newspaper clippings and other sundries, place them next to the photographs, and then, with the air of a man who has completed the first step of an exhausting job, close the zipper on the leather envelope and put it on the floor next to his chair.

It was only the first step. Then came the search through various jacket pockets until the small black notebook was found and added to the row on the desk. This was followed by a pack of cigarettes, a lighter, a package of chewing gum, a pencil, a ballpoint pen, and an eyeglass case, and by now Frank's face was usually a fine shade of purple.

The eyeglasses wound up the performance with a flourish. Heavy of frame, splendidly executive in appearance, they would be removed almost tenderly from their case, held up to the light for inspection, breathed on, polished, and finally donned by

Bruno with an air of rich satisfaction that was the last straw to Frank.

'Are we ready *now*, Mr Manfredi?' he would roar, and the thunder of that fine, round baritone would freeze new stenographers at their desks.

Nor, as Frank had discovered, was there any way of speeding up the routine. Any effort to do that seemed to wreak havoc with Bruno's otherwise efficient memory, send him fumbling helplessly through his papers with pathetic, long-winded apologies, and take twice the usual time to clear up the business at hand.

'Of course, I know why he's doing it,' Frank had once complained to Murray after a particularly harrowing session. 'And if I was a little bit hard on him when he started here it was only because I like to see a man sit down, spit out his business fast, and be on his way. But he's made his point now, so let him be done with it.' Then he added after morose reflection, 'You know, I don't even believe the crazy son of a bitch *needs* glasses.'

The trouble was that by the time Frank was dead and gone what had started as a way of badgering him had become ingrained habit. Watching Bruno neatly lay out his materials in the familiar row on the desk, Murray felt a weary sympathy for everything Frank must have felt on such bygone occasions. But, wiser than Frank, he waited until Bruno had finished the ritual, and then waited another full minute on his own account before saying anything.

'Where's Lou?' he asked mildly. 'He was supposed to be here with you, wasn't he?'

'Right now he's on that trucking deal. You know, that Dawson guy who thinks his drivers are hijacking his deliveries.' Bruno unwrapped a piece of gum and popped it into his mouth. Then he lit a cigarette and inhaled luxuriously, his jaw never missing a beat. 'About those records, he made contact with the clerk, but so far no dice. He can't say why. He figures maybe the heat is on because of Wykoff.'

'Maybe.' Murray nodded at the assortment of papers on the

desk. 'Who helped you put all this together? You didn't do it yourself, did you?'

'Jesus, you're getting worse than Frank,' Bruno said indignantly. 'That new kid Rigaud backtracked some of the leads I gave him, but the legwork is all mine. Here, you want to see my shoes?'

Murray declined the offer. 'What does it add up to?'

'About Miller? I don't know. As far as catching him with the goods right now, we don't have a thing. Either he's a reformed bookie, or he's putting up the best front anybody ever did. But there's some items here that might be interesting. Let me run through it, and you'll see for yourself.'

'Run,' Murray said pointedly. 'Don't walk.'

'Sure, Speedy.' Bruno dug into his papers. 'Here's his birth certificate. Born New York, 1915. And his high-school record, and some poop from the yearbook when he graduated. Honours in mathematics – that's the bookie blood starting to show – member of the tennis team, member of the dramatic society.'

It struck Murray that Arnold Lundeen, one way or another, had a surprising affinity for people who were interested in dramatic societies. He found himself thinking of Ruth, and impatiently thrust the thought aside. 'So far,' he told Bruno, 'all that's missing is the grey-haired mother and the faithful dog. When do they come in?'

'Will you let me do this my own way?' Bruno demanded. 'Now, listen. In September, 1933, Miller enrolled at NYU. Three months later they gave him the heave-ho right out of there.'

'Why?'

'For peddling examination papers. Him and two other guys were in a little racket to steal test questions and sell them off to the other schoolboys. It all came out in the newspapers when Miller's people sued for readmission, and I've got a couple of clips about it here. Think they're worth anything to Harlingen?'

'I'll leave that up to him. What happened to Miller after that?'

'Well, we lose him for a couple of years, and then we pick

him up doing office work for the Bindlow Resort Corporation. That's the company that runs the Acres – you know, that billion-dollar hotel up in the Catskills. Private airport, private swimming pool for every customer, private dining room for left-handed people – you ought to see the book they put out. It's like Radio City with trees.'

'What's Miller got to do with all this?'

'Plenty. The guy who owns it is Daniel Bindlow, and he's got no family of his own, but he's got one niece, Pearl. In 1940 Miller hit the jackpot; he went and married this Pearl. She's not much to look at maybe, and she's five, six years older than Miller, but he must have figured that, what the hell, half the time he's with her the lights'll be out, and the other half he can sit and read her uncle's bank account. Anyhow, he played it for keeps.

'Then in 1942 the army grabbed him, and he was in for about a year. He got out on a hardship appeal. His wife kept having nervous breakdowns or something while he was away, and she was in and out of sanatoriums until the Red Cross put in a pitch for her.

'After that he went to work for Bindlow again, and here's where it gets interesting. Bindlow was having all kinds of trouble running his place those years. The help was looking for more pay, so he had a couple of strikes, and he also had basketball trouble.'

'Basketball trouble?'

'I thought that would goose you. You know how those hotels hire college teams to play for them in the summer; it's one of the biggest things up there. The kids are supposed to be waiters and bellhops and such, but they're getting their dough to play ball, and everybody knows it. Bindlow's trouble was that he couldn't buy himself a winner. The customers wanted to bet on the home team, but every time they did it they lost their shirts. So Bindlow dug himself up a guy who could take care of everything for him. The labour trouble, the basketball trouble, everything in one nice package. A real little miracle worker. Who do you think?'

'Miller,' said Murray. 'Who else?'

Bruno stubbed out his cigarette in the ashtray before him and leaned back in his chair smilingly. 'Guy name of George Wykoff,' he said gently, 'that's who else. Fix you up with the union, fix you up with a basketball team, fix you up with anything you want, if you can pay for it. Which Bindlow could.'

'Where'd you learn all this?' Murray asked.

'I got hold of a programme for a game they had up there around that time, and Rigaud located one of the guys listed on it. I had a long talk with this guy for the price of a drink. It's all written down there. He says you can use whatever you want of it, he don't care. He says the way they got a winning team at the hotel was that Wykoff paid other teams to dump games to them now and then, but at the end of the season Wykoff ran off with most of the pay-off money. They all hated his guts.'

'And what's this got to do with Miller?'

'Well, when Wykoff took off at the end of the season, Miller and Pearl went along with him. That must have been the beginning of their tie-up. Then Miller showed up in New York making book over on the West Side and using his Songster Company for a front. Songster is still in business, by the way. Miller sold it to a guy named Billings last summer, and I had quite a parley with this Billings. Know what kind of outfit it is?'

'Theatrical agency?'

Bruno waved a disdainful hand. 'Nah, that's way out of Billings' class. This is a real sucker trap. What it claims to do is write words to music or music to words, whichever way the suckers want it. A lot of noodles in the farm land figure they can write songs, see? If they send the music to Billings he writes the words for them, or if they send the words he writes the music. They pay plenty for this, and in the long run they wind up with some copies of the song, and no harm done. Billings says what the hell, there's nothing against it in the postal regulations, so he don't worry. He's got a broken-down piano in there and a rhyming dictionary, and he says as long as the supply of suckers holds out he figures to make a living. When Miller ran the place, Schrade used to handle the song-writing angle for him.'

Murray reflected on that. In a way, he thought, you had to admire Miller for the unerring way he gravitated toward the graft, the payola, the swindle. Even in choosing a front for an illegal operation he was driven to choose something which was a swindle in itself. It was the kind of fine instinct that would let him know exactly what cop to pay off, and how much to pay him, and how to have the cop take the rap when the time came. A very smooth fish swimming easily in very hot water, because that was his natural habitat.

'What's he up to now?' asked Murray. 'I mean, Miller.'

'He's back with Bindlow again. Mostly he's in the New York office here, but when there's a big holiday rush at the Acres he goes up there for a stretch. Kind of assistant manager.' Bruno lit another cigarette, and bent over the desk to study his report. 'Anyhow, let me fill in the details.

'He and his wife live over on West End Avenue. No kids, but they got a little poodle dog. There's some kind of nurse for Mrs Miller, too; from what the doorman said, she was taken pretty bad around Thanksgiving. Miller works ten to five, takes a cab home about five-thirty, stays in mostly, and then goes for a walk with the dog around eleven. Dresses fine, reads the *Times* in the morning, the *Telegram* at night, also weekly *Variety*. Eats lunch in that classy place downstairs from Bindlow's office, Terwilliger's. And the whole time I tailed him he never said a word to a living soul outside of the waiter there. What do you make of that?'

'Just playing it safe,' Murray said. 'Bindlow probably took him back on that basis.'

'I guess so. Anyhow, Bindlow should talk. He's the one who got Wykoff into the picture in the first place.' Bruno handed a photograph to Murray. 'Here's how Miller used to look around then. I had the lab blow this up from a snapshot in an old advertising book the Acres put out. He looks about the same now. Heftier, and without so much hair, but you could still tell him from the picture, all right.'

The picture was that of a tall, well-built young man in shorts standing before a tennis net, a sweater thrown casually over his shoulders, a pair of tennis rackets held under his arm. He was squinting into the sunlight, a smile flashing whitely out from a tanned face, blond hair tousled in the breeze. It was obviously a picture aimed at luring hopeful spinsters to the Acres, and, thought Murray, must have been highly effective in its function. He could imagine the cloud of despair that had risen over the Catskills when Pearl Bindlow herself had grabbed off this prize.

Bruno came around behind Murray's shoulder to study the photograph with interest. 'Don't look much like any bookie you ever met, does he?' he commented. 'Looks like he's getting ready for the Olympic Games or something.'

Murray said: 'You have to be an amateur for that. This one was born a professional.' He tossed the picture on the desk. 'Is that the works?'

'That's it.'

'Nothing about Lundeen? No reason why Miller might have wanted to frame him? No possible tie-up between them?'

'What's that mean?' Bruno protested. 'You know I gave you everything I had. It's all right down here.'

'All I saw right down here,' Murray said, 'is a smart bookie who pays off the cops when he has to.'

'Well,' said Bruno, 'that's the whole story, isn't it?'

Murray smiled. 'I know. I just wanted to hear you say it, that's all. It shows what a smart detective you are.'

'Smart enough to know when I'm being conned,' Bruno said coldly. He thumped the leather envelope back on the desk and started to load it. 'You want me to work on Miller any more?'

'No, Schrade is next on the list. Dig up what you can on him.'

'After I take a day off. I'm bushed. Home at two AM, Up at seven – I don't even remember what Lucy and the kids look like any more.'

Murray had been prepared for this. Lucy Manfredi was a round-faced, bustling woman who took a dim view of her husband's vocation, and who regularly declared open rebellion against it. 'No day off,' Murray said. 'I'll call up Lucy and explain things.'

Bruno yanked at the zipper of the envelope. 'You'll have a tough time with her. Not about me, either. She keeps asking why you never come around any more. She thinks since you got to be a big shot, maybe you got a swelled head.'

'She knows better than that. Tell her I'm just leery of those over-age girl friends of hers she keeps shoving at me.'

'Monsters,' Bruno agreed sombrely. 'But you know how a woman is. She sees a guy with money going around single she gets sick all over. Anyhow, I'll tell her about it tomorrow. It wouldn't hurt me to take a day off and show my face around the house.'

'You'll be working on Schrade tomorrow,' Murray said. 'And on your way out tell Mrs K. I want to see her.'

Bruno stopped at the door. 'Sure, boss,' he said unctuously. 'That's right, boss. Yes, sir, boss. Anything else, boss?'

'Yes,' Murray said. 'Leave that Miller report here. I'll be using it.'

He waved aside Mrs Knapp's omnipresent pad and pencil. 'I'd like to make a date with you for tonight,' he told her. 'How would it be if I picked you up at your place around eight?'

'Very flattering. What is it, a subpoena?'

'No, we won't be serving any papers. I want to talk to one of the witnesses in the Lundeen case, Ira Miller. This stuff here is Bruno's report on him, and there's plenty of material on Lundeen in the files. Read up on it when you have time this afternoon. It'll tell you as much about him as I can.'

'All right. Is this a come-as-you-are?'

Murray surveyed her thoughtfully. 'Maybe a little less chic would be better. Hardly any make-up. Cotton stockings—'

'Good heavens!' said Mrs Knapp.

'Well, you know what I mean. Something a little less eye-catching than those.' For a woman in her sixties she had excellent legs. 'And a sort of maiden-aunt hat, if you can find one.'

'I think I can. Whose maiden aunt am I supposed to be?'

'Nobody's. You'll be an old schoolteacher of Lundeen's – no, we'll make that a settlement-house worker who knew him back when, and who just got wind of the trouble he's in. You simply can't believe it. He was such a *nice* boy. Now you've come to his lawyer to speak up for him and have insisted on telling Mr Miller to his face that you're sure a terrible mistake has been made. How does that sound to you?'

'Terribly touching.'

Murray laughed. 'I know it's corny, but if it opens the door that's all we want. Care to make it a party?'

'I'll be ready at eight,' said Mrs Knapp.

8

The building occupied by the Millers was an ornate and weathered pile, a monument to the era when apartment houses were designed to look as much as possible like castles on the Rhine. Its elevator rose ponderously to a dismal accompaniment of rattling chains, and the sound of his footsteps along the corridor leading to the Millers' door echoed hollowly in Murray's ears.

'What'll you bet,' he whispered to Mrs Knapp, 'that whoever answers the bell is wearing armour and carrying a halberd?'

It was not a knight, however, but a Valkyrie who opened the door. A blonde, strapping figure of a woman clad in a gleaming white uniform, she stood stony-faced, barring the way.

Mrs Knapp smiled a gently hopeful smile. 'I'd like to see Mr Miller,' she said, and Murray had the feeling that she was thoroughly enjoying her role. 'Is he in?'

'He is not here,' said the Valkyrie. 'Mrs Miller is here, but she cannot see people. She is sick.'

Murray silently cursed Bruno Manfredi and all his works, but Mrs Knapp seemed unperturbed. 'Oh, I'm sorry to hear that,' she said. 'It isn't serious, I hope.'

The Valkyrie shrugged. In that one small gesture she made it clear that it wasn't serious, that Mrs Miller was a fool who pampered herself, and these strangers were a nuisance. 'You call up tomorrow on the telephone,' she advised. 'Mr Miller will be here.'

'Hilda,' said a pleasant voice behind her, 'you are being rude, aren't you? You know one doesn't keep people standing outside like that. Do come in, please, you people.'

The Valkyrie sighed so that her corset creaked audibly. 'Mrs Miller,' she said without turning her head, 'why do you walk around? You must lie down and rest.'

'I'm tired of resting. I want to have company. Now, do let them in, Hilda, or you'll spoil everything.'

When Hilda moved aside in ungracious invitation Mrs Knapp glanced at Murray, and he nodded. Pearl Miller led them into a living room so vast that even a grand piano in one corner seemed no more than a normal part of it.

'How lovely to have company,' she said. 'How lovely, lovely. Do sit down, won't you? No, not there. Toto uses that, and he sheds horribly. It doesn't matter, though, if you wear dark clothing, does it, because he's inky black all over, and he's just an angel. Usually he goes for his walk at bedtime, but he was so pent up today that my husband took him out right after dinner.' (Murray silently apologized to Bruno.) 'But they should be back very soon, and then you'll see for yourselves what an angel he is. You don't mind my telling you all this, do you? I'm just *full* of good talk.'

Her hand moved vaguely as she spoke, weaving a slow, meaningless pattern in the air. With a sense of shock Murray realized that despite the desiccated hand, the scrawny body lost in the heavy chenille robe, the faded complexion, the livid shadows under the eyes, this woman was twenty years younger than Mrs Knapp and looked years older. Then, when the sleeve of the robe fell back, he saw the tell-tale bandage around her wrist. Pearl Miller followed his eyes and stood studying her own upraised arm with a puzzled interest. She suddenly dropped the arm and tugged the sleeve down.

'Isn't that silly?' she said brightly. 'I cut myself.'

Murray clicked his tongue sympathetically. 'How did it happen?'

'It was an accident,' said Pearl gravely. 'Don't you think it was an accident?'

'Of course I do. What kind of accident was it?'

'Oh, very messy. Do you like to hear about accidents? I don't think they're good talk at all.'

'I do,' said Mrs Knapp. She sat on the edge of the over-stuffed couch next to Murray, a worn handbag balanced on her knees, the archetype of genteel social worker. 'And look how the newspapers write about them. They know people are interested.'

'I don't like the newspapers,' said Pearl. 'I won't read them. My husband reads them, but I don't think he should.'

'Why?' asked Murray. 'Because they printed things about him?'

'They did that, too.' She eyed Murray warily. 'You're not from a newspaper, are you?'

'No.'

'I'm so glad. Now let's talk about something else. Do you like the theatre?'

'Very much. Do you?'

'Oh, yes, but not as much as my husband does. You have no idea. I tease him about it sometimes. I say: "Ira, if you ever run off and leave me some day, it won't be for another woman. It'll be so you can go on the stage." Of course, it's just teasing. He wouldn't really do it, would he?'

'You mean, go on the stage?' Murray asked. He had the feeling of being led blindfold, step by uncertain step, across quicksand.

'I told you that was just teasing. I mean – go away. It can happen, you know,' she assured him solemnly. 'It happens all the time.'

'My dear, you shouldn't even think about that,' Mrs Knapp said. 'I'm sure you're very happily married.'

'Oh, I am. I am very, very. But I used to think about it.' Pearl smiled in faraway recollection. 'Isn't that strange? I used to worry about it all the time. After we were married people would say to me: "Pearl, you've got to keep your eye on him. Pearl, you've got to watch out with that kind of man." People in the family, friends, they all said it. You see, they didn't know how kind he was. All they knew was that he was so handsome and smart, and he worked with somebody like Georgie Wykoff. But even Georgie respected him for being such a good husband. Nobody was ever a better husband. Did you see *Time Out of Hand* when it was on Broadway?'

Murray dimly remembered it as a play which had closed after a brief struggle against bad reviews. 'Yes,' he said. 'I did.'

'Did you like it?'

Her tone gave him his cue. 'Very much.'

'I'm glad. My husband helped finance it, you know. We both thought it was perfectly beautiful. Why do you think the critics didn't like it?'

Murray shook his head. 'It's hard to say.'

'You see? You don't even know why yourself. But I'm sure you were angry about it, weren't you?'

'Yes, I was.'

'I was, too. Oh, how I hated those critics. We all waited in Lindy's that night until the man came in with the papers, and when we read them I just hated those critics enough to kill them. Ira was so proud of the play – it was what he always wanted to be doing, produce a play – and then he had to sit there with all our friends, and make jokes about how bad it was. But I knew how he felt. I know everything he feels. Isn't that funny? I know everything about him. Even the things I don't want to know.'

'That's the way it should be,' said Mrs Knapp reassuringly.

'Yes,' Pearl said placidly, 'that's the way it should be. Would you like some coffee? I've been so pleased about your coming to visit that I've quite forgotten to be a good hostess. It does get lonely at times without company. I think it's because this apartment is so enormous, isn't it? You know, when it's empty it can be the emptiest place in the whole world. That's what happens when there's no children, you see. All my friends tell me that. They all have children, so they know. We thought we'd have a family when we first moved in here, but we never did, and we still live here.' Her hand went to her mouth in a small fluttering gesture, and she smiled uncertainly. 'That piano was going to be for our little girl. It seems a terrible waste now, doesn't it? I don't know how to play it at all.'

It was a dog that suddenly broke the terrible spell she was weaving, a small black poodle that dashed into the room at her, its feet scrabbling on the hardwood floor, its body wriggling ecstatically. She patted it with one hand while fending it off with the other. 'My beautiful Toto,' she crooned. 'Beautiful boy. Did you have a good walk?'

Then Miller stood there, a triumphant Hilda beside him, looking at them all with slow astonishment. He was the Miller of Bruno's photograph, but the body was thicker now, the hard line of jaw concealed by a heavy jowl, and the face tired and unsmiling.

'What is this?' he said. 'Who are you people? My wife's a very sick woman. She's not supposed to be seeing anybody.'

'I'm not sick!' Pearl clutched the frantic poodle to her so tightly that it yipped in protest. 'I had an accident, but I'm all better now. You know it was an accident, don't you, Ira? You told me so yourself. You said—'

'I know, I know.' Miller went to her, lifted the dog gently from her arms, and handed it to Hilda, who took it with obvious distaste. 'It was an accident, but you were all upset after it, and that's like being sick, Pearlie. You know you're not supposed to get excited about anything, and now look at you. Is that the way you take care of yourself? Is that the way you keep your promises to me?'

She drew his arm through hers, and looked up at him coquettishly. 'Let me stay with the company, Ira. Please?'

'Some other time. Right now you get to bed and try to sleep. You should have been sleeping all the time I was out. You've got a lot to make up.' He detached himself carefully and led her to the door. 'Hilda, lock up the dog, will you, and then see that Mrs Miller's taken care of.'

Hilda was the image of righteousness. 'I told her,' she said. 'When the doorbell rang she just—'

'God damn it,' Miller said in a deadly voice. 'I'm paying you a fortune to take care of her, not argue with her. Now go on and do it!'

She departed, her broad back rigid with outrage, and Miller closed the door behind her. When it clicked shut Murray saw Mrs Knapp's hands tighten convulsively on the handbag, and had a graphic insight into what she must be feeling. She had helped serve papers before, but this was something different. Then it was usually a case of being on the outside, wondering how to get in. Now it was a case of being on the inside, wondering how to get out. Which, as any mouse in a trap would admit, was a far more uncomfortable matter.

The trouble was, he knew, that Mrs Knapp had no idea how much she resembled the genuine article. The sweet old gentlewoman loaded with the milk of human kindness. The settlement-house lady eager to turn aside wrath with a soft word. Our Mrs Knapp. If she could see herself as Miller was undoubtedly seeing her she would feel a lot better. Unfortunately, she couldn't.

Miller himself seemed divided between embarrassment and annoyance. He started to sit down in Toto's chair, thought better of it, and stood there hunting in his pockets until he found a pack of cigarettes. He offered it to his callers, and Murray took one – it was Frank Conmy's theory that a man was always subtly flattered when you took a cigarette he offered you – while Mrs Knapp smiled beatifically and shook her head.

'I don't smoke,' she said.

'I smoke too much,' said Miller. He lit a cigarette for himself, and Murray saw that his hands were trembling. 'Well, I've got reason. I'm only sorry you people had to walk in on something like this. I guess you know that whatever Mrs Miller was saying to you – whatever she was talking about – well, it wouldn't be too logical. She had this accident a little while ago, and it just sent her off balance. She's loaded with this Reserpine stuff now – this tranquilizer – so she's on sort of a jag all the time.'

'How awful,' said Mrs Knapp. 'She's such a lovely woman.'

'She's a saint,' Miller said heavily. 'She's too good. She bleeds for everybody. Let me tell you, it's crazy to be like that in this world. But what do you do when somebody is made that way? How do you talk her out of it?'

'You don't,' said Mrs. Knapp. 'She has a right to be that way.'

'You think so?' Miller shook his head. 'I don't. You can be just so good, and then they nail you on a cross, and where are you? And where are all the people who care about you? You think you're helping them, but you're killing them, too. What do you think happens inside of me every time I look at her? Do I have to tell you?'

Murray saw the opening and seized it. 'I'm afraid you won't convince Mrs Knapp about that,' he said. 'She used to work for the Downtown Settlement House, and as a matter of fact, she's here to help somebody she knew there a long time ago.'

Miller looked puzzled. 'Help somebody?'

'Somebody you know. Arnold Lundeen.'

'That cop?'

'Yes. Mrs Knapp was very close to him at the settlement house. When she heard about the trouble he was in she came to me and asked to see you personally about it. She's sure a mistake has been made, and wanted to clear things up.'

What interested Murray was Miller's reaction to this. This, he thought, is the spot where another man laughs, swears, or rages. But not Miller. The small frown, the pursed lips, the sober concentration, all indicated only a sympathetic interest, a warm desire to listen and help. It was a beautiful performance. With a witness like this on the stand, LoScalzo could impeach the President of the United States.

'I'm sorry,' said Miller, 'but I don't completely understand. What mistake has been made? And where do you come in?' he asked Murray. 'Are you a friend of Lundeen's?'

'I'm associated with his lawyer on the case.' 'Associated' was always the perfect word, suggesting, as it did, everything and nothing. 'My name is Kirk, if you want to check on it. Anyhow, I explained to Mrs Knapp that it's pretty unusual, this business of coming to you directly, but, as I found out, she can be a pretty stubborn woman.'

Mrs Knapp bridled. 'I can be, when it's a case of seeing justice done.'

'Sure, sure,' said Miller soothingly. 'But where do I come in?'

Murray saw that Mrs Knapp's hands had relaxed their grip on the purse. Like a good fighter she had been keyed up waiting for the bell, and now that it had rung she was prepared to answer it like a champion. The story of an Arnold Lundeen *sans peur et sans reproche*, who as a child, a youth, a man, could do no wrong, emerged like a Hollywood epic of the slums.

'So you see,' Mrs Knapp concluded, 'when I heard about the terrible charges against him I just *knew* it was a mistake. He couldn't be dishonest. It isn't in him to be. Mr Miller, couldn't you have picked the wrong man? Couldn't you have forgotten what really did happen? That's possible, isn't it?'

Miller had maintained the sympathetic interest throughout the recital. Now he showed some impatience.

'Let me answer you this way,' he said. 'It's also possible that there are some honest cops in New York, but so far I never met any. No, you don't have to look at me like that, lady. I've dealt with more cops than you'll know in a lifetime, and every one of them was looking for a handout, and waiting to twist your arm if you didn't come across for them.

'Sure, in my line of work – and I'm well out of it, thank God – you expect it, you play along with it, it's part of the business. From *your* angle a cop is somebody in a nice uniform who helps you across the street sometimes, who chases crooks, who's always Johnny-on-the-spot when some kid gets his head stuck in the subway turnstile. But, lady, that's because you're always on the right side of the street. Come over to where I was, and you'd have your eyes opened. Whether it's an apple, or a five-dollar bill, or a thousand dollars, there's always a cop waiting to help himself.

'What makes you think this Lundeen is any different? Because he was the nicest kid on the block, the way you tell it? No, that's not the way it goes, because if he was such a nice kid he would never want to be a cop in the first place. The kind of kids who want to be cops, they're the kind who have an itch to push people around and to collect graft when they're still in kindergarten!

'And what happens to somebody who gets on the force and isn't a born grafter? They make him one, that's what! Where do you think Lundeen would be if he didn't collect from me, so he could pass on a cut to the captain, the inspector, the politicians right at the top, so that they'll have enough to give your settlement house a few pennies and help keep kids honest? It's a joke, lady; the whole thing is one big joke on people like you. All any cop or any politician is looking for is the ice, the pay-off. That's what Lundeen was looking for, and that's what he got. And if you want my advice, you'll write him off as a dead loss. Let his lawyer here worry about him. Does that answer your question?'

Mrs Knapp looked wide-eyed at Murray, who nodded. 'Speaking for the lady,' he said, 'I imagine it does.'

'All right then,' said Miller. He pulled a handkerchief from his breast pocket and mopped his forehead, which was glistening with sweat. 'I'm sorry I had to talk like that, but it all goes back to what I was telling you about – well, about people being bleeding hearts. They have no right to put themselves out for somebody who isn't worth it. It's not natural. It only makes trouble.'

'There's one more thing,' said Murray. 'If you—'

'Forget it,' said Miller in a hard voice. 'I told the lady what she wanted to know, and that's it. Anything else I have to say I say only in court. And in case you think I'm a little bit dumb about all this, mister, I'll tell you one thing I worked out all by myself. This lady never got the idea to look *you* up; nobody goes to such trouble for the fun of it. You were the one who pulled her into this.' He brushed aside Mrs Knapp's protest. 'I'm not saying everything she told me isn't true. I'm just saying it's a shame to drag a nice old lady into this, so you could soften me up for the trial. I hate to tell you what that makes you look like, mister.'

The elevator lurched downward, its chains rattling balefully. 'What I want to do now,' Murray said, 'is get over to the office and tape what we remember of this while it's still fresh. How about it?'

'All right,' said Mrs Knapp, but there was an unusual note in her voice. Murray noted with concern that she looked very old and very tired.

'Are you sure?' he asked. 'You seem a little frayed around the edges.'

'Just reaction.'

'That's natural. It was a sweet session, wasn't it? Well, when it's on tape we can write it off. After that, we'll run over to some good late place, and I'll stand you coffee and cheese cake. Lindy's, let's make it.'

'No,' said Mrs Knapp abruptly. Too abruptly.

It took him a moment to understand. 'You mean because of Mrs Miller sitting there listening to her husband make sad jokes about his show? All right, we'll go somewhere else. You name it.'

'That wasn't any accident,' Mrs Knapp said, unheeding. 'That was a suicide cut, wasn't it?'

'I guess it was.'

'And she's such a dear. She's such a pitiful little thing. I sat there listening to her, and I wanted to say something that would – oh, God,' said Mrs Knapp with intensity, 'sometimes I hate all men!'

Murray had the feeling that this was unfair both to Ira Miller and his sex in general, but Mrs Knapp's mood hardly invited argument. Then, to his relief, the elevator stopped, and its door slid open invitingly. But Mrs Knapp did not move. He looked at her, and realized with alarm that she was crying. Head averted, handkerchief in hand, she was silently and helplessly crying.

It was, in its way, a revelation.

9

He slept badly that night, and at five in the morning settled on a brimming glassful of brandy as an emergency measure. He arrived at the office at noon, conscious of a dark brown taste in the mouth and a weariness deep in the bone.

'This,' he told Miss Whiteside as he examined the appointment book on her desk, 'is one of those days when, in the immortal words of Joe Jacobs, I should have stood in bed. How many did I miss?'

'Quite a few,' said Miss Whiteside unkindly. 'I made other appointments for most of them, but this one here – this Mr Scott – said he would wait until you showed up. He went out for lunch, but he said he'd be right back. He was very anxious to see you.'

'This would be a better world if people weren't so persistent, but if that's the way he is— What in God's name are you reading there, Miss Whiteside?' Murray studied the cover of the magazine with interest. It was adorned with a photograph of a reigning Hollywood queen, her low-cut gown gaping wide open as she leaned forward into the camera. Underneath the picture a caption in bold type asked, 'Why Were Her Panties Found in the Wrong Bedroom?' 'You shouldn't show this kind of stuff around here, Miss Whiteside. You'll scare away the better class of client.'

Miss Whiteside's sense of humour was not her strong point.

Her face went bright red, and she abruptly thrust the magazine into Murray's hand. 'It does not happen to be mine, Mr Kirk. It was left here by that Mr Scott. He works for it or something.'

'Oh. Well, I'm sorry I misjudged you, Miss Whiteside. It's just that nowadays you never know—'

'Let me tell you, Mr Kirk, I wouldn't be caught dead reading something like this.'

'I'm sure. What's this Scott like, Miss Whiteside?'

'Oh, very nice,' said Miss Whiteside. 'A very classy type.'

He was all of that, Murray saw at a glance when Scott was ushered in. A trim man with iron-grey hair and a face as hard and smooth as polished flint, he would have made a flawless model for a whisky advertisement, posing, glass in hand, before a fireplace. Put him behind the wheel of a yacht off Sand's Point, Murray speculated, or behind an expensive shotgun on the Eastern Shore, and he'd be right at home. He had the look. He had the sound, too, when he spoke. The voice was a cool and positive reflection of Harlingen's.

'You're late, Mr Kirk, but there's no need to apologize. Personally, I detest people who ask one to explain away a lateness like a tardy schoolboy. You'll notice I haven't given you my card. There's no need to. My credentials are right on the masthead of this copy of *Peephole*. I'm its publisher. As for my excursion here – the mountain coming to Mahomet, so to speak – don't give it a thought. There are aspects of my business which I prefer to handle this way. The reason is obvious,'

'Of course,' said Murray. It suddenly struck him that the worst possible prescription for a hangover was time spent with a monumental egoist.

'*Peephole*,' said Scott, 'is the biggest thing in publishing today. Our circulation is five million a month. Our news-stand sales are skyrocketing. *Peephole* means money, it talks money. If you have any doubts about that, Kirk, take a look at this.'

Murray leaned forward to read a slip of paper Scott held up before him, and saw that it was a cheque for five thousand dollars payable to Conmy-Kirk. 'Very inspiring,' he said. 'But if you don't mind my asking, Mr Scott, what's it supposed to inspire me to?'

'You know my magazine, Kirk? You've often read and enjoyed it, haven't you?'

'Not too often, I'm afraid. It always seems to be about the same old things happening to people who should know better. It loses some of its flavour after a while.'

'Not for our mass of readers, it doesn't. Maybe you have other interests, Kirk, but our readers *want* to read about the same old things happening to people who should know better. Just as long as those people are glamorous public figures. Figures in the entertainment world, especially. I don't care whether they're singers, dancers, actors, directors, or writers – they all have a skeleton in the closet. And *Peephole*'s readers want to see that skeleton. They want the names, the dates, the places, the words spoken, and pictures, if there are pictures. They want, in brief, just what you've got stocked away in those filing cabinets behind you. Do I make myself clear?'

'I'm not sure. My impression is that you're offering me five thousand dollars to go out and dig up scandal about various celebrities. Is that it?'

'No, it isn't. I have agencies working on that angle for a great deal less, Kirk. What I want from you is material you've already got in your case files. It so happens that my man in California used to work for Frank Conmy, and he told me that your files here are loaded with red-hot material on some of the biggest people in show business. Those tapes and photos are the lifeblood of *Peephole*. Give me first pick of them, and I'll top the price of any competing magazine in the business.

'Now get this straight, Kirk. I don't want entry to your files; I don't want anything to do with them. All you have to do is go through your master index, write down the name of anyone who might be of interest to *Peephole*'s audience, and give me that list. I'll pick fifty names from it, and take the files on just those fifty people, sight unseen. That's one hundred dollars apiece, Kirk.

Five thousand dollars for an hour of your time. It's a gamble for me, but I'm a willing gambler. And there are no other demands put on you. I'll have truckmen come here and pick up the load at my own expense.'

'I see,' said Murray. He pressed his hand to his forehead to ease the pounding there, but it didn't help.

Scott frowned at him. 'What's the matter? Headache?'

'Yes, but it's really—'

'A headache is nonsense,' Scott declared. 'Here, let me show you why,' and the next instant, to Murray's surprise, the man was coming at him from around the desk, hands extended like the hands of a strangler seeking a victim. There was no fending them off, either. They bore down on Murray's neck, digging in, twisting, and grinding with bone-cracking force. Surprisingly cold, hard hands, too. *They are the hands*, Murray thought wildly, with an almost macabre relish, of a *Thing sent to haunt me because I have been a sot*. His nose an inch from the desk, he struggled against the uncontrollable laughter that rose in him, and managed, in the crisis, to turn it into a sputter.

'Relax, man,' said Scott. 'Relax, and get the full effect.' He twisted his victim's jaw, there was a climactic pop of vertebrae, and the hands were removed. When Murray warily raised his head Scott was standing there patting his brow with a handkerchief and breathing hard.

'That's better,' said Scott. 'Damn it, Kirk, you've got fine bone structure, but look at the way you're fouling it up. You're a man, not an animal, for God's sake. Sit straight. Walk straight. Be a man all the way down that spine. And take my advice – see a good chiropractor. A chiropractor made a new man of me.'

Murray managed to restrain the comment which rose to his lips. 'I'll think about it,' he said.

'Don't think about it. Do it. And that reminds me that I'd like to settle our business and be on my way.' He held out the cheque. 'I'm sure the terms are satisfactory.'

Murray looked with brief longing upon temptation, and then

closed his eyes to it. 'Sorry, Mr Scott, but I don't think they are.'

'That's your privilege, Kirk. What price are you asking?'

'That depends. All I know so far is that I seem to be in the middle of a seller's market. Before I make any decisions I'd like to look around and see what confidential files are being quoted at.'

A small crack showed in Scott's composure. 'Now you're talking like a sharper, Kirk. I'm surprised at that.'

'That's your privilege,' said Murray. His headache, he discovered, was as bad as ever.

'All right, we're both businessmen. I'll raise the ante another thousand. But for that figure I want your word that I'll be getting the real goods. Sex, dope, prison records – those are the circulation builders. And whichever it is, it's got to involve a celebrity the man on the street knows and wants to read about. If I can't get good stories out of fifty per cent of your list, I'm taking a loss.'

'That's a nice sales talk, Mr Scott. However, no sale.'

The crack in Scott's composure was very wide now. 'Look, Kirk, let me enlighten you about something you aren't taking into account. I approached you directly, because I feel it's good business to deal with the man in charge when you can. But you know and I know that loyalty doesn't mean a damn to the kind of people who work in your line. You've got a big organization here, and there isn't anyone in it who wouldn't sell you out to the highest bidder. In view of that, why do you force me to go behind your back and deal with some double-crossing employee? Isn't it better for you to make the sale yourself and draw a profit from it?'

Murray stared at the man with unblinking fascination. 'Well, I'll be damned,' he said softly.

'But you do get my point?'

'Oh, I do,' said Murray. 'I do.' He buzzed for Mrs Knapp, and when she appeared he swung his chair around to face her.

'This is important, Mrs Knapp. I want you to draw up a list of our clients, past and present, who might be regarded as celebrities. That means anyone the man on the street knows and wants to read about.' He nodded at Scott. 'You don't mind my borrowing your definition, I hope?'

Scott was the image of pleased urbanity. 'Not at all.'

'Good. After that, Mrs Knapp, when any one of our men asks to see a file included in that list he's to write out his reason and sign it. If you think the reason is the least bit fishy, report to me at once. Then I can—'

'Good heavens!' cried Mrs Knapp as the door slammed behind Scott with the impact of a bomb bursting. 'What was that about? The man must be out of his mind.'

'No, he's just terribly, terribly hurt. Anyhow, get to work on that list, Mrs Knapp. Or better yet, put one of the girls from the stenographers' pool on it. Pick the stupidest one we have. That kind has an uncanny eye for celebrities.'

This day, Murray decided after a lunch that had been delivered to his desk lukewarm and totally unpalatable, was destined for small troubles and many of them. He was convinced of that when Bruno called at two o'clock to announce that their bird had flown. Eddie Schrade had disappeared from his Coney Island address, seemingly into thin air.

'What do you mean, disappeared?' Murray said. 'Did you ask around? Did you cover the whole neighbourhood?'

'All day, so far. The only character who looks like he might know something is the guy who owns the trap where Schrade was living, and he's not talking. Jesus, nobody wants to talk around here. You should see this place in the winter, Murray. It's like the end of the world.'

'What about it? You're not there on a sightseeing tour, are you? Do you think LoScalzo's behind this?'

'He could be. He needs Schrade to back up Miller, or he's got no case. Maybe Schrade is the one he's worried about.'

Murray pondered this until Bruno wailed, 'Talk to me, boy, talk to me. It's cold and lonely out here.'

'You miserable coward. Listen, are you near a post office?'

'There used to be one around here. What've you got in mind, Murray, the Brother Frank play?'

'We'll try it,' Murray said. 'Two postal cards and two letters, and make sure you don't address them so light that they wind up in the dead-letter office.'

'Roger and over. Say, who'll be Brother Frank?'

'I will,' said Murray, 'so write those things to Brother Murray.'

'Okay. See you in the morning then.'

'No, hold on a second.' Murray drew a pad toward him and carefully started to doodle a Palmer Method exercise in circles. 'You remember when Jack Collins was in town last year he said something about a new angle he had out on the Coast, but he wouldn't say what it was?'

'Yeah.'

'And you remember I told you afterward that if his angle was to sell off tapes and pictures to the dirt magazines we'd have to get a different agency to handle assignments out there?'

There was a silence. 'I get it,' said Bruno at last.

'What the hell,' Murray said, 'I know how you feel about him, Bruno – you were always buddies, he's got that job in LA waiting for you any time you want it – but I can't let that make any difference. If our big clients hear we're tied in with his kind of deal we can write them off tomorrow. You understand, don't you?'

'Sure, I understand. But, Murray, you could still be making a mistake. Every agency on the Coast is doing the same as Jack's. The whole goddam state of California is bugged from top to bottom. You take one of those Hollywood babes, if she don't think there's a microphone under her mattress she can't sleep nights. With a gold mine like that around, you can't blame Jack for wanting to cut in, can you?'

'I'm not blaming him,' Murray said; 'I'm ditching him until he cuts loose from those magazines. He's a nice guy, but he's no use to me right now, Bruno. I'm telling it to you straight so you'll know there's nothing personal in this.'

'Screw that,' said Bruno, 'you don't owe me anything,' and then the operator's voice cut in, remote and melodious. 'Deposit five cents for the next five minutes, please,' it said.

'Chisel from somebody else, sister,' said Bruno, and hung up.

Murray slowly replaced the phone, and then out of the dark complexity of his thoughts realized that Miss Whiteside was regarding him from the doorway with a peculiar expression. *Now what?* he wondered.

'There's a girl here to see you, Mr Kirk,' said Miss Whiteside. Her voice was as peculiar as her expression.

'A young lady?'

'A girl,' said Miss Whiteside coldly. 'A little one with a big mouth.'

It was introduction enough. He knew, even before she made her entrance, that it was Megan Harlingen.

10

Entrance was the only word for it. No tragedienne walking on stage for her big scene – certainly, no tragedienne who might weaken under the handicaps of a nose made glowing pink by the cold, conspicuously grimy knuckles, twisted stocking seams, and a tendency to wobble on high heels – could have done better. Megan was indifferent to the handicaps. Her overcoat was draped casually over her shoulders. The skirt of her bouffant pink lace dress ballooned out over an assortment of crinolines and swayed languorously as she moved. Her hauteur was magnificent.

'I'm very glad I was *finally* allowed to see you,' she told Murray. 'There are some people—'

'She said she needed car fare to get back to school,' Miss Whiteside cut in, 'and I said you were busy, and I'd be glad to oblige. And then – well, I'm surprised you didn't hear the fuss right through the door, Mr Kirk!'

Megan's lip curled. 'I did not make a fuss. I simply made it clear that I cannot possibly accept money from strangers.'

'You sure did!' Miss Whiteside retorted inelegantly, and for the second time that afternoon the office door was slammed shut with explosive impact.

It seemed to jar Megan. She essayed a smile, and then, in the face of Murray's stony silence, removed it. 'I'm sorry,' she said weakly. 'I really didn't mean to make her angry.'

'No?'

'No, I really didn't.'

Murray sighed. 'In that case, Megan, let me reveal a deep, dark secret to you. Miss Whiteside is one of those eccentrics who *will* get angry when someone is rude to her. Come to think of it,' he added with bleak significance, 'she's a lot like Mrs Donaldson in that respect.'

'Mrs Donaldson? Oh, you mean Didi.'

'I mean Didi.'

'Isn't that a curious name?' Megan said brightly. 'Wherever did she get it, Murray?'

He looked at her blandly, and remained silent.

Megan abstractedly started to gnaw a thumbnail. 'I guess she told you what happened, didn't she? I mean, about what I said to her?'

He nodded.

'Well, she shouldn't have. She only did it so she could look unspeakably heroic and pitiful. If you weren't a man you'd know that right away.'

'I don't think so, Megan. She had a choice of either clouting you one in front of company or unburdening herself to me, and I'd say she made the charitable decision. But what gets me is why you made that crack to her in the first place. What was the point of it?'

'I'm sorry, but I would rather not say. I'm sure you wouldn't understand.'

'Don't pull rank on me, sister. Just answer the question.'

'Well, all right!' Megan said despairingly. 'I only wanted – is she your girl friend?'

'She is not, and don't change the subject.'

'Then I suppose she's your mistress, isn't she?'

'Megan!' He said it with outrage, because he had an idea it was the noise expected from him. Expected, at least, by propriety, if not by Megan. Actually, for the first time since he had dragged himself out of bed that morning he felt that the day was bright with promise, and life full of unexpected little bounties.

Megan did not seem to share that feeling. 'I don't care,' she said sullenly. 'She looks like a mistress.'

'Megan, since you probably don't even know what the word means—'

'I *do* know. It's in lots of books. And the man who lives downstairs from us—'

'Mr Walters?'

'Yes, Mr Walters. Well, he has a mistress, and I saw her myself. He brought her up to a party one night, and she got drunk, and they had a *shattering* argument. She said everyone else there was in analysis and she wanted to be in analysis, too, and he said it was too expensive, and she went home crying. I was right there when it happened.'

Murray wistfully thought of the tape recorder locked away out of reach. 'That's very interesting, Megan, but just a little bit irrelevant. What I'm waiting to hear is why you were rude to Didi.'

'I *am* telling why, and I didn't mean to be rude. I was just merely hinting to her in the nicest possible way that she looked all wrong.'

'She did?'

'Of course she did. Her dress was cut down to here, and when she crossed her legs her skirt was up to here so you could see she was wearing black lace underwear when it was hardly lunchtime, and perfume so you couldn't breathe, and all that fur and jewellery just for visiting. It was too perfectly disgusting for words.'

'A hopeless case,' Murray agreed sombrely. 'It's a wonder you had the courage to tackle it.'

Megan's eyes narrowed. 'And that isn't all. The way she was hanging on to you – well, maybe you didn't mind, but you don't know how it *looked*. I mean, wouldn't you think a grown-up woman has enough strength to walk into a room without hanging on to people and fixing their ties and patting their hair all the time? Especially with everybody sitting and watching?'

Sudden comprehension smote Murray full on the brow. He

looked at Megan now, positive that he recognized the classic symptoms of jealousy.

'Megan, Miss Whiteside said you needed car fare to get back to school. What are you doing away from school, anyhow?'

'Oh, that. Well, we're supposed to work on medieval costumes, and Miss Vincent gave me permission to go to the Forty-second Street Library after lunch and make notes about them. I mean, as long as I got back in time for rehearsal. So then I found out I didn't have money to get back, and I knew your office was around here, and I looked in the telephone book. It's perfectly all right to be out of school if you have permission. Everybody knows that. It's unspeakably progressive there.'

'I'm sure it is.'

She had a handbag the size of a small valise slung on her arm, and he deftly twitched it away and turned it upside down over the desk. From it poured an amazing trove, ranging from lipstick-smeared tissues to paper clips, and among the trove, naked and accusing, were some crumpled dollar bills and a scattering of coins. 'Well?' said Murray.

Megan swallowed hard. 'Now, isn't that funny? I looked and looked—'

'Really?'

'Oh, yes.'

'Oh, no. You happened to be around here, and you thought it would be just dandy to drop in for a visit. But you ought to know that—' He stopped short, a golden prospect opening before him. 'Megan, who's in charge of your rehearsal?'

'Miss Vincent.' Megan forlornly started to sweep her horde back into the handbag. 'And she did so give me permission.'

'I believe that. You don't talk about her personal affairs in school, do you, Megan? About the case your father and I are working on?'

'I never say a *word.*'

'Did you ever mention me to the other ki— to anyone there?'
Megan nodded.

'What did you tell them?'

'Only that you're a real private detective, and I know you. They think it's utterly breathtaking and heroic.'

'That's very kind of them. And to show there's no hard feelings, I'll tell you what I'll do. I'll drive you back to school myself. Think we'll have time on the way for a sundae at Rumpelmayer's?'

'You will?' said Megan dazedly. 'I mean – oh, yes!'

Obviously, it was a day bright with promise for all lovers.

The pink lace dress was embellished with a large chocolate stain by the time they arrived at the school, but neither that nor the fact that rehearsal was already in progress could keep Megan from walking on air as she paraded Murray down the aisle of the auditorium. At a glance the surrounding seats appeared to be empty, but then, here and there, heads popped up like frogs surfacing on a lily pond. The eyes fixed on Murray, however, had no glazed and froggy indifference in them. They gleamed with avid interest.

On the stage Ruth Vincent, a tulip rising above a wind-swept patch of weeds, was putting her class through its uncertain paces. A company of villagers was in the throes of a morris dance accompanied by the mournful, reedy wailing of a recorder. The instrumentalist – Murray surmised that this must be the hapless William Hollister Three – sat in a chair tilted back at a precarious angle to the wall, and paid no attention to Ruth's efforts at conducting. The dancers gaily bounced back and forth and paid no attention to the recorder. Then, magically, the sounds of recorder, of thumping feet, and of intermittent giggling faded into silence. Ruth, wise in her office, looked around to see why, and one look was enough.

Watching her walk up the aisle toward him, Murray had to marvel at himself. He was thirty-five years old, sound of mind, and certainly neither a libertine nor a romantic. He had learned the hard way that what separates the men from the boys is the ability to weigh and measure emotions carefully before doling them out. Youth was the hot time, the time when the kettle was always boiling and never empty, the time for the foolishness of excess. But a full-grown man, as Frank Conmy put it, is someone with sense enough to count his fingers after he shakes hands with anyone, including his own mother. And Murray marvelled, because, while he knew this was the indisputable truth, he also knew, looking at Ruth Vincent, that in him was all the heat, the foolishness, the constriction in the belly, of his seventeen-year-old counterpart, and was glad of it.

This is my beloved, he thought, and, recklessly scrambling his poetry, *She walks in beauty, like the night—*

She walked in temper as well, but Megan, who might have been expected to quail before it, only rallied with banners flying. Clearly working on the assumption that the way to avoid disaster is to plunge into your story fast, tell it breathlessly, and omit all compromising details, she rattled away for two minutes without a break. At the conclusion of the narrative Murray had a dazzling picture of himself as a St George in armour, one foot manfully propped on the body of a dying dragon, while Ruth looked highly sceptical.

'And what about your dress, Megan?' she said. 'You certainly weren't wearing that one when you left here at lunchtime. Do you always change into party clothes when you go to the library?'

That was the most unkindest cut of all. Megan's shoulders dropped, her lower lip trembled, her eyes filled, and Ruth looked stricken. 'Oh, never mind,' she said hastily. 'Get up on the stage and find your place, Megan. And don't ever dare—' But Megan had already fled. It was hard to tell, as she galloped on to the stage, where she was instantly enveloped by chattering class-mates, whether she was laughing or crying.

Murray said to Ruth: 'You remind me of Mark Twain's wife. You know, the time she wanted to show him how ugly his swearing sounded, so she tried it herself, and he told her that she had the words right, but the music wasn't there. I think Megan's got you buffaloed.'

'Megan's got everyone buffaloed.' When Ruth smiled a small dimple appeared near the corner of her mouth. No, not a dimple, he saw, but the faint tracing of an old scar. And trust the gods to put it where it would make her even more beautiful. 'But she really went too far this time,' Ruth said. 'She had no right to bother you with her nonsense.'

'It wasn't any bother. Cross your heart and promise not to tell, I was faced by something bigger than both of us. She's got a fearful crush on me. I think it's called an unspeakably heroic crush.'

'Oh? You seem pretty much pleased about it.'

'Sure I am. I like girls to have crushes on me. I'll admit that in Megan's case there's a discrepancy in age, but after all, Juliet was only fourteen, wasn't she?'

'She was, but she never had to worry about flunking French and algebra. I hate to blight love's young dream, my friend, but Megan's a complete featherhead as it is. If you encourage her at all, she'll be impossible to handle.'

'I see. Well, would it be considered encouragement if I waited until you were finished here, and drove you home afterward?'

'I'd rather you didn't.'

'Why not?'

'For one thing, I live down on Barrow Street in the Village. I'm sure it's out of your way.'

'It isn't. Try again.'

'And I know you'd be bored silly, sitting through this rehearsal. We'll be here for another hour.'

'I'll enjoy every minute of it. I can just sit and watch that girl there. The one who's crossing the stage now. My God, she isn't fourteen, too, is she?'

'Who? Oh, that's Evvie Tremayne. No, she's sixteen. And will you *please* turn around. She's only walking like that because she knows you're looking at her.'

Murray obediently turned his back to the stage. 'You see? And you said I'd be bored. Now you only have one excuse left.'

'Oh, damn!' Ruth said in exasperation. 'I've been trying to tell you politely that I don't want you to take me home. Isn't that enough?'

'No, because I wanted to talk to you about Arnold, and this looks like a perfect chance to do it. It might be very helpful to me.'

He had been saving that as a trump card, confident it would take the trick, and it did. Ruth looked apprehensive. 'What about him? I mean, there's nothing wrong, is there?'

'I didn't say that. It's just a matter of getting some personal information about him, but if you—'

'That's ridiculous; you know I want to help any way I can. I'll be with you as soon as I'm finished here. No, don't sit there; you're enough of a distraction for this crew as it is. One of those seats in the last row would be better.'

He took a seat in the last row, and, despite the magnificent confusion on the stage and the sleep-provoking thump of couplets delivered with all stress on rhythm and none on sense, was able to get a fair idea of what it was all about. The village, it seemed, had been invaded by a devil who was now busily instructing its inhabitants in the delights of sin. Especially, if one judged by the male villagers, in the delights of whacking each other over the head with rolled-up play scripts whenever teacher's back was turned. Then, at the height of the orgies, noisily symbolized by the morris dance, Death in the person of Megan Harlingen entered to serve a grim warning. The villagers were led by her to the brink of hell itself and shown the varied punishments awaiting them unless they repented in time.

Largely because Death had difficulty in remembering her lines and had to be prodded through them, word by word, there was no time to unveil the final scene. Instead, the curtain came down on a speech by Ruth, delivered with ringing sincerity.

'Megan,' she said, 'you have a flawless memory for anything you've ever seen in the movies or on television right down to the commercials. It is really a remarkable memory in its way. Can't you, for heaven's sake, apply one small fraction of it to *this*?'

But, Murray thought, even without its final scene the play's happy ending was inevitable. The villagers, with the possible exception of Evvie Tremayne, reform; they return to their proper medieval lives; they save themselves for their medieval purgatory. About Goodwife Wanton he was not so sure. She might think she was going along with the crowd, but nature was betraying her every undulating step of the way. And why not? as Frank Conmy would have said. Wasn't that nature's business?

It was. Take a man who's sitting on top of the world – on top of the St Stephen, at least – and who has health, wealth, and women, all in fair measure. He knew what he wanted, and now it's his. He has it made. And then along comes nature telling him that the full sum of this isn't worth one of Ruth Vincent's fingernails. Telling him, in effect, that all he's living for now is to take and keep Ruth for himself.

It could be done; it had to be done. The sole obstacle was Lundeen and the way she felt about him. If the man went down protesting his innocence and his purity of soul to the bitter end, he'd be a martyr to her afterward, and martyrs are perversely attractive objects to women, by and large. So the one problem was how to wrap up Lundeen so tight and sink him so deep that nothing could be salvaged of him. He had to be finished off so thoroughly that there wouldn't be more than a bad memory left of him while he rotted away his two-and-a-half-to-five in jail That was it. That was everything. After that there would be no problems left, at all.

In the car Ruth said: 'If you're showing the traditional male annoyance at having had to wait for a woman, please don't. I told you it would take time.'

'What? Oh, I'm sorry. I wasn't thinking anything like that.' He drove with his eyes fixed straight ahead, careful not to turn and look at her profile, or even glance at the slender legs outstretched beside his. 'I happened to be thinking about the play.'

'Thinking what about it?'

'Oh, about the way Death always pops up in those old

moralities to scare people back to righteousness. But since even the dumbest peasant knew his days were numbered anyhow, would he really scare that easily?'

'Sure he would. After all, it wasn't just a matter of dying. It meant closing your eyes one minute, and then opening them in front of the gates of hell where the sign said *All hope abandon, ye who enter here*. That should have been enough to terrify anybody, don't you think?'

'Except the righteous, of course.'

'Oh, you know how the righteous are; they're always the most terrified of all when it comes to facing judgement. And it was literally a time of judgement. Death was only something that brought you before the Judge.'

'A sort of glorified cop?'

Ruth drew in her breath sharply. 'Yes.'

'Not in *Everyman* he wasn't. Seems to me that in *Everyman* Death was police, judge, and jury all in one. Real Star Chamber stuff, as our friend Harlingen would say. How do you figure that?'

'You mean, you've read *Everyman*?' Ruth said in surprise, and clapped a hand to her forehead. 'Oh, damn! *That* certainly sounded condescending, didn't it? But it really wasn't meant to be. Or was it?'

'I leave that to you,' Murray said impassively. 'In all fairness though, I ought to tell you that I sometimes read books. I look up the hard words in the dictionary.'

'That's a sound policy. Would you mind my asking a highly impertinent question?'

'It all depends.'

'Well, I'm not being condescending this time. I'm being curious. How did someone like you happen to become a private detective in the first place?'

'I was seeking worldly advancement. How'd you happen to become a schoolteacher?'

'Oh, predestination, I guess. I was the little girl who took charge of the other kids on the block as far back as I can remember. Taught them games, read to them, made up plays to act, generally ran them ragged. And loved it. I mean, *I* did. Not being conversant with the latest educational theories at the time, I never bothered to ask if they did.'

'What block was this?'

'Same old block. Barrow Street. My family's owned the house there since the Village was really a village. It's kind of an interesting house, too, if you don't mind weird plumbing.'

He noted that no invitation was included in this, but let it pass. 'You don't live there alone, do you?'

'No, both parents are present and accounted for. Dad's a history teacher up at Columbia.'

'He is? That's my old stamping ground.'

'Well, what do you know,' said Ruth. 'When did you go there?'

'I didn't. I went to City. But my father ran a grocery across the street from Columbia – I think he was friends with every teacher there – and let me tell you, no one ever worshipped more devoutly at those gates than I did. Did you know that a miserably underrated Columbia team once went out to California and beat mighty Stanford in the Rose Bowl? It took me years to get over that. I must have been run off the campus twenty times that spring trying to get the autograph of every man on the squad. College football has never been the same since then.'

Ruth groaned. 'That's what you think. Did you know that after you left Harlingens' Saturday Ralph had that television set blasting away all afternoon with one game after another? There I was working with Megan in her bedroom, and I couldn't even hear myself talk. And then Dinah would drop in now and then to explain over the noise that a medieval play was all a mistake to start with. So let's not underrate college football. It had me so unnerved that I seriously considered working on a new play altogether.'

'Which one?'

'Oh, something by that Welsh poet, Evan Griffith. It's perfectly beautiful, and a lot of fun. Have you read him?'

'I've read him. Didi was a friend of his.'

'Of *Evan Griffith*?'

'Let's not underrate Didi, shall we?' He risked looking at her now, and found that she was regarding him with the open-mouthed wonder of a child. 'Jesus, what's so wonderful about knowing Evan Griffith?'

'Because it is. Because he – oh, never mind. Did you know him, too?'

'No, I just met him once.'

'Well, what was he like?'

Murray considered that. 'Very talented.'

'You know that isn't what I meant,' Ruth said impatiently. 'What was he like in person?'

'Didi can tell you better than I can. Ask her about it some time.'

'All right, I will,' Ruth said firmly, and then peered inquiringly through the windshield. 'Why are we turning off here? It's only Fifty-seventh Street.'

'Because I want to go down the Drive. It's roundabout, but we'll miss the traffic. And I wanted to talk about Arnold without worrying about the traffic. After all, that's what we're here for, isn't it?'

'Yes,' Ruth said. 'What about Arnold?'

'Well, you remember when he came up to the office and recorded his story of the story?'

'Yes.'

'That's what I'd like you to do now. Make believe I'm a recorder and just tell me all you can about him from the time you two met. Don't worry about how personal you get, or how irrelevant something may seem to be; it's all grist for the mill. Would you mind doing that?'

'No. But wouldn't it be better if Arnold did it himself? I'm only—'

'We'll get to that some other time. Meanwhile, this is a necessary part of the picture. Make believe I'm not even here, that you're talking out loud to yourself. You'd be surprised how much help this kind of thing can be when a report is being put together.'

The elevated drive unwound along the Hudson River piers, and Murray drove at an easy speed, watching the sun slowly settle into the Jersey hills across the river, keeping an eye on the big ships berthed along the way, trying to identify them by the markings on their stacks before he reached them, listening to Ruth with half an ear as she talked. But most of all, he was conscious of the girl's body next to him, her head back against the seat, her knee almost touching his. It would have been easy to rest an arm casually along the back of that seat, to move a knee the fraction of an inch necessary to provide an electric contact. But he did not. He drove at an easy speed, and listened to her talking about Arnold Lundeen.

She had met Arnold in high school. She had never dated or even known any other boy before or after Arnold. He was the only one. At first it had merely been a matter of helping him sometimes with his studies, because he was a poor student, and then suddenly they were going together all the time. This was a feather in both their caps, if you wanted to look at it that way. Arnold was a school hero pursued by all the girls in his classes, and she herself had been – well, boys had always tagged around after her, even though she never encouraged them to. So both she and Arnold had, in effect, made enviable conquests.

After he graduated, Arnold had trouble finding a place for himself. He couldn't get a steady job because he was of draft age, and no company would risk training him and then losing him to the army. So he hung around with one of those local gangs of leather-jacketed boys who admired him for his past glory. She hated that. Not because there was anything criminal about the boys, but because they were like lost souls without any direction in life, and Arnold was head and shoulders above them. She had fought this out with him several times, and then the whole thing was settled by the draft, anyhow.

He was overseas most of his time in the army, but wrote voluminously. His letters were sometimes so intense that they were embarrassing, but they were always touching. The one bad spell came about because of the picture. He had written her for a picture of herself in a bathing suit, and she had, after consideration, refused to send one. Their next letters became so violent about this silly business that she finally sent him a picture which – well, all she could do was hope he wasn't showing it around like a prize trophy. Not that she couldn't understand why he had brought up the whole thing in the first place. He loved her, he was proud of her, he wanted everyone to know why. It was a compliment, really, although a distressing one.

When he came home he immediately looked for work, but now, ironically, he was unskilled and untrained; there was no worthwhile job open to him. It was her father who first had the idea of the police, and it was he who pulled a few political strings to make sure that Arnold would have no trouble getting his appointment. On the day he got the appointment Arnold proposed to her. She hadn't wanted to accept – there were several reasons for that – but he had finally persuaded her to wear his ring without setting any date for the wedding.

He got along well as a uniformed policeman for a while; so well that he was picked for duty with the Vice Squad. Things changed for the worse after that. He hated his work, hated the business of tricking prostitutes into accepting his money in dirty hotel rooms, hated the way bookies jeered and threatened when he arrested them, hated the feeling that everyone he knew was always silently accusing him of taking graft. And he had been afraid to ask for a transfer to different duty, because then both the men on the squad and in the rest of the force would eye him with double suspicion.

That was how matters stood when LoScalzo struck his blow. Now, all that was left was the hope that justice could be had in court. That there was some way of assuring it, of taking the bandages off those blind eyes so that they could clearly see Arnold Lundeen's innocence.

'I don't like that statue,' Ruth said wearily. She turned to look at Murray, her head still against the seat. 'I never liked it. I remember when I was a little girl I once wondered why it was blindfolded, and even after I found out it seemed all wrong.'

Murray had timed the trip perfectly. He turned the car into Barrow Street and pulled up before the house Ruth pointed out.

She made no motion to get out, and, almost abstractedly, he let his arm fall across the top of the seat so that it brushed her hair.

'Cigarette?' he asked.

'No, thanks.'

He thrust the unopened pack back into his pocket. 'Funny thing,' he said. 'This is the first time since we met each other that I've seen you even halfway relaxed.'

'It is? I guess it is. Maybe I just talked myself out. You're a good listener.'

'And you've been needing one for a long time. Even if it is somebody you almost took apart a couple of weeks ago for saying that Arnold was guilty. Say, how do you know I still don't feel that way about him?'

'Because you don't.'

'How do you know?'

'Well,' Ruth said slowly, 'it's a little involved, but what it comes down to is that you're not really the stereotype you wanted me to think you were. You know, that cynical, hard-bitten private-detective role you were playing. It's not you. Not at all.'

'Since that's probably intended to be a compliment, thanks.'

'You're welcome. Now I have to run along. If you don't mind.'

He closed his hand on her shoulder and felt her go rigid against it. 'Look,' he said earnestly, 'your trouble is that you're going around with the pressure on you all the time, and that makes no sense at all. Arnold has not been tried and found guilty; he is not locked up somewhere; you don't have to run inside to write him a letter or bake him a pie with a file in it. I mean it. There's no reason in the world why you and I couldn't go somewhere to dinner, and then you—'

She furiously wrenched her shoulder from his grasp and fumbled for the handle of the door. Murray watched with astonishment her frantic efforts to open it. 'Jesus!' he said. 'What's all this about? I'm not trying to force you to do something you don't want to do. All you have to do is say no.'

He reached over and thrust open the door. She got out and faced him from the sidewalk.

'In that case,' she said: 'no!'

11

The Brother Frank routine was an ancient and familiar one at the agency. Murray skipped his shave the next morning, and a few minutes after he walked into the office with an itching jaw, Bruno arrived carrying a battered valise and a week-old copy of the Chicago *Tribune* that he had picked up at the out-of-town newsstand on Times Square. Neither of them said anything about their previous day's passage on the phone, and there was nothing in Bruno's manner to indicate that he would make any issue of it. This did not surprise Murray. Any showdown on Collins, he knew, would be held in abeyance until after the Christmas bonuses had been handed out.

Bruno's letter and cards with the Coney Island postmark on them had been delivered in the first mail, and Mrs Knapp had already laid them out on the desk. The job of daubing the postmarks with a touch of India ink to blur the dates, erasing the addresses, readdressing them to a non-existent *M. Schrade* at a dummy number in Chicago, padding the valise with sheets of the *Tribune*, and shaking up the few articles of wear in it to eliminate all traces of Lucy Manfredi's neat hand at packing took no more than ten minutes.

Lou Strauss came in while this was going on and seated himself comfortably on a corner of the desk. 'That's what I like to see,' he told Murray: 'the boss going to work with the rest of the slaves. That's what I call democracy in action. Who's the pigeon?'

'Schrade,' said Murray. 'Remember the name?'

'You don't have to be so sarcastic, because that's what I'm here to talk about. Say, don't you have a bottle to go in that bag? Who do you know ever took the train from Chicago without a pint on him?'

'Let me worry about that,' Murray said. 'What about those Miller and Schrade records? Did you get them?'

'No, but let me tell you.' Strauss reached down and reflectively scratched an ankle. 'There's something funny going on, Murray. You know how that guy at Records always co-operates? Now, all of a sudden, he's very careful. Three, four times I get in touch with him, and he don't know, he'll see me later, we're getting nowhere. Then yesterday he calls me at home in the morning to have dinner with him at a chop suey place, and we'll do business. I meet him, we sit down at the table, and one minute later what do I see at the next table but a snoop.'

'How did you know?' Murray asked.

'I know, all right. It was the old newspaper act. He wasn't eating anything, just drinking some tea, and he had the newspaper open up to his nose, with the eyes over it. I been in this business a long time, Murray. I know the newspaper act when I see it. So I stopped right there, because what's the sense of monkeying with a frame-up like that? I gave the money back to Mrs K. when I came in. It wouldn't buy anything but trouble, anyhow.'

'You're sure about all this?'

'I'm sure. After we ate I walked this guy from Records a couple of blocks, and the snoop was with us until I said goodbye. Believe me, I was careful not to even shake hands.'

'All right then, we'll let it go at that. You're on another assignment now, aren't you?'

'I'm on a crazy trucking deal looking for hijackers that ain't there,' Strauss said, aggrieved. 'At my age Mrs K. thinks I need muscles, so I'm a helper on a truck. But who knows?' he said philosophically as he took his departure. 'With a little luck I could get a rupture and retire on workmen's compensation.'

The valise was ready now, and Murray turned his attention to Bruno's letters and cards. Both letters and one of the cards mentioned the woes of the music writing business and asked for money. These were tucked away in the valise. The other card was short and to the point. *Dear Brother Murray, it read: I am in trouble very bad and will tell you when you hit New York. My address is the same.* The signature was an undecipherable scrawl.

Murray put this one into his coat pocket, then picked up the valise and posed for Bruno. 'How does it look?'

'Good enough. Maybe you could use some more wrinkles in that overcoat. Roll it up and sit on it in the cab.'

'I'll do that. You didn't put anything with a New York label on it in the bag, did you?'

'No, it's the same old Chicago stuff we always use. And be careful with this guy when you talk to him. He knows I was there yesterday, so he might smell something. Don't push too hard.'

'You mean, not if I want to come back with all my teeth.'

'That's what I mean,' said Bruno.

Before he left, Murray spoke to Mrs Knapp. 'I want you to call Mrs Donaldson for me,' he told her. 'Start phoning her at noon, and keep ringing until you get her. Tell her I'll be around at seven this evening to take her to dinner. Tell her it doesn't matter what else she had planned, this is very important.'

'All right,' said Mrs Knapp, and then said in mild reproof, 'I suppose you'll be gone all day, won't you?'

'Probably. Why?'

'Because you're letting an awful lot of work pile up here, Mr Kirk. Look at it. There must be three days' mail in that basket. And these contracts should have been sent out yesterday, but you haven't even read them yet. And all these expense accounts to okay. I know you're taking a special interest in the Lundeen case, but really, you can't afford to neglect everything else for it.'

'I see. Well, Friday you can lock me in here and not let me out until everything is cleared up. Fair enough?'

'Yes, if you mean it. Oh, and there's something else you ought to know about. One of the girls – that Mae Bridges – was transcribing a tape, and I caught her making an extra copy of the report. She said that it was all a mistake, that she didn't know she had the extra carbon in her machine, but of course she was lying. I checked her locker and found another report in the lining of her coat.'

'Hell,' said Murray, 'the way things are getting to be they'll have to pass a copyright law to take care of us.'

'Do you want to talk to her about it?'

'No, you can handle it. Try to find out who she's dealing with, and then fire her, whether she tells you or not. And pass the word along to Inter-American and Fleischer to be on the lookout for her. I owe them a couple of favours, anyhow. And whatever you do, don't forget about Mrs Donaldson. Tell her I'll be there at seven on the dot.'

It was a long ride out to Coney Island, and when Murray left the cab he had the feeling of having arrived in the middle of a ghost town. On his few previous excursions to the place it had been brightly lit, loud with the thunder of scenic railways, and jammed with people who moved in a sluggish current along the outside of the sidewalks, making their way past the hungry ones who were packed in front of the concessions. Now the concessions were boarded up, the scenic railways were desolate skeletons, and the only sign of life was a faraway sound of carousel music, the merest tinkling of music, carried along the avenue by the wet salt wind which blew steadily from the beach. Some optimist was making a pitch for the last customer of the year, and it had an uncanny quality in that damp, grey desert.

The boarding house was as grey and shabby and lifeless as everything around it. It was a huge barn of a place, evidently built at a time when cupolas and fancy wooden trim were the latest things. A sagging porch ran entirely around the house, and when Murray crossed it to ring the doorbell the boards underfoot creaked at every step.

The man who answered the bell was as round and solidly

made as a beer barrel, and even more unshaven than Murray. He chewed steadily at the stub of an unlit cigar as he eyed his caller up and down.

'You lookin' for a room?' he said.

'That's what I'm looking for. I'm Eddie Schrade's brother in from Chicago. Want to tell him I'm here?'

The man removed the stub of the cigar from his mouth, thoughtfully squeezed it into cylindrical shape, and replaced it.

'We ain't got no Eddie Schrade.'

The valise dropped from Murray's hand. He pulled the postcard from his pocket and read it with bewilderment. 'Are you kidding?' he said. 'He told me right here this was the address.'

When he held out the card the man took it and read it, front and back, his brow knit with concentration. Then he handed it back to Murray.

'He used to live here. He don't live here now.'

Murray said: 'Jesus, that's a nice touch. A whole day on the train because he puts up a holler for me, and then he takes off somewhere. Well, where can I find him?'

The man hesitated. It was barely perceptible, but it was there, nevertheless, and it was all Murray wanted to see. 'I don't know where he went to. What's it my business?'

'Maybe it's not. Maybe he just figures I'll walk around the streets and look for him. This is a big town for that kind of deal.'

The man surveyed the wasteland beyond his porch. 'It's a big town, all right,' he agreed.

Murray thought this over, rubbing his jaw slowly. 'Well, whatever Eddie expected me to do I can't go around like this. I must look like hell. Is there a barber shop near here?'

'Next block down. Across from the subway.'

It was the Moment of Truth. Murray picked up the valise, half turned away, then turned back. 'Say, would it be all right to leave the bag here meanwhile?'

'Stick it in the hall, if you want. Nobody'll touch it.'

The sign in the window of the barber shop said TWO CHAIRS – NO WAITING, which proved to be accurate up to a point. There were two chairs, but there was only one barber, an elderly and near-sighted man, and he was hard at work on the tresses of a pimpled youth. Murray picked up a magazine and stretched out in the other chair, prepared to kill time, then found himself inexorably drawn to the spectacle in the mirror.

After every few snips of the scissors the boy would pull his head nervously away from them. 'Stoopid,' he would say, not unkindly. 'Go easy, stoopid.'

Then the snipping would resume until the boy would stop it again. 'Oh, stoopid,' he would sigh. 'Stoopid, stoopid.'

It went like this until the barber was finished, and the boy snatched the comb from his hand to add the last touches himself. Peering into the mirror, he swept back the long hair on each side of his head, and delicately, with a little finger, flicked the curls down the centre until each ringlet stood erect, and one flopped forward over his forehead. When he walked out Murray saw that he was wearing dungarees so tight that they encased his scanty buttocks as the sausage skin encases the sausage.

The barber took notice of it, too. 'See?' he said to Murray. 'All the boys today, they look like girls. All the girls, they look like boys. What the hell you gonna do?' Then he used a gesture straight from Calabria to indicate what he would like to do, given the chance.

He was a good barber, a deliberate worker who stepped back to study the effect after every few strokes of the razor, and Murray had no objection to that. The landlord would have all the time he needed to open the valise, examine everything in it, and verify the credentials there. Of course, that also gave him time to phone Schrade if he wanted to, but that was in the lap of the gods. Everything that could be done had been done.

When Murray got back to the boarding house the man was still working on the cigar stub, but his mood had considerably softened.

'You know,' he said, 'first I figured you didn't look anything like Eddie, and then I figured maybe I'm wrong. Anyhow, all of a sudden, it came to me where he moved.'

Murray said: 'Man, you just saved my life. I was all ready to head back to Chi on the next train.'

'Well, you don't have to. And maybe I can save you even another trip back here. Did you know Eddie walked out of here owing me twenty bucks?'

Murray had anticipated a figure nearer fifty. He paid the money, got the address, and left, feeling that he had just earned Arnold Lundeen a net profit of thirty dollars.

Apparently Eddie Schrade was a man who liked the smell of salt water. His new address was across the borough in Columbia Heights, not far from Brooklyn Bridge. The house was an old apartment building, but it seemed to be clean and well kept. Offhand, one would have said that Schrade had improved his station in life by moving here.

His name wasn't over any of the bells in the hall, but the name plate to apartment 3B was missing. Murray walked up two flights of stairs to 3B and knocked on the door.

'Who is it?' a voice said from inside. 'What do you want?'

'DA's office, Eddie,' Murray said with his head close to the door. 'LoScalzo sent me over. I have to talk to you.'

The door suddenly opened to let him in, and then closed quickly behind him as he stood there blinking. The shade had been drawn down full length over the single window of the room, and the glare from a naked electric bulb hanging at eye level was blinding. It took a few seconds to focus on Schrade. He was small and scrawny, and the fringe of hair around an otherwise gleaming bald head looked like an unkempt tonsure. His features were sharp and very much alive in a twitching, mouselike way.

'What is it now?' he said querulously. 'What do you want? Don't I get any peace at all?'

'Maybe not,' said Murray. 'Fact is, I don't work for LoScalzo, Eddie, I'm handling some business for a fellow name of Lundeen.'

Schrade looked as if he were going to collapse. He shrank back against the wall in a quaking terror. 'You get out of here! You got no right to be here!'

'That's no way to talk, Eddie. I'm not here to hurt you, am I?' Murray calmly sat down with his back to the light, and held out a pack of cigarettes. 'Help yourself.'

'What is this? For a lousy cigarette I'll be your friend all of a sudden? You think I'm crazy? Now get out of here, because I'm not talking to you!'

'Why not?' Murray lit a cigarette, and Schrade's eyes followed every motion of his hand with fascination. 'What have you got to hide, Eddie?'

'Me? I got nothing to hide. But I'm not talking. Especially, not to you, the way you push in here with a phony story.'

'Eddie, Eddie,' Murray gently chided him, 'you're not looking at this the right way. You're not looking at it the right way at all. I have a big agency behind me. What's to stop me from having somebody tail you day and night? Would it make you feel better to know that every step you took there was a man tailing you? Of course it wouldn't. How do I know that? Because I wouldn't like it myself. That's why I thought that the way to handle this was to sit down like intelligent people and talk it over. Am I wrong in that? Does that make me a heel?'

Schrade's face went through a whole series of twitching contortions as he considered this. 'You mean,' he said, 'that we talk it over, and then you and this Lundeen stay out of my hair? Why should I believe that?'

'You can take my word.'

'Your word, your word! Next thing you'll kiss your pinkie and tell me honour bright. Even Miller don't like to talk now, he knows what the cops might do to him. What makes me different from him?'

'Because Lundeen'll do what I tell him to do. And if you're wondering about me, ask anyone about Conmy-Kirk. We don't do business by double-crossing.'

'Yeah? How did you get in here except by double-crossing?'

'Eddie, don't tell me you're the kind of guy who thinks every little joke is a double-cross. Are you really such a country boy?'

'I don't like jokers,' Schrade mumbled. 'When you're all upset jokers ain't funny.' He slowly edged away from the wall and held out a hand. 'Give me a cigarette. Give me the pack, so I don't have to go out later.'

Murray tossed him the pack, and Schrade lit a cigarette. He drew in deeply, then exhaled a cloud of smoke and shook his head wonderingly at it. 'How did I get into this?' he said. 'A peaceful man, and here I am holed up like a gangster in the movies. A composer – an artist, mind you – and I got to worry about a crazy cop shooting me in the back some night!' He waved the cigarette at Murray. 'Go on, ask me how I got into it.'

'All right. How?'

'That's a good question. For doing favours, that's how I got into it. I'm surprised I didn't get into trouble a long time ago, the way I do favours for people.'

'Like being a stand-in for Miller?'

'Naturally. He knows who the sucker is, the good-natured one. He runs in looking like he's going to drop down on the spot. "Do me a favour, Eddie," he says. "They got me down for the count, and I need a stand-in. You got to do it, Eddie," he says. Hoo! If I knew what was coming—!'

'When did this happen?'

'When do you think? The day with that cop, that Lundeen. But what difference does that make?

'I said to him, "Ira, what is it? What kind of trouble could be so bad?" But believe me, I didn't have to ask. What other trouble could it be for a bookie except cops?

'What kills me with Miller is that he's not like a bookie at all. He's an educated man. A college man. He's got a fine, respectable wife. In business he could be anything he wants. So what is he? A lousy bookie from Broadway!

'And you know why?' Schrade demanded. He poked a finger into his meagre chest. 'Because there's something in here – a bug, a worm – something that's always figuring angles, always looking for the easy dollar. Ah, so what's the use.'

'What happened then?'

'You mean, what didn't happen! He says to me, "It's the cops, Eddie. Somebody from plain clothes grabbed me near the Garden and shook me down for everything I had on me. A thousand dollars bet money he grafted from me. But it's more than that. He wants a stand-in so he can make an arrest, and I don't have time to fix it up with anybody else. You'll have to take the arrest for me, Eddie."

'How do you like that? I'm sitting there writing a song – my head is all full of beautiful music – and the next thing, I'm invited to do him a favour by getting arrested!

' "Ira," I said, "there's a lot of favours I'd do you, but this is too much. I don't know a thing about horse betting. I wouldn't even know what to say."

' "A baby could do it," he said. "Look, Eddie, you'll just stand downstairs with the slips and stuff in your pocket until he comes along, and I'll be near the corner to tip him off it's you. That's all you do, you stand there. Then when he makes the arrest you put up a little fuss so it'll look legitimate, you go to court and pay the fine, and that's the whole thing. You're a first-timer, Eddie, you got nothing to worry about. I'll cover the fine, and give you fifty for yourself in the bargain."

'Maybe he thought he was making it sound easy, but let me tell you that he was making everything in me turn to water. I'm a plain citizen, all my life I'm only interested in staying out of trouble, so who am I to go around asking for it?

' "I can't do it, Ira," I said to him. "I'm a nervous wreck as it is. Something like this could kill me."

' "*You're* nervous?" he said. "Eddie, this'll be my sixth rap. It means—"'

'Hold it!' Murray cut in. 'Did Miller really say that?'

'Say what?'

'That this would be his sixth rap. That they might throw the book at him now.'

'Sure. And then he said, "Eddie, if that happens, my wife will go crazy. You know what she's like. And there's something else, Eddie. If anything happens to me I'll have to close up Songster. Then look at the spot you'll be in."

'So there it was. His wife, the business, everything was suddenly on *my* shoulders. What could I do? What could anybody do? Did I know that later on they'd get the goods on Georgie Wykoff, so that the DA would look up first-time arrests to find the stand-ins? I didn't even know what time it was, that's how dumb I was.

'I took the arrest, it worked like Miller said it would, and so far, so good. Then they caught up with Wykoff, and the house fell in on me. They got me in front of the grand jury and started to sweat me, and they wouldn't take no for an answer.

'It turned out that being a stand-in wasn't so bad; they didn't even bother about that. But if you tell lies to the grand jury they got you on perjury and a million other things. Does that cop, that Lundeen, think I should cover up for him on account of the fifty bucks Miller gave me? You can tell him for me that he made a lot more money being crooked than I got for doing a favour.'

Schrade drew on his cigarette now with the serenity of a man who has cleared his conscience. 'Well,' he said, 'that's how it happened. And now that I told you, I want you to play square with me. I want you to keep that Lundeen away from me like you said.' He held up a warning finger. 'I'm taking your word on that.'

Murray said, 'Did he ever approach you or threaten you up to now?'

'So what if he didn't? He could still get ideas before the trial.'

'All right,' Murray said, 'you won't have to worry about him any more. I'll take care of him.' When he stood up he raised the window shade and turned off the light. 'For one thing, it'll cut down your electric bill.'

At the door Schrade laid a hand on Murray's arm. 'Wait a minute,' he said. 'You know, when you first walked in maybe I got the wrong idea about you. But seeing you're a nice fellow really, I got a little proposition to make.'

Murray waited expectantly.

'It's like this,' Schrade explained. 'With somebody else running Songster and all, I got myself a job now playing piano with a little combination. Just violin, piano, and sax, but very good. It ain't union, but who cares? What the union don't know won't ever hurt it.

'Anyhow, if you got any kind of a wedding or an affair where you want music, just get in touch with me. As a favour, I'll give you a big break in the price.'

'I thought you decided not to do any more favours for people,' Murray said.

Schrade smiled a golden smile. 'Not people,' he said. 'Just bookies.'

12

Didi was an inveterate table hopper. The third time she returned from a foray around the dining room Murray pointed to her chair and said, 'I'm giving you fair warning. If you get up from there once more, I am going to break your beautiful arm. Now set and stay set.'

She looked unchastened. 'Sweetie, how you do go on. I can't help it if I *know* people, can I?'

'You can, and don't waste your time fluttering those eyelashes at me. I could see from here that that character you were just talking to didn't have the dimmest idea who you were.'

'Oh,' said Didi. 'Well, maybe we never exactly met before, but he's Ted Holloway, who produced a couple of those TV things I was on. He's putting together that big new panel show now, and I thought it would be kind of cute if I could help out. Anyhow, we hardly even talked about me. We talked mostly about you. That man with him is Wallace Crowley, and he won a Pulitzer Prize. He wants to write a book with you.'

'We'll do it first thing tomorrow. Now, will you listen to me, please?'

'I *am* listening. I can perfectly well eat and listen at the same time, can't I?'

'I hope so. Remember Ruth Vincent, the girl you met at the Harlingens' that time? The one you raised such a fuss about?'

'Yes.'

'Well, you don't have to look so suspicious about it. All I

want you to do is arrange a little get-together at your place, and invite her. But fix it so that there's no unattached man around for her, because that'll be my department. Will you do that?'

'I will not!'

'Oh, fine,' said Murray. 'I thought you were out of that mood.'

'It is not a mood,' Didi said icily.

'The hell it's not! If you can give me one real reason—'

'I already did, and you know it. I don't like that girl, Murray. I don't think she'd be good for you. And I will not be party to any—'

'Hold it, Mother Carey, and let's stick to the point. You're working up to the kindly advice bit, and I didn't ask for that. All I asked for was one real reason why—'

A hand was laid on Murray's shoulder, and he looked up to see Crowley, the Pulitzer Prize winner, swaying over him. 'Mr Murray Kirk, the great detective,' said Crowley with alcoholic tenderness. He sat down heavily. 'Don't mind if I sit here, do you?'

'Sure I do,' Murray said, 'but don't let that bother you any.'

'Many, many thanks,' said Crowley. He was glassy-eyed drunk, but still in fair command of his tongue. 'Many, many, many thanks. And more to come.'

'Later,' Murray said. 'Not now. Some other time, *amigo*.'

'Right. Lady here—' Crowley winked hugely at Didi, and then, pleased with himself, winked again '—lady here says you know all about detective business.'

'Wrong,' Murray said. 'Look, pal, why not try some other table? Maybe you'll have better luck that way.'

'Ha!' said Crowley contemptuously. 'Modest. So modest. Makes me sick to see man hide his light under a shovel.'

Didi reached over and patted his hand consolingly. 'Never you mind that, sweetie. Murray's one of those people likes to be coaxed. Just you go on and tell him about the book.'

Crowley blinked. 'The book?'

'Sure enough, sweetie,' Didi said encouragingly.

'Oh, the *book*. All about ole McClellan. Ole George Brinton McClellan, west mar—' Crowley stopped to untangle that one '—worst maligned bastard in the whole Civil War. That's who *he* was.'

He tilted forward to arrange a knife and fork on the table. 'See? Here's ole Robert E. Lee. Here's ole George McClellan. But no G-2, no Military Intelligence. You follow?

'Ole George says, "I can whip the ass off Robert E. Lee, but I got to know how many soldiers in his army first." He sends for sneaky ole Pinkerton, best damn detective in the whole world. "Mr Pinkerton," he says, "you go find out for me how many soldiers ole Lee's got."

'Pinkerton comes back. "Sire," he says—' and Crowley almost careened out of his chair as he executed a sweeping salute '"—sire, ole Lee's got a million men. Even worse. He's got a million *million* men! Worse than that, sire, they're armed to the teeth! They got cannons, mushrooms, swords, and galore!"'

Didi looked at Murray. 'Cross my heart—' she said helplessly, but whatever else was forthcoming was cut short by Crowley, now in full flight.

'Ole George listens to this,' he said, cupping a hand behind his ear, 'and he's sick about it. Why? Because he doesn't know that every word ole sneaky Pinkerton told him is a lie! Every word of it is right from under the horse's tail. All he knows is he can't whip any million *million* soldiers. So he sits it out until Marse Lincoln dumps him, and everybody in the whole world thinks he's a bum. You follow?'

'I follow,' said Murray.

'Right. But who was the one made a bum out of him? It was ole sneaky Pinkerton, that's who! Ole great detective telling a bunch of lies. What I want to know is, why'd he do it? Stupid, maybe? Somebody paying him off, maybe? You know detective business, so you tell me. Say, what's your name, anyhow?'

'Sheridan,' said Murray. 'Old Phil Sheridan.'

Crowley exploded with laughter. 'Son of a bitch, that's great!' he bellowed, pounding the table delightedly. 'Your name's Murray Kirk, sneaky ole detective, but I like you!'

'Mr Crowley—' said a waiter behind Murray.

Crowley brandished a steak knife over his head. 'Here comes the cavalry!' he yelled. 'Here comes old Phil Sheridan!'

The maître d'hôtel suddenly appeared with two other waiters. 'Mr Crowley,' he said, 'I think we'd better help you to the lounge.'

Murray pushed Didi into the revolving door and whirled her out to the sidewalk. 'Ole Didi,' he said when he joined her there. 'Ole Didi and her friends.'

'Sweetie, I've been trying to tell you and tell you, and you just won't listen. Will you please listen for one second?'

'Nope.'

'You will, too! I've been trying to tell you that he wasn't one bit like that when I was talking to him before at his table. Not one tiny bit.'

'You mean, *Who would have thought the old man had so much booze in him?* Hey, that's pretty good! Ole Frank Conmy himself would have liked that one. He was always the man for a juicy Shakespearian paraphrase.'

'It stinks,' Didi said wearily. 'And it's freezing out here. Where'll we go now?'

'To the St Stephen.'

'The St Stephen! But it's only nine o'clock! *Nobody* goes home at only nine o'clock.'

'Who cares?' Murray said. 'Let's live dangerously for once.'

He was measuring off two snifters of cognac in the kitchenette of the apartment, when he heard Didi's voice raised from the bedroom.

'Murray, what's happened to all my things? I can't find them in the closet, and it's like an icebox in here.'

'Then get out of there and look in the bottom drawer of the dresser. And stop yelling like that. What'll the neighbours think?'

'Oh, blank the neighbours,' said Didi, as he knew she would. When she emerged in a sheer ivory negligee he was waiting on the couch, warming a glass in each hand. She took one and idly held it up to the light. 'Why'd you put everything away in the dresser like that, Murray?'

'Oh, that was because of the cleaning woman. She is now one of Father Divine's happy band, and she's been going around so full of saintliness that a halo is beginning to form. Anyhow, I felt bad, because every time she opened that closet door I knew she felt bad, so I did something about it. End of story.'

'You mean that?'

'Sure I mean it. You don't think I could make up anything as implausible as that on the spur of the moment, do you?'

'I guess not. And you really are a doll, aren't you, sweetie?' Didi stretched herself out comfortably with her head on his lap and her ankles crossed over the arm of the couch. 'I thought it was the management or something, and I was going to be real huffy about it.'

'Hell, no. The management is highly moral, all right, but only about the cheaper rooms. And don't try to drink upside down like that. You'll choke yourself.'

'I will not. Just you watch and see.'

He watched and saw with admiration.

'Say, that's a pretty neat trick. Where'd you pick it up?'

'Oh, down Amarillo way when I was a little kid. Used to drink upside down from the spigot all the time. Made up my mind I could learn to do it, and kept at it until I could.'

'That's the stuff.' Murray finished his drink, and took a deep breath. 'Didi, are you listening?'

'Uh-huh.'

'Then listen good. When do we have that little house party where I meet Ruth Vincent?'

'Well, if you aren't the man with the one-track mind! And

you can stop rubbing my tummy like that. I don't want you rubbing my tummy while you're asking me to help you seduce somebody!'

'Who the hell said anything about seducing? And it's not your tummy. Only little girls have tummies. This is your belly.'

'Well, whatever it is, you can just stop poking it. I'm not fooling, Murray. You make me feel downright indecent.'

'I'm sorry,' Murray said. 'I guess I'm not very bright sometimes.'

Didi sat up and swung her feet to the floor. 'I guess you're not,' she said, and then studied his face with perplexity. 'Murray, what is it with this girl? Are you in love with her?'

'I am. Isn't it the damndest thing?'

'You mean, *marrying* love?'

'Yes.'

Didi was silent for a long while. Then she shivered and drew her feet up under her on the couch. 'It's cold,' she said. 'Why don't you make a little fire in that old fireplace? Doesn't seem much sense to a fireplace without any fire in it.'

He had been expecting her to say any one of a number of things, and was grateful that none of them was forthcoming. 'I'll get you a blanket,' he said. 'It's too much mess making a fire.'

'No, it isn't. First make the fire, and then you can get me a blanket and another drink, please.'

Obediently he went to work until he had built up a fair blaze, and then went for the blanket and another snifter of cognac. When he returned she was sitting on the floor in front of the fireplace, idly poking a stick into the ashes of the kindling. He handed her the drink and draped the blanket over her shoulders. 'Warmer now?' he asked.

'Some. No, don't sit over on the couch. Pull that chair up here so I can lean on you.'

He pulled up the armchair, and Didi let her head fall back against his knee. 'Isn't that funny?' she said. 'Why'd they ever go and put fireplaces in a hotel like this, anyway?'

'Not fireplaces,' Murray said; 'just one fireplace. This is the only one in the building. Back in the Depression, when they'd do anything to keep a tenant, Frank had them make it for him. He told me it wasn't much of a job, but I have my doubts.'

'He must have been awful cold-blooded.'

'Just the opposite. He claimed that he never met a pretty girl in all his life who could resist getting down on the floor in front of an open fire. And once she was on the floor—'

'Why, the old goat!' Didi said in a shocked voice.

'Smart old goat. Look where you are right now. Anyhow, it's a natural symbolism. Pretty girls always like to play with fire.'

Didi gently patted his knee. 'Not all of them, sweetie. Not the one you're carrying that big old torch for. That one is all schoolteacher.'

'Skip it,' Murray said.

'I will not. All right, I will. But I can talk about you, can't I?'

'Is there any way I can stop you?'

'No, there isn't.' She turned around to face him. 'Murray, did you know you were two different people, as different as different could be? Did you know how bad that could be for you?'

'Why? Two can live as cheaply as one, can't they?'

'Oh, stop. You *are* two different people, and one of them's in that office all day, or in court, or on a job someplace, and he can be the coldest, hardest, most sarcastic thing on two feet. And the other – tell me something, Murray. The time you started taking me places – I mean, right after Donaldson gave me the divorce – why did you do it?'

Murray took the empty glass she thrust at him and set it on the floor. 'You ought to know why. I thought you were kind of nice.'

'No, you didn't. I was a mess. I was just a scared, lonely, weepy mess. And you knew that, didn't you? That's why you came walking in right out of nowhere with a whole load of flowers and a big old bottle of perfume, wasn't it?'

'Was it?'

'Yes, it was.' Didi banged his shoe with her fist. 'And that's your *other* side. That's the Murray Kirk who's kind and considerate and worries about how people feel and never laughs at them when they're a little dumb sometimes.'

'I never said you were dumb any time,' Murray protested. 'And will you quit doing that to my foot? You'll break a toe.'

'I *am* dumb sometimes.' Didi banged his shoe even harder. 'But I am also smart enough to know that you're two different people, and it's no good to keep them separate the way you do. All that happens is that one side watches the other, and doesn't do anything to *help*. If you'd only put them together for once, you'd see how utterly crazy it is to go around swooning over this beautiful statue of a stuck-up schoolteacher. Oh, what's the use!' she said, and wheeled around to face the fireplace. The stick she had been playing with was nearby, and she picked it up and flung it into the blaze.

'This is a hell of a note,' Murray remarked to her back. 'Have you ever heard me say one word against Evan or Alex or anyone else *you* were ever interested in?'

'No, but I never told you I wanted to marry them, did I? You know Evan already had a wife, and I certainly don't expect to marry Alex, for God's sake.'

'Why not? He seems to be a nice enough guy, all in all.'

'I told you a long time ago why not. I wouldn't marry any man in the world didn't have money. I mean real money, too, not just a lot of talk.'

'I guess that takes care of Alex, all right.'

'Well, I can't help it. He's a lamb, but all he's got right now is what I give him. If we got married he wouldn't even have that much, because then the alimony would stop.' Didi shrugged listlessly. 'Who knows? Maybe I'll go marry good old Donaldson again. He's sure got himself worked up for it.'

'That's a switch, isn't it? Last time I asked—'

'Oh, what do you care!' Didi said irritably. 'Just bring me another drink, please, and stop picking at me.' She flung herself around to face him again. 'Besides, what makes you think this girl would come to a party just because I invite her? She doesn't look like the friendly type one bit.'

'She'll come. She's crazy about Evan's poetry, and I told her you used to know him. Build that up. Let her know you'd be glad to talk to her about him. Bring in a couple of that crowd that used to hang around him, and let her know she'll meet them, too. Only thing is, don't tell her I'll be there. That might make a problem.'

'Oho,' said Didi. 'I can see it might. Murray, something already happened between you and that girl, didn't it? What was it?'

'I don't know. I can't quite figure it out myself.'

'Did you make a pass at her or something?'

'Now you sound like an army doctor asking an inductee about sex life. Can we avoid the clinical note, please?'

'Then you did,' said Didi with conviction. 'And I bet you got a nice, hard kick right where it would do you no good at all.'

'Thank you.'

'You're welcome. But I still don't know. Suppose I do take care of this for you – I mean, suppose I go to all this trouble and everything. What would I get out of it?'

'What do you want?'

'Well—' She put her little finger into her mouth and sucked it thoughtfully while she regarded him with narrowed eyes. 'You could buy one of Alex's pictures. That's the very least you could do.'

'Very least!' Murray said, and then had to laugh. 'Didi, everything that guy paints is the size of a circus tent. What would I do with anything that size in this place?'

'Oh, aren't you the dashing lover! Well, as it happens, there's lots smaller things in his studio, and that's where your precious party'll be Saturday night. And you better bring your cheque book, too. That's your ticket of admission.'

'You blackmailer,' Murray said admiringly. 'All right, it's a deal. One small picture, hand painted. I'll bring in the bottle, and we'll drink to that.'

Two hours later, with the bottle empty and the fire guttering out, she was sound asleep on the floor, curled in a foetal position under the blanket. She was still there the next morning, but now completely out of sight under the mound of additional blankets and the mink coat which Murray had courteously piled on her before making his own unsteady way to bed. Only a gentle rise and fall of the mound gave notice of life underneath it.

When he left the apartment he closed the door very softly behind him, and, out of deference to the chambermaid's delicate sensibilities, left the DO NOT DISTURB sign dangling from the knob outside.

13

A large part of the morning was spent trying to locate Harlingen – he was in court, Dinah Harlingen explained over the phone, but she wasn't exactly sure which court – and then, after Mrs Knapp had located him on the basis of this slender clue, waiting for him to get to the office. By the time he arrived Murray had brought the Lundeen file up to date and had prepared a discreetly censored outline of it. He and Harlingen put in a long session over the outline.

It was clear that various items in it, and especially the notes on Schrade's story, did not make Harlingen too happy. Not that Conmy-Kirk wasn't doing a good job, he hastened to assure Murray. On the contrary, it was doing a damn fine job. After all, fit all this stuff together the way Murray had done, and what did you have but a perfect picture of LoScalzo's line of attack. Miller's five previous convictions would seem to give him a motive for paying an exorbitant bribe, and that was the springboard. Then Miller would testify that the stand-in arrest had been arranged at the very time Lundeen was away from Benny Floyd. And then Schrade would step up and swear to his own part in the affair, and that was it. Why, the Conmy-Kirk report was as good as a blueprint of the prosecution's whole case!

Trouble was, however, that knowing a man's line of attack didn't automatically provide you with a satisfactory defence against it. Take the time element, for example. If LoScalzo was out to prove that the deal had been arranged at the very time

147

Lundeen was with this floozie Helene, she'd *have* to take the stand, wouldn't she? She was the only one who could alibi Lundeen, wasn't she?

'What about it?' Murray said. He had been looking forward to this part of the discussion with relish. 'My money says that the jury'll take one look and go for her as big as Lundeen did.'

'That isn't the same as believing her. And it isn't what I meant, anyhow. Can you picture how this will hit Ruth? It'll be awful. I don't even know if Arnold would allow me to put that woman on the stand. I'll have to talk to him about it. And I should talk to the woman, too. She may—'

Murray felt a quick alarm at the way his trump card was being snatched from his hand. 'Hold on,' he said. 'As far as Lundeen is concerned, there's no point making an issue of this thing until we have the whole case lined up, and he can see he has no choice in the matter. And with Helene – well, I'd say that the best thing is for you to stay away from her altogether for the time being.'

'Why?'

'Because the situation with her is a little more complicated than I might have made it look. It's sort of a touchy set-up.'

Harlingen shook his head. 'I don't understand.'

'Well, Helene has a husband. He was probably right there on the scene that day, along with her and Lundeen.'

Harlingen immediately brightened. 'But what's wrong with that? I think it's fine. It couldn't be better. It gives us a corroborating witness, and it certainly proves that Lundeen and that woman—'

'No, it doesn't.'

'It doesn't?'

'You'd have to see the old coot to know what I mean. He's about forty or fifty years older than the girl and looks like a toadstool, but even more poisonous. My hunch is that he gets his kicks watching through the keyhole.'

'My God!' said Harlingen.

'That's only part of it. He's also one of those types who are a little offbeat when they talk to you. The kind who can suddenly cut loose in the witness chair and turn everything into a holy show. As a witness he'd be murder. Of course, since I know my way around him and the girl now, I can handle them pretty well. That's why I think you'd do better to leave them to me until it's really necessary for you to step in.'

Harlingen looked like a man who had found an especially loathsome serpent twining around his arm and was still shaken by the experience. 'Yes,' he said. 'Yes, I see your point. If you're on good terms with them I wouldn't want to endanger that.' There was no regret in his voice when he said it. 'And after all,' he went on with growing assurance, 'if the woman does testify, she doesn't have to explain what happened in detail, does she? She could say that Arnold was an old friend. That he dropped in for a cup of coffee. At least we'd be sparing Ruth that much.'

'Except for one thing,' Murray said blandly. 'The woman under discussion happens to be a hot-looking redhead about twenty years old, and her figure – well, to put it in nice language, she is extremely well endowed. LoScalzo will know the score as soon as he takes one look at her. He is going to kick that cup of coffee right out of her hand.'

Watching Harlingen digest this information, Murray was surprised at the degree of his own honest sympathy for the man. And still, he wondered, what was wrong in feeling that way? Harlingen was, by any standards, a decent person. From the evidence, he was a good husband, a good father, and a good friend. And he had guts, too. He could have spent a soft life as a well-kept office cat, but at his age he had thrown that over and gone out to roam strange alleys and to battle tougher and smarter cats who knew the terrain from the start. A foolish decision, true. A decision that reeked of the genteel do-goodism, of the compulsive idealism that now and then infected people of Harlingen's class and type. A decision finally triggered by a forty-dollar-an-hour psychoanalyst who knew he had to deliver something for his fee. And yet it took guts. Within certain limits you couldn't help liking a man with that kind of spirit. And there was no law on the books that barred a Ralph Harlingen from growing up eventually and exercising common sense to match the spirit.

Murray considered this, and then said to Harlingen, 'Do you mind my asking you a personal question?'

Harlingen smiled. 'Well, when somebody starts off with that question I usually find out later that I do mind. That's just a joke, really. What did you want to know?'

'Oh, whether you've changed your mind about Lundeen, at all. I mean, about his being a nice, clean-cut, innocent cop who's been framed by a pair of villains for some unknown reason.'

'No, I have not,' Harlingen said. He was clearly nettled. 'And from that somewhat sardonic tone I take it that you haven't changed your mind either. That surprises me. It really does.'

'Why should it?'

'Why? Because of the evidence you yourself went out and got. *This* evidence,' said Harlingen, slapping a hand down on the papers before him. 'All right, I grant it proves Arnold was a fool. Perhaps a little more than a fool. But by the same token it happens to prove that he is not guilty of perjury. I don't see how you can dispute that.'

'Oh, but I can. And do.'

'I still don't see how,' Harlingen said stubbornly. 'The girl's story alone—'

'—takes care of about twenty minutes. It does not take care of one minute before or after that.'

'But Lundeen was with Floyd the rest of the time. You heard Floyd say that yourself.'

'Yes,' said Murray, 'I did. And whether he's been splitting the graft with Lundeen or is just a real good pal I don't know, but he was lying like an old master. Not that I don't give the boy credit. Baby face and all, he isn't going to change that story for anybody. Not you, not LoScalzo, and not the Recording Angel either. He'll stick with it to the end, and it won't bother him one bit. You don't make the grade with the Vice Squad, and pal with a guy like Lundeen, and let little things like graft and perjury bother you any.'

Harlingen opened his mouth to say something, and then closed it. He sat rubbing his hand slowly back and forth over his close-cropped hair in abstraction. 'No,' he said at last, 'I don't believe it.'

It was the way he said it that pulled Murray up short. The flat finality of it. The notice that the evidence had been reviewed and was politely rejected. It gave Murray the feeling of having run headlong into a hard object he hadn't known was there; and that, as he told himself, was a strange feeling to have evoked in you by someone like Ralph Harlingen.

'All right, then you don't believe it,' Murray said. 'But LoScalzo does, and he's going to bang away at it at the trial until he's got the jury believing it, too. That's what they pay off on in your line of work.'

Harlingen did not seem disturbed by this, either. 'I know what you mean,' he said. 'I've been seeing quite a bit of LoScalzo during the past week.'

'You have? Where?'

'In court. I've been sitting in a back row as an observer at this trial he's working now.' Harlingen shook his head admiringly. 'He's a good man.'

'Worried about that?'

'No, the funny thing is that I'm not,' Harlingen laughed shortly. 'Maybe it sounds like the most godawful conceit, but I'm sure I have what it takes to make a good trial lawyer. I can think on my feet, I can speak well, I can really hit hard if I have something to hit with. I mean, I'm not just saying this. Of course, I've only tried a few small civil suits, but I was good at it. My father once admitted as much, and I suppose you know how he was about doling out compliments. Or is this turning your stomach? I warned you it would sound like godawful conceit.'

'No,' said Murray, 'a little of that can be a big help to a lawyer. Fact is, the one thing I couldn't handle in law school was public speaking. Only reason it didn't bother me too much at the time was that I pictured myself winding up ultimately as the brains behind somebody else's mellow voice. Made a nice picture, too, until reality set in.'

'I never knew you studied law,' Harlingen said with surprise. 'Where was that?'

'Oh, St John's, in Brooklyn. One jump across the bridge.'

Harlingen nodded gravely. 'Well,' he remarked with an air of knowing what was expected of him, 'they've turned out some good men there.'

Murray was wickedly tempted to ask him to name a few, but restrained himself. 'Let's back up to Lundeen again,' he said. 'Have you seen him lately?'

'Yes, he was at the house Sunday morning. We worked out a list of people who might testify as character witnesses.'

'Such as?'

'Well, one's an old friend of his who's now doing very well in real estate. Very much the sort to impress a blue-ribbon jury.'

'Might be. Who else is there?'

'Quite a few. A minister and several church vestrymen. And there's a policeman who was on the beat with Arnold when he was in uniform. He was there when Arnold captured an armed bandit and won a citation. Did you know he had won a citation?'

'No. And I don't know if that's admissible in this case. Is it?'

'It may not be. Even so, I want to get the fact before the jury. It doesn't matter if it's struck from the record later, as long as the jury's heard about it.'

'It's worth a try,' said Murray. 'Is that the list?'

'No, the last one is Arnold's old high-school principal. A Dr Charles Fuller down at Greenwich High. I spoke to him on the phone yesterday, and he remembered Arnold very well. It seems that there had been some sort of incident at the school – hoodlums attacking a student, or something like that – and if Arnold hadn't come along in the nick of time it might have wound up pretty tragically. It isn't always—'

Murray felt every nerve tighten. 'That kid who was attacked,' he said casually. 'You didn't get his name by any chance, did you?'

'No, but that doesn't matter. What matters is the testimony itself, especially coming from a man like Fuller. But, as I was saying, it isn't always easy to get someone like that on the stand. He might be talked into it, but I'm not sure.'

'Tell you what,' Murray said abruptly. 'I'd like to take a crack at him myself this afternoon. I have to be down in that neighbourhood anyhow.' he added to forestall any objections. 'It won't be any bother.'

He said very little more during the remainder of the discussion, and what he thought, while Harlingen meandered along his loquacious way, was largely unprintable. Most of it concerned lawyers who had only one case to handle, thus having all the time they needed to talk a man to death about it, as if it mattered a damn to him.

Dr Fuller was an elderly man, not long before retirement, with oysterlike pouches under his eyes, and a few hairs carefully drawn across his otherwise naked scalp like the strings of a violin. When he spoke, it was in measured accents, his voice the complacent rumble of a kindly sage offering enlightenment to the peasants.

Yes, he assured Murray, he remembered Arnold very well. Not an exemplary scholar, perhaps, but certainly an outstanding student. A fine athlete. A natural leader. Few others in the school's history had ever won the honour of being elected president of the Student Council for two successive terms. A remarkable achievement, especially for a boy who came from the home Arnold did. Drunken, abusive parents who never helped the boy an inch of the way. No background at all. It was a sad day when people like that—

Murray shifted in his chair. 'There was some sort of incident, wasn't there?' he prompted. 'I think Mr Harlingen mentioned an attack on a student—'

Ah, yes. That had been an atrocious affair. The student in

charge of the supply room in the basement had gone down to lock it at the final bell when two young hoodlums who had been ransacking it seized her and dragged her inside. There was no question about their intentions. They were simply brute, unreasoning animals. If Arnold had not heard the girl scream, and, at considerable risk to himself, driven them off, it would have been an absolute tragedy.

'Do you remember her name?' Murray asked.

Yes, as it happened, Dr Fuller did remember the girl's name. But he was not at liberty to divulge it. Both the police and the child's parents had impressed that on him very strenuously. Very strenuously indeed. That was entirely understandable, of course. The girl was entitled to protection from the tabloids and from neighbourhood talk. It was to everyone's credit that the affair had been handled so discreetly. It would have been outrageous if the school's reputation had been blackened by an affair like this for which it was in no way responsible. Why, the girl herself—

A few blocks away, on Eighth Street, Murray found a bar with comparatively well-lit booths. He spread his street map out on a table in a far corner, anchored it with a bottle of beer, and studied it carefully. Then he folded the map and went to the telephone.

Victory Hospital was the nearest, but, it briskly informed him, it had no ambulance service. 'St Alonsus takes most of the ambulance calls around here,' the girl at the switchboard said. 'Anyhow, if you need an ambulance, mister, you ought to call the police. They'll take care of it for you right away.'

St Alonsus was more helpful. Yes, it had operated an ambulance service ten or twelve years ago. In fact, it had operated an ambulance service fifty years ago. Records? Well, the one to see was Sister Angelica at the reception desk. She'd know all about it.

The craggy-faced nun at the reception desk found time between incessant phone calls to shake her head regretfully at

Murray. 'I'm sorry,' she said, 'but before I show any medical records to you I must have the superintendent's permission. And he's not here now.'

'I'm not interested in medical records, Sister. All I want to see are some ambulance drivers' reports from around that time. Aren't they kept separately?'

'Oh, yes. Yes, they are. I'm sorry, I didn't understand. Sister Maria Gloria may be able to help you find what you want. She's in charge of our old records.'

Sister Maria Gloria was a diminutive Chinese woman with a shy smile and eyes that shone with earnest helpfulness behind a pair of old-fashioned steel-rimmed spectacles. She listened to Murray with concern, and then guided him down a long corridor, her skirts whispering plaintively over the waxed floor. When she threw open the door of a dingy storeroom a reason for the concern became immediately apparent.

The room was a shambles of records, an Old Curiosity Shop of records. Bound volumes of them of every size and shape crowded wall shelves to the ceiling. Bundles of them tied with cord towered high in shaky columns. Stacks of them were piled on a window sill. And each rung of a ladder in the middle of the room was decorated with an individual volume.

'Of course, these are *old* records,' Sister Maria Gloria hastily explained, as if to point out that even in a well-run hospital one cannot expect efficiency to extend to the darkest corners. 'Some of them are very old. A hundred years old. If you touch the paper it breaks apart. We do not want that to happen, so we must be very careful.'

'The ones I want,' Murray said, 'are the ambulance-call reports from around ten years ago. Do you think you can find them?'

'Oh, yes,' said Sister Maria Gloria, and looked around at the shelves doubtfully, 'but it will take a little time.'

It took two hours of tedious search, and long before then Sister Maria Gloria's wimple was grey with dust from the shelves, and her nose badly smudged.

'There is this thing,' she said, as she finally stacked the desired volumes on the top rung of the ladder which had been cleared for the purpose, 'this microfilm. Do you know about it?'

'Yes,' said Murray.

'It is wonderful,' said Sister Maria Gloria fervently. 'All these books, and you could hold them in one hand like this.' She held out a small hand with fist clenched to show him.

Murray laughed. 'Well, maybe a little more than that, Sister.'

Sister Maria Gloria looked shamefaced. 'Yes, it would take more than that. I was exaggerating. But it *is* wonderful. And,' she sighed, 'it does cost so very much.'

She stood out of the way in a corner telling her beads while he painstakingly went over each entry in the first book. The second book went faster; it included the months of July and August, which he could skip entirely. And then in the third book his finger, slowly moving down a page, was transfixed by the entry he had known all along must be there.

Emergency receiving 4:05 p.m., it read. *Ruth L. Vincent – white – female – fr Greenwich H.S.*

Written in a careless scrawl. Written probably by some tired intern or driver who had seen too many of these things to care much, one way or the other. But written there, nevertheless, for Murray Kirk to find when the time came.

He turned to Sister Maria Gloria, and she put away her rosary and took the book from his hand. 'You have found what you were looking for?' she asked.

'Yes,' said Murray. 'I found what I was looking for.'

'How very nice,' she said, glowing. 'I prayed that you would.'

'And I prayed you would, too,' he said solemnly, and smiled at her bewilderment. 'No, I'm not teasing you, Sister. In my office there happens to be the finest microfilm outfit you can imagine, and a high-priced photographer who's always glad to find a use for it. You bring these books to him, a few at a time, and you'll make him a very happy man. He'll do your work free of charge.'

'Oh, no!' said Sister Maria Gloria aghast.

'Don't you want to be able to hold all these books in one hand?'

'Oh, yes,' said Sister Maria Gloria weakly. 'But it is like paying me for what I do here. You must not pay me for that.'

'I see. Then would it be all right if I offered this as a gift to the hospital itself?'

From the dawning light of wonder behind those spectacles, he knew it would.

14

He had completely forgotten his good intentions of clearing up office detail on Friday, but Mrs Knapp had not. No sooner had he taken off his hat and coat than she appeared, tight-lipped and forbidding, a grim priestess bearing votive offerings to the gods of efficiency. In her arms was the basket of unanswered mail, unsigned contracts, and unread reports. Close in her wake came Gene Rigaud, drafted from his labours on the executive files to transport the Dictaphone machine.

'And,' stated Mrs Knapp before departing, 'there isn't one single appointment on your pad for the whole day. I told Miss Whiteside to make sure of that.'

Faced with the inescapable, Murray went to work, but by noon found himself struggling futilely against a mounting restlessness. Finally he went to the window to watch the crowds in the street below. They didn't offer much of a spectacle – the bleak grey of the sky made everything in sight seem lack-lustre – but they were certainly better to look at than the tedious litter of papers on his desk.

The trouble was, he reflected, that Conmy-Kirk was now past the point where it could be handled as a one-man operation. Of course, much of that was his own doing. Once he had understood the depth of Frank's lonely need for him – Bruno had opened his eyes to it the day he told Murray that it was like money in the bank – he had argued endlessly and vehemently in favour of expanding the agency to the absolute limit. Did it make any difference that there had been more to the argument than an interest in piling up money for Frank? That he knew Frank would have to lean more and more heavily on him as the agency expanded, until a full partnership was inevitable? Not at all. It had been fair exchange, and Frank would have been the first to say so.

As a matter of fact, what he needed now was someone to walk in and serve him as lieutenant half as well as he had served Frank in his time. But where could you find that someone? The more you considered the possible candidates the more you realized that Scott, despite his brutal self-assurance and his crackbrained worship of the spinal column, had come uncomfortably close to the bull's eye with his remark about loyalty. Bruno was the likeliest candidate, but he was much too close to Jack Collins. Gene Rigaud, young, smart, and hungry – he could be another Murray Kirk in the making – was already too close to Bruno. Burke, the retired police captain who was running the payroll-guard service in fine style, seemed to be too close to half the cops in the city, and was also a little bit too hard-boiled and smart for his own good.

Murray smiled at the thought of someone like Ralph Harlingen taking the job, and was suddenly reminded that he had not yet reported to Harlingen on his interview at the high school. He had the call put through, and, after he explained matters on the phone, was pleased to note that Harlingen accepted the unfavourable verdict on Fuller without demur.

'Yes,' Harlingen said, 'he sounded like an old windbag when I talked to him, too. Of course, that doesn't always count against a witness, especially someone in Fuller's position. I have the feeling that no matter how old a man gets, he still finds a high-school principal a pretty imposing object, and that's what I wanted to hit the jury with here. But you're probably right. If he's going to make such a big thing of Arnold's bad home life as a kid, it could have the wrong effect altogether.'

'It could,' said Murray. 'Also, I gathered that he hadn't been in touch with Lundeen for quite a while. You don't need anyone up on the stand rehashing ancient history. Your best bets are people who've known Lundeen since he joined the cops.'

'I know that.' Harlingen sounded a little miffed. 'I made that point to Arnold when we prepared the list. Fuller is the only exception on it, and you can see why.'

'I suppose so,' Murray said. 'Oh, by the way, was Ruth there when you and Lundeen discussed Fuller? I mean, when he told you about the time he saved that kid who was being mobbed?'

'Why, yes. No, wait a second – I don't believe she was. She must have been off with Dinah somewhere at the time. I remember that, because usually she's right in the middle of these discussions, but she had very little to say that morning. She seemed very much under the weather emotionally. That's not surprising, of course. She's been under almost as much of a strain as he has.'

'I guess she has,' said Murray, and let it go at that. 'Yes, I'll keep in touch. Have a nice weekend.'

From all the evidence, he told himself jubilantly as he put down the phone, Lundeen is now running scared. He is running very, very scared, indeed. He would never have risked exposing the secret of that high-school episode if he wasn't. And what must have taken place between him and Ruth when he told her he wanted to do so—

Murray returned to the pile of papers before him almost lightheartedly.

At four-thirty, when he was near the bottom of the pile, Miss Whiteside came in to announce that someone wanted to see him right away. 'I know Mrs Knapp said you weren't to be bothered today,' she said worriedly – she had a wary regard for Mrs Knapp's injunctions – 'but this seems awfully important. It's somebody from the District Attorney's office. He says his name is Myron Kramer.'

It took Murray a moment to recall the name. Then he

realized that his caller was Felix LoScalzo's leg man, and found himself not at all disturbed by the realization. If anything, what he felt for LoScalzo – and he was willing to extend the feeling to LoScalzo's representative – was a pleasant kinship. For the time being, he was one of them. They were all professionals together; they spoke the same language; and, most intriguing to contemplate, they were gunning for the same bird, each in his own way. That was the case in a nutshell, although it was hardly LoScalzo's business to know it.

Kramer was tall and slim, with blazing red hair and a host of freckles on his youthful face. He looked eighteen, and was probably about twenty-eight. Nowadays, Murray knew, every district attorney's office, every United States Attorney's office in the city, was loaded with this kind of underling. Young Harlingens all, they had no soft berth with the old man waiting for them. So they piled into prosecutors' offices where they could fetch and carry until the baby fat they bore from law school was melted off, and were then put to work trying unimportant cases until the legal muscle was built up. In the end, they made good lawyers who knew their way around a courtroom as well as a contract. Kramer, with his youthfully earnest face and shrewd eyes, seemed to be a superior example of the type.

He also proved to be a young man who did not waste words. Mr LoScalzo, he said briefly, would be out of court in a few minutes, and looked forward to seeing Mr Kirk in his office when he got back there. It was important that they have a little talk.

'About what?' asked Murray.

'Articles 54 and 70, I think,' Kramer blandly replied.

Article 70 was the old pitfall for inept private detectives, disorderly conduct, but Article 54 was something else again. 'Disorderly conduct and conspiracy,' Murray said. 'You sure there's nothing else on the agenda? Sepulture? Barratry? Duelling? Nothing really fancy?'

Kramer smiled. 'I wouldn't know,' he said. 'After all, I'm just the guy who empties ashtrays around the place.'

I'll bet you are, Murray thought as he reached for his hat, *you cute little cobra.*

LoScalzo was a big man. Big in height, big in girth, his huge head surmounted by a shock of unkempt white hair, he sat there peeling an apple with a paring knife which circled the fruit in a smooth, continuous motion. The peel, coiling into a plate on the desk, looked as if it were being run out of a machine. Murray recognized the performance as a variation of Bruno's briefcase act, and a dull one at that. He turned his attention to the rest of the room, and found that the one object of interest there was a glass jar nearly full of water, and with what appeared to be some shapeless wads of black gum pressed against its inside wall. Without looking up from the apple LoScalzo jerked his head toward the jar. 'Know what they are?'

They were the first words he had spoken since Murray had been ushered in and left there with him. They had been a long time coming.

'No,' Murray said, 'I don't.'

LoScalzo put down the knife and apple and heaved himself out of his chair. He went to the jar, and, using a pair of sugar tongs that had been lying next to it, he carefully lifted one of the blobs from the water.

'Bloodsuckers,' he said affectionately. 'Or, if you're fussy, leeches. Couple of months ago some of the boys raided a barbershop on the Bowery that was peddling rotgut in the back room, and they brought back these little jokers along with the evidence. Some of the barbers down there still use them for black eyes. Just plant them on the swelling, and they're supposed to do a fine job of bringing it down. Ever see one close up?'

He thrust the tongs near Murray's face, and the slimy thing they gripped writhed in a slow, blind motion of protest. Murray felt his gorge rising, but forced himself to sit rigid and unblinking. It was not easy. He had always had a revulsion for crawling things, and this one was like some monstrosity dredged up from his blackest nightmares.

'Most people don't like these jokers,' LoScalzo said. He finally dropped his captive back into the jar, and Murray's breathing became easier. 'I don't know why, but that's the way it goes. Take even a nervy guy like you. For a second there, it looked like you were all set to heave up over that nice expensive suit, so I guess you don't like them either. Isn't that a fact?'

Murray did not vouchsafe an answer to this, and LoScalzo did not seem to expect any. He fitted himself into his chair, picked up the apple, and bit a chunk from it. 'With me,' he pointed out, 'it's different. Bloodsuckers might turn your stomach, Kirk, but not mine. What makes *me* want to heave up is the kind of bastard who stakes out an apartment until he can catch a sick woman alone in it – a woman who's this far away from being a mental case – and then hire some beat-up old actress to go along with him and fool the woman into talking about her husband's troubles. That's what can really set me off, Kirk. Or don't you know what I'm talking about?'

It was the tone as much as the words that did it, and in that instant Murray's complacent sense of kinship vanished in an explosion of blind rage. Then he caught hold of himself. If there was anything LoScalzo wanted – if there was anything he had been aiming at with his whole performance – it was just this. It had almost worked, too, and Murray turned his wrath against himself for that. He had known that the cape was being waved in front of his nose to draw him on, had certainly suspected the blade behind it, and yet had been lured perilously close to wildly charging it and being left for dead. What LoScalzo would have to be taught now was that he was in the ring with the wrong bull.

'No,' Murray said, 'I don't know what you're talking about.'

'I see.' LoScalzo bit into the apple again, and chewed away steadily while he weighed this. 'Then you deny that, while acting for a client last Monday, you and some woman entered the home of Ira Miller in his absence, and spoke to Mrs Miller there?'

Murray smiled. 'You know I can't deny something I haven't been charged with. Are you charging me with breaking and entering?'

LoScalzo smiled in return. 'I'd like to,' he said pleasantly. 'God knows how much I'd like to, Kirk, just to teach you it doesn't pay to split legal hairs with me. But I won't. What you and your accomplice were up to when you worked on Miller to change his testimony was conspiracy. And what you and another accomplice were up to when you tried to tamper with official records is also conspiracy. And all for one client, too. You must be in a real sweat about that client, Kirk, to put yourself on the spot for him this way.'

'What spot?' Murray asked derisively. 'If you thought you could make a case out of this, would we be sitting here talking about it? The hell we would. I'd be downstairs getting finger-printed before you were finished peeling your apple.'

LoScalzo's eyebrows went up. 'Who said anything about a case?' he asked mildly. He put the core of the apple into the plate, and carefully cleaned his hands with a handkerchief. 'All I had in mind was a little hearing before the State Director of Licences.'

That had an unpleasant sound, and the more Murray considered it, the more unpleasant it sounded. The business of the police records was no problem, because Strauss had been smart enough not to walk into the trap set for him. But the business of Ira Miller was something else again. Miller and that ironclad nurse of his would make murderous witnesses at a hearing, and since Miller himself must have raised this issue with LoScalzo in the first place, there was no question about his willingness to appear as a witness. No question about the nurse, either. She'd jump through a hoop, if Miller told her to. And the thought of what they would have to say, and how they would say it, led to only one possible conclusion.

'All right,' Murray said resignedly, 'as the old joke had it: I get the point; you can take away the knife.'

'Not yet,' said LoScalzo. 'Not so fast, mister. I want to wait until Lundeen's been brought to trial, and Miller's taken the stand against him. Then we'll see.'

'See what? You don't really expect Miller to run out on you, do you?'

LoScalzo held his hands wide, palms up, in a sad gesture. 'I'm a simple man,' he said. 'A *paisan*. When I hear the dog who just tried to run my witness off the stand ask that question I get confused. What is it, Kirk? Are you dumber than you look, or are you so smart I can't follow you?'

'Dumber,' Murray said promptly.

'Good. Just keep that in mind, and stay far away from my witnesses after this.'

'And then?'

'Then maybe you'll be able to hang on to your licence, and not have to worry about making an honest living digging ditches.'

'Thanks,' Murray said. He was only too glad to get up from his chair. 'And let me know when you run for governor. You can count on my vote.'

It was the wrong joke to make at the wrong time. He knew it from the way LoScalzo rose to face him across the desk; the man's collar suddenly seemed to be chokingly tight around the bull neck.

'Kirk,' LoScalzo said in a deadly voice, 'some time when you're not busy framing divorce evidence do me a favour. Go through the newspapers and find out for yourself the kind of publicity I'm getting on this job. The kind of political build-up I'm getting. How many people know about me, and how many give a damn.'

'Look,' Murray said, 'you know I was only kidding.'

'Nobody kids me about this, Kirk. Nobody at all. You want to know why? Because for thirty years I handled a practice that made me more money and got me into more dirt than I ever thought could wash off. When this job came along I took it like you take a steam bath – to get clean again. And nobody is going to dirty it for me!'

He meant it, Murray knew. Savonarola on the scaffold could

not have meant it more passionately. 'I'm sorry.' Murray said. He held out his hand. 'I'll remember that.'

LoScalzo looked down at the hand, and then raised his eyes. 'Go on,' he said wearily. 'Get out of here, before I throw you out.'

It was not the words which cut deepest. It was not the rejection of the proffered hand. It was the look on LoScalzo's face then. The same look, Murray knew, that he himself must have had when he was suddenly confronted by the nauseous thing LoScalzo had lifted from the jar for his benefit.

15

The distorted image of LoScalzo was with him through a series of horrendous dreams that night, and then – it seemed no more than a minute – after he had given up caring and sunk a thousand miles deep into dreamless oblivion, the ringing of the phone shrilly started him out of it.

It was Mrs Knapp. And, thought Murray, blearily aware of the daylight that flooded the room, it was Saturday morning. So it must be important.

'There were two calls for you after you left yesterday,' Mrs Knapp said. 'One of them was from Mrs Donaldson. She wanted to remind you to be at Mr Princip's studio tonight. She said to tell you that everything was taken care of, whatever that means.'

'Good. Who was the other call from?'

'George Wykoff, Duchess Harbor, Staten Island,' Mrs Knapp said as if she were reciting an incantation, and Murray suddenly came wide awake. 'The phone number's unlisted, but he left it with me so that you could get in touch with him as soon as possible. Do you have pencil and paper handy?'

'Hold it a second,' Murray answered, and lay back with his eyes closed to consider this development. Right now, he knew, there was a fair chance that one of LoScalzo's bright young men was crouched in a thicket of telephone wires in the depths of the St Stephen listening to every word. But it was too late to do anything about that, too late to do anything but curse the fisherman's luck that lured a big one like Wykoff – a killer whale among sharks – to your bait, when all you could do was stand there with your hands tied and watch him get away.

'Hello, are you there?' said Mrs Knapp.

'Yes. About that phone number, Mrs Knapp, just tear it up. Forget about it. Is that clear?'

One of Mrs Knapp's virtues was that nothing ever had to be repeated to her. 'I understand. Is there anything else, Mr Kirk?'

'No,' said Murray. 'That's it.'

The building that housed Alex Princip's studio fronted the small rectangle of Gramercy Park; with its series of balconies and wrought-iron balustrades it might have been conveyed wholesale from New Orleans. The studio itself was large enough to serve as a basketball court, and when Murray walked in he found it filled with people, noise, and smoke. It was easy enough to pick out Alex in the crowd – he bulked a head taller than anyone else there, and his face, ferociously bearded and gleaming with sweat, shone like a beacon in the fog – and Didi was, of course, in attendance on him.

'Say, what is this?' Murray said to her. 'I was aiming at a little get-together. This looks like the gathering of the clans.'

'Well, don't blame me, sweetie.' Didi was concentrating on a pitcher of martinis which she swirled with practised hands. 'I asked hardly any people to start with, but they all wanted to bring somebody, and I couldn't say no, could I?'

'You could have tried. I'll admit I'm flattered, considering this is all for little old me, but there are times—'

'Oh, stop,' said Didi. 'And you don't have to be so flattered. The only reason it's like this is because you're paying for it. I mean instead of a picture. It'll be on your bill from the St Stephen, because they're supplying everything here. They were very co-operative.'

'I'll bet they were. Is Ruth here?'

'I said she would be, didn't I? She's over there somewhere.'

He worked his way through the crowd in the direction pointed out; it took him an anxious minute to locate Ruth.

Then he caught sight of her, half-hidden by a circle of admiring males as he knew she would be, and evidently enjoying herself. A couple of the admirers were familiar to him. One was Ted Holloway, Didi's whilom TV producer. The other, a chunky little man with the face of a leprechaun, had been one of Evan's intimates. He had introduced himself to Murray, that night of the bard's memorable display in the West Side saloon, simply as The O'Mearagh, an unappreciated poet with far more talent than Evan, but with considerably less sexual ardour.

'That's what does me in,' he had explained sadly. 'We're right back to the minnesingers again, when it was a case of sing to the count and – if you'll excuse the expression – screw the countess. I am a man violently given to moderation. There's no place for the likes of me in this neo-codpiece age.'

Watching Ruth handle the circle around her, Murray saw that things were well under control. The party was in that phase in which interested males were surveying prospects, but were not yet ready to do anything about it. Then his view was momentarily obscured by a waiter – he recognized the man as a regular from the St Stephen Grill – who, with loaded tray held high, swam into ken as effortlessly as an eel slipping through seaweed. The waiter recognized him, too. 'Nice party, Mr Kirk,' he said, lowering the tray. 'Have something?'

'No, thanks,' said Murray, and the man next to him said, 'Well, I will,' and helped himself to a sandwich. Then he turned a darkly tanned, well-fed face to Murray. 'Kirk?' he said. 'Say, I know you. You worked for Frank Conmy, didn't you?'

'Yes.'

'I thought so. Chipman's the name. Joe Chipman. I used to run the agency that booked Frank's radio interviews. Too bad about him, wasn't it? But, of course, he was an old man when his time came.'

He had sold his agency a couple of years ago, he explained in answer to Murray's polite query, to go into independent film production with a partner on the Coast. 'I talked myself into it,' he said. 'When I handled the agency I spent so much time telling producers that movie business was on the upgrade that I finally got to believe it myself. I had no idea what a clever con man I was.'

A handsome, grey-haired woman came up and looked at the remnants of sandwich in Chipman's hand. 'Oh, Joe,' she said reproachfully.

Chipman sighed. 'How much sharper than a serpent's tooth is a wife who counts calories. Hannah, Mr Kirk here is a real, live private detective. When you find him following you some day you'll know the jig is up.'

Hannah Chipman smiled at Murray. 'That'll be the day. Are you a friend of Alex, Mr Kirk?'

'Not quite,' said Murray. 'More the friend of a friend.'

'Alex, the vulgar Bulgar,' Chipman said. 'I got him his first job designing some sets for United Television that were real gems, and now look at him. Maybe you don't know it, Kirk, but he was quite a painter before he got started on these Duco and chickenshit masterpieces of his.'

'Oh, Joe,' said his wife.

'Well, that's what they are,' Chipman said placidly. 'After all, I was raised on a New Jersey chicken farm along with a couple of thousand Leghorns. I shovelled enough guano in my time to know it when I see it.'

'What're you in town for?' Murray asked. 'Just taking in art shows?'

'No, I'm in on the expense account. My angle is package deals where you put together a star, a director, and a story, and then go beg for financing. The trouble nowadays is with stories. Stars and directors I can shake off trees, but not stories. Right now I'm combing Broadway down to the last flop on the chance that MGM hasn't already bought everything. *Kapeesh?*'

'I *kapeesh*,' Murray said. 'But you'll have a job making good pictures out of what I've been seeing this season.'

'*Good* pictures? Who said anything about *good* pictures? Wake up, my friend. Look around you at our brave new world. The movies are all drive-ins today. It's where the kids go so they can muzzle in the car, and the family people go so they can dump baby in the playground while they catch up on their sleep. You think any of them are worried about how good the picture is? All they want is something on the screen so they've got an excuse for being there.'

'Oh, God,' said Hannah Chipman, 'here we go again.'

Murray said to Chipman: 'Come to think of it, I know somebody – strictly by way of business, that is – who backed a show called *Time Out of Hand* two or three years ago. Ever hear of it?'

'I not only heard of it, I had the pleasure of turning it down when they were trying to peddle screen rights. That desperate I never was. Why?'

'No particular reason. How much would you say something like that cost to produce?'

Chipman shrugged. 'Depends on a lot of things. Eighty thousand bucks is rock bottom, but it could run to plenty more by the time you get done adding up this and that. If you want the figures all you have to do is look up the copy of the *Wall Street Journal* where they announced the incorporation of the play company. That'll give you the bad news in detail. One thing about financing a show—'

'Joe,' said his wife. 'if you can't find something else to talk about, I am going to scream.'

'Isn't she cute?' commented Chipman. 'She hates these business trips, because all you do on them is talk business.'

'And talk and talk,' said Hannah Chipman. 'And you know you won't have a single story property to show for it when we get back to the Coast.'

'Maybe not,' Chipman said, 'but maybe there's something else we can take along with us.' He nudged Murray. 'Have you seen *that*?' he asked mysteriously. 'Can you picture it in Technicolor?'

Murray looked, and saw that he meant Ruth, who, with her brow knit in a frown, was intently listening to a harangue by The O'Mearagh.

'Very nice,' he said.

'Oh boy, have *you* got a gift for expression,' said Chipman. 'My friend, what you are now looking at is more than very nice. It is something aimed at stirring up even the knotheads who inhabit drive-ins. I've been watching her right along—'

'I know, dear,' said his wife.

'—I've been watching her right along, and my uncanny producer's eye tells me that there are vistas opening for all concerned. How anyone can look so much like a primrose on a river's bank and yet send out such tiger-lily vibrations I do not know, but that I'll leave to her analyst. All I'm interested in are those vibrations. Are you getting them?' he asked Murray.

'Clear as a bell,' said Murray. It struck him that the Chipmans, while unpredictable, might help cushion the impact when he presented himself to Ruth. 'You want to meet her?'

'I sure do,' Chipman said with alacrity. He turned wonderingly to his wife. 'How do you like that? He knows her, and he's been standing here killing time with us. Have you ever seen such self-control?'

'Not since I've known you, I haven't,' said Hannah Chipman.

By now the circle around Ruth had yielded to The O'Mearagh, leaving him in sole possession. He was not happy at the intrusion of the newcomers, and that did not surprise Murray. What did surprise him was the nature of Ruth's greeting to him. Her hand in his was warm and responsive, her voice altogether friendly. 'I'm so glad you came,' she said eagerly. 'There's something I wanted to tell you.'

With the memory of her panic at their last parting vividly in mind he had expected anything but this. Then he took in her flushed cheeks, her shining eyes, and the empty glass she was holding, and realized that Didi's explosive martinis had been at work here. It was also clear that they had been at work on The O'Mearagh as well, but with different effects.

'Movie people,' said The O'Mearagh with loathing after introductions had been made. He stared hard at Chipman. 'Ah, but there's the bloody mercenaries of the arts for you. There's the carrion birds of culture.'

'Please,' said Chipman. 'I've been trying to keep it from my wife. What do you want to do, queer me with her?'

The object of his concern patted his shoulder encouragingly. 'Don't give it a thought, dear,' she advised him. 'You just go be a nice successful mercenary. I'd like it.'

'I'll bet you would,' Chipman said balefully. 'You succubus. Or is it incubus?'

'Succubus,' said Ruth. 'Do you know anything about Edward the First?' she asked Murray. 'I mean, the Plantagenet one?'

'Only what I read in the papers,' Murray admitted, dazzled by this change of pace. He took the glass from her unresisting hand. 'How many of these things have you had so far?'

'Oh, two or three,' Ruth said airily. 'We've been arguing about Edward. The O'Mearagh's planning a long work about the massacre of Celtic bards Edward was supposed to have ordered, and I've been telling him that story was discredited a long time ago. It's as false as all that nonsense about Richard the Third.'

'I know Richard the Third,' announced Chipman. 'He's the one who had those kids killed in the Tower, the dirty incubus.'

'He did *not*,' said Ruth.

'I beg your pardon,' The O'Mearagh interposed heatedly, 'but he most certainly did. And I will state my principles plainly. I'm against all this whitewashing of scoundrels being done by a gang of professional jackasses looking to glorify the bloody British Crown. They're tearing the heart right out of the immortal body of literature, that's what they're doing!'

Chipman raised a magisterial hand. 'Objection overruled,' he said.

The O'Mearagh gave the impression of pawing the ground in his rage. 'What the hell do you mean by that?' he demanded. 'Whose side are you on, anyhow, mister?'

Chipman pointed at Ruth. 'I'm on her side, the way any

red-blooded American boy would be. And I mean that no matter how much those kids in the Tower asked for it, you can bet Richard never dared lay a hand on them. Why? Because their grandma wouldn't let him! Just ask my mother-in-law about that. She'll tell you.'

'Joe,' said Hannah Chipman coldly, 'that is not funny.'

'Funny!' cried The O'Mearagh. 'It's sheer blather! And,' he said, narrowing his eyes at Chipman, 'if you don't know what you're blathering about, mister, kindly do not blather at all.'

Chipman took a deep breath. 'Would you care to go outside and repeat that?'

'I would!'

'All right,' said Chipman, 'go ahead and do it. Meanwhile, I will be talking business to this lovely intellectual who might – just barely might – be interested in a screen test. How about it?' he asked Ruth. 'Maybe it'll pan out and maybe it won't, but there's no strings attached. All I want is some footage to see if the camera can catch those vibrations. Are you interested?'

'Sort of curious,' said Ruth, 'but not really interested. You know, they were his nephews, not his sons.'

'Who?' asked Chipman in bewilderment.

'Oh, you know who. The princes in the Tower were Richard's *nephews*, not his sons. The way it went, the succession to the throne—'

The O'Mearagh, who had been thinking his own dark thoughts, suddenly plucked Chipman's sleeve. 'Mister,' he stated in a voice that turned every head in the vicinity toward him, 'I think you've very much insulted me. Will you own up to that like an honest man?'

'Not me,' said Chipman without rancour. 'I'm a born coward. I never insult anyone but children and old ladies. Little old ladies,' he added, and held his hand a foot from the floor to illustrate.

The O'Mearagh was not to be denied. 'I said you've very much insulted me, mister, and I do not like it. I do not like it especially, when it comes from a big, fat, gutless slob with the reek of the Hollywood charnel house on him. What do you think of that?'

Murray did not wait to hear Chipman's answer. And the last he saw of the scene, as he grabbed Ruth's hand and dragged her out of the storm centre, made a remarkable tableau. The O'Mearagh's fist was bouncing ineffectually off Chipman's well-padded shoulder, while, almost simultaneously, a large leather handbag wielded by Hannah Chipman was landing flush against the side of The O'Mearagh's startled face. To add to the picture, the handbag had burst open on the impact, and the air all around seemed full of its flying contents.

Hannah might not have known it, thought Murray, but no one could have struck a sweeter blow for Edward the First.

16

The world outside the house was cold and empty, made fitfully alive by a tearing wind. Under it the naked trees along the block thrashed in unison, and the old-fashioned street light overhead swung in a reluctant and groaning arc at the end of its pole.

Murray stopped on the sidewalk at the foot of the steps and said, 'Hold on, you want to catch something fatal?' and Ruth stood obediently while he buttoned her coat. The warmth of her body surrounded him then, her face was perilously close, and the only defence he could mount against this was to frown, to thrust the coat buttons into place with brusque efficiency, to be the kindly but indifferent male attending to little sister. 'Still set on walking?' he asked. 'It's a long way home in weather like this, and I've got the car parked right around the corner.'

'I'd rather walk. And the weather's wonderful. It makes things look like a *Walpurgisnacht*.' She looked up at the clouds scudding across the face of the moon. 'See that? Probably a witch flying by right now.'

'It is not. She'd have been spotted by radar and shot down before she got past Long Island. Shot down like a supersonic dog.'

'Perish the thought,' Ruth said. The tapping of her high heels made a quick obbligato to his footsteps as they moved off down the street, and, he observed, she walked careful inches apart from him. 'Perish radar. Perish everything that does away with witches and warlocks and wonders. *Step on a crack, break your mother's back*,' she sing-songed cheerfully, picking her way across a stretch of broken pavement, and then let out a small yelp. 'Oh, poor mother! But that wasn't my fault, was it? There are more cracks than pavement here.'

'That ought to console poor mother,' Murray jeered. 'Not that she didn't have it coming to her. Any woman who lets her drunken daughter fool around with witchcraft—'

'If you don't know what you're blathering about, will you please not blather? I hardly ever fool around with witchcraft any more. And am not drunk. I have an exceptionally active liver which either does, or does not do, something to the alcohol I ingest, so that it is impossible for me to get drunk. Right now I am merely seeing things through a glass lightly. Nothing wrong with that, is there?'

'Not a thing,' Murray said devoutly. 'It sounds like the ideal state.'

'It is exactly that.' She sighed with pleasant recollection. 'Lordy, what a night. What a pluperfect night. I didn't stop talking from the time I got there, and I loved every minute of it right up to the knockout. There must have been five years of talk bottled up in me, and plenty of nice, crazy people to listen and argue back. And I like people to argue back, damn it. I hate the mealy-mouthed breed who smile and pat you on the head, instead of having it out.'

'So I gathered. By the way, while all the handshaking was going on – you know, before the fireworks started – you said there was something you wanted to tell me. What was it?'

She pondered this, and shook her head blankly. 'I don't know. There was something, but now I can't remember what. Isn't it awful?'

'Terrible. Try talking about something else. Maybe that'll bring it back.'

'Talk about what?' she laughed, and then hiccuped. 'Oh, God,' she said despairingly, 'now I've got the hiccups. Everything is breaking down all together.' They had reached Fourth

Avenue, and she braced herself with both hands against the mailbox at the corner there, shaken alternately by wild, helpless laughter and a series of shattering hiccups. 'Everything!' she finally managed to say. 'Mind, body, and soul. I feel like one of Alex's pictures. What do you make of those pictures?'

'They remind me of life in the linoleum works,' Murray said. 'You know, the standard treatment in these cases is to whack the patient a few times on the back. Suppose I—'

'You will not. And don't go trying any other homespun remedies, either. It's the remedies that kill, not the hiccups. Besides, they've gone away. At least, I think they have.' She stood at attention with eyes closed to test this, and then drew a cautious breath. 'They have. The ostrich treatment always works. If you close your eyes it's not there.'

'Could be. Or was it talking about Alex's painting that did it?'

'No, and anyhow I wasn't talking about it for that reason. You said to talk about something at random, and that's what I picked. But you'll have to co-operate. How about some deep down, vital opinions on the subject?'

'Not from me,' Murray protested. When they turned south along the avenue the wind was at their backs, and he gratefully felt life returning to his numb features. 'What makes you think I'd have any?'

'Oh,' Ruth said carelessly, 'Mrs Donaldson would, for one.'

He glanced at her face, but it was all innocence. Too innocent, he decided. 'What about Mrs Donaldson?'

Ruth shook her head. 'I'm sorry, but that slipped out. I shouldn't have said it.'

'Skip the vain regrets. What about her?'

'Well, nothing, really. It's just that she confided to me – and I quote – that you were positively brimming with deep-down, vital opinions. You were sort of a cultural angel always hovering nearby with the Word. Or didn't you know?'

'Sure, I knew,' Murray said with foreboding. 'But I didn't

know you two had any chance to swap notes about it. When did all this happen?'

'At the gallery this afternoon. When she called up to invite me to the party – and honestly, it sounded more like an Evan Griffith Memorial than a party the way it was described – she loudly hinted that the price of admission was attendance at the gallery before the main event, and a few polite cheers for Alex. Of course, I said yes. The next thing I knew, she had singled me out of the mob there, backed me into a corner, and was talking to me a mile a minute. A lot of it was about you.'

'Good or bad?'

'Oh, some of each. Did you know you were a fragmented personality and terribly vulnerable?'

Murray winced. 'I suppose that's a direct quote, too?'

'Word for word. But that's all right; she said Evan Griffith was the same way, so you're in good company. She gave me quite a lecture about Evan. Seems that her job had been to mother, cosset, and service him, in return for which she could count on a swift kick in the teeth now and then. It sounded perfectly delightful.'

'I didn't notice her minding very much,' Murray said. 'For that matter, it's not much different with Alex. She asks for it.'

'I know. I saw her with Alex at the gallery, and it killed me to watch her. She was so terribly possessive and eager and wanting to cluster around, and he – well, it wasn't anything really brutal – but he just kept shoving her away. It was pathetic, that's what it was. Doesn't she have any pride? Doesn't she realize how pathetic it is?'

'It wouldn't make any difference if she did. Look, while you two were hanging over the back fence, did she say anything about this guy Donaldson she used to be married to?'

'Only enough to let me know there was an ex-husband in the offing. Why? What did he do, beat her up regularly?'

'Maybe worse,' said Murray. 'Fact is, she got him dead to rights on an adultery charge. No, I'm not fooling,' he said in answer to Ruth's look of suspicion. 'I think that catching Donaldson in bed with another woman did a lot more damage to her than any kick in the teeth. And that's an expert opinion. In my business you get to be quite an expert on adultery, any size, any shape.'

'So I've heard,' said Ruth, and her tone – something in it – jabbed a nerve already made raw by LoScalzo.

'It's a business, all right,' Murray said. 'The same kind Ralph Harlingen is in, or Arnold, for that matter. We're all in the same barrel together, regardless of what kind of licence gets us into it. Or didn't you know you had to have a licence to run an agency in New York?'

'I never thought of it one way or the other. And I don't know what you're being so crabby about. Just because I made a perfectly harmless joke—'

'In that case, skip it.'

'Why do you keep telling me to skip things?' Ruth said irritably 'I want you to understand – oh, never mind. Let's hear about Mrs Donaldson. She was a lot better company than you are right now; I'll say that much for her.'

She had the power, he realized, to mollify him as readily as she could anger him, and it was not unpleasant realization. 'All right,' he said, 'she came from a no-account family in Texas that kept goats in the yard, and by the time she was sixteen she couldn't take any more of the family or the goats, so she went off to marry a millionaire. Naturally, she wound up in Dallas.'

'Naturally. And this Donaldson was the millionaire. A goat of a different colour, you might say.'

'No, *you* might. But he was the one, all right. She worked in his office, and he started taking a fatherly interest in her, and then a different kind of interest, and it wound up with them getting plastered one night and running off to get married. The funny thing was that she wasn't any beauty contest winner then; she didn't have a fraction of the looks she has now, and he still went and married her. She thinks it's because she was a virgin, and he found he couldn't do anything about it except by marrying her. Guys like Donaldson are great ones for *prima noctis*, if you know what I mean. They can have almost any woman they want, but it takes that one unplucked fruit on top of the tree to really make their mouths water. And the fact that it might be a gawky seventeen-year-old kid doesn't seem to make any difference. Anyhow, it didn't in this case.

'Still and all, she said it worked out pretty well for a while. She made a big project out of being the dandy little housewife, the kind you see in the magazine ads – it wasn't hard, because she had a bunch of Mexican help to do all the work for her – and he was the loving husband, and seemed to get a big kick out of it. What she didn't know at the time, of course, was that when he was away from home on business – and he was away plenty – the business was always women.

'She didn't find that out until they came to New York, and he really made a holy show of himself. I don't know whether he didn't care by then if she found out, or if he thought she wouldn't, but it would have been hard for her not to. All she ever reads in the papers are the gossip columnists, and he was a natural for every columnist in town. He was not what you might call discreet about his amours.

'So one day, without saying a word to him about all this, she just went out and dug up a lawyer out of the phone book. Her luck he happened to be somebody who used our agency, and that's how I came to know her. I was along with her and the photographer when Donaldson was caught in the act. And I saw what it did to her. That's why I say it was worse than a kick in the teeth. It was.'

'Not for long,' Ruth said. 'She seems to have gotten over it very nicely.'

'That's the point I'm making. She didn't get over it. It's the thing that shaped her into what she is now.'

Ruth said caustically: 'But whatever she is now, she apparently adores men; she just goes to pieces around them with love and devotion. If finding her husband was unfaithful really meant anything, it would work the opposite way, wouldn't it? It would make her despise men.'

'No,' said Murray, 'it wouldn't. You've got a nice theory there, but it doesn't happen to fit Mrs Donaldson. The only thing she despises is herself. She'd call me a liar if I told her that to her face, and she'd mean it, too, but it's the plain truth. In her heart she feels inadequate. She feels there's something she was supposed to provide in marriage – maybe sexually, maybe intellectually, whatever it is – that she didn't provide. So what she did with Griffith, what she's doing now with Alex, is overcompensate. She picks out some man she admires, and, by God, she's out to prove to herself that she can be the perfect mate for him. The indispensable woman. That's what Donaldson did to her. He knocked the props right out from under her.'

Ruth looked at him curiously. 'You like her a lot, don't you?'

'I don't know. I pity her a lot. How much can you really like someone you pity?'

He was deliberately aiming close to the mark with that, the thought of her tie to Lundeen uppermost in his mind, the need to rip apart the tie, to hurl Lundeen into limbo suddenly possessing him like a physical hunger. But Ruth only continued to look at him with appraisal, the scarred corner of her mouth drawn into a crooked little smile.

'Quite a fragmented personality,' she said at last, and he felt that he had missed the mark completely.

'Thanks,' he said. 'And vulnerable. Don't forget the vulnerable.

'And vulnerable,' she said.

She was lost in her own thoughts the rest of the way home, and Murray could only wonder what the thoughts were without daring to intrude on them. It made a silent walk, but not an unpleasant one for him, because when they crossed the street at Union Square under the menacing headlights of the late traffic he drew her arm through his, and she did not withdraw the arm or make any objections. To that extent, at least, he told himself, he had taken physical possession, and had to smile inwardly at what Frank Conmy would have remarked about this peculiar game of love he was playing, and the devious way he was forced to play it, step by wary step.

Frank had always maintained – using the Anglo-Saxon terminology to express himself – that there was only one question to ask a woman when you felt an itch for her, and it was her business to answer yes or no, I will or I won't, no fuss and fancy footwork, no guitar solos under the window or carriage rides through the park behind a smelly horse, but yes or no, and to hell with her if it was no. Love, said Frank, was a biological urge with a pretty label on it. It was something cooked up by people who wrote popular music or advertising copy to help them sell their merchandise. And anyone who doubted that ought to be locked up for his own good, before he found himself with a wedding ring through his nose and being led along like an ox to the slaughter.

Because Frank did not take kindly to disputation on his pet opinions, and because this opinion itself seemed to be weighted with logic, Murray had never given much thought to it, but had accepted it for what it was intended to be, wisdom for the good of a disciple's soul. But he thought of it now, and of the way Frank looked delivering it – the big face red with a hectic flush, one hand sloshing brandy around the balloon glass, the other chopping the air with sharp strokes to emphasize a point, the voice booming out eloquently – and he found the thought a little painful. Maybe Frank had been talking good sense to him at the time, but the pressure of Ruth's arm against him now made it seem only querulous and tinny and pitiable, and it hurt to think of Frank that way. Hurt, but couldn't be helped. So much for Conmy, the old philosopher, Murray reflected uncomfortably.

At the door of the house Ruth fumbled in her purse for the key, and then suddenly faced him and said, 'You know, there is something to that Freud thing, after all. I mean, about forgetting things you subconsciously want to forget. What I wanted to tell you back at the party was like that. I just remembered what it was.'

'That's fine. But if it's something you don't want to talk about—'

'I do want to talk about it. I really do. It was about the last time you brought me home – the way I acted. I was sick about it afterward, and I didn't know how to apologize. I wanted to call you up, but every time I picked up the phone I'd start wondering what to say, and I'd put it down again. I suppose that's what happened when I saw you at the party. I started off fine, and then first chance I had I just went blank. But I'm not blank now, thank heaven, so I can tell you that I did behave badly that time, and I do owe you an apology.'

The cold wind whipped at him, sent dry leaves scraping past his feet, but he stood there looking at her, warmed by a marvellous quickening of the blood. 'The funny thing is,' he said, 'I was going around the same way. I thought it was my fault.'

'It wasn't.'

'Then what was it?'

'I don't know.' They were speaking in hushed night-time voices, close together in the doorway, and a passing couple eyed them with interest. Ruth waited until they had gone by, and then said half-angrily, 'I was afraid, I suppose. What difference does it make?'

'None, as long as you're not afraid now. Are you?'

'Yes.'

'Of me?'

'Yes. Oh, I don't know. Why must you take everything I say so seriously? I told you it was like a *Walpurgisnacht*; everything's all mixed up right now. And I did drink a lot. That's obvious, isn't it?'

He put his hands on her shoulders and shook her once, very gently. 'Are you really afraid of me?'

'Oh, please,' she said, but there was no resistance to his

hands, none of the effort to pull away from them that he had been prepared for.

'Are you?' he demanded.

'No.'

'Good. Then when will I see you again?'

'You can't!' she said in alarm. 'I mean, not this way, as if we were dating or something. Don't you understand that?'

'Tuesday would be fine for me,' Murray said. 'I don't have anything scheduled for the afternoon, so I could meet you after school, and we can take it from there. Dinner, theatre, and a lot of talk. How does that sound?'

'It sounds like everything else that happened tonight. It doesn't mean anything. I'm not listening to it.'

'Then listen. Tuesday's the day. I'll pick you up at the school.'

'I don't want you coming around the school.'

'Then we'll make it the house here. At seven.'

'Isn't there any way I can make you understand?' Ruth said in bewilderment.

'I don't see how, unless we sit down together and put our minds to it. We can do that Tuesday.'

'I don't even know if I'll be free then. Besides, I can always call you, can't I? If there's some way I can arrange things—'

It was a gambit not even worth casual notice. 'You know what'll happen,' Murray said. 'You'll keep picking up the phone and putting it down, and think of the wear and tear on your nerves. It's better to settle it right now.'

'You mean, settle it your way,' Ruth said helplessly. 'Oh, all right, if you're going to be so damn stubborn—'

Walpurgisnacht, he thought, when she was gone and the door had closed behind her. And Christmas to come.

17

Late Tuesday afternoon Mrs Knapp came into the office to tell him that she had the theatre tickets for him, that a table for two had been reserved at Le Pavillon, and that George Wykoff had been phoning at regular intervals. He had been expecting to hear from Mr Kirk, and what was going on there, anyhow?

'What did you tell him?' Murray asked.

'Oh, just that you weren't available. From the way he sounded he wasn't very happy about it.'

'That's his tough luck,' Murray said. He described to her the gist of his talk with LoScalzo, and Mrs Knapp said, 'Well, in that case we certainly don't have any choice, do we? I'll take care of it if he phones again. I'll tell him you're out of town or something. Did you know that a couple of agencies are going to be called to Albany for hearings on illegal wire tapping next week?'

'No, where'd you pick up that information?'

'Somebody from Inter-American told Mr Strauss about it. The ones they've grabbed aren't competitors, unfortunately, just a pair of small operators, but can you picture how this will stir up things in Albany now? They don't know one agency from another up there. It would be the worst possible time for us to get into any kind of trouble.'

'It's always the worst possible time,' Murray said.

On the way back to the St Stephen to dress for dinner he

bought an evening paper, and while soaking in the tub he read it, starting with the comic strips – Mary Worth's latest protégée was in a real mess this time – and wending his way through the sports section to land in Dr Marie Zinsser's *People's Problems*, a long-winded column, couched in psychological gobbledegook, and dedicated to the proposition that anyone who wrote in for advice must be guilty of something to start with.

The first letter struck a familiar note.

Dear Dr Zinsser,

Right after we got back from our honeymoon my husband said he wanted his mother to live with us a little while. Even though she is mean and bossy I said all right, but it is three years now, and I am so unhappy all the time I could die. How can I make my husband understand that it is wrong for his mother to live with us while she can afford to live by herself?
Edith

Murray read the answer with fascination.

Dear Edith,

When you say 'wrong' don't you mean it is only 'wrong' for you? The lives of two other people are involved in this, you know, and I am afraid that unconscious antagonisms in you prevent you from taking this into account. One must understand his own motivations fully before he—

It was an answer, Murray had to admit, squarely in the great Zinsser tradition.

While dressing, he put Berrigan's 'I Can't Get Started' on the phonograph and set it for replay. He briefly considered his neighbours in the apartment next door, dismissed the thought, and turned up the volume of the machine. There were only two suites on the top floor of the St Stephen, and the couple who occupied the other one – a retired rear admiral and his wife – had acute hearing partly compensated for by a sense of humour.

They would tolerate three replays of any record at the peak of its volume, and then would knock at the door in good-natured protest. When Murray opened the door, one or the other would say, 'Now, hear this!' which was his cue to say, 'Aye, aye, sir,' and turn the machine's volume down.

But what he needed now, Murray knew, was loud music and strong drink. Even an old sea dog would appreciate his feelings if he ever got one look at the reason for them. Murray poured himself the strong drink, downed half of it, and took the remainder to the bedroom as sustenance while he finished dressing. Pushing the cuff links into his shirt, he mentally framed his own letter to Dr Zinsser.

Dear Dr Zinsser,
    I am a romantic-type fellow who is hopelessly in love with a girl who imagines she is engaged to a cop who is under indictment for perjury. Tell me, do you think I have any right to expect a wedding present from a man in jail?

The familiar knock sounded just as Berrigan had completed his third mournful round of the song, and while Murray was still trying to draft a proper Zinsserite answer to himself. He loudly goose-stepped to the door and threw it open. 'Aye, aye, sir,' he said.

The man standing there blinked at him. It was not the admiral. It was a chauffeur in dark livery, his driver's cap held close to his chest in both hands. A compact little man, a head shorter than Murray, with a slightly battered-looking face and bright, black shoebutton eyes.

'Hell,' said Murray, 'I'm sorry. I thought you were somebody else.'

'My name is Caxton, sir,' the chauffeur said. 'I'm from the Clientele Limousine Service. Are you Mr Kirk?'

'Yes, but I don't think I'm the Kirk you want. I didn't order any car.'

The man looked with puzzlement over Murray's shoulder

into the empty room beyond. 'Do you have someone else here who might have called, sir?'

'No. You can see for yourself there's nobody else here.'

'Well, thanks, Mr Kirk,' Caxton said, and when he said it Murray knew that he had been beautifully taken. But there was no time to make any move now, no time for anything but regrets. Not after the man flipped the chauffeur's cap aside with one hand to show the gun held in the other, its barrel in a straight line with Murray's belly. It was an ugly-looking gun, made even uglier, somehow, by a stubby, two-inch barrel. 'Go on,' said Caxton. 'Back up.'

Murray backed up. It was the first time in his life, including his army service, that he had ever found himself looking into the business end of a gun, and the sight washed all the bravado out of him, leaving a sick and helpless anger in its place. Caxton followed him into the room and slammed the door shut with his foot. He frowned with distaste at the phonograph. 'Turn that thing off,' he said. 'How can you stand all that noise?'

Murray switched off the phonograph and faced the gun again. It struck him that if the man had really intended to use the gun then and there, he would have wanted as much noise as possible around him to muffle the sound. For what it was worth it was an emboldening thought.

'What's all this about?' Murray said. 'Who put you up to it?'

'Nobody put me up to anything, Mr Kirk. I mean, if you're trying to make out I'm some kind of hood you got me all wrong. I'm very legitimate. Six Caddie limousines working for me, and ten guys on the payroll, and a half interest in a nice garage – that's legitimate, ain't it?'

'Sure,' Murray said. 'Especially the way you go out and get customers with a gun. Who owns the other half of the nice garage? George Wykoff?'

'Maybe he does, and maybe he don't,' Caxton said blandly. 'Whichever way it is, Mr Wykoff happens to be a very good friend of mine. I mean, he's the kind of a friend where if he says, "I wish I could get close to a certain Mr Murray Kirk," why, I'm glad to fix it for him. Do him a favour, you might say. Mr Wykoff's got a lot of friends like that. Few days ago he got all bothered because a certain Mr García – some greaseball who runs a lunch stand over on Eighth Avenue – was being kind of mysterious about things, so last night one of those friends got sore about it and jumped all over Mr García. He's up in Montefiore Hospital now. I mean, in case you want to drop in on him with a box of candy or something.'

So that, Murray thought, was what his five-dollar tip had bought the little Puerto Rican with the sad face and the bright, fixed smile.

'You could have left him alone,' he said bitterly. 'He doesn't know anything.'

Caxton shrugged. 'That's what he kept saying, but it's none of my worry, Mr Kirk. I'm just telling you about it, so you'll know what the score is. Now, how about getting your coat on and taking a little run out to Staten Island with me? The car's right downstairs.'

'What happens if I say no? You shoot me and drag the body along to Wykoff? Maybe he'd rather have me in shape to talk.'

'Oh, if that's what's bothering you,' Caxton said. He held out the gun to Murray, who took it incredulously. 'It's not loaded. I always say anybody carried a loaded gun around with him is sooner or later going to have it blow off when he don't expect it to. This way it just comes in handy so people'll listen when you want to talk to them.'

Murray broke open the gun and saw the empty chambers inside. Then he flung it aside with the wild joy of combat flaring up inside of him. What happened next was hard to understand. He was looking up at Caxton – *up* when he had just been on his feet lunging at the man – and he found that he was sprawled on his back, his head almost in the ashes of the fireplace, the hot salt taste of blood filling his mouth. Caxton stood like a Colossus over him, looking down at him pityingly.

'The bigger they are,' he said. 'Especially when they got a glass jaw. Anyhow, you don't have to take it too hard, Mr Kirk.

You look in the records for Billy Caxton you'll see fifteen kayoes out of thirty-six decisions. And always classy opposition. I was a real good banty-weight in my time.'

Murray turned sideways, putting his weight on one elbow, and grabbing at the man's booted legs with his other arm. Caxton stepped back and kicked him in the ribs hard enough to drive the breath out of him and leave a vacuum in his chest for liquid pain to rush into and fill up. 'You dumb son of a bitch,' Caxton said dispassionately, 'now can you see why I don't need any gun to handle you, or any three big slobs like you?'

He watched silently as Murray pulled himself unsteadily to his feet, using the fire screen as support, and then said, 'Maybe you still don't get the score, so I'll tell you about a couple of other friends of Mr Wykoff's. I mean, you'll be real interested in this. They parked right behind you when you went down to Gramercy Park Saturday night, and they hoofed it all the way down to Barrow Street with you, just to get a good look at your friend. Very pretty, they tell me. A real gorgeous piece. Now, how would you like it if some crazy character jumped all over her the way he did with García? Or maybe got the idea to heave a bottle of acid into her face, so she wouldn't be so pretty any more? That would be too bad, wouldn't it?'

There was no more blood in his veins, Murray knew, but only a terror like beads of ice crawling through them. 'Listen to me,' he said; 'if anything happens to her—'

'Oh, sure, Mr Kirk, but that's up to you. Meaning, we take a run out to Staten Island, you tell Mr Wykoff what he wants to know, and then you forget all about it. What is it, yes or no?'

'Yes,' Murray said.

'I thought it would be.' Caxton looked him up and down, and it was clear that he was relishing what he saw. 'You don't look like such a big shot any more, Mr Kirk, the way you did when you opened that door before. Fact is, you're just a dirty mess. Go on and change those clothes. And when you talk to Mr Wykoff you can forget what happened here. It might get him all upset.'

18

The ferry from Battery Park docked at St George, the small, hilly metropolis of Staten Island. From there it was a twenty-minute drive to the village of Duchess Harbor. The car rolled noiselessly through the village – a cluster of shabby stores and an abandoned movie house – and entered a narrow road which wound along the shoreline past several handsome estates. Wykoff's was the most remote of these.

Wykoff was at the dinner table with two guests when Murray was ushered in. Seen at close range the man looked years older than he did in his newspaper photographs. His face was sallow and deeply lined, his eyes creased at the corners by a network of wrinkles. He was wearing an expensive suit, but it hung on him in a way that suggested he had lost a good deal of weight recently. All in all, Murray noted, he looked like the epitome of the harassed businessman, which, no doubt, was exactly the way he saw himself. His voice, when he took notice of Murray, was loud and high-pitched.

'You didn't eat yet, did you?' he said without any preliminaries. 'No, I guess you didn't. Here, sit down and they'll fix a place for you. You can skip the soup. It only makes you gassy, anyhow.'

It was clear that whatever business Wykoff had with him would keep. Murray sat down at the foot of the table, and the Japanese major-domo who had taken him off Caxton's hands at the door set his place with the dexterity of a man producing rabbits out of a hat.

Wykoff said: 'You don't know these people, do you? This is Mitchell Dowd, my lawyer. This is Mrs Dowd. Her name is Mona. Did you ever hear of a song about "Oh, Mona"? I was telling her about it, but she says she never heard it. What'll you have to drink?'

'Nothing,' Murray said.

'Ah, don't give me that,' Wykoff said, and nodded at the Japanese. 'Bourbon for the man, Joe. Make it the good bourbon.' He waved a spoon in Murray's direction. 'This is the guy I was telling you about,' he said to Dowd. 'Murray Kirk. He runs that big agency. A real sharpshooter. He don't look like you'd expect, does he?'

'Not very much,' Dowd said. He had the grave, self-satisfied air of a lawyer whose richest client is in serious trouble. 'Glad to know you,' he told Murray.

His wife was a tall, languid girl with doll-like features and sleepy eyes, flawlessly made up so that her face gleamed waxily in its perfection. She had probably been a showgirl in the recent past. 'Meetcha,' she said.

'My pleasure,' Murray said. He downed the bourbon at a gulp and winced when it stung the cut in his mouth.

'What I mean is,' Wykoff remarked, 'now and then I run into a guy in the private-detective line he's always a creep. Always a Broadway suit and a dirty shirt. So I see somebody like Kirk here who's got a little class, it's very interesting.' He peered near-sightedly at Murray. 'You go to college maybe?'

'Yes.'

'I thought so. Now, tell me something. How do you like the way this place is fixed up? I don't want you to crap me, y'understand. I want your honest opinion. How does it look to you?'

'I haven't seen it yet,' Murray said. He wondered if Wykoff's phone was being tapped and decided it probably was. Which meant that even if Wykoff would let him use it, trying to call Ruth would be a bad move.

'It's mostly like this room,' Wykoff persisted. 'What do you think about it?'

The room with its starkly designed, blond furniture and bleak grey wall-to-wall carpeting was a perfect example of what Frank Conmy had called Antiseptic Modern. It was strikingly like the Harlingens' apartment.

'Very nice,' Murray said. 'It's got real class.'

'That's on account of Mona,' Wykoff said. 'She did the whole thing from top to bottom. Sixteen rooms and thirty thousand bucks' worth of stuff in them, and my baby girl here handled the whole deal. She made it a real showplace. Didn't you, baby?' he asked Mona.

Mona gave Murray the feeling that she was always on the verge of stifling a yawn. She roused herself from her lethargy long enough to shrug deprecatingly. 'I liked doing it,' she said in a small voice. 'It was fun.'

'That's what she says,' Wykoff told Murray, 'but it was a lot of work, believe me. She had to take apart everything that decorator guy I had in here messed up for me. You should have seen that guy, Kirk. A real fag from off Park Avenue with the hands always going around in the air like this, and with one screwball idea after another. You wouldn't believe some of his stunts. I'm away in Vegas while he's working on the parlour, and when I come back what do I see? Everything red and black like a Chinese whorehouse, and right in the middle of the floor he's got a little merry-go-round! In my parlour he's got a merry-go-round, the crazy bastard! You know the kind, like those little ones they pull around on a wagon for kids to ride on. That's what's in my parlour, all painted up and ready for me to take a ride on. That's what I'm supposed to pay him for, putting merry-go-rounds in my parlour. Let me tell you, he's still waiting to collect. Do you honest-to-God think there's people who like that kind of thing in their houses?'

'I guess so,' Murray said. 'I never heard of a Park Avenue decorator starving to death.'

'Well, this one'll starve to death if he's sitting on his round little fanny waiting for my money,' Wykoff said. 'And you know what his trouble is? He's got no class. He's faking it. Real class is something inside you, y'understand. I don't mean you have to be born with it or any crap like that, y'understand, because I personally know some society people don't have it any more than a monkey. What I mean is, you put some work into it, you can wind up with real class, so people couldn't even tell you didn't pick it up at home when you were a kid. Naturally, you don't have money to go with it you're just a poor slob. But when you got money *and* class back to back, Kirk, you're in the driver's seat. What do you think of that?'

Dowd said – and there was a warning in the way he said it – 'You can see that George feels very strongly about this.'

'Why not?' said Murray. 'It makes sense.'

'It makes good sense,' Wykoff assured him. 'Now, let me tell you something funny about class. I mean, about the way you can get it right inside of you when you're not even looking for it. You know anything about wine?'

Mona said to Dowd, 'Would it be all right if I—?' and then there was a deadly silence as Wykoff turned to face her. He put his spoon down and rested both hands flat on the table.

'When I'm talking,' he said softly, and his face was not pleasant, 'you shut up. I already told you about that, didn't I? When I was a kid I was brought up so when one person talked everybody else shut up. That's the way I want it now!'

Mona fixed her eyes on her plate. She was caught between two fires, Murray saw. Dowd was glaring at her from across the table with unconcealed anger. 'I'm sorry,' she said.

Wykoff was not mollified by this. 'What is it? You're tired of hearing me tell about this? You don't have to con me. Just give me an honest answer.'

'I'm sorry,' Mona said. 'I was just feeling headachy.'

Wykoff picked up his spoon. 'Then take an aspirin and don't make a production out of it.' He pointed the spoon at Murray. 'Where was I?'

'You asked me if I knew anything about wine.'

'Oh. Well, what I wanted to tell you is something funny that happened to me account of learning to drink wine. Real French wine, y'understand. The imported stuff. How I got on to it is because sometimes when I was in a fancy eating place I'd see customers lapping it up, and it was mostly the kind of place and the kind of customers with a lot of class.

'So what bug do I get when I'm down in Miami once with nothing but time on my hands? I got to find out what's with this wine deal. Frankly, the first few times I tried the stuff I never thought it made any sense, because it always tasted spoiled. But then I got hold of a guy in my hotel – you know what a *sommelier* is?'

'Yes,' Murray said.

The answer did not sidetrack Wykoff. 'It's a guy with a big chain around his neck, he's in charge of all the wine,' he explained. 'So I hired this *sommelier* to sit down with me and tell me all about what's what. And with all his jabber the one sure thing I picked up was that if you were a greenhorn you would start with a sweet wine for a table wine, but then if you wised up it would be too sweet, and you'd want stuff that was drier and drier. When you talk about wine you don't call it sour, y'understand. You call it dry. I mean, if you're talking about good wine, not Dago red.'

Wykoff leaned forward intently. 'And you know what? It happened just like he said it would. I am not handing you the crap, Kirk. I am sitting here and telling you that I started with what they call Château d'Yquem which is real sweet, and then I moved over to some stuff called Graves, and I finally wound up with Chablis, which is as dry as hell and strictly for the experts! Right now if you put a bottle of Château d'Yquem in front of me for a table wine I would gag on it, because it would taste like candy to me!

'So now, y'understand, I can be with people who were maybe brought up on French wine all their life – you know, the kind of snotty characters get all dressed up for the opera – and I can drink it right along with them and enjoy it without faking. I don't care how fancy the people are. I can call the *sommelier* over and order the right wine and not look like some kind of creep who don't belong there. And remember, I was brought up in a house where they drank out of the bottle and ate with their hands. Now you get what I mean about having real class inside of you, and all you got to do is work at it a little?'

'I get it,' Murray said.

When they finally arose from the table Wykoff surprised him by asking. 'You play any bridge, Kirk?' because, offhand, bridge would hardly seem to be Wykoff's game. On second thought Murray saw that his surprise was unwarranted. What with one thing and another, bridge was bound to be Wykoff's game. It had Real Class.

'I'd rather talk business,' Murray said. He did not try to conceal his impatience.

'Ah, there's plenty of time for that,' Wykoff told him. He placed a hand over his belt buckle and patted himself there. 'Fact is, y'understand my stomach is a little bit shot, and the doctor laid it on very heavy about not doing any kind of business until I digested. Anyhow, the *$64,000 Question* comes on TV pretty soon, and if we start talking we'd only have to stop then. I don't miss that show, no matter what. What I figured, we could get in a couple of rubbers up to the show, and then afterward we talk turkey. You know, I only been playing bridge a little while, Kirk, but I am absolutely sold on it. Here is the one game in the world you can play for no money at all, and still get a kick from it.'

It was a touching speech, but, as it turned out, the stakes were five cents a point – just enough, as Wykoff said, reversing his field easily, to make it a little interesting – and since Wykoff and Dowd who played partners shared an almost uncanny rapport, the bill came high. When the major-domo came in to announce that the television set was warmed and waiting, Wykoff ran his pencil down the score sheet and reported that the total was eighty dollars and change.

'Call it eighty bucks even,' he told Murray graciously. 'You and Mona both pay me. Mitch and I got a little deal on where any time we play partners I take it all if we win, but I got to pay the whole tab if we lose. That's how I am. I hate to think I might be costing somebody money because my game is off or something.'

'That's how I am, too,' Murray told Mona as she opened her purse. 'It's all right, I'll pay the tab for both of us.' His one consolation had been the discovery that she was not as sleepy as she looked. Not only had she played capable bridge, but at one point, when he had stretched a leg out under the table he had found it pressed against hers, and they had played through the rest of the session sharing a warm and stimulating contact. Even so, Murray reflected, at about two dollars a minute it was high-priced consolation.

Now Mona looked at him with what might have been surprise. 'Well,' she said on a rising note, 'aren't you the real good sport?'

When Wykoff and Dowd went off down the hall in the direction of the television set she lingered to apply fresh lipstick, and Murray politely lingered with her. 'You play a solid game,' he said. 'Too bad we didn't get a few breaks.'

'Oh, that.' She studied her handiwork in the mirror of a small jewelled compact. 'They cheat all the time, you know. Didn't you catch on?'

'No.'

'I thought maybe you did, because it's kind of crude, really. You know, the way you hold the cards, or the way you announce bids – that kind of jazz. It's not Mitch's fault. George likes to do it, so Mitch just strings along.'

'And George always collects for both of them. He must be pretty far ahead of you by now.'

'Ahead of me?' Mona looked at him blankly. 'Aren't you silly? You don't *really* think it cost me thirty thousand dollars to furnish this dump, do you?'

The room where they viewed the show was a shrine to television. An immense set was centred in one wall, and every seat was arranged to face it. In the corner was a small bar attended by the Japanese, now garbed in a white jacket. The only object that seemed out of place was a Christmas tree in the back of the room, a stately tree glittering with tinsel and glass ornaments.

'George has a couple of nephews who bring their families around on Christmas,' Dowd explained when he saw Murray staring at it. 'How many kids do they have?' he asked Wykoff. 'Six, isn't it?'

'Seven, God bless them,' Wykoff said tenderly. 'The cutest kids in the world, but wild Indians, the whole bunch of them. That's why I got the tree in here along with the television. At least with the tree and the television together you can keep them out of your hair a little.'

The *$64,000 Question* was received with the reverence usually accorded a church ceremony. No one spoke, and in the reflected light from the set Murray saw Wykoff sitting open-mouthed, his face vacuous with wonder and admiration, literally sweating it out with each contestant in the isolation booth. When it was all over he wiped his brow with a handkerchief, a man who had been through a profound emotional experience.

'Tell me something,' he said to Murray. 'You think the fix is on with this show? I mean, you think it's all on the level?'

'Why not?' said Murray.

'I don't know why not,' Wykoff said, 'but it better be on the level. I'd hate like hell to think some lousy TV show was making a sucker out of me every week.' Mona, looking drugged, was seated between him and Dowd, and he patted her thigh. 'Be a good girl, baby. Turn the set off now, and then beat it. Maybe the cook's still in the kitchen, you can talk things over with him. Get yourself a new recipe. I'll tell you when it's all right to come back.'

He waited until she had left the room, and then drew two cigars from his pocket. One he handed to Dowd. The other he fitted into an amber holder and lit for himself. It reminded Murray of a time long ago when Frank Conmy had put him in his place by carefully not offering him a cigar.

Wykoff drew deeply on the cigar, which seemed to leave a sour taste in his mouth. 'All right, Kirk,' he said in a hard voice, 'stand up.'

'Why?' Murray asked matter-of-factly. 'I don't have anything to talk over with the cook. I'm loaded with recipes.'

'Don't be so smart, Kirk. When we talk business we do it my way. That means Joe frisks you before we start. It won't hurt any.'

'You've been watching too much television,' Murray said. 'I don't carry a gun.'

'I'm not worried about guns. But I hear they make tape recorders now, you could stick one in your tooth, for Chrissake, and nobody would know. So let's get with it. Up on the feet and hold out the hands.'

Murray stood up slowly, and the Japanese said, 'If you don't mind, Mr Kirk,' and went over him thoroughly. It was a professional frisking, down to the way his wrist watch, wallet, and pen were removed and examined. The Japanese returned them to him. 'You know how it is, Mr Kirk,' he said.

'Sure, Joe,' Murray said. 'What'd they have you doing in the big war, counter intelligence?'

'Three years of it in the South Pacific, Mr Kirk. My CO looked something like you, too. I didn't like his face, either.'

The atmosphere around him, Murray saw, was certainly frosting up in a hurry. As if to confirm this, Wykoff said, 'I'll let you in on something, Kirk. Joe ain't very big, but he's even tougher to handle than Billy Caxton. And I figure from that lump on the jaw you already found out about Caxton. So if you don't want a busted arm to go along with that jaw, y'understand, you'll sit down and be a little gentleman. I don't go for rough stuff myself, y'understand, but if a guy walks in here and asks for it I'm entitled to protection, ain't I?' He turned to Dowd. 'If it happens like that I got the law on my side, don't I?'

Dowd looked uncomfortable. 'I don't think Kirk is looking for trouble,' he said. 'He seems to be a smart young fellow.'

'Smart?' Wykoff said with elaborate surprise. 'A creep like

him hires himself a fancy limousine to cart him out here with everybody looking, he walks into my house which is the last place he should be, God knows, and you call him smart? Believe me, if I didn't know how Mona gets so upset about everything he would have been bounced out of here as soon as he stuck his nose in the door.' He drew on the cigar, evidently savouring it now, and darted a sidelong glance at Murray. 'Y'understand what I'm saying, Kirk?'

'Yes.'

'That's good, because I really got you hung up by the thumbs, don't I? How do you think your friend LoScalzo would take it, if it got back to him you were out here trying to put the muscle on me?'

'I don't know,' Murray said affably. 'Anyhow, I thought he was your friend. That's what a lot of ex-cops are saying nowadays.'

Wykoff's face darkened. 'Don't you worry what they say, Kirk. Before I went down for the count they made enough off me, so I don't owe them a handshake now. And as far as LoScalzo goes I'll let you in on something. Anybody who's my friend don't fix me up with two years on Riker's Island.'

'Now wait, George,' Dowd protested. 'You're not there yet, are you? The appeal hasn't even been reviewed yet.'

'Ah, lay off,' Wykoff said impatiently. 'Don't oil me, Mitch, don't fix me up with any grease job, because that's not what I'm paying you for. We both know the appeal don't stand a chance. I'll put in my time, all right, but what I want Kirk to know is, one squawk from me, and he'll be right there in the same place. You hear that, Kirk?'

'Yes.'

'Then sit down and listen.' Wykoff waited until Murray, taking his time, had made himself comfortable, then said, 'First, what's with this cop Lundeen?'

'It's no secret. I'm doing a job for him.'

'There's more to it than that, Kirk. A guy like this Lundeen, y'understand, is nobody. The only guy less than him is somebody goes around the park, picks up papers on a stick with a nail in it. So this nobody Lundeen suddenly gets a lawyer name of Harlingen which I hear is the classiest kind of Wall Street stuff. Is that right, Mitch?'

'It's one of the outstanding law firms in the country,' Dowd agreed.

'Right. In the whole country, y'understand. And the kind of place it is, no ordinary cop could even get in the side door. Then that ain't enough, so this Lundeen shows up at the Conmy-Kirk agency, which is also very classy. And who does his job personally for him there? The big cheese himself! Mr Murray Kirk, who can sit around and collect an arm and a leg for unscrewing some millionaire creep from his wife, don't want to bother about such stuff now. Not now, he don't. All he wants to do is get off his fanny and hustle around on a case for a down-and-out cop!' Wykoff sat forward and jabbed a finger into Murray's knee. 'Only this cop ain't really so down-and-out, is he, Kirk? He's got a lot of pull somewhere, He's got big people backing him up. Who are they, Kirk? What's their angle?'

'No angle,' said Murray.

'No? Then how come the Harlingen office is handling the case?'

'It isn't. The old man's son left the office to take the case on his own.'

'Why?'

Murray smiled. 'He's an idealist. He wants to be the new Clarence Darrow.'

'You kill me,' Wykoff said wearily. He turned to Dowd. 'What do you make of this, Mitch?'

'It's not very convincing, I'm afraid,' Dowd said. 'I can look into it, if you want me to.'

'You do that,' Wykoff said. He regarded Murray with narrowed eyes. 'How about you, Kirk? You in on this, because you're maybe some kind of an idealist, too?'

'No, what happened to me is pretty funny. I went overboard for Lundeen's girl friend, and I took the case to prove to her he was guilty. Then when they've got him locked up I figure to marry the girl. That's all there is to it.'

Wykoff's face indicated that he did not think this was pretty funny. It took him time to find words, and when he did they came out choked with black rage. 'You miserable, double-talking monkey,' he said thickly, 'who do you think you're fooling around with? You think I'm so stupid I'd believe one word of that?'

'No.'

'No. But it's all right to kill time with. If I ask you about it again, you tell me the same thing, and we go around and around that way. Is that it?'

'Yes.'

Wykoff stood up threateningly, and Dowd came to his feet almost at the same moment. He laid a restraining hand on Wykoff's arm. 'Listen to me, George,' he said. 'Either you get hold of yourself, or I walk out of here right now. You've got to consider my position, too.'

Murray felt an old familiar knot tighten in his belly. He had estimated from the start that Dowd's presence was his surest safeguard, because Dowd was obviously a man who wanted no part of violence. Not, at least, if he might be a witness to it. Without his company anything could happen, and, according to Bruno Manfredi's sombre philosophy, it probably would. It came as a relief when Wykoff pushed aside the restraining hand and sullenly said, 'What're you making such a fuss about? You think I want to get you mixed up in some trouble? You're worse than a fat-assed old woman.'

Dowd's face reddened. 'Maybe I am, but I've got sense enough to see you're not getting anywhere this way. Why not come to the point? You want Kirk to drop this case, no matter who's behind Lundeen or what he has up his sleeve. All right, put it to the man that way, and see what he's got to say about it. He's no fool.'

'Thanks,' Murray said. 'Only I'm not so smart either. What's George here got against Lundeen?'

Wykoff said with venom, 'He's making trouble for Ira Miller, that's what. No, don't go giving me the fishy eye, Kirk. If you don't know how things stand between Ira Miller and me you better find out quick, because it ain't any joke. I'm not talking about somebody just happened to work along with me, y'understand. Ira Miller is like my kid brother. He's high class and his wife is high class, too. They're the finest people I know in the world, and they got enough trouble without you pushing them around like Ira says you did. That means all I want is to comb you out of their hair, and, between you and me, I don't care how I do it!'

It was said with a savage intensity that left no doubts about Wykoff's sincerity, and Murray knew that he had struck a fine vein to explore. He laid his hand over his heart. 'That gets me right here, Wykoff. But if you don't see me crying, it's because I already met Ira Miller. If you want my honest opinion, he is hardly what I would call the kid-brother type.'

'Who the hell wants your opinion? What do you know about it, a professional sneak like you?' Wykoff held up a trembling forefinger. 'Let me tell you something, Kirk. In my whole operation there was just one man who could run a losing book and get away with it. Right in the middle of town, in the fattest district I had, Ira Miller ran a loss for me one year after another, and I never blinked an eye! He was into me for fifteen, twenty thousand dollars, and it didn't bother me, because that's how it is with us two.

'No one ever double-crosses George Wykoff, Kirk. No one, y'understand? If anyone else ran a losing book like that he knows what would happen to him. Only Ira Miller could do it, because when he said it wasn't his fault I knew he was telling the truth. The bets went bad, the cops kept pushing for bigger graft, that's how it went. My own accountant knew every book in the organization inside-out used to say to me, "Ira's running in hard luck, but he's strictly on the level." And he didn't have to tell me. You think when it comes to a showdown between Ira and your cop that Ira ain't on the level? You better think again!

'So now you know something, don't you? And if you got any brains, Kirk, tomorrow you'll tell this Lundeen to take a jump for himself. I don't care who's in back of him or why. You do what I say.'

'That's a fine proposition,' Murray said. 'What do I get out of it?'

'Your neck. What more do you want?'

'Oh, some way of backing out of the case. Take those records you were talking about. If you look them up right now and give me evidence that Miller paid off Lundeen, I'm in the clear. That's the kind of thing the people I'm dealing with would understand.'

'Yeah?' Wykoff said coldly. 'And what makes you so sure the records are right around here?'

'Where else would they be? You wouldn't keep them in a bank vault where they could be impounded, would you? You wouldn't turn them over to somebody who could bring the income-tax people down on you like a ton of bricks, would you? What's the odds they're right under your mattress while we're talking here?'

Wykoff regarded him curiously. 'You been wasting your time,' he said with unwilling admiration. 'I could have used somebody like you in my business. Well,' he asked Dowd, 'what do you think? You think it's all right?'

'I don't see why not,' Dowd said.

'But you'll have to take my word for it,' Wykoff warned Murray, and when Murray looked doubtful he said, 'You got a lot of gall, Kirk, the way you take over. All right. Mitch here can look at the books with me and back me up. Will that suit your royal highness better?'

'The date was May third,' Murray said.

There was no mystery about where the records were kept. The door he heard opened was that of the room directly across the hall; the sound that followed was that of a wooden drawer being creakily pulled out. It was the purloined letter all over again, he reflected. Put it under everybody's nose, and it would be the last place they'd look for it. He smiled at Joe, who leaned on the bar watching him warily. 'Take it easy, soldier,' he said. 'Can't you see the war is over?'

He got up and strolled to the window, humming the theme from 'I Can't Get Started'. It was snowing. The first real snow of the winter, and where else but out in the wilds of Staten Island. In the winter, he thought, he and Ruth would head up to the mountains for the skiing. If she didn't know how to ski, so much the better. He himself was the world's worst skier.

Dowd said behind him, 'No question about it, Kirk. Miller made a pay-off to Lundeen May third just the way he said he did.'

'Well, all right,' said Murray. 'We'll have a drink on that.'

He travelled back to the St Stephen in Caxton's limousine. Dowd had offered him a lift to Manhattan, but Wykoff had curtly said, 'No, Billy's waiting to take him,' and that had settled it.

. Caxton, it turned out, had been briefed before the departure.

Just before they drew up to the St Stephen he said, 'I'm glad everything worked out all right, Mr Kirk, you know what I mean? So now you forget about it, and make time with that piece down in the Village. A real nice girl. You want to make sure nothing happens to her.'

He had a great sense of humour, Caxton did.

19

The banquet department of the hotel had been busy that night. The lobby was crowded with people in evening clothes ready for departure, but delaying it, because what had been a picturesque snowfall in Staten Island was an icy rain here, sluicing down savagely, daring them to come out. So they stood in small clusters, be-minked and overcoated, loudly repeating endless goodbyes, complaining about the weather – you wait all year for the Affair, and look at the lousy weather! – and peering anxiously through the dripping glass of the revolving door to see if some passing cab had been lured up to the marquee.

When Murray pushed his way through them they refused to give ground. One man said irately, 'Hey, you!' and as Murray turned he knew what his own expression must be, because the man looked taken aback and weakly said, 'Well, you ought to watch out, mister,' more in apology than protest.

On the other hand, Nelson, the assistant night clerk who ordinarily wore a professional air of distaste for the world at large, looked relieved to see him. 'You've been getting calls pretty steadily all evening, Mr Kirk. Nothing wrong, is there?'

'No,' Murray said. He took the message slips Nelson handed him, and moved to the side of the desk to rifle through them.

There must have been a dozen. Mrs Donaldson. Miss Vincent. Miss Vincent. Mrs Knapp. Mrs Donaldson. Mr Harlingen. Mrs Donaldson. At least half of them were Didi's, which was unusual. As a rule, she never called more than once in an evening. If he didn't answer she would let it go at that.

When he got up to the apartment he had barely opened the door when the phone sounded. He sat down on the bed without taking off his overcoat, hoping against hope that it was Ruth. The clock on the night table, he saw as he picked up the phone, said twelve thirty, which might still allow him time to see her tonight.

It was Didi. 'Murray,' she said, 'I'm so glad you're finally in, you just have no idea. Can you come over here now? Or would you like it better if I came over there? It won't be any trouble for me. I've got the car parked right handy.'

'Not tonight, Didi. We'll have to make it some other time. I'll call you tomorrow.'

'Oh. I suppose you've got someone there with you. Is that it?'

'No, but it doesn't make any difference,' he said impatiently. 'I told you I'd call you tomorrow.'

'Murray, please. I want to see you now. I want to talk to you. I never say no if you ask me, do I?'

That stung him hard. 'What do you do, keep a record of it?' he demanded angrily. 'Look, Didi, you know how you are. Whatever's bothering you can wait, can't it? Why don't you just try to sleep it off?'

There was a long silence. 'You don't mean that,' Didi said at last.

'Oh, yes, I do,' he said, and took a mean pleasure in saying it. Then it struck him that her voice had sounded odd. 'What's the matter? Do you have a cold?'

'No,' Didi said, 'I'm all right. Kind of weepy, but it's, no, never mind. I told you I was awful dumb sometimes, didn't I?'

That was all. She hung up on that cryptic note before he could answer, leaving him with the empty humming of the dead line in his ear, and a hot resentment at the way she had chosen now, of all times, to dump one of her moods into his lap. Or was there another, more acute reason for the resentment? There was, he knew. He had finally, after all these years, fallen victim to her peculiar talent for masochism. For the first time since they had known each other he had treated her the way every other man she knew sooner or later treated her. Kirk, the Great Exception, had joined the club, and that pathetic Mrs Donaldson who so rejoiced in a slap across the face could now claim a perfect score. Was it his fault? The hell it was, Murray told himself. Any good, capable masochist could make a sadist out of a saint, and he was no saint to start with. And he had his own problems to solve.

Ruth must have been within arm's reach of her telephone when it rang. 'Man, I could kill you,' she said breathlessly. 'Where are you calling from? You're not hurt, are you?'

The query painfully reminded Murray of his bruised jaw and the place on his ribs where Caxton's shoe had found its mark. But as far as he was concerned, Ruth's breathlessness was all the ointment he needed. 'Not a chance,' he said. 'What happened was that something came up suddenly, and I couldn't even leave word for you. It's quite a story.'

'Well, it better be,' she told him with unmistakable relief. 'Considering the fuss I kicked up around here, you'd better make it an epic The O'Mearagh himself couldn't beat. I've been calling everybody. I even had Ralph dig up your secretary's home number, but she didn't know any more than I did.'

Which explains the messages, Murray thought, glancing at the crumpled slips of paper on the bed. Then he realized that it didn't. Not quite.

He said, 'While you were at it, did you call Mrs Donaldson, too?'

'Yes, she was at Alex's.'

'What did she have to say? I spoke to her a few minutes ago, and she sounded a little offbeat. I was wondering about it.'

'Oh? Well, I explained to her about how worried I was, because I was supposed to see you tonight – last night, that is –

but that you had simply disappeared into nowhere. Then she — we talked a bit, and that's all. What makes you think there was something wrong?'

'I don't know,' Murray said. 'But don't let it bother you. I've got something more important on tap, anyhow.'

'Yes?'

'It's about Arnold, but I'd rather not discuss it over the phone. Can I get together with you and Ralph at your place now, or do you want to make it tomorrow?'

'Make it now,' Ruth said. 'I'll call Ralph and have him here. Is it good or bad?'

'It's not good,' Murray said.

Ruth was waiting at the door when he arrived, and while he was hanging up his dripping hat and coat on an old-fashioned wall rack he observed that she was still dressed for an evening out, and that the shapeless woollen cardigan she had thrown on over her pale blue, brocaded sheath in no way lessened its effect on him.

Ralph, she said, would be there soon. He had been up when she phoned him, because Dinah's folks were in from Philadelphia, and they had all been sitting around and talking at the Harlingens'. Dinah's parents were Quakers, Ruth added gratuitously, as if under a nervous compulsion to make conversation, and really the most enchanting people. They worried all the time about the way Megan was being brought up, but Megan had once told her that when she was with them in Philadelphia they spoiled her worse than anybody. Trust Megan to know a good thing when she saw it.

Ruth's father came tramping up from the cellar during this recitative. In his slippers and robe, his few remaining hairs clipped close to the skull, and with a good humorous face and fine eyes, Vincent was the passable facsimile of a monk out of Balzac. He greeted Murray cordially, and explained that he had been down in the cellar to check possible seepage there because of the rain. The original foundation of the house had been built over a supposedly dry brook bed – a branch of the Minetta, most likely – but every time it rained hard enough the brook mysteriously came to life.

'She's alive and kicking now, all right,' Vincent said, not over-concerned. 'If you want some fine fishing tomorrow, this is the place for it. We'll have the boats out.'

'Tommy, you're impossible,' Ruth said. 'You promised Mother you'd have it fixed last summer, didn't you?'

'Did I? Well, I'll have to get her a life preserver, instead. You know,' he said to Murray, 'Ruth's been telling me a great deal about you, and I have a hunch I once knew your father. I can see a distinct resemblance when I look at you. Was his that store near the south gate on Broadway?'

'Yes.'

'Isn't that the damndest thing? I'm positive he's the one. That was, oh, around twenty-five years ago, during the early part of the Depression. I was on my fellowship then. I used to drop in for a sandwich and milk there, because it was the cheapest place in the neighbourhood.'

'He wasn't much of a businessman,' Murray said.

'No, I suppose he wasn't. But he was a great conversationalist, as I recall. The most ingenuous sort of Utopian, and full of wonderful, visionary schemes for the improvement of mankind. He used to write verses about them, and make everyone who came into the store read them. Of course, a lot of us lived with visions in those days. We were all firebrands of one sort or another. But I don't think your father was a firebrand in that sense. He seemed to have a different spirit. Luminous, you might call it. You can see how well I remember him.'

And here, Murray thought, we have another member of the cult, another one of that jolly band of middle-aged intellectuals who got through the Depression with their pride in one piece, and who wistfully look back on it now as the Great Adventure. He had met others of this breed before, and found them as readily identifiable as only cultists can be. Full of talk about that bright time when they were all paupers together, when Ideas

Not Money was the common currency, where there was an Intellectual Ferment in the Air. Full of talk about the snows of yesteryear, and never asking what had become of the old men who were paid ten cents an hour to shovel it away.

But this particular member of the cult, he knew, happened to be Ruth's father, and the smart thing to do was tread warily and speak softly. So he trod warily and spoke softly until Harlingen arrived, rain-sodden and full of apologies about the time it had taken him to drive down, and Vincent said a round of good nights and went upstairs. Watching him go, Murray found almost with annoyance that he liked the man. It made him wonder how anyone of that calibre could remotely think of allowing his daughter to marry an Arnold Lundeen. Under any conditions, it wasn't possible that he could be happy about it.

Harlingen was very much at home here. He made his way unerringly to a liquor cabinet in the living room, and searched through it, holding up one bottle after another to the light to read the label.

'Sherry,' he complained. 'Sherry, and again sherry. You know what the trouble is? Those kids in Tommy's classes keep reading novels where college professors are always drinking sherry, so comes Christmas they load him up with the stuff. I wish somebody would write a book where college teachers only drink Scotch. Good twelve-year-old Scotch, preferably.'

He finally came up with an almost empty bottle of whisky and poured out three drinks. When he had served the others he downed his own with a gulp and a shudder. 'All right,' he said to Murray, 'I'm ready for the bad news. It isn't too bad, I hope.'

'I'll leave that up to you. Do you remember when we were with Benny Floyd at the lunch stand that day, and I said I wanted to yank the grapevine and see if we could stir up Wykoff?'

'Yes.'

'Well, we stirred him up.' Murray turned to Ruth. 'That's what happened to our date. Wykoff sent over a tough to fetch me along to Staten Island, and I wasn't offered any choice about it, either.'

Part of Ruth's untasted drink splashed into her lap. 'Oh, no!' she said.

'Wykoff?' said Harlingen in astonishment. 'A man in his position trying a stunt like that? Why, if the authorities—'

'What authorities?' Murray said. 'Look, let's not kid ourselves. If it's anything to do with Wykoff, LoScalzo's the man in charge, and right now LoScalzo would like nothing better than to leave me for dead. But that's not the point. What I'm getting at is Wykoff's angle. Evidently, my working on the case bothers him. He wants me out. And to prove to me that I might as well get out he offered me the evidence that Arnold was guilty.'

'He couldn't have!' Ruth said. 'There isn't any such evidence, unless he made it up!'

Harlingen waved a silencing hand at her, his eyes fixed on Murray. 'What evidence, Murray?'

'Wykoff's got his records locked up in the house there,' Murray said. 'And he's got a record in black and white of the pay-off Miller made to Arnold on May third.'

'In what form?' Harlingen said witheringly. 'A signed receipt?'

The atmosphere around him, Murray saw, was as chill now as it had been when he was in Wykoff's television room. *Wherever I am*, he thought, *there is no man's land*, and he had never found the thought more bitter since the day he had walked into Frank Conmy's office and learned to do things Frank Conmy's way. It was the look in Ruth's eyes that made it bitter.

He said in defiance of that look: 'You know damn well there's no signed receipt, but that doesn't mean anything. Wykoff ran his racket like a business. He's that kind of man; you'd have to meet him to appreciate it. He's the kind of man who brings you out to see him at the point of a gun, and then has his lawyer on the spot so everything'll be handled the right way. If you told him he was just another racketeer he'd probably give you a whole line about how you can't legislate morality, and being forced to do illegally what should be legal, and all the rest of it. But because he is that way he's kept records of what went on while he was running the bookies around here. And he does have a record of Arnold's graft. And it means that Miller and Schrade are telling the truth. Maybe you don't know it, Ralph, but the toughest man to handle on the witness stand is a crook who finds himself telling the truth for the first time in his life and is glad to make the most of it. That's what you're up against here, so you can see how much of a case you've got.'

Harlingen said: 'It seems to me we've run through a routine like this before. You didn't get me here at this hour just to repeat it to me, did you?'

'No, I wanted you here to listen to some advice. First thing tomorrow you get Arnold into town and explain all this to him. Then see if he won't appear before the grand jury again and recant his testimony. If he won't, see if you can't get him to plead guilty to a lesser count of the indictment. Perjury in the second, let's say. I don't know if LoScalzo would be interested in making a deal, but he might be talked to on that basis. The only trouble is that he's holding the winning hand and knows it.'

'Is that the only trouble?' Harlingen said. 'What kind of hand are you holding, Murray? I wonder about that.'

'What does that mean?' Murray asked.

Ruth came to her feet and confronted him, her arms clasped over her chest, her fingers digging hard into the sleeves of the sweater. 'You know what it means,' she told him scathingly. 'How much did Wykoff pay you to say this, that's what it means. Well, how much was it? More than Arnold could pay?'

It left Murray with the feeling he had had after Caxton had hit him. Worse than that. He had been hurt by Caxton, but he had not been afraid. He was afraid now. 'Ruth,' he said, 'I swear that I never took a penny from Wykoff. He didn't offer me anything, and I didn't take anything.'

'You mean, all he did was tell you what to do, and you're doing it,' she said sweetly. Too sweetly. 'He threatened you.'

'No,' Murray said, 'he didn't threaten me. He threatened you. He had us followed Saturday night, and he's got you marked. It doesn't mean anything as long as I don't step on his toes, but even so, starting tomorrow I'm assigning a man to keep an eye on you until all this blows over. You won't have anything to worry about.'

'I won't have anything to worry about? Oh, please, *please*, let's not drag this down to the level of melodrama. You don't really think it makes it any more convincing, do you?'

He wanted to hit her then. He could feel all through him the release he'd get from the impact of his hand against her face. She must have sensed that, too. She took an involuntary step back as he stood up, and that rather pleased him.

'What're you afraid of?' he asked her. 'A little melodrama? You know I'm only hamming it up. The whole thing's a big joke.' He looked at Harlingen, who was not smiling now. 'Same as what happened to that little Puerto Rican who ran the lunch stand we were at. Remember him, Ralph? A genuine bystander, wasn't he? That is, until Wykoff got the idea he knew more than he was telling, and had a couple of the boys send him to the hospital for repairs.'

'You don't mean that,' Harlingen said.

'You want to call up Montefiore right now, and ask how the patient is doing? The name is García. Oh, he's probably listed as an accident case, but I wouldn't let that fool me, if I were you. I know how sensitive you are about anybody fooling you.'

'That's not very funny,' Harlingen said.

'No? Well, I'm only laughing to keep from crying. How would you feel in my place? Or you?' he asked Ruth. 'Do I sound more convincing now?'

She shook her head furiously. 'No,' she said with hard emphasis. 'No. No. No!'

'My God, don't you know me well enough by now to trust me?' he pleaded.

She said: 'I thought I did! I thought – oh, what's the sense of going through all that? I was wrong, that's all. I was so wrong. And Arnold was right.'

'About what?'

'About you. The last time I talked to him about you he said I was being stupid. He said anyone who trusted private detectives was stupid. They were all the same. They were dirty, rotten cheats who'd do anything for money. Anybody who came along could buy them, because that's the kind of business they were in – selling something dirty to people who could pay for it!'

When you were sufficiently enraged, Murray found, you really saw red. Ruth – Harlingen – the whole room around him wavered in a reddish haze. He said hoarsely, 'And sure as hell, Arnold is the judge, jury, and executioner in this case, isn't he? He's Death right out of your pet play. He's a mighty smart cop who knows all the answers. By God, every day he's on trial I'll be the first one in court and the last one out. It'll be a pleasure to watch them break him wide open!'

'I believe that,' Ruth whispered. 'Oh, how I believe that now. But whatever happens, Murray, take my advice. Don't order theatre tickets or make restaurant reservations for a celebration, if you're expecting me to celebrate with you, a big joke.' He looked at Harlingen, who was not smiling hands in the moonlight. 'Up to now you've been making good time, I'm ashamed to say. You've been taking me for a lovely ride. But here's where I get off. Your friend Mrs Donaldson would like that, I'm sure!'

Harlingen, who had been following this with growing concern, could not contain himself any longer. 'Like what?' he said explosively. 'Have both of you gone crazy? You're acting like a pair of neurotics on a binge. Is that what we're here for?'

'Will you please shut up?' Murray said in a dangerous voice. He wheeled on Ruth again. 'Go on, let's have it. What's Mrs Donaldson got to do with all this?'

Ruth clasped her hands together hard enough to make the knuckles show white. 'She rounded out the picture for me this evening. I didn't tell you all about our little talk on the phone, did I? That's because I was still on that lovely ride, and I didn't want anything to spoil it. Not even when she asked me if you had gotten your money's worth out of me for what her party had cost you. Yes, she put it exactly in those words, and you don't have to look so shocked about it. She's jealous, of course. That's what you ought to worry about. Not about some comic-book gangsters shooting me, but about her shooting you, because she doesn't like you to chase around after other women. She may forget how pathetic she is and do it some night!'

Murray said: 'Is she the only one who's jealous? What would you say Arnold was right now? You must have told him some interesting things about me to heat him up like this.'

'Yes,' Ruth said, 'I did. If I had sense enough to keep my mouth shut I wouldn't have to be sorry about it now. But Arnold and I have never been much on concealing things from each other. We've never gotten the fun out of being devious and dishonest that you do. You need practice to enjoy it, don't you?'

'I suppose so,' Murray said, and then pushed conscience aside. 'Why don't you ask Arnold about that?'

'I think we're all in a mood,' Harlingen interposed, and looked at his watch. 'No wonder. It's almost two, and since we're only talking in circles—'

His intentions were good, Murray knew, but if there was anything bound to put Ruth on her guard it was the apprehension in that voice. And Ruth was on guard immediately. 'What do you mean?' she asked Murray. 'What are you getting at?'

The image of Lundeen lay in his hand, his own wax doll whose time had come. He slowly crushed it in his fist. 'Ruth,' he said, 'Arnold's been playing you for a fool right along. He's got another girl on the string who's not only sleeping with him, but who thinks he's going to marry her. He'll have a hard time getting out of it when she sets the date.'

Ruth looked at him open-mouthed, and her expression was one of sheer incredulity. 'My God,' she said, 'what a mind. It's fascinating. It's absolutely fascinating.'

'It's not that fascinating,' Murray said, and I looked at Harlingen.

'Go on, tell her, why don't you?'

'Tell her what?' Harlingen said angrily. 'Hearsay doesn't mean anything. Whatever I know about that girl is from your report.'

'Which applies to Wykoff, too,' Ruth pointed out. 'And Miller. And anyone else you'd care to name, doesn't it?'

She was triumphant now, Murray saw. She had Harlingen on her side, and truth and justice and righteousness. It was almost a shame to knock all the fine sentiment out of her.

'Get your coat,' Murray told her.

'I'm sorry,' she said. 'I've got to be ready for a day's work in a few hours. I don't feel like going out now looking for adventure.'

'It won't be any adventure. You're going to meet Arnold's little friend, whether you want to or not. Get your coat.'

Harlingen said: 'This is ridiculous, Murray. What are you going to do, wake up everybody in New York at this hour to prove a point? Can't it wait until a sensible time?'

'No,' Murray said, 'it can't. In your language, Ralph, I'm a nice friendly fella, but in the last eight hours I've had a gun pulled on me, been manhandled, swindled at bridge, black-mailed, and called a liar more times than I can count. And I'm going to finish up in style. Either Miss Vincent here gets her coat and comes along peaceably, or I drag her out into the rain by the scruff of her neck. And if anybody tries to stop me I've got eight hours of misery I'm itching to get rid of at one wallop. I'm not fooling, Ralph. Nothing will happen as long as every-body stays in line. I think you know what I mean. You must have had days like this, too.'

'I know what you mean,' Harlingen said, and, strangely enough, he sounded sympathetic. 'But you're going about this the wrong way, Murray.'

'Let me worry about that,' Murray said.

Ruth looked from him to Harlingen and back again, measur-ing them, making up her mind. 'All right, I'll go with you,' she said, 'and for one reason only. I want to see how you handle the rest of this performance. It's been so dramatic and touching up to now I'd hate to spoil it for you.'

'It gets better as it goes along,' Murray told her.

Eighth Avenue was a rain-washed void; the side street was as barren of life and even darker. The single bright spot on it was the OOMS FOR ENT sign, which had been draped with a holly wreath, and which sent out a flickering blue track of light across the glistening sidewalk.

Murray bore down on the doorbell with a heavy thumb, not releasing it until the old man opened the door and stood there squinting at them in the dimness of the vestibule. He was dressed in long woollen underwear which gaped open between the buttons showing white hairs on a scrawny chest, and he was barefooted. 'You don't belong here,' he said. 'Ought to call the cops. Know what time it is?'

'I know what time it is,' Murray said. 'I want to talk to Helene. Tell her Arnold Lundeen sent me. Tell her to get ready for some bad news.'

He had been right when he had told Harlingen that Helene could take care of anything that came her way. She had the vocabulary – made even fouler and more violent by the way she spat out the words at Ruth, giving them meaning instead of using them as mere punctuation for what she had to say. She had the temper, so that Murray warily kept close to her, knowing that if it exploded full force somebody was going to get hurt. And she had the letters, a shoe box half full of Lundeen's letters, which, in the long run, was all she needed.

They were not well written, they were full of misspellings, but they were, in their way, masterpieces of direct statement.

Baby I wish I was with you tonite because then we would . . .

Helene baby sometime I can't sleep because I think about you and what we could be doing. We could . . .

I bet you miss me plenty. I bet right now you would like me
to . . .

When this trouble is over we will make up for it plenty baby.
We will chase the old man out for 24 hrs and then we will . . .

There was nothing perverse in the letters, Murray saw.
Nothing a psychopathologist would raise an eyebrow at. Lundeen was, in fact, singularly unimaginative about his desires and
his expression of them. But even the unimaginative can provide
an impact when it is set down in the explicit language that
Lundeen used. Ruth looked at one letter too many. Then she
wildly ripped it across, ripped it again, shredded it as if that
would obliterate it completely.

Murray got an arm around Helene's waist just as her hand
caught at Ruth's hair, grasping it, pulling the head down. He
managed to force the fingers back and loosen their grip so that
Ruth staggered free, and then he found that he had a fight on
his hands. Helene was wearing only a flimsy nightgown. With
his arms locked around her he could feel the muscles bunch
under it, had to ward off the knee kicking up at him, had to
avoid the sharp white teeth trying to tear at his shoulder, his
cheek. She fought him, cursing him steadily, while the old man
stood there useless, staring at them with blank eyes and scratching his chest vacantly as he stared. It might have taken a minute
– two minutes – before the girl was wrestled into the bedroom,
the door slammed shut against her, and the key turned in the
lock.

When Murray looked around, Ruth was gone.

20

He ran through the hall calling her name, dimly aware of spectres in nightclothes who hung over the banister of the staircase above him, following him with avid eyes. Ruth was not in sight on the street. He looked up and down its emptiness, his heart hammering, and then, at a guess, raced toward Eighth Avenue. Luck was on his side. He saw her half a block away on the avenue, walking rapidly, her head bent against the driving rain. He caught up with her near the corner and grabbed her arm, swinging her around to face him.

'Where do you think you're going?' he said. 'What kind of fool trick is this?'

She looked at him dazedly. Her coat was open, her dress soaked, her hair a wet tangle. 'I'm all right,' she said. 'Let me be.'

'Sure you're all right. You look like something that was fished out of the river. Come on, let's get back to the car and go home.'

'No.' She tried to pull away from him, but yielded when he would not relinquish his grip. 'Don't you understand? They always wake up when I come in late, and talk about everything. I don't want that now.'

'You mean you'd rather walk around the streets until you meet up with some hoodlums? Suppose you're not as lucky as you were back in school? They could leave you with a lot more than this to remember them by.'

He touched a finger to the scar at the corner of her mouth, and she shrank back. 'How do you know about that?' she whispered. 'Who told you.'

'Nobody told me. Or maybe you did, a dozen different ways. But what does it matter? Let's go home and settle it some other time.'

'I told you I didn't want to go home.'

'Well, where else is there to go?' he asked. Then he said with deliberate cruelty. 'How about my place? That's a thought, isn't it? We could go up there and celebrate the post-mortem with a few drinks and have a real ball. Does that sound better to you than home or the hoodlums?'

'If that's what you want.'

It was what he wanted, but not this way. Unexpectedly and shockingly she was telling him that the game was over and that it was all his, but he had the outraged feeling that her tone of indifference, her sudden, incredible surrender was somehow cheating him out of his triumph. What he had fallen in love with was a woman of flesh and blood, of fine-drawn nerves and taut fibres, a whole woman who mixed humour with anger, grace with temper. What he was being offered as a trophy was the shadow of all this. He would have to be a fool to imagine it was anything more.

In the face of that, he wondered, what was he to do? Take her to her home, and shut the door against her and temptation together for the time being? But what would happen once the door was shut? What were the chances of its ever being opened to him again? What would she feel tomorrow when she was no longer alone with him in this empty and unreal night world which was made to order for illogic?

He stood in torment, afraid to answer his own questions, knowing he had to, one way or the other, but afraid to, afraid to move this way or that, caught in the middle, hung up by the thumbs as Wykoff would say, and feeling the chill of the rain and of his own fears oozing through to his marrow. *Not even sense enough to come in out of the rain*, he thought in bleak self-mockery, and pulled Ruth, unresisting, into the shelter of a doorway. 'Did you think I meant it?' he asked her, inwardly pleading with her to say no, to solve the problem that way and let things be as they were. 'Did you really think I meant it?'

'Yes,' she answered, 'I thought you did.'

The sidewalk before them was a series of puddles, and a traffic light on the corner, a solemn robot directing non-existent traffic, turned them into pools of red and then green and then red again as Murray watched.

'All right,' he said at last, 'you wait here. I'll have the car around in a minute.'

The lobby of the St Stephen had long since been deserted by the banqueters when they entered it. A few charwomen swung mops back and forth over the marble floor and paid them no attention, Nelson behind the desk looked up from a stack of index cards he was sorting and then discreetly looked down again, and the elevator man put aside his *Daily News* and piloted them upward in tactful silence. It gave Murray the feeling, as it had on similar occasions, that a genteel conspiracy was being carried out on his behalf, but this time, unlike the others, he was annoyed by that.

In the apartment he drew off Ruth's coat and found it spongy-wet in his hands. She was probably wet to the skin, he conjectured, and wondered how to tell her to get out of her clothes and into something dry without making it sound like a ridiculous overture to seduction. He had made up his mind to follow her lead, to play the Dutch uncle as readily as the billy goat if that was what she wanted, but now he found himself faced by an idiotic impasse which made either role seem untenable. If it were anyone else but Ruth, he knew, it would be funny.

He temporized by saying, 'I guess you could stand that drink now, couldn't you? Anything special you use?'

'No,' Ruth said, 'I don't want anything. It would make me sick.' She leaned forward a little, supporting herself with a hand on the phonograph cabinet. 'There's something wrong with me. I feel cold. I'm freezing.'

He was no expert, but it didn't need an expert's eye to see that there was something very wrong with her. Her skin was taking on a leaden pallor, her lips turning a deathly blue under it, and she was shuddering fitfully, trying to fight against it with her eyes closed and her teeth clenched, but not succeeding. 'I'm so cold,' she gasped, and when he got an arm around her, her weight sagging against him, he could hear her teeth chattering. 'Oh, God, I'm so cold.'

The tab of the zipper at the back of her dress was lost somewhere under a fold of the collar. He fumbled for it with fingers as numb as if they had been anaesthetized, cursing it and every other maddening device like it, and finally managed to rip it down its full length, pulling the dress from her as it fell apart to the hem, pulling off her sodden shoes almost with the same motion of his hand. Half-dragging, half-carrying her, he got her into the bath room, Shoved open the door of the stall shower, and turned on the hot-water tap full force. The water jetted down in a blast of steam. He felt the scalding pain of it on his arm from a remote distance, turned on cold water to lessen the heat, and pushed Ruth under the shower, holding her there, supporting her with one hand, forcing her head down with the other, while the steaming spray drenched him blindingly.

It was rough treatment, but effective. When he finally turned the water off and released her she leaned back weakly against the wall of the shower, but with fatigue and not sickness now, her chest heaving, her skin no longer that terrifying ashen grey, but coloured by the glow of returning warmth. Like that, her hair in dark, dripping strands, her brassière and step-ins plastered wetly to her body, her stockings held by some kind of garter-belt contrivance which drew taut lines against the milky-white flesh of her thighs, she was far more disturbing to Murray than he had bargained for. Far more disturbing, he surmised, than if she were naked and ready for his embrace. And wasn't she herself aware of that?

Apparently not. Because when he said brusquely, 'How do you feel now?' she made a wry face, obviously ashamed of her weakness, and just as obviously not concerned with the appearance she made before him. 'Better,' she said. 'Almost human.'

'Should I call the doctor? There's one right downstairs.'

'No, I really am better. Just a little weak in the knees, that's all.'

Her lips quirked in a pale smile. 'You must think I'm pretty much of a mess, don't you?'

He had no intention of yielding to the smile. 'Maybe I do,' he said, and turned away from her stricken face to take a bath sheet from its rack and hand it to her. 'I guess you can be left to yourself now. Get out of those things and wrap up in this while I dig up something for you to wear. I'll wait for you inside.'

He left her holding the bath sheet, looking after him with a clouded expression, and the expression was with him when he went into the bedroom and pulled off his own soaking-wet shirt and undershirt. Well, what did she expect him to do, he asked of the Unseen. Take her then and there? Make a martyr out of her on the spot, so that she could get it over with, once and for all? He swept the litter of telephone messages from the bed, crushing them in his fist and flinging them aside, and then dragged the bedspread loose and dried himself with it, rubbing his back and chest hard until he struck a painful spot in the ribs. In the mirror it showed as a beautifully drawn bruise, the exact shape of Caxton's heel, and the sight of it added more fuel to the fire Murray felt kindling in him. It was a dangerous fire, he knew, recognizing the symptoms of roaring temper unleashed by a host of grievances, and he revelled in it, stoking it furiously, feeling it engulf him and make him godlike.

In the living room there was another fire to attend to. She was going to get the royal treatment, no less. Glowing embers to poke at prettily, soft music for the nerves and hard drink for the blood, and never let it he said that Kirk didn't know how to rig up a production when it was called for. He scraped aside the residue of ashes and charred wood from the centre of the fireplace, using a convenient log for the purpose, but when he straightened up from his labours the leering face of Frank Conmy was there, watching from the shadows, and the ghosts of women Frank had known in his virile years, women as doll-faced as Mona Dowd, coy and languorous, waiting for the inevitable before the hissing flames, and the shade of Didi sprawled there snoring unmusically – the whole crew on hand for the performance when Ruth would walk in, a virgin for the immolation, the altar ready, the priest armed.

With all the strength he could summon up he hurled the log into the fireplace. It drove into the ashes, whirling them up in a gust of powder around him, smashed into brick and mortar with the explosive crash of cannon fire, rebounded into the fire screen, knocking it over with a great, resounding clatter. The room was full of noise – shattering, deafening, soul-satisfying noise – and then out of its last echoes he heard Ruth's voice behind him. 'What happened? What's wrong?'

He wheeled to face her. She had the huge towel wrapped tight around her from shoulders to knees and was clutching it to her breast with both hands, a smaller towel was wound around her hair in a turban, and her eyes were wide with alarm. She was the most unbelievably vulnerable thing he had ever seen in his life – the doe ready for the taking, and yet dead and gone forever once you've taken it – and the realization triggered the full explosion in him.

'Wrong!' he said hoarsely. 'God Almighty, you ask me that? It's you! You're what's wrong!'

'What are you so angry about?' Ruth said in bewilderment. 'All I meant—'

He cut her short with a furious gesture. 'You think you're not wrong? You think I can find it in me to blame Arnold for that girl? The hell I can. I pity him. I've never even been near him, and if I was I'd hate his lying face on sight, but, Jesus, how I pity him for what you've been putting him through! A big, healthy animal like that stuck on the Snow Maiden. That's the picture, isn't it? Well, isn't it?'

'I don't know,' Ruth said desperately. 'I don't understand why you're acting like this. You're being irrational.'

'Oh, no, I'm not. I'm being so rational that it hurts. I'm cutting right down to where it bleeds, because this is going to be settled here and now. Tell me something. You've never in your life let any man handle you, have you? Not even Arnold.'

She looked at him stunned. 'Am I supposed to be ashamed of that?'

'No, it can be a policy with a lot of merit to it. But what made you change your mind about it? You knew what your coming up here meant. Why did you do it?'

'I wanted to.'

'You wanted to,' Murray said scornfully. 'Isn't that a wonderful break for me? All I do is say the word, and everything that's been coming to Arnold all these years is mine to collect. But why not? I'm smarter than Arnold, no matter how you look at it. He never did understand why you were the Snow Maiden, did he? No, like any ignorant character out of the gutter he thought that's the way a woman is when she's a well-bred, high-toned intellectual. She's purer, somehow. Her glands don't function like ordinary people's. Maybe after she's married she'll warm up – you can hope for that, anyhow – but until then all you can do is hang around and admire her and keep other men away.

'That was what you used him for, wasn't it? You had the horrors after what happened in that school basement, you had a permanent case of nerves worked up over it, but Arnold made it easy to live with. He didn't make any demands on you himself, because he was so damn awe-struck by your fine ways, and he was a living guarantee that no other man would make demands either. He even made it easy for you to lie to yourself about it. After all, he was the one who saved you, you owed him something, so what better way to pay him off than with the kind of loyalty you can use as a chastity belt? Isn't that what it amounts to? Isn't that the God's honest truth about that ring you're wearing?'

He was shouting now, advancing on her as his voice lashed at her, but she made no move to retreat. She seemed rooted to the spot, staring at him as if he were a golem approaching her, menacing and inescapable. It was only when he grasped her arms that she reacted, and, unwilling to release her hold on the towel, she strained away from him, her face anguished, her body arching back so that if he had suddenly let go his hold she would have fallen.

'It's not true!' she gasped. 'It's not true!'

'Stop lying to yourself! It is true! You know it is!' He shook her hard as she moved her head back and forth in blind denial, and the turban knotted around her hair loosened and fell to the floor, the hair tumbling to her shoulders. Holding her like that, seeing her like that, he had an overwhelming sense of *déjà vu*, of having lived through this before in some obscene, almost forgotten dream, until he remembered that the first time he had seen Helene it was like this, her hair spread wet on her shoulders, her body half-revealed by the towel wrapped around it, and knew that the mastery over Lundeen, over Ruth Vincent, over Fate he had felt then was far away now. Out of hand. Gone. 'It is true!' he pleaded in his agony to recapture it. 'Tell me it is!'

'If that's what you want me to say, yes! Now let me go. Please, let me go. You're hurting me.'

He shook her again as she writhed in his grip. 'Don't make it sound as if I'm putting words in your mouth. Say it so that I know you mean it.'

'Yes,' she cried out, 'I do mean it,' and then she crumpled, the high defiance ebbing from her as he held her pinned against the wall. 'Why does it matter so much to you?' she asked piteously. 'It's all changed now. Don't you know that it is?'

He said: 'All I know is that you've picked me to be a cure for hurt pride, some kind of medicine to help get Arnold out of your system. But why me? You made it plain enough in front of

Ralph Harlingen what you thought about me and my business. It's a dirty business, you said, and it makes dirty people. All right, I'll buy that. But in that case aren't you moving down too far below your class? Aren't you doing me too much of a favour, considering what I am?'

'The way you say that—' Ruth looked at him wonderingly. 'You don't hear yourself, do you? You mean it to be sarcasm, but it isn't. You really believe it. You're defensive about it.'

'The hell I am. You're defensive when you've been pushed into a spot you can't get out of, and you want to rationalize it. Nobody pushed me into this spot. I walked into it for a good reason, and with my eyes wide open. The day my father—'

He was cut off in mid-sentence by the telephone. It rang St Stephen fashion, a brief, warning tinkle, followed by a long pause. Then it tinkled again, making a small, eerie sound in the hardbreathing silence of the room.

There is not and never will be any escape from the telephone, Murray thought, and turned toward the bedroom. 'It must be your people,' he said. 'What do I tell them?'

'I don't care.'

But it wasn't her people. It was Nelson calling from the desk downstairs, and his voice was a fine blend of unction and polite distaste. 'Mr Kirk, you understand how much I dislike registering a complaint but the tenants of the apartment next to yours – that's Admiral and Mrs Johnson – after all—'

Murray slammed down the phone and waited, daring it to ring again. Ruth had followed him into the bedroom, and he said, 'It wasn't for you.'

'I know,' she said, dismissing it. She sat down on the edge of the bed and looked up at him. 'What were you going to tell me about your father?'

'Nothing.' The clock on the night table said five, he was numb with fatigue, physically and emotionally, and the last thing in the world he wanted to talk about now was his father.

'I want to hear,' Ruth said. And then she said surprisingly, 'I have a right to hear.'

Maybe she had at that, Murray thought, trying to understand why. He took a cigarette from the pack on the dresser, and then jammed it back into the pack, sure he would find the taste of it in his mouth acrid and unpleasant. 'There's not much to hear,' he said. 'He was a well-meaning fool. He went broke and my mother died at about the same time – I was starting high school then – and those years the only job somebody like that could get was being a janitor. So that's what he was, a janitor for a tenement building in the neighbourhood there. He got a basement room and a few dollars a month for it, and I hustled packages for the women who shopped at the supermarket and had put him out of business, and that's how we got along. Sounds like something out of Dickens, doesn't it?'

'I don't know yet. What happened after that?'

'Not much. It might have been a lot worse, if it weren't for the people in the building. Mostly Puerto Ricans, the bunch of them, just landed here. They were all crazy about him, they acted as if he was Jesus Christ come to earth for them, and that made it easier to take. There was this couple – Julio and Marta Gutiérrez – with five kids of their own, and they practically brought me up. I ate with them, slept with them – the old man didn't like me sleeping down in that miserable basement room – and I guess I was about the most important member of the family, as far as they were concerned. All my father worried about was that I became a great lawyer; the eating and sleeping part didn't bother him very much. He had a whole beautiful plan worked out. I would become a great lawyer and then a great statesman like William Jennings Bryan, his pet hero, and then I would be right in position to settle all the world's problems for him. You can see what a pathetic crackpot he was.

'When I came out of the army he still had that bug, and as far as I was concerned, being a lawyer was as good as anything else, so I went through the mill and wound up clerking for a firm downtown. I won't even tell you what salary I got, but I can say that if it wasn't for Marta's cooking every night I would have been a damn hungry law clerk.

'Then one day they took the old man to hospital. It wasn't anything dramatic; he was shovelling snow in front of the building during a freeze and he got pneumonia. They took him to the city hospital and he died there a few days later. It was what happened after that that made the difference.'

He drew the cigarette from the pack again and lit it this time, and the taste was, as he had expected, bitter in his mouth. He wondered if he were coming down with something, the way he felt. The sensation of chill permeating him must have been what Ruth had gone through before.

'What was it that happened?' Ruth asked.

'It was a farce. I couldn't raise the money for a funeral, and there they were, waiting for me to take him away and bury him. I almost went crazy trying to get three hundred bucks in cash together, and in the end it was the Gutiérrez bunch and some other people in the building took care of it for me. They were all at the funeral, too. I think they loved the old man because with his weird Spanish and all he used to talk to them as if they were people, and he liked and respected them. They don't get very much of that. It'll be a long time before they do, if ever. So you can see why they would make a big thing of him.'

'Yes,' Ruth said, 'I can.'

'When I left the cemetery that day,' Murray said, 'I knew that I had had it. I went right from there to the Conmy office, where there was a job open, and a chance to make real money, and a chance to be a human being. I know it sounds funny to hear talk like this when things are so different nowadays, but it wasn't funny to me then. I never went back to that law office I was working in, and I never turned around. I went straight to where I wanted to go, and that's why I can say I'm not being defensive about it. I know why I'm here, and any time I forget why, I can always take down the dime notebook the old man used to write his poetry in and remind myself. There's no place in this world for well-meaning fools. It's tough enough when you've got brains and know how to use them.'

He watched Ruth, waiting to see how she took this, wondering if she understood the depths of his feeling about it. When she slowly shook her head his heart sank. 'No,' she said tonelessly, 'it's not like Dickens, at all. It's like Murray Kirk.'

'I'm sorry about that. Next time I tell it I'll try to work it up a little better.'

She turned this aside with a shrug. 'I must be getting home,' she said, as if there had never been any question about it in the first place. 'What do I do about clothes? My things are sopping.'

So that was that, Murray saw. The party was over, the time had come to say goodbye and not *au revoir*. He indicated the bottom drawer of the dresser where he had stored Didi's belongings. 'There's some stuff there – sweaters and skirts – and a pair of fancy mules that'll do for shoes. They're Didi's,' he said, hoping to draw some response to this, no matter how tart, 'so they'll probably fit well enough. And you can use one of my coats.'

She remained indifferent. 'All right. How long would it take to call a cab here?'

'You won't need any cab. I'll drive you home.'

'I'd rather you didn't.'

'I'd rather I did. There's a certain hard-boiled gentleman who may be taking a close interest in you.'

'I don't think so,' Ruth said.

'You mean, you don't believe so.'

'That's right. I don't believe so.'

Murray said evenly: 'And you still think I'm playing on Wykoff's side. In spite of what you saw tonight.'

'Yes.'

'What does it take to convince you?' he asked. 'Do I have to bring you the evidence against Arnold wrapped up in a pink ribbon?'

'You could never do that,' she said.

He gave up then. There was no longer any chance of penetrating the wall she had built around herself, no sense battering himself against it when every blow only seemed to reinforce it. So he drove her home in silence, her answer to him the final words spoken between them.

When he returned to the apartment the first grey light of dawn was showing at the windows. The blue dress still lay in a heap at the foot of the phonograph cabinet, the high-heeled slippers, their toes curling as they dried, near it. In the bathroom her undergarments and stockings were neatly draped over a towel rack, the newspaper he had been reading in the tub the evening before – a hundred years before – just as neatly folded on the sink.

He swept everything together into a damp bundle – underwear, stockings, dress, slippers, and newspaper – balled them together and flung them into the disposal can in the kitchenette. Then he went into the bedroom and picked up the phone.

It took Mrs Knapp a long time to answer, and when she did her voice was thick with sleep. 'Mr Kirk,' she said blurrily, 'there's nothing wrong, is there?'

'No,' Murray said, 'but I won't be getting to the office until very late. Meanwhile, I want you to assign a couple of men to keep an eye on Miss Vincent. Ruth Vincent, have you got that? It's protective service, but she's not to know anything about it. Take care of that as soon as you get in. Oh, yes, and you can close the file on Lundeen. Conmy-Kirk's finished with the case.'

'We are?' Mrs Knapp sounded puzzled. 'Then who do we charge Miss Vincent's expenses to? isn't she—'

'All I said was that Conmy-Kirk is through with the case. But I'm taking it over on my own now. Any expenses in regard to it can be charged to me. Not the office, but a personal account right here at the hotel. Just charge it all to Murray Kirk.'

Part Three
Kirk

1

Leo McKenna – and Leo would have been the first to admit that he knew as much about burglar-alarm systems as anyone in New York City – said that it could not be done. He leaned over the desk, his head close to Bruno Manfredi's, and studied the crude sketch Murray had made of the device in Wykoff's window. It was obvious at a glance that Leo did not like what he saw.

'Right off,' he said, 'I can tell you one thing. What you're showing me here is the standard photoelectric system which we don't even feature any more. It's the same in my business as in everything else today. You improve, or you go under. You give them more and better for the money, or some bastard like Hoch or Garfield moves in with a system that's got fins on it or chromium or something, and steals a customer right out from under your nose. That's why when we now get a customer who wants one hundred per cent security, and money is no object, we push our new ultrasonic system. Let me tell you, gentlemen, that is the system. Floor-to-ceiling protection, no dead spots—'

'Ah, come on,' Bruno said. 'Will you quit selling so hard, Leo. We don't want to buy a system. We only want to know if we can beat this one here.'

'I was getting to that,' Leo said. 'My professional opinion is that you can't. Not unless you have an inside man working with you. That's only my professional opinion, of course, but you know how I rate in this business.'

Murray shifted in his chair. 'But a photoelectric system can leave dead spots in the corners of the window where the beams don't reach,' he said. 'Isn't there any way of getting past them and disconnecting the alarm from inside?'

Leo looked hurt. 'I gave you my professional opinion, didn't I? What more do you want? Look—' he drew a pencil from his pocket and outlined the rectangle of a window '—you've got the eye of the beam midway up the window frame. From there the beam fans out wide right across the whole glass. At the most you've got a couple of little dead spots at the top and the bottom, and you don't even know how big they are. Maybe big enough for a finger; maybe big enough for a hand. So right there you don't even know how much room you're operating in.

'But let's say you can get a hand through. You cut out the glass, you get your hand inside, and then what? I'll guarantee you won't short-circuit that system by monkeying with the eye. All you'll do is set off every alarm in the house. You see what I mean? This isn't like one of those jerk systems where the alarm goes off only if you try to raise a window, so you can clip a wire when you get the moulding off. This is the real thing. You put a finger into that beam, and it'll sound like a war starting. Naturally, that's only my professional opinion, but if twenty years in this business don't mean anything—'

'Sure it means something,' Murray said. 'How do they power this system? From the main fuse box?'

'That's right, but it has its own lead, so you can't cut it off by short-circuiting something else in the house. Gentlemen, when the underwriters certify a system as Grade "A" they take all this into account and a little more besides. Of course, my company stands behind the ultrasonic as the one and only system for the man who wants the best, but I have to admit that the photoelectric is entitled to genuine respect. I don't say this grudgingly. I've been in this business twenty years, and I always—'

When he was gone Bruno said: 'That's only his professional

opinion, of course. But my professional opinion is that he knows what he's talking about. How do you feel about it now?'

'I don't know,' Murray said. 'I'm thinking it over.'

'Thinking it over! Thinking what over? Jesus, you've got a house wired up like Fort Knox, you've got three, four hoods hanging around looking for trouble, you've got a house-breaking rap waiting if something goes wrong, and do I have to tell you something'll sure as hell go wrong? What kind of thing is that to think over?'

'Wykoff's got something I want,' Murray said. 'What do you expect me to do, tell him to mail it to me?'

'Why not? That makes just as much sense as trying to get in there and take it for yourself.'

'No, because I can take it for myself. I have a good idea how to do it, if I can count on you to help.'

'Thanks,' Bruno said. 'It isn't every day I get such a wonderful chance to get beat up and put in jail. But I wouldn't want to take advantage of you, Murray. Do somebody else the favour.'

'There's two hundred dollars' worth of favour here,' Murray said. 'Does that change your mind?'

'No.'

'All right. How much would?'

'One million dollars,' Bruno said. 'All in small, dirty bills. Or make it clean bills, if you want, and I'll dirty them myself.'

'How much?'

Bruno said seriously: 'Look, a joke is a joke, but don't push it too far. Right away it stops being funny.'

'Do you think I'm joking?'

'No, and that's what worries me. Let me put it to you straight, Murray. In all the time Frank was here he never got himself into any deal like this, and that's why he died rich and happy. If you want to go the same way, don't get any ideas in your head that can blow up this whole place along with you. You remember what Frank used to say? He used to say this agency was a business, it's got to be run like a business. But it's even a bigger business than when he was around, and maybe you're not the only one who's got an interest in it. Maybe I've got an interest in it, too. Maybe I want to protect my interest.'

'What are you talking about?' Murray said. 'What's all this about an interest? Do you mean your job?'

'No, I don't mean my job. Didn't Jack Collins get in touch with you? He was supposed to call you this week.'

'Well, he didn't. And if you're so anxious to put things to me straight, you can start with this. What's Jack Collins got to do with you and me right now?'

'That's for him to say when he calls.'

'Suppose you say it.'

'All right,' Bruno said, 'it's about him buying in here. What the hell, you can't run this place alone any more. Don't you think everybody knows that? It's built up so big now, you don't know what's going on half the time. But if you take in somebody like Jack as a partner, why, you've got one of the best men in the country with you, and you can live it up a little for yourself. He's got the cash, he's got the know-how, so put you two guys together, and you could have the biggest thing around outside of the FBI.'

'You think so?' Murray said. 'And what's your interest in this proposition? Or are you just a friend of the groom?'

'You don't have to be so snotty about it, Murray. Remember me? I knew you when you didn't have a pot. As for getting an interest, sure I'll get an interest. I've had a percentage coming to me for a long time, and this way I'll finally get it. But not from you. It comes right out of Jack's end. He knows I'm worth it, just the way Frank did and you do, but he's not afraid to give it to me.'

'That makes three partners,' Murray said. 'Are you sure there's nobody else on the waiting list?'

'As far as I'm concerned,' Bruno said, 'three is just right.'

'As far as I'm concerned,' Murray said, 'I won't even pick up that phone when Jack calls, unless I've got this Wykoff thing all cleared up.'

Bruno digested this in silence. 'I don't believe it,' he finally said. 'You'll never get another partnership offer like this as long as you live. Jack's loaded right now, and he's got money behind him, too. He'll pay whatever you want for a half share. You wouldn't throw away a deal like that, just to put the squeeze on me now. Not you.'

'You knew me when I didn't have a pot,' Murray said. 'From then to now have you ever caught me lying to you?'

He waited while Bruno stood there unhappily arguing this out with himself. And he kept his face impassive when Bruno said: 'You louse. But it's no ten-cent job. I want a thousand bucks for it, and I want the cheque before I walk out of here tonight.'

'Five hundred,' Murray said, but when Bruno stubbornly shook his head he said, 'All right, a thousand. But you'll have to work for it.'

'How?'

'First of all, get out to Staten Island and rent a car there from one of those Drive-in-Yourself places. Nothing flashy. If you can get something plain black, so much the better. Then make a couple of runs past Wykoff's house. Try it through the tunnel and Bayonne, and then try it with the ferry, and see which way you make better time. Do it around nine at night, because that's when we'll go out there. Tuesday night around nine. Wykoff should be in then, because they show the *$64,000 Question* at ten, and he'll be watching it.'

'In?' said Bruno. 'What do you want him in for?'

'Because that's how we get in. The other thing you have to do is get yourself an outfit. Some kind of high-class workman's outfit, because you'll be a repairman for Staten Island Utilities. You'll need identification cards and a receipt book, too, so have Mrs K. arrange for that at the print shop we use over on Sixth Avenue.'

'And then?'

'Then you stay away from here. If you've got anything to say, call Mrs K. at home; I'll tell her to wait in evenings just in case. Tuesday, you pick me up in front of Lüchow's restaurant at eight. If I'm not there, keep going around the block, and whatever you do, don't get yourself a ticket while you're rigged up like that.'

'Lüchow's,' Bruno said. 'The condemned man—'

'You're a cute kid,' Murray said. 'What made Jack decide to move back to New York? Did they run him out of California?'

'He's leaving before they can. This *Peephole* thing is going to bust wide open. Criminal libel and a couple of other things. Would you want to hang around and take a rap for that, if the stupid magazine loses out?'

When Bruno showed up before the restaurant Tuesday evening it was in a black Chevrolet of respectable vintage. The car swerved toward the curb, Murray jumped in, and it slid back into the cross-town traffic almost without a change in speed.

'Which way do we go?' Murray asked, and Bruno said, 'It takes about the same both ways. I figure we'll go by ferry so you can brief me while we're crossing, and we can make the run back through the tunnel in case somebody's tailing us. You can't shake anybody off when you're on a ferry. But why did I have to rent this job? What was wrong with my car?'

'Nothing, except that this one's got Staten Island plates, and yours has Queens County plates. Suppose somebody takes a look and starts wondering why a Queens car is on a repair job out in Staten Island?'

'I didn't think of that,' said Bruno.

'No, you were probably too busy fixing up Lucy with another baby. How did it feel to be home on a four-day vacation with pay?'

'All right,' Bruno said, 'and I wasn't fixing up Lucy with any babies. I was fixing up the house for Christmas. Only she made me go to church Sunday. You know how long it's been since I was in church?'

'Too long. It must have done you a lot of good.'

'If I get home in one piece from this screwball deal, I'll know it did. Otherwise—' Bruno shrugged, and then on second thought crossed himself. 'I talked to Jack long distance last night,' he said. 'He won't be calling you. He's flying in right after the holidays to talk things over. I told him it's better that way.'

'He knows where to find me,' Murray said.

'I hope so,' said Bruno.

The ferry was almost empty when they made the crossing, and the sound of it – a slow thumping of engines, a rhythmical splash of water against the hull – gave Murray the feeling that he was, for the time being, infinitely far removed from the overpowering noise and pressure of the city. That was the thing about boats, he reflected. While you were on them there was nothing you could do but mark time. And it might explain why he had the obsession to own a boat, and why he had never gotten around to buying one.

He said to Bruno: 'Here's the way we'll work it. You're on an emergency call from the utilities company, because there've been complaints about power failure in the neighbourhood. When you're in the house telling Wykoff about this, see if you can't get five or six feet down the hall opposite the French doors there. I'll keep an eye on you from outside, because there's a window looks right through those doors. If things go wrong, take off your cap and scratch your head, and I'll head back to the car, but try not to let things go wrong. Your big job is to get down to the cellar and get the fuses out of the box, so that the alarm is cut off. Then give me a count of a hundred, put everything back, and get away. Make a good front all the time, though. Give them a receipt for the call, look official, don't try anything offbeat. You have any idea how a repairman would do it?'

Bruno nodded. 'I got better than an idea. Yesterday I put the fuses in my house on the blink, so I could watch one of those guys in action. I know the routine. I'm even dressed up the way he was. Didn't you notice?'

'Now I notice. Was he wearing one of those patent-leather

bow-ties, too? I didn't even know they made those things any more.'

'What do you mean? Where I come from, a well-dressed electrician would just as soon be caught without his pants as without one of these things. It makes all the difference.'

'Not on you it doesn't. What about the identification cards and the book?'

'Right here in my pocket. I filled in some of the book to show I been on a couple of jobs. And I got a box with some tools in it on the back seat. But what happens if Wykoff calls back the utilities company while I'm there, to see if I'm on the level. Any guy who spent all his life ducking subpoenas knows all the tricks we do. How do you figure to get around that?'

'Easy. When we land at St George, pull up someplace where there's a phone and I'll show you.'

In the first available candy store Bruno leaned against the open door of the phone booth and slowly peeled the wrapper from a bar of chocolate while Murray dialled.

'Staten Island Utilities,' said the voice at the other end of the wire. It was a woman's voice, charged with efficiency. 'Emergency service. What is it?'

'Look,' said Murray plaintively, 'my name is Waggoner, and I live out here on Shore Lane in Duchess Harbour. There's something funny happening to the power around here. The street lights keep going off, and it's very annoying. Can't you people—'

'The street lights?' the woman said. 'We haven't been getting any complaints about that, sir. If there was any failure on the line it would show up here. Are you sure you aren't mistaken?'

'Of course I'm sure. I'm telling you in plain language that something's wrong with the lights around here, and I want a man out to fix them. You have my name and address, young woman. Take my word for it, I am not in the habit of playing practical jokes!'

The woman's voice now bore the weary resignation of one who has listened too often to unwarranted complaints from lunatic consumers. 'Very well, we'll send a man out as soon as possible, Mr Waggoner. It may take a little while, but he'll be there.'

'He'd better be,' Murray said, and hung up.

Bruno swallowed the last of the chocolate bar. 'You know,' he said admiringly, 'you just sounded like the most miserable crab on Staten Island. You really did, man. What that poor dame must think of this Waggoner, whoever he is—'

'He's got a house near Wykoff's,' Murray said. 'Come on. Now we move fast.'

The trip to Duchess Harbour had taken twenty minutes in Caxton's limousine. Bruno shaved that to fifteen minutes by keeping a heavy foot on the gas, and a wary eye out for stray policemen along the way. When the Chevrolet turned off the highway into the road leading to the shore Murray slipped off his overcoat and shoes, and Bruno, observing this, said, 'Now I see I really got myself into something. What are you supposed to be – Kirk of the Commandos?'

The knot which had been withstood so far tightened in Murray's stomach. It pressed up against his diaphragm, and breathing became difficult. 'That's me,' he said. 'Watch out when you get to the driveway. The garage is on this side, and there were a couple of guys hanging around it last time. Best thing is to come in around the other side, and slow down when you're near the corner of the house, so I can jump off there.'

He had the door already open as the car passed the corner of the house, and he jumped out, skidded and almost fell on ground which was icy-hard and slick under a film of frozen snow, and then regained his balance and ran, crouching low, to the side of the building. Light showed behind the lowered Venetian blind in the window there, but the window itself was a foot above his head. He braced his hands on the sill and cautiously drew himself up until he was resting on his forearms, his stockinged feet dangling free. Hanging there like that, he found that every sound around him was magnified and distorted. Everything became approaching footsteps; the wind flicking at the cuffs of his trousers was a restraining hand laid on him. It cost him an effort not to look around at the threatening unknown. Not that it would do any good to look, especially if something was there. In his position he was a perfect target – the classic sitting duck – for anything aimed his way. It was hard to gauge whether it was that chilling realization or the bitterness of the night air that was numbing him into helplessness while he strained to see through the slats of the blind.

It seemed an endless time before Bruno finally came into sight in the hall. Joe, the major-domo, was with him, shaking a doubtful head, and then Wykoff himself appeared, along with a man who might, from the looks of him, have been one of the nephews Dowd had referred to. He towered a head over Wykoff, but he had the same vulpine features, the same sulky air about him.

Bruno was apparently having a hard time of it, but was playing his hand well. His manner was one of indifference, mild puzzlement, the manner of a man who finds himself the innocent victim of a misunderstanding between a corporation and a customer. He spoke casually, shrugged, looked at his receipt book with a frown – and then Wykoff turned away from him and headed directly toward the window from which Murray dangled.

That, Murray saw, was something he hadn't taken into account. The phone was on a table not five feet from the window. When Wykoff picked it up and dialled, his back was toward Murray. But as he started to speak he slowly turned, his eyes abstractedly fixed on the wall, the window, passing over it, and for that moment he was, as far as Murray knew, looking directly through the blind into Murray's eyes. It seemed impossible that the man didn't see him. But nothing showed on Wykoff's face except interest in his phone conversation. Then slowly he turned away, nodded, replaced the phone. He must have called the utilities company, must have been satisfied by what he had been told. He gestured at Bruno, and Bruno, still magnificently unconcerned, still the man who could take a job or leave it, whichever suited the customer, followed Joe out of sight down the hall.

Murray let his feet down to the ground. To the best of his recollection there were two windows in the living room he had just been looking into, two windows in the dining room beyond it, and then there was the room with the desk in it. He counted his way along the side of the house and waited, watching the glow of light from the living-room windows and from the upstairs windows above them. In his mind's eye he saw Bruno at the head of the cellar steps, moved with him downstairs, and followed as Bruno crossed the cellar to wherever the fuse box was.

Still the lights shone from the house, the naked trees thrashed around him making warning noises, and the wind whipped at him. There was no sign that anything had happened or was going to happen to those maddening lights. Nothing to say that Bruno hadn't been lured into the cellar where he might be lying now with a bullet in him. And how was that going to be explained to Lucy and the four kids? What right did a man have to play with people's lives, because he had a furious need for a woman who wanted no part of him, anyhow?

Murray never saw the lights blink out. They might have been out for a minute or an hour; the only thing he knew was that there was blackness all around him, every window in the dim greyness of the wall towering over him was now a black patch instead of a lighted eye. He knew it must have happened while his mind was wandering, and he swore at himself for that and for precious seconds wasted.

He heaved himself up to the sill and pushed at the window frame. It slid up an inch and then stopped. He pushed harder, balancing precariously on his knees and using both hands, but either the frame was jammed or there was a safety catch holding it. If it was jammed – but there was no use thinking about that. The thing to do was try the catch first.

The outside of the sill was very narrow. It was hard finding a foothold on it after he had gotten himself up to a standing position there, and meanwhile Bruno must be well through his count of a hundred. Murray pulled the glass cutter from his pocket, ran it in a semi-circle around the point where he calculated the catch would be, and worked the glass loose from the frame. He had calculated correctly, the catch was directly above the opening he had cut. He reached in and turned it, and with one heave pushed the window up the full way.

The room was a well of darkness. He lowered himself cautiously into it, holding his breath as he passed through the invisible wall ordinarily provided by the electronic eye, half expecting the alarm to go off next to his ear. Then he was inside. He swiftly drew down the window behind him, and turned on the flashlight which was the second of the three tools he had brought along with him.

The third tool was a chisel meant to serve as a jemmy, and if the desk didn't yield to it – he couldn't keep that thought from rising in his mind – he would have no second chance. The desk was there against the wall. He tried the top drawer, hoping against hope that was unlocked, but it remained immovable. He slid the chisel into the narrow crack over the lock and struck it hard with the heel of his hand. The noise startled him. He stood there poised for a second blow, but afraid to deliver it, feeling the time running out on him lightning fast. It was the sound of voices in the distance that released him from his paralysis. Wykoff was grumbling about something; it was clear that if power wasn't restored in time for the *$64,000 Question* the Staten Island Utility Company was going to have to answer for plenty. If a lousy electric company wanted to monkey around—!

Murray struck the chisel again. It drove deep, he bore down on it, and felt the drawer give. He inched it out, saw with cold foreboding that it was empty, and tried the next drawer below it. There was a binder there with a sheaf of paper in it. He turned the light on it, saw the columns of figures headed by cryptic initials, thrust it inside his shirt, and got to the window as fast as he could. Once outside that window and with it closed behind him he could breathe again. He balanced on the sill, shoved the window down, and dropped clumsily to the ground. He was not a second too soon. Still crouching there, shaken by the fall, his foot bruised by a stone he had landed on, he saw the lights of the house go on. It was that close, he knew. Close enough to have gotten him a broken skull or worse if George Wykoff kept his ledger in the bottom drawer of his desk instead of the middle drawer. Close enough to make him even more terrified after the event than he had been during it.

All he wanted to do now was get into the waiting car and be away from there. The car was the symbol of everything that was beautiful and desirable in the world. It was a refuge on wheels. It was a way of getting as fast as possible to some place where he could lock himself in, soak up alcohol until his blood warmed up again, and look with equanimity on the fact that he had just too damn much imagination to be a really brave man.

He made his way toward the car, limping a little, one hand pressing the binder of papers to his chest. The rear door of the car was open – it took Bruno to realize that a door would have to be left open for this exigency – and he went through it, huddling out of sight on the floor there, the door left open behind him. Then Bruno came out of the house, thrusting his receipt book into his pocket, tossing the tool box on the back seat with a flourish, slamming the car door, getting into place behind the wheel, starting the motor so that Murray felt the vibration of it through him like the feeling of life beginning again.

The wheels spun on the icy road, the car lurched forward, found traction, and moved down the driveway, bouncing as it went over the small rise leading to the road away from George Wykoff. It turned into the road and Bruno stepped up its speed so that the small vibration was transformed into a gentle, swaying motion. He reached around and slapped Murray on top of the head.

'Tell me something,' he said. 'Is it true what they say about a guy's hair turning white if he's scared enough?'

2

As they emerged from the tunnel into Manhattan, Bruno said, 'Where to?' and Murray said, 'Make it your place. Wykoff might check the office and the hotel in a little while, and I don't want to be around when he does. Meanwhile, we can look over these papers, and see what they're all about.'

'If that's what you want,' said Bruno.

The Manfredis lived in a frame house that fronted on a deadend street, and whose back yard overlooked a cut of the Long Island Railroad where now and then could be heard the slow rumble of passing freight trains. The house was an old one but well kept, and a good deal of Bruno's own handiwork had gone into it. Bruno, as Murray had learned years ago when he had been drafted without warning to help lay a flagstone walk, was a devotee of the do-it-yourself school, and it was his beloved house, more than anything else, that had anchored him to New York when Collins had offered him a good job on the Coast. Which, as Frank Conmy himself had once grudgingly admitted, was a break for the agency. You didn't come by a man like Bruno every day of the week.

Lucy Manfredi was seated at the kitchen table drinking coffee when they walked in. In a pair of worn slippers, her house dress down at the hem, her hair in pin curlers, and with a newspaper propped before her against the sugar bowl she looked like an exaggerated picture of weary domesticity. She raised her eyebrows at the sight of her husband's companion.

'Well, what do you know?' she said caustically. 'Look at the great man himself. I'm surprised he even came in here when one of my ugly girl friends might jump out of the closet and grab him.' She pointed an accusing finger at Murray. 'You got a nerve, you, with that kind of talk. You ought to be ashamed.'

'Me?' said Murray. 'What did I do?'

'You know. He knows, too.' Lucy turned the finger on Bruno. 'Didn't you tell me—'

Bruno sighed. 'I told you. Now let him alone, because he's already got a girl friend. And what's it your business, anyhow? Just fix up some coffee for us, and stop worrying about who's getting married to who. Or would you rather have a shot of hard stuff?' he asked Murray.

'A shot,' Murray said. 'A big one.'

He had a big one, and then another, while Lucy regarded him with unabashed interest, her elbow planted on the table, chin cupped in her hand. 'Who's the girl friend?' she asked. 'The crazy one from Texas you had here that time?'

'Maybe.'

'Maybe. Ah, you're still talking like that, Murray; you're still old Mr Careful. Say, you know what I think? I think you're turning into one of those guys who's so scared of marrying the wrong girl they never get married at all. They just dry up and get mean. You wait and see if that don't happen.'

'All right, if that's what you want, I'll wait and see.'

'You can't have any kids that way,' Lucy warned.

'That's what you think,' said Bruno. 'Look, I told you to let him alone. Now will you clear up this table so we can get some work done? And then go inside and watch television.'

Lucy deposited dishes in the sink with a clatter. 'I don't want to watch television. I got a bellyful of television. I want to sit right here in my own kitchen, and read my newspaper, and tend to my own business like I always do. *If* you don't mind.'

She plopped herself down into her chair and picked up the newspaper, defying them. Bruno said helplessly to Murray, 'If you want me to fix up a table inside—'

'Hell, no,' Murray said. 'It's all right the way it is.'

'Thank you,' said Lucy from behind the newspaper.

Murray laid the binder on the table. The sheets of paper it enclosed were tissue thin, but even when pressed tight together they bulked as large as a good-sized volume. Bruno drew up a chair alongside Murray's, and they studied the first pages together.

'It's from this year,' Bruno said, 'but that's all I can make of it. What do you make of it?'

The pages were divided into a series of columns, each column a solid row of figures. Murray ran his finger along the horizontally ruled line at the top of a page and said, 'Some of it is easy. We'll skip this first one – 11B1 – because that's probably a code for the exact date. But then we've got $220 under *gr*, which must be the gross receipts for that day, and $140 under *nt*, which would be the net amount left after bets were paid off, and then *Immediate Cash Expenses*, which, I'd say, is incidental expenses they deducted from the net. And next we have 13E277, which is a code for something else. What we want to work out first, are these dates. Then when we hit May third and see a thousand bucks marked down we know we've got Lundeen pegged right. He probably took a lot of graft, but the only payment that means anything to this indictment is the one on May third.'

'Wait a second,' Bruno said. He peered closely at the page. 'I thought so. Somebody's got a real sense of humour in that outfit. You know what *Immediate Cash Expenses* stands for?'

'Sure. It's outlay. Whatever it cost that day to run the operation.'

'And how. You look at those initials there, friend, and you're looking at I-C-E for ice. The old payola. The graft. And right next to it here, Murray, these are shield numbers. They marked down the number of every cop who collected from them. That's what this 13E271 is. Now why should they want to go to all that trouble? What difference does it make, as long as the payoff was made?'

'A lot of difference. Every cop whose number is down here must have been a bagman, a captain's man, and his job was to collect and pass it along to the man over him. But what happens when some big shot says to Wykoff, "You missed a payment last week. How about that?" Then all Wykoff has to do is check his records here and say, "We paid one hundred bucks or whatever it was to a cop with this shield number." And they catch the double-crosser right at the source.'

'Do you mean that Lundeen—?'

'That's what I mean. Lundeen collected from Miller, all right, but he tried to keep it all himself instead of passing it on to the higher-ups. He was a marked man after that; the word must have gone out to get him as soon as anybody had a chance. And when LoScalzo grabbed Miller, that was Miller's chance.'

Bruno said with awe: 'What a beautiful set-up. What a beautiful, beautiful set-up. You get the picture? While we're sitting here with this one book in front of us, there's somebody – some guy on top of the whole organization – and he's got forty, fifty of them from all over the country to play with. Maybe a hundred! You know how much money that comes to, Murray? Jesus, you can't even figure it! And the way they run it, so whoever's in charge can put his finger right down on a page and say, "This corner in Chicago pays off so much a week, and this cop here wants so much for a cut." I mean, this is a way to operate something.'

Lucy lowered her newspaper. 'Look, lover boy,' she said. 'Don't go getting any ideas.'

'Ideas?' Bruno threw out his arms in an appeal to the heavens. 'That's fine,' he said. 'Thanks for advising me about it. Now if somebody comes along and asks me do I want to run the gambling syndicate for the whole United States I know what to tell him. Otherwise, I wouldn't know what to say. And it could happen tomorrow, couldn't it?'

'From what I'm reading in this paper,' Lucy said, 'anything could happen tomorrow.'

'Will you two quit?' Murray said. 'Look, Bruno, this date

thing doesn't make sense. Here it starts with 11B1 and figuring 11 for the month and 1 for the day you've got November first. But the series runs up to 11B38, so that's out, because no month has thirty-eight days. Right?'

'Yeah, but suppose that B is the day, and – no, that don't make sense, either. Anyhow, what've they got all these B's for? The whole page is full of them. The whole book.' Bruno flipped through some pages and then stopped short. 'Wait a minute. Here's an M. Maybe there's some others, too.'

He went through the pages more slowly. 'Sure there is. Here's S, and here's Q – what the hell, Q – and here's X. I guess that's all. Now what do we have?'

Murray checked them off on his fingers. 'B, M, Q, S, and X. Five of them. Hey, that's something. What comes in fives, boy?'

'Basketball players.'

'Boroughs,' said Murray. 'The five boroughs – Brooklyn, Manhattan, Queens, Staten Island, and X for the Bronx. How much would you want to bet on that?'

'No bet,' said Bruno. 'But that's a fine system of figuring dates you got now. If this column is all locations, it means there's no dates in the whole book, except for the year they got down on that first page.'

'My friend,' Murray said. 'Well, there's only one way to work on it. I'll take this left-hand page, and you take the right-hand page, and we'll go over them a few times to see the pattern. Then we'll switch around.'

'How about doing it tomorrow?' Bruno suggested. 'It's kind of late, and you can get cross-eyed looking at these numbers.'

'Now,' said Murray. 'And get some pencils and paper. They might help us.'

They didn't, At the end of an hour of experimentation, with dates substituted for numbers and then applied to a section of the book at random, the problem looked hopeless. 'I think the best thing to do,' said Bruno out of the middle of a yawn, 'is get this Lundeen's shield number, and then go through the whole book and hope it turns up somewhere. Maybe we'll go blind doing it that way, but this way is getting us nowhere, Murray.'

'I'm not so sure. Do you have any numbers missing from a sequence? My page runs right through from 11B1 to 11B38 but then the next number is 13B1. But where are all the 12's?'

Bruno sleepily scanned his page. 'Not here,' he reported. 'This runs from 13B2 all the way up to 21B1, but – hey, the 19's are missing!'

'You've got it cold,' Murray said. 'The 12's are out, the 19's are out, and if you look ahead you'll find the 26's are out, too. Every seventh number must be out. There's seven days in a week, but there's no work on Sunday for these bookies.'

Bruno jubilantly flipped pages again, and then clapped a hand to his forehead. 'Maybe some bookies like to work even when the horses don't run, Murray. Here's the 26's.'

Murray felt the rage mount in him. 'What the hell was Wykoff trying to do – fool the Russians?' He studied the column that Bruno indicated. 'How can that be? What's the next one missing?' Bruno scanned a series of pages. 'The 123's,' he said, and Murray saw the light in a blinding flash.

'Bruno,' he said, 'if you want to write the month and day the short way, how do you do it? Take today, December twentieth. What's the shortest way of writing that?'

'Twelve-twenty,' said Bruno, and then blinked as the light hit him, too. He snatched at the book. 'Look at this. 11B1 is one-one-Brooklyn. January first, Brooklyn. And that means January second and ninth and sixteenth and twenty-third are all out. There's no 12B, 19B, 116B, and 123B. All of them were Sundays.

But what's this number after the B stand for? This B1?'

'That's the territory in Brooklyn. It's the code number for the district, however they marked it off. But one thing is sure, they didn't manufacture maps for this. They used some kind of ordinary map, something handy for them. Maybe election districts. Something like that.'

'Yeah, but where does that leave us? I don't have any maps like that around.'

Lucy was deep in a crossword puzzle. 'There's maps in the telephone books,' she said. 'Maybe that's what you need.'

It was, although they missed on their first try, using telephone zones. Then Bruno said, 'There's this other map here of postal districts and they all have numbers, too. What's the highest number Wykoff had down for Brooklyn there?'

Murray turned pages with furious haste. 'It's B38.'

'And,' said Bruno, 'the highest number of these Brooklyn postal zones is 38.'

They looked at each other with tired approbation, and Lucy said: 'You're both so smart. If I didn't tell you about the telephone books—'

'I know,' Bruno said. 'How did I ever get along before I got married?'

Lucy smiled. 'You're both so smart.'

'Now the acid test,' Murray said. 'We've got to put down Lundeen in code and see if he's here. That was May third in Manhattan – 53M, that would be – he collected a thousand dollars graft, and his shield number—' Murray struggled to remember and found that when he closed his eyes to concentrate the only thing sharply defined for him was the pounding of a pulse in his forehead. 'I'm not sure. I think it was 32C something-or-other.'

Bruno was following this with a pencil. 'All right, so now we got 53M and from this map here Miller's district was number 19 – so we look through the records of 53M19.' He arranged his glasses on his nose and thumbed through pages of the binder, squinting at them closely. Then he stopped and looked around at Murray. 'Friend,' he said, 'meet Mr Miller and Patrolman Lundeen.'

53M19, the line read: *gr $870 nt $480 $1000 – 32C720*

The bed in the guest room had a swaybacked mattress that sounded to Murray as if it were stuffed with corn shucks – an assurance, he told himself grimly, that there would be little sleep for him this night – and after a moment's contemplation of this bleak prospect he was sound asleep. He awoke in darkness wondering where he was. Then he became aware of the metallic *clunk-clunk* of an endless freight train passing by his window, and remembered. Remembered, too, the stray thought that had prowled all through his dreams, staying just out of reach. A man. An identity. A name—

He slid out of bed, shuddering as his feet touched the floor, which was as cold as the snow-encrusted ground outside Wykoff's house, and groped around for the light. With his eyes narrowed against its glare he looked at his watch and saw that it was not quite six o'clock. He debated trying to get back to sleep, and decided against it. Now that he had that name on his mind it would be impossible, anyhow.

Wykoff's record book was on the dresser. He took it into bed with him and opened it. The name was in the book – it was the only name in the book written out fully – and while it shouldn't have meant anything to him, it did. It was signed in a fine, round hand at the end of each month's records, obviously attesting to the accuracy of the figures that preceded it. *Okay – Chas. Pirozy, CPA*, it said; the signature and pedigree of a Certified Public Accountant proud of his professional standing, and not afraid to go down on the record, as long as the record was safely locked up in Wykoff's charge. What Chas. might feel now, Murray thought, was something else again.

But it was not that thought that bothered him. It was the feeling that the name was familiar, that somewhere he had met it before, which affected him like a gnat hovering before his nose. But where? He sat with the book propped on his knees trying to match the name with someone who might have had reason to mention it to him. It had to be someone who knew Wykoff, who was close to him – Miller, Schrade, Caxton, Dowd, possibly Mona Dowd – no, it didn't seem to be any of them. He could have sworn to that.

Harlingen? Now why, Murray wondered, should the image

of Harlingen keep interposing itself. He was brooding over this when he heard a noise at the door, the sound of a fingernail tapping against it. 'Murray,' Bruno whispered, 'are you awake?'

Murray opened the door and observed that Bruno was in pyjamas and was not alone. Riding piggyback on his shoulders was the youngest and smallest Manfredi, who, also garbed in pyjamas, kept his balance by a tight grip on two upstanding tufts of his father's thinning hair. When he saw Murray he bounced up and down on Bruno's shoulders, his eyes bright with interest.

'Quit it,' Bruno commanded amiably. 'I saw your light on,' he told Murray, 'so I wondered if it was too cold in here. You need another blanket or something?'

'No, I'm all right. I was just wondering where I heard that guy's name before, that one who handled Wykoff's books. You know how it is when you start wondering about something like that. Not that it matters any.'

'I know. But wouldn't it be in Lundeen's file?'

'If it was, I'd remember it. I know that file backward and forward. Funny thing, though, it keeps reminding me of Harlingen. No, wait a second, not Harlingen – Harlingen's kid. But what would she have to do with it?'

'Well,' Bruno said, 'Harlingen said he always keeps her in touch with everything. He's afraid she'll have a nervous breakdown on him, if he doesn't. Maybe he told her, and she told you, and that's how it went.'

'I think you've got the wrong slant on Harlingen,' Murray said. 'Anyhow, let it go. It'll come to me sooner or later, if I don't bother about it.' He indicated Bruno's rider. 'Which one is this?'

'Oh, this one? This one is Vito,' said Bruno. 'He's a big boy now. Last time you saw him he was wearing diapers, but he don't wear diapers any more. That's why we go for a ride every morning this time. Isn't that so, Vito?'

Vito waved an arm behind him, pointing at something. 'No Sanny Cross,' he said querulously.

'What's that mean?' Murray asked. 'Oh, no Santa Claus. Sure there's a Santa Claus, Vito. Don't let your father hand you that stuff.'

Vito bounced up and down and pointed again. 'No Sanny Cross,' he protested stormily. 'No Sanny Cross. No Sanny Cross.'

'Ah, turn it off,' Bruno said. 'This is a real character, this one,' he told Murray. 'Saturday, I took the whole gang to the show at the Music Hall, and afterward we ate at the Automat. So while I'm down in the men's room with Vito, who walks in and lines right next to him but one of them charity Santa Clauses. You know, all done up with the white whiskers and the red suit and everything. The poor kid'll never get over it. Now, every time I take him to the john he figures to see Santa Claus there. Don't you, Vito?'

Vito was not paying attention. He leaned forward and poked a finger at Murray's face. 'Din,' he said in a melting voice. 'Din. Din.'

'What's he saying now?' Murray asked.

'Who knows?' said Bruno. 'Half the time the only ones who can make out what he's saying are the other kids, so if they're not around I'm really flying blind.' He settled Vito firmly on his shoulders. 'You ought to get back to bed before you freeze your feet. That linoleum is murder in cold weather.'

Murray shook his head. 'No, I'll get dressed and get going. This thing about Harlingen and his girl is too much on my mind, and if I get to his place before she leaves for school I can talk to them both about it. I'll leave Wykoff's book here, and what you have to do is take it to the office and have the lab run a film of it. As long as we've got a film of it put away safe, we've got Wykoff backed into the corner. I don't think he'll try any rough stuff then, what with the Treasury Department ready to give its right arm for this book. It must be worth about five hundred years in jail for the guy on income-tax evasion.'

'You don't think LoScalzo wouldn't give his right arm for it, too?' Bruno said. 'You know what it could mean to him in this investigation? Man, that bundle of paper is the hottest thing in town right how. Drop it on the floor, it'll send up a cloud like an atom bomb.'

'Well, don't drop it. Matter of fact, don't go in alone to the office. Call up Mrs K. and tell her to send a couple of men out for you, and then one of them can take that Chevvy back to Staten Island. And if you smell trouble coming, call for the cops. Don't you go being a hero. Lucy's got enough on her hands without having to take time off to visit you in the hospital.'

'That's so, isn't it?' said Bruno, and then he said awkwardly, 'You know, Murray, now that we're talking like this, I wanted to tell you something. I mean, the way I popped off about that partnership and all – well, I felt bad about it afterward. But it's such a big thing for me, Murray. What the hell, you work all your life, and then you get turned out like an old horse, and where are you? But if you've got a piece of good business you don't have to wake up in a sweat all the time, worrying about things. You see what I'm getting at, don't you? There's Vito here and three others, and maybe they got brains enough for a good education, and where's the money coming from, the way things cost today? And maybe Lucy gets sick – you know how women are when they get older – and there's operations and stuff, and that's more money. I got plenty of money troubles in the head, Murray; it's the only reason I blew up like that. With all I'm making I just can't get ahead of the game. But if you and Jack can get together—'

'I'll talk to him when he gets here,' Murray said, 'but I can't make any promises until I get his offer. If it's a case of some extra cash right now—'

Bruno shook his head. 'I don't want any handouts, Murray. I don't take handouts. All I want is a little percentage. You won't ever be sorry about it, either.'

'We'll see,' Murray said. 'Will I be able to get a cab around here this early?'

'Sure. You tell them you want to go into Manhattan they'll be glad to take you.' Bruno bumped the back of his head gently against Vito's chest. 'Uncle Murray's going away, Vito. What do you say?'

Vito pointed angrily behind him, and opened his mouth.

'Ah, don't start *that* again,' said Bruno.

3

The cab pulled up at the St Stephen a few minutes after seven, which, Murray estimated, allowed him just time enough for a quick shave and a change of clothing before he paid his visit to the Harlingens. It was going to be an interesting visit, he knew, and not for the reason he had given Bruno. What he hadn't told Bruno – after all, it was none of his business – was that Harlingen was the means by which a single page torn from Wykoff's binder would be presented to Ruth Vincent, pink ribbon or no pink ribbon. Chances were that if he tried to approach Ruth himself, he'd be left out on the sidewalk like a frustrated Romeo bellowing up to his unwilling Juliet that he had the goods on Paris, and that was not for him. He wanted no part of that. But Ruth would listen to Harlingen, and if the three of them sat down together—

When he pushed open the door of his apartment there was no mistaking the scent of perfume that hung in the stale air of the living room. Didi was asleep in the armchair there, her feet tucked under her, her coat wrapped around her. Murray stood looking down at her until she opened one eye and returned his look with disinterest. Then she yawned prodigiously, a shuddering yawn, and huddled down, wrapping the coat tighter around her.

'Well, where have you been?' she asked.

'Out,' Murray said. 'What was I doing? Nothing.'

'Nothing,' said Didi. 'Sweetie, aren't you the chivalrous one?'

She stood up with a show of anger, and then gasped and clutched the chair for support. 'Oh, God, both my legs are asleep, Murray! They're all prickles. It's killing me. Will you please do something?'

'You do something. I've got to be out of here in twenty minutes.' He walked into the bedroom, and Didi cautiously relinquished her hold on the chair and hobbled after him, groaning at every step.

'You're despicable,' she told him. 'Don't you even want to know why I'm here? Aren't you interested one little bit?' She flung herself face-down on the bed. 'Oh, God, now they're coming back to life! It's not funny, Murray. Will you please rub them and stop acting like that? I don't care if you've been in bed with that girl all night. It's medical attention I'm asking for, you utter stinker, not sexual!'

He stopped undressing and turned around to slap her legs mercilessly until she yelled and kicked out at him. 'Quit that!' she said. 'The way you let me sleep on that floor, I just got over being black and blue because of you.'

'You ought to have that set to music. Anyhow, you had it coming. That was a nice filthy crack you made to Ruth, wasn't it?'

Didi rolled over on her back and sat up to face him. She pulled her skirt primly over her knees. 'Was it? Did it hurt her feelings, poor little thing?'

'Jesus, what's gotten into you? You're acting like every woman you ever hated. You used to point them out to me and tell me what bitches they were for meddling in people's affairs just to build up their miserable egos. Now you're worse than any of them.'

'Thank you.'

'Don't thank me. Just go some place else to get it out of your system. The further away, the better. Otherwise—'

'I am going away,' Didi said, and the way she said it pulled him up short. 'That's what I came here to tell you, Murray. I wanted to say goodbye, because the plane leaves at eleven, and we probably won't be seeing each other again. I'm sure Donaldson wouldn't like it, especially since it's you.'

'Donaldson?'

'We're getting married again. It'll be in Dallas, because he wants everybody there. You might see it in *Life*; he's trying to get them to send some photographers.'

'I didn't know *Life* was interested in re-marriages,' Murray said, and Didi's face went white.

'You've got quite a filthy tongue yourself, haven't you, Murray?'

'I'm sorry,' he said, and meant it. 'I shouldn't have said that. I'm sure everything'll work out fine for both of you. After all, Donaldson's older and smarter now, and – well,' he concluded lamely, 'it ought to work out fine.'

'But you don't really believe that, do you?' said Didi. 'You don't, not really.'

'Why shouldn't I?'

'Because you're no fool, and you don't have to sound like one for my benefit, Murray. You know what's going to happen just the way I do. It'll be very nice to start with, and then, oh, in about two or three months Donaldson'll take to going away on those awfully important business trips, or coming home at four every morning, and then people will start to act all sorts of ways when I'm around – you know, so terribly kind and sympathetic, and a tiny bit amused, of course – and then the columnists will start to print those little hints with initials that don't hide anything at all, so when I pick up a paper I—'

He could not restrain himself any longer. 'Then what are you doing it for?' he demanded. 'What right do you have to let yourself in for something like that?'

'Because I have to!' she said passionately. 'I have to, Murray. I can't wait around all my life for something to happen. In no time at all I'll be thirty years old, and men don't marry you when you're that old. Don't look at me like that when I say it, Murray, it's true. You don't know what it's like when you're a woman. Even when you're twenty you start getting scared to look in the mirror, because you know how quick you get old, and there's no way of stopping it. It's the worst thing that can happen to you, and there's no way of stopping it at all.'

'But why Donaldson? Alex would be a lot better than that, money or no money.'

Didi smiled at him. Rather, the corners of her mouth twisted into what would have been a smile if there had been any humour in it. 'You think so, Murray? Suppose somebody told you that tomorrow you could have whatever else you wanted, but you'd have to give up all your money for it, would you do it? No more St Stephen, no more big car, no more anything – but everything the way you told me it was when you first came to the agency. Would you want that? And old clothes, and a sick little three-room flat with bargain-basement furniture in it. And worrying yourself to death about nickels and dimes every minute you're awake – would you really want that?'

He tried to weigh his answer, and then shook his head. 'I don't know.'

'Yes, you do. Especially when you've had it so good. That's when you never want to go back to the way it used to be. Even Donaldson is better than that. Even your agency. And you hate your agency a lot more than I hate Donaldson.'

'I never said that.'

'No, you never did, did you? You never said a lot of things. Like right now. You know damn well that right now all you have to say to me – all you have to do—'

She was silent, and he stood there rigid in the face of her silence, afraid of what was coming next, not wanting to hear her say it. But it remained unsaid. They looked at each other, the room oppressive with their unspoken thoughts, and that was it. Didi suddenly stood up, arranged her hair, pulled her dress into place. 'Well,' she said brightly, 'there's no sense saying goodbye all day, is there?'

'No.'

'But I'm real glad it was like this,' she rushed on. 'I mean, not with both of us being huffy about things. I hate it when people go off being huffy, don't you, and then they're sorry for it afterward, but it's too late to help. I left the key on the dresser there. Whatever clothes I've got here you just give away to somebody. It would be all kinds of indecent if I took them along to the wedding, wouldn't it?'

In the living room she flung the coat over her shoulders and slowly ran her hand over its sheen. 'You marry a man like Donaldson who figures to let you down with a bump,' she said with a sort of defiance, 'you'd be surprised how soft you land when you're wearing something like this. Know what I mean, sweetie?'

'Yes,' said Murray. 'I know what you mean.'

The scent of her perfume remained in the air around him when she was gone. It was, he knew, a very good and very expensive perfume called Joy.

The effect on Harlingen of the page from Wykoff's records left nothing to be desired. When he opened the door to Murray he looked in robe and slippers like a man in the pink, a man ready to go ten rounds with a tough fighter. But when, behind the closed doors of his study, the paper had been laid on his desk and explained to him figure by figure, he looked weary and beaten, a man who has just gone ten rounds with a fighter who was a little too tough. He said, 'It doesn't leave much of a case for Arnold, does it?'

'No, it doesn't.'

Harlingen pursed his lips. 'Still, if LoScalzo calls this record into evidence, he'll have to have Wykoff testify as to its authenticity. And if Wykoff decides to lie about it—'

'I'm sure he would.'

'Well, then you yourself would have to testify as to how you got possession of it. Would you want to do that?'

'No.'

'But how can you avoid doing it? It seems to me—'

Murray shook his head slowly. 'I'm not giving this to

LoScalzo,' he said. 'I never intended to. Why should I when he's got his case won without it?'

Harlingen caught the meaning of that at once. 'You mean, you're giving it to me as final proof of Arnold's guilt, is that it? It's my cue to go to LoScalzo and make a deal as soon as possible.'

'Yes,' said Murray, 'that's it. It's my impression that you're working for Lundeen because you're sure of his innocence. Now that you've got proof of his guilt, I want to see what you'll do about it. Go to court and know he'll be perjuring himself every step of the way, or make a deal with LoScalzo? It's a nice point, Ralph. If you stay in criminal law, you'll find yourself running into it again and again. And nobody's ever worked out the answer to it. Maybe you'll be the one to do it.'

'Not I,' Harlingen said, and then he looked at Murray with a curiously penetrating eye. 'As a matter of fact, Murray, I think that if anyone can come close to the answer, it'll probably be you.'

'Thanks, but you can count me out.'

'You were out, Murray,' Harlingen said pointedly. 'What made you come back in again?'

'You don't have to be coy about it,' Murray said. 'I want Ruth to see this piece of paper. I want her to know once and for all the kind of grafter and liar Lundeen is. After that, I'll consider the account settled.'

'No, you won't. After that, you'll go out and get yourself blind drunk. You'll pick up the first woman who comes along and go to bed with her and get no pleasure from it. You'll beat your head against the wall trying to get Ruth out of your mind, and you won't be able to. That's how you feel about Ruth, Murray, and we both know it. But I told you that night that you were going about it the wrong way. All you've been trying to do is tear down Arnold, blot him from sight. And all you've managed to do as far as Ruth is concerned is tear yourself down.'

Murray's hand shot out and caught the collar of Harlingen's

robe, almost dragging the man from his seat. 'Did she tell you that? Is she so blind—'

'It's too early in the morning for this sort of thing, Murray,' Harlingen said calmly, and without making a motion to free himself, waited until the hand was removed. 'She told me nothing, but she didn't have to. You see, even though she may despise Arnold for carrying on with that girl – even though she's already given him back his ring because of that – she's bound to him by a kind of loyalty that transcends personal emotions sometimes. She feels he's not guilty of the crime he's charged with, and it's that feeling she's being loyal to. And the only thing that could change it would be his own confession of guilt. Now can you see what you've been trying to fight against?'

'But it doesn't make sense! I've proven the case against him a dozen different ways!'

'You've proven nothing. You started off with a rank bias, and you've let it influence you right along. You've brought whatever was sold you, as long as it was evidence against Arnold. Miller, Schrade, Wykoff – anyone who stood against Arnold was automatically on your side. Anything you could lay your hands on, every statement made to you, this paper right here, wasn't material to be put to the test and analysed objectively, but a weapon to be used against Arnold. And the saddest part is that you've been going around with the smug assurance that you're on the side of the angels. You're proving to Ruth that you're a better man than Arnold is. You're putting another crooked cop in his place. What the hell, man, you don't even make a good cynic! You reek with self-righteousness!'

Murray felt the heat of temper roaring up in him. He fought against it, beating it down. 'Are you talking for yourself, or for Ruth?'

'I'm talking for Arnold Lundeen,' Harlingen said. 'He happens to be my client.'

'All right, then I want Ruth to speak for herself. I want her to see this piece of paper and then tell me what she thinks.'

'That can be arranged. I'll have her come here this evening, and you can be here, too. Will that be convenient for you?'

'It'll be more than convenient,' Murray said. 'It'll be a positive pleasure.'

'I don't think so.' Harlingen hesitated. 'You know, I've been meaning to call you up about something, but since you're here—'

'Yes?'

'It's about what you said that night. That is, you said Ruth might be in danger. I've been wondering—'

'You didn't have to,' Murray said. 'There's a man watching her all the time. But don't tell her about it. It's all right to keep someone under surveillance, but if they find out and turn you in, you're liable to public disorder. I'd hate to see any of my men pulled in for that, because I told you about this.'

'Well, in that case . . .' Harlingen said. He smiled. 'You know, Murray, I wish we had gotten to know each other under different circumstances. I have a feeling—'

'That's nice of you,' Murray said, and saw the smile instantly vanish from Harlingen's face. He leaned forward and pointed to the signature at the bottom of the paper on the desk. 'I've got something I wanted to ask, too. That accountant's name there – do you recognize it?'

Harlingen studied it. 'No. Am I supposed to?'

'Probably not. Is Megan out of her room yet, do you think? I'd like to ask her about it.'

'Megan? Why Megan?'

'I don't know. But I have the damnedest feeling she once talked to me about this man, and I'd like to check on it.'

'Well,' said Harlingen doubtfully, 'if that's what you want—'

Megan was at the breakfast table with her mother. She sat pale and drooping over a plate of scrambled eggs, listlessly stirring them with her fork. When she saw Murray she smiled wanly. 'Hello, Murray.'

'Hello, Megan,' said Murray. 'I missed you when I came in. How are things going?'

'Oh, all right, I guess.' Megan reversed the direction of the fork, and her mother said in a voice of restrained desperation, 'Megan, will you stop doing that, and eat. Those things must be ice-cold by now.'

'They are,' Megan said with loathing. 'They're unspeakably disgusting. I can't eat them.'

'Megan!' said her father.

Megan started to eat her eggs. 'Isn't it awful?' she said to Murray. 'I just have no appetite in the morning. I think I have a delicate stomach.'

'You have no such thing,' said Harlingen.

'I do. I think it's psychosomatic.' Megan turned toward Murray. 'Murray, when you were at the school that time did you like the play?'

'Very much.'

'Well,' Megan said eagerly, 'we're giving it Friday afternoon, because that's when the Christmas party is, and tickets are only a dollar. And it's for a disgustingly good cause – old ladies or something. You could come if you're not busy then. You could even bring somebody.' And then she said with gallant resolution, 'You could bring Mrs Donaldson. She said she liked anything to do with the theatre, didn't she?'

Murray felt an unexpected pang at that. 'Yes, but she's not in town now. And I probably will be busy then.'

'Oh.'

'I'm sorry,' Murray said. 'But even if I can't go, would you do me a favour?'

'Oh, yes.'

'Well, there's a man – Charles Pirozy – and I think you once spoke to me about him. Do you remember that?'

Megan looked blank. 'No, I don't.'

'You don't recall the name at all?'

She shook her head. 'No, I don't, Murray. Oh, yes, I do. He was on television.'

'On television? What would he be doing on television? He's an accountant.'

Megan looked up at the ceiling, her eyes glazing over. It was obviously her method of bringing memory into play. 'He *was* on television,' she said remotely, and then turned to Murray, her eyes now glowing with recollection. 'Only he wasn't exactly *on* it; they were talking about him. Remember after we got done watching Private-Eye Brannigan, that newscaster came on? He said Charles Pirozy was killed in an accident. He said a hit-run driver— What's the matter, Murray? It *is* right, isn't it? Why are you looking like that?'

The file on Lundeen was suddenly open before him, everything in it whirling down on him like the deck of cards whirling down on Alice to end her dream. A whole deck of cards, all jokers, fanning out before him while he stared at it wide-eyed and wondering, Frank's voice in his ears telling him to turn away and forget it – put it aside when there was everything to lose and nothing to gain – and other voices trying to drown that warning out, yammering at him to forget Frank Conmy, to forget all the hard lessons learned—

He saw the Harlingens watching him with bewilderment. They heard no din; it was all inside himself, and to end it he had to move one way or the other. He moved, and the voice of Frank Conmy was heard no more.

'Ralph,' he said, 'I think we've broken the case wide open. Don't tell Ruth anything about it yet. Don't tell her anything about the talk we had. I've got to run now, but I'll keep in touch with you. Just sit tight.'

The last thing he heard as he went through the door was Megan's voice raised in baffled query to her parents.

'But what did I say?' she asked.

4

(New York City, November 25) Charles Pirozy, 60, was struck by an auto late last night and dragged for two blocks before his limp body dropped from the hit-run vehicle, police believed.

Pirozy, a resident of New Rochelle, was found unconscious in East Sixty-second Street about thirty feet east of Madison Avenue at 10:10 p.m. by a passer-by.

He died in an ambulance en route to Roosevelt Hospital.

At Sixtieth Street and Madison Avenue police found a hat and gloves which were identified as belonging to the dead man.

Police said Pirozy apparently was hit by a car at that corner as he emerged from his office in the building there. He was then carried on the front of the auto to Sixty-second Street. When the car turned east into Sixty-second Street, they theorized, the body was dislodged and dropped off.

Bruno put down the newspaper clipping and picked up the police report. 'That's a great way to go,' he commented. 'What's this report say about it?'

'A lot,' Murray said, 'considering there were no eye-witnesses. The car was a last year's model, green Buick, and it was going more than forty at the moment of impact.'

'How'd they find that out?'

'Condition of the body, some paint stains on his coat that they analysed, some other little things. You can't get away with anything nowadays. Remember that, next time you aim at a pedestrian.'

'I'm like that with pedestrians,' said Bruno. 'But what's it all add up to? What makes you think the car is up in the Catskills right now?'

'Because as soon as this happened, the police were out looking for it, and a smart man would hide it out at the Acres, where nobody would think to look. You know, it's funny the way that car jumped into my mind as soon as the kid remembered about Pirozy. That is, it's funny the way the picture of *no* car came into my mind. It's like that Sherlock Holmes bit where they broke the case because the dog didn't bark. Did you ever read any Sherlock Holmes?'

'I got four kids,' Bruno said. 'When would I get time to read anything?' He walked to the window of the office and drew aside a corner of the curtain to look down at the street. 'What a life,' he said. 'Yesterday we're running like hell to get away from Wykoff. Today you call him up to wait downstairs so I'm scared to even move out of here. I wish we could go down now, and get it over with. How much longer do we have to wait, anyhow?'

'Until Rigaud calls from the Acres and says he located the car. Figuring it took him two hours to drive up there and another half-hour to hunt around, it shouldn't be long now.'

'I hope you're right,' Bruno said, his eyes still fixed on the street. 'Look at that! A cop walks right by and don't even give him a ticket. You got to be in a Caddie limousine not to get a ticket for parking like that. Now the chauffeur's getting out again to wipe the hood; that makes three times already. Say, is he the guy that flattened you?'

'He's the one.'

'Such a little guy? He must be a head shorter than you.'

'He said he used to be a fighter. I believe him.'

'Even so,' Bruno said. Then he shrugged in self-deprecation. 'Ah, what am I talking about? When I was a kid I went into the Golden Gloves once, and I only lasted until the other guy had a chance to catch up to me. He was a little guy, too, but what a monster! I'm telling you, Murray, he had hair all over him like an ape; you stick a glove into him it was like sticking it into a haystack. And all he wanted to do was kill me. I knew it right from the bell, so I—'

The telephone clicked demandingly, and Murray reached for it. 'That's Rigaud,' he said. 'Go out to the switchboard and listen in on the extension there.'

He heard Bruno pick up the receiver of the extension as Miss Whiteside's voice came lilting over the wire. 'It's your call, Mr Kirk. Mr Rigaud calling person-to-person from the Acres,' and immediately after, Rigaud's voice broke in. 'It's me, Mr Kirk, and the car's here, the way you said.'

'Where are you calling from?' Murray asked. 'Can anyone hear you?'

'No, I'm in one of the stores here in the hotel.'

'All right, what kind of car is it, and how does it look?'

'It's a green Buick sedan, last year's model. There's a wrinkle and some scrapes on the right front fender, still fresh, no rust marks yet. There's a little dent in the grille next to it, and some stains on the grille that're probably blood. And the headlight on that side is twisted off base a couple of inches. I don't think anybody's been near this job since it was put here.'

'Did you find out who put it there?'

'Yes, one of the garage hands was called down to New York to pick it up in a rush the Saturday night after Thanksgiving. He said they told him to pick it up in a garage in the city and just run it back here and put it away.'

'Who told him to do that?'

'He said it was Mr Bindlow. That's the big cheese around here.'

'Bindlow?' Murray's heart sank. 'Are you sure about that?'

'Yes, but he said the car don't belong to Mr Bindlow. He says it belongs to another one of the bosses around here. Ira Miller.' Murray's heart rebounded. It took him a second to find his voice. 'That's great, Gene. That's fine work. Now what you do is this. Get to the nearest town there – there is a town around there, isn't there?'

'Yes, about two miles away.'

'Good. Get over there and talk to the sheriff or the police chief or whatever he is. Tell him—'

Bruno's voice suddenly cut in. 'Hold it, Murray. Anybody from the Acres can buy and sell those local cops for a dime. You don't want them; you want the State Police. You hear me, Gene?'

'Sure,' said Rigaud. 'I go to the State Police, and then what? Hey, is that you, Bruno? Jeez, you ought to see this place here. It's—'

Murray said sharply, 'What is this, Old Home Week? Listen to me, Rigaud. Get the licence number of that car and then head for the nearest State Police barracks. Show them the New York police report on the accident, give them the licence number and description of the car, and tell them you want it impounded immediately. Tell them if they have any questions about it to call here and ask for Mrs Knapp. Do you have that straight?'

'I got it, Mr Kirk.'

Murray put down the phone as Bruno ambled back into the room and closed the door behind him. He looked at Murray musingly. 'Ira Miller,' he said.

'Ira Miller,' said Murray. 'That's what I meant when I was telling you about the Sherlock Holmes bit. As soon as the Harlingen girl spoke her piece I remembered there was one thing missing from your report on Miller. No car. No car at all. How likely is that for a man like Miller? Especially when he has to travel back and forth to the Acres on business every so often. The dog that didn't bark, and the car that wasn't there. You know, Frank would have liked that touch.'

'It's the only thing he would have liked about this whole case,' Bruno said. 'All right, you've got the car and you've got Miller. But Lundeen's still up the creek, and Miller's still safe on high ground. What about that?'

'Let me answer a question with a question,' Murray said. 'Do you play chequers?'

'Sure, I play chequers.'

'All right, that's what we're going to do now. Like this.'

Murray pushed three paper clips into a line on his desk. 'Here's Wykoff, here's Schrade, and here's Miller – three pieces that we're setting up. And when they're all set up we jump them – one, two, three – and take them off the board all in one shot.'

'And what happens if one of those pieces gets out of line before we're ready? What happens to us then?'

'Then—' Murray said, and drew the edge of his forefinger across his throat.

'That's what I thought,' Bruno said. 'Now I'm sorry I asked. All right, let's get it over with. It might be cold out, but every minute Wykoff's sitting there is only making him hotter.'

'No, first check with Mrs K. about Schrade. Who's watching him now?'

'It's supposed to be Leo Morrisey.'

'Then ask her when Morrisey called in last and what he reported.'

Bruno, ordinarily a slow-moving man, departed and returned with fair celerity. 'She says he called about twenty minutes ago, and Schrade is still there. Is that good?'

'Very good. Now we go to work.'

'Oh, if you knew how happy that makes me,' Bruno said.

He waited in the doorway of the building, holding the portable tape recorder, while Murray strolled a few paces along the street and stopped to look in the window of the tobacco store there. Using the window as a mirror he watched Caxton leave the car and approach him.

'Mr Kirk?' Caxton removed his cap and held it to his chest, a gesture befitting the dignified chauffeur of a dignified magnate. 'Mr Wykoff says that if you want to speak to him, would you please step into the car? It's right over there.'

'I know it is. But you tell Mr Wykoff for me that I want to speak to him right over here. Tell him he could use the fresh air.'

Obviously, it was not up to Caxton to make decisions as long as Wykoff was on the scene. He retreated to the car, and in the shop window Murray saw him talking animatedly to Wykoff. There were other reflections in the window as well, Murray noticed; the reflections of two-dollar betters passing up and down the street. Men and women of all sizes, shapes, and conditions of life, they walked by, not knowing that the man they glanced at as he was helped from his limousine – a man conservatively dressed, prepossessing, possibly an Elder Statesman – was what they had ordained with their two dollars. He had held the power of the High Justice, the Middle, and the Low over them for a long time, and they knew nothing about it and cared less.

Wykoff moved alongside Murray, and the two of them stood studying the contents of the window, the handsome pipes and exotic tobaccos which, as any passer-by could see, were their sole interest in life at the moment.

'The price,' said Wykoff. 'What's the price?'

'Cheap,' said Murray. 'No cash involved. Just a couple of favours I want you to do for me.'

Wykoff cast an admiring eye at a meerschaum. '*You* want! Who are you to tell me what you want, you son of a bitch? I want my book back. That's what I'm here for.'

'Two books,' said Murray. 'I've got a little machine upstairs that makes two out of one. One for you and one for me. Mine is in a box along with my life insurance. But I've got a surprise for you, Wykoff. If you make a deal with me now you can have both of them. I hate to say it, but your records aren't worth anything to anybody.'

'That's what you say. What kind of deal?'

'An easy one. First, I want you to drive me over to Brooklyn and wait there while I clear up some business. Then, around nine o'clock tonight, I want you to show up at Ira Miller's apartment. And I want you to bring LoScalzo along with you. That's all there is to it, and you'll get your books tonight at Miller's. It's the biggest bargain you could ask for.'

Wykoff tilted his head to read the price tag on the meerschaum. 'You call that a bargain, making trouble for Ira? Take

277

it from me, Kirk, I don't sell Ira down the river for anybody or anything. And what's this about LoScalzo. Since when do I give LoScalzo his orders? If you knew what he was like—'

'I know, but you can make up some story that'll get him there. And as far as Miller goes, you'll be there to take care of him, won't you? And it's either that, or no book, Wykoff. You're hung up by the thumbs.'

'You think so?'

'Don't stall, Wykoff. Make up your mind quick, or start wondering who gets those records first – LoScalzo or the Treasury Department.'

Wykoff turned away from the meerschaum. 'Get in the car,' he said.

'I've got someone who has to come along with me.'

'All right, both of you. What the hell do I care?' said Wykoff, but when Murray signalled Bruno out from the concealing doorway he looked momentarily surprised. Then he recovered himself. 'Oh, it's you,' he said sourly. 'How come you ain't around fixing people's fuses any more. Did you get a promotion or something?'

There were sounds emanating from behind the door of Schrade's room, the sounds of a piano badly played. When Murray knocked on the door the sounds abruptly ceased. 'Yeah?' said Schrade. 'Who is it?'

'It's Murray Kirk, Eddie. Remember, a couple of weeks ago you told me if I ever needed a little band to play at an occasion—'

The door swung open. 'Come on in, come on in,' said Schrade. 'I'm glad you're interested. If I—'

Murray pushed him back into the room, and Bruno slammed the door and stood menacingly against it. Schrade gaped at them both. 'Say, what is this? What's going on here? You better watch out with the rough stuff, because I don't like it.'

'That's too bad,' Murray said, 'because the guy who sent us

here does. But maybe you'll get used to it, Eddie. Maybe after a couple of lumps you won't even mind it.'

Schrade found it hard to swallow. 'What guy? What are you talking about?'

'What guy?' Murray turned to Bruno. 'He wants to know who sent us. You want to tell him?'

Bruno smiled grimly. 'Sure. George Wykoff sent us. Is that any surprise?'

'I don't believe you!' Schrade cried. 'You're a couple of fakers. What would Georgie want with me? What does he care about me?'

'You little double-crosser,' Murray said, 'he cares plenty. You didn't really believe that story I told you last time, did you? It was George sent me then, because he heard all about you and Miller and Pirozy, but he wanted to give you a chance to come clean. You had your chance, Eddie, and you blew it. What do you think of that?'

No one made a move toward him, but Schrade retreated until he was backed against the wall, hands extended as if to fend off oncoming disaster. 'I'm still telling you, you're both fakers. How could George know something that ain't so? You're not working for him. You got nothing to do with him. Now go away before I let out a holler and really make trouble for you. You hear me? Get out of here, both of you!'

Murray took the tape recorder from Bruno, placed it on the table, and opened it. 'Eddie, you've got one more chance coming to you. George didn't want to see it my way, but I convinced him I could get a straight story out of you. That's what I'm trying to do now. If you come clean, you're out of it altogether, and Miller has to answer for himself. Just talk into this thing, and when George hears it he'll know what side you're on. Go ahead, it won't bite you.'

Schrade looked at the recorder and seemed to gather courage. 'Who are you from?' he demanded. 'That Lundeen, isn't it? You think George Wykoff would send anybody out to make people talk into this thing? What kind of fool are you trying to make out of me?'

'Eddie,' Murray asked pleasantly, 'do you know what George Wykoff looks like?'

'Sure, I know what he looks like.'

'And Billy Caxton. Do you know him?'

'I know him, I know him. I seen him around.'

'All right, Eddie, take a look out of your window and tell me what you see around now.'

'What for? What are you trying to do now?'

'I'm trying to do you a favour, Eddie. Take a look out of that window and you'll see what I mean.'

'You think I'm so stupid?' Schrade said, but he sidled along the wall toward the window, and then cautiously turned to look out of it. He fell back with a gasp, his eyes starting out of his head, his arms flailing out blindly, and when Murray caught hold of him it was like supporting a sack of flour that had been punctured, its solidity oozing out of it in a steady stream.

'Now will you talk, Eddie?' Murray asked.

Eddie talked.

They waited in Murray's car – Murray and Harlingen – across the street from the Gothic pile where the Millers lived, and shortly before nine they saw Wykoff enter the building. A few minutes later a cab pulled up and disgorged LoScalzo. He paid the driver, pulled himself through the door the way a swollen cork is drawn from a bottle, and walked into the building. He was hatless, and his overcoat was thrown over his shoulders like a cape.

'Always the ham,' Murray said, and then as Harlingen was about to push open the car door he said, 'No, wait a minute. Let them get settled upstairs first. It'll run smoother that way.' He patted the tape recorder on his lap. 'You sure you know how to handle this thing?'

'Yes.'

'And you know how the stuff in the briefcase is arranged. It's all in order.'

'I know that,' Harlingen said. 'Look, will you stop worrying about me? I told you once that when I had something to work with I knew what to do with it. Now I've got something to work with.'

'Yes, but it won't be like any courtroom you ever saw,' Murray warned. 'There's no ground rules, nobody's presiding, nobody to appeal to. And there're three characters up there—'

Harlingen laughed. 'Let's go,' he said, 'before you convince me.'

The Valkyrie opened the apartment door, and did not seem surprised to see them there. 'Here is more,' she announced over her shoulder, and Pearl Miller behind her said, 'Oh, how nice! It's like a party, isn't it? And Ira never told me a thing about it.'

She trotted ahead of them into the living room. 'Ira, dear,' she said anxiously, 'here's more company, but you never told me anything about it, and there's nothing in the house for them. What am I going to do?'

'Do?' said Miller, and the expression on his face intrigued Murray. There was no surprise in it – of course, Wykoff would have passed along a warning about this encounter at the first opportunity – but only a polite gravity, a frowning concern at this invasion of his household. It was a look Murray recognized from his previous visit here. The look of a man who had hoped to settle down for the evening with a good book and a well-worn briar, and who finds, instead, that he must play host to some well-meaning but uninvited guests. 'There's nothing to do, Pearlie,' he said cheerfully, and patted her shoulder. 'Don't you worry about it.'

'But coffee?' Pearl Miller looked around at the assemblage in the room. 'You would like some, wouldn't you? And I do make such good coffee.' She put her finger tips to her mouth, and when her sleeve fell back Murray saw that the bandage was gone from her wrist. 'I do make good coffee, don't I, Ira?' she asked uncertainly.

'The best.' He steered her toward the door, an arm around her waist. 'Now you go in the kitchen and Hilda will help you make it. And tell her to keep the dog in there. You know George doesn't like him around.'

Through all this, LoScalzo had sat sunk in the deepest armchair in the room, his big body relaxed, his eyes veiled and watchful. In his own way, Murray surmised, LoScalzo was as good a poker player as Miller. He knew that something was going on, and he was willing to sit and study his cards with an expressionless face until he knew what. Then he would be ready to get into the game.

Harlingen walked over to the piano which stood at the far end of the room. He placed the tape recorder on the piano bench and laid the briefcase next to it. He looked, Murray thought with concern, like a college instructor warming up for a lecture. And when he introduced himself his voice had a staid professorial quality. 'And now,' he said, 'let's get down to cases. My client, Patrolman Arnold Lundeen—'

LoScalzo came to attention, 'Hold it, counsellor. I've already warned your man here—' he glowered at Murray '—against any intimidation of my witnesses, and I now repeat that warning to you. Don't let zeal get the better of you. Whatever song and dance you want to display, bring it before the bench.'

'Mr LoScalzo,' said Harlingen imperturbably, 'I have now been warned. In return, let me say that if I were to bring my information before the bench you would wind up looking like the biggest damn fool in town. To save yourself from that, let me put on my song and dance first, and reserve judgement until afterward. This whole thing will take ten minutes, and I assure you that I won't make one statement during that time which isn't backed up by evidence I will place in your hands here and now. Is that fair enough?'

He had roused LoScalzo's curiosity, Murray saw, and then wisely he did not allow LoScalzo time to put curiosity aside.

Without waiting for an answer, Harlingen drew the binder of Wykoff's records from the briefcase, and Wykoff's eyes were instantly riveted on them. 'First,' said Harlingen, 'I'd like to establish the identity of one Charles Pirozy, whose name is in these records I hold here. But because the records are confidential, I will waive showing them publicly and ask Mr Wykoff to identify the party in question. Would you do that, Mr Wykoff?'

'Sure,' said Wykoff. 'He was my accountant. A very high class person, believe me.' His fingers twitched for the binder, and Harlingen handed it to him.

'There's a copy of this, too,' Wykoff said. 'A film, it should be. Where is it?'

Harlingen looked apologetic. 'I'm afraid it's in the bottom of this bag,' he said blandly, 'but I'm sure we'll find it when we get everything else cleared up.'

Wykoff looked daggers at Murray, but Harlingen gave him no more time to enter a demurrer than he had LoScalzo. 'And now that we know who Charles Pirozy is,' he said quickly, 'let's hear some statements about him from an interested party.'

He pressed the switch on the tape recorder. There was a faint humming, and then Eddie Schrade's voice emerged loud and panicky.

'George,' it said, 'you got to be reasonable. You hear me, George? This is Eddie Schrade, and you got to listen. It was Pirozy and Ira worked that swindle on you. I swear it was. I didn't want any part of it. I even said to Ira—'

'Shut that off!' It was Ira Miller, now without the aplomb. He was on his feet shouting, his face twisted with fury. 'Where do you come off to try a trick like this? Who do you think you—'

And it was George Wykoff who restored order with a small gesture. He snapped his fingers as one would to bring a dog to attention. 'Shut up, you,' he said.

'But, George, do you mean you'd listen to that? It's not even Eddie! I know Eddie's voice, and I tell you—'

'I said to shut up. It's Eddie, and he's talking to me. Me personally, y'understand? Shut up so I can hear what he says.'

'It worked like this, George,' said Eddie Schrade's voice out of the silence that followed: 'Pirozy said Ira stood in good with you, so they could make it look like a losing book and get away with a lot of dough. Especially if Pirozy covered up for Ira. So they did it. They made it look like a lot of bets had to be paid off all the time, and they also fixed it so it looked like the cops were getting a lot of ice they weren't really getting. Then Pirozy really got his hooks in Ira, because Ira dropped such a pile on his show—'

Harlingen switched the recorder off. 'The show referred to,' he said to LoScalzo, 'was a play called *Time Out of Hand*, which had a run of four performances three years ago. Here is a copy of the *Wall Street Journal* showing the incorporation of the play company, and the amount invested by Ira Miller, the largest shareholder. It amounted to $52,000, all of which he lost. He was then in serious financial difficulties.'

He turned on the machine again. '—he would do anything to make it back. So they took you for more and more, George, but I never got a dime from it. I swear, not a dime. Not even chicken feed. You got to believe that, George. You know I'm a small-timer. What would I have to do with such big money?

'And then when Ira got scared and wanted to back out, Pirozy wouldn't let him. He said he would tell you about it, and you would kill Ira, but that he would get off, because he knew how to get around you. He would say to Ira, "I need a hundred" or "I need a couple of hundred," it didn't matter how much, and Ira always had to shell out, and then make it look like a pay-off to the cops.'

Murray's voice cut in. And Murray, hearing it, felt the curious embarrassment he always did in listening to playbacks of himself. 'How about Lundeen?' his voice asked. 'What happened to him that day, Eddie?'

'Ah, he never got a nickel from Ira, the dumb cop. It was a real arrest, strictly on the level, only Ira marked down he paid a thousand dollars to Lundeen, so he and Pirozy could split the money. Pirozy wanted the arrest, because he had to show George on the books how many cops in the district were collecting big graft, and how much ice it cost to keep operating. Only Ira didn't want to take the arrest himself, because he had too many already – you know, arrests on his record – so he paid me a couple of bucks to go out and take some bets and be the pigeon for him. He said if I wouldn't do it he'd get somebody else to run Songster for him, so what could I do?'

'But what about Lundeen? Why was he the one to be framed?'

Schrade's voice was a fine mixture of surprise and sarcasm. 'Why him? Because he was the one who came along that side of the street right then! Why else?'

Harlingen shut off the machine with finality, and LoScalzo lurched forward in his chair. 'That's interesting, counsellor,' LoScalzo said, 'but it happens to be the unsubstantiated statement of one man. What about this Pirozy? Can you produce him?'

'No,' said Harlingen, 'I can't.'

'Why not?'

Wykoff had been staring at Miller like a man watching a monster take form before him. He turned the same expression on Harlingen now. 'Sure you can't, you four-flusher,' he said coldly. 'Pirozy was killed in an auto accident a month ago. So how about that?'

'Plenty,' said Harlingen. 'Because even after the grand-jury investigation closed down your shop, Pirozy kept his hooks in Miller. He still blackmailed him regularly, and still threatened exposure to you if he failed to pay on demand. And what ended that was Pirozy's death – not by an accident, but by murder.'

'Murder?' echoed Wykoff dazedly. 'That's a terrible thing to say. It was an accident, I tell you. I know all about it.'

'You do?' said Harlingen. 'Then I've got news for you. On Thanksgiving night here in the city, Charles Pirozy was deliberately run down and killed by a car which was today impounded by the New York State Police.' He reached into the briefcase. 'Here is the original police report on the accident, so called, and here is the memorandum of a phone conversation I had with

Lieutenant Baker of the State Police confirming his action. This was not another hit-run accident. Not when the car – the murder weapon, in fact – has been identified as the property of Ira Miller.'

They looked at Miller then, LoScalzo and Wykoff did, but Miller did not reel and fall and grovel. By some magic, Murray saw, he had been restored to himself. He was once again the self-possessed Miller of yore.

'That accident happened Thanksgiving night?' he demanded of Harlingen.

'Yes.'

'Then what's this all about?' Miller said hotly. 'That whole night I was up at the Acres, and I didn't get back to the city until eight the next morning after I got a call that my wife was in bad shape. The man who gave me a lift back to town will tell you that. A thousand guests up at the Acres will tell you that. So why drag *me* into this? Why smear me with a charge that won't hold up for a minute?'

LoScalzo was evidently someone who not only hated loopholes, but also the people who clumsily left them open. 'In that case—' he said angrily to Harlingen, but Harlingen shook his head regretfully.

'I did not charge that Ira Miller drove the car that killed Pirozy,' he said. 'He did not. But there was someone else – someone whose every interest was bound up with his, who knew every facet of his life, who knew all about the hold Pirozy had on him, and, most tragically, who decided out of absolute and unquestioning love that the one way to ever break that hold was to run down and kill Charles Pirozy.'

There was a crash. Pearl Miller stood at the door, an empty tray in her hands, shattered cups and saucers at her feet, a dark stain of coffee creeping outward in the rug beneath them. Then the tray clattered to the floor, and she clapped her hands over her ears as if to shut out what she had heard and all comprehension of it.

'Ira,' she cried out, and all the agony of the ultimate betrayal was in her voice, 'you said you'd never tell! You said you'd never tell!'

And her answer was not in anything Miller said, but in the look on his face then. Whatever the man was, Murray saw, whatever he had been or would be, there would always be a place for him in Purgatory and a chance for the long climb out of it.

Ira Miller was a man completely in love with his wife.

5

Near Broadway was an Automat still open, and while Harlingen went off in search of its phone booths Murray deposited coins in various slots. He was already on his second sandwich when Harlingen returned.

'Mission accomplished,' said Harlingen, and then looked at the array of plates on the table. 'Say, you must be hungry.'

'I am. First time today I've thought of eating, thanks to your friend Arnold. What did he have to say?'

Harlingen sat down and placed his hat on the chair next to him. 'Oh, he wasn't too coherent about it, but that's natural, I guess. Just kept saying, "That's wonderful, that's wonderful," and then something about being glad to get away from those so-and-so frying pans. He's told me a few times how he hates being a short-order cook. He probably quit the job the minute he hung up the phone.'

'Why not?' said Murray. 'He's got a bright future ahead of him. No departmental trial to worry about now, all that back pay coming to him from the force, and Helene waiting. What could be sweeter?'

'Yes,' Harlingen said, 'but as far as Helene goes—'

'And you can't go any further than that.'

'You know what I mean, Murray. She put him in a very bad spot, and he knows that now. He may feel differently about her after what he went through.'

'He may, but I don't think she feels differently about him.

And a woman who's enough in love with a man can be pretty unpredictable. Any time you have doubts about that just think of Pearl Miller.'

'I'd rather not,' Harlingen said with a depth of feeling. 'God, what an experience! The way that poor soul—'

'I know. Ralph, do you intend to keep on practising criminal law?'

'Yes.'

'Then brace yourself, because you're going to see a lot of tears before you've done. That's what criminal law comes down to – women sitting in back of a courtroom and crying their hearts out for all the worthless men in their lives. In view of that, do you still feel that this is the job for you?'

'Yes, but why are you so concerned about it? What are you getting at, Murray?'

'A proposition.'

'What kind?'

'A partnership. You and me. Harlingen and Kirk, if you want it in alphabetical order.'

'A partnership?' Harlingen knit his brow trying to understand. 'But your agency – I mean, you'd be in a peculiar position, wouldn't you?'

'No, because I'm selling the agency. I've had an offer to sell a percentage of it, but I'm selling the whole works. I don't know what kind of deal it'll amount to, but under any conditions I'm walking out. And I think you and I would make a good team.'

'We might at that,' Harlingen said. And then with good-natured malice, 'Didn't you once remark that with your brains behind someone else's mellow voice—?'

Murray shook his head. 'Let me tell you something, Ralph. I got you into Ira Miller's apartment tonight, but that's all. You had no right to be there, no right to present anything in evidence there, no right to talk to those people the way you did. But you did it, and you got away with it, because, as they say around my office, you were always on top of the case. I gave you some papers and a tape, but you had to be the one to use them against that cageful of tigers. And no one could have done it better. If I didn't think so, I wouldn't have brought up this proposition in the first place. I couldn't work with someone I didn't respect.'

'I know that, Murray, and I appreciate the compliment, but there are other things to consider, aren't there? Your attitudes and mine don't always match. Wouldn't that make trouble?'

'It might. But we'll push and pull a little and manage to come up with the right answers together. That's how it is in law. Get two people doing it and you've got a partnership. Get nine people doing it, and you've got the Supreme Court. See what I mean?'

'Yes,' Harlingen said, 'I see what you mean.'

'Then is it a deal? You'll have to decide quickly, Ralph. If I sleep on this I may wake up with a different point of view, but right now, judging from the way the world looks to me, I'm your man.

'But why?' Harlingen asked. 'If you think you're going to do better financially—'

'No, I don't. In fact, I know I won't do anywhere near as well financially. But it comes down to something you said, Ralph. Do you remember telling me I didn't make a good cynic?'

'Yes.'

'Well, you were wrong. I made a damn good cynic, because it never entered my mind for one minute that Lundeen was innocent, and that's about as far as you can go in that direction. It was a blind spot in me that the agency made. It was the way Frank Conmy would have thought and felt. And I don't want to be another Frank Conmy, Ralph; it scares me to think of winding up like that. The agency poisoned him with suspicion of everybody and everything in this world, and I can't let that happen to me. But it will if I stay with the agency. You understand what I'm saying, don't you? You're the kind of person who should. That's why I'm telling you that if you say the word I'm your man.'

'Let's use the word partner, instead,' said Harlingen. 'It's got a nice ring to it.'

When Murray broke the news to Mrs Knapp the next afternoon she took it with surprising calm.

'Well, I'm sure you know what you're doing, Mr Kirk,' she said. 'And, of course, Mr Collins will be a very good man to have in charge. Mr Conmy always thought highly of him while he was here. And I understand that he's done very well on the Coast, too. When will you be leaving?'

Then Murray realized that to her there never really was a Frank Conmy, a Murray Kirk, a Jack Collins. There was only an Agency, and its undisturbed efficiency was all that mattered. So doth efficiency, he mused, blight a soul.

'I don't know,' he answered. 'Collins will be coming in next week, but then there're papers to be drawn up and so on. It may take a month or so. Why?'

'Because there are a great many details to attend to, Mr Kirk. There's this business of the nun, for instance, I don't—'

'Nun? What nun?'

'She came here from St Alonsus Hospital this morning, and a man with her had a whole load of records to be microfilmed. She had a letter from you that says it's to be done free, but if we tie up the machine for that—'

'Then we'll buy them their own machine, Mrs Knapp, if that's the only other way out of it. If you get delivery on it next week it'll make a nice Christmas present.'

'It'll make a very expensive Christmas present. And there's a great deal of correspondence on your desk, Mr Kirk. Would you mind taking care of it before you go home for the day?'

'I'll do that. Meanwhile, Mrs Knapp, have one of the men get some big, empty boxes from the lab – you know, those cartons that the photographic paper comes in – and tell him to bring it to my office. And there's a list of more or less newsworthy clients you had made up when that man from *Peephole Magazine* was here. I'd like that, too.'

'Why?' asked Mrs Knapp.

It was the first time she had ever questioned one of his instructions. He was, he saw, no longer on top of the case.

'Because I'm in the mood for it,' he said shortly. 'So let's get with it, Mrs Knapp.'

It was slow work checking the files against the names on the list. When he was finished with the job and had two boxes well laden he called downstairs to McGuire, the building manager, and learned that the building had no furnace. Never did have, in fact.

'No, sir,' McGuire said, 'we pipe in our heat from the New York Steam Company, Mr Kirk. I'm surprised you didn't know that.' From his tone he was clearly gratified that there was something that he could instruct a tenant on. 'If you want to get rid of that stuff, best thing to do is find some place with an incinerator. Or send it down here, and we'll give it to the disposal man when he comes around.'

'Thanks,' Murray said, 'I'll find an incinerator.' If he had any doubts about it, the note of rising interest in McGuire's voice settled them completely. And there was always the fireplace at the St Stephen.

But as it turned out, whoever had built the fireplace hadn't allowed for the burning of such odds and ends as Murray crammed into it. The tapes sizzled and smouldered; the films sent out a smoke that shrouded the apartment in an acrid fog. It was only when all the windows had been drawn up and the door opened and held in place by a book that a proper draught swept up the chimney. Then Murray squatted down before the fire and fed handfuls into it, blotting out vain regrets as he did so.

Near the bottom of the load was a set of photographs, and one of them caught his eye. It showed in excellent detail the wife of a hapless polo player and the muscular young man who was her interest of that month caught by the photo flash during a moment best veiled in darkness. Murray studied the picture with interest, marvelling at the way a woman could wear – even though otherwise unclad – a look of total insouciance at such a disastrous time. Her lover, on the other hand—

'Fifty artistic poses, fifty,' said Ruth at his shoulder, and he looked up at her dumbfounded as she stood there, the same Ruth who had stood there a week, a lifetime before, yet somehow different. Then he scrambled to his feet, realized with angry embarrassment that he was still holding the picture, and pitched it into the fire.

'I'm sorry,' Ruth said. 'I knocked, but you were so busy that you didn't hear me, and I just walked in. I didn't know you were pasting up your album.'

'How long have you been here?'

'Long enough to have memorized the details of that picture. Who was it? Anyone I know?'

'Hardly. It isn't anyone I know, either.'

'Oh, Murray, stop looking like that. Don't you know I'm teasing? Really you can be—'

'Let's not go into that. When people walk in without invitation to insult me, it's too much. Now you tell me whether I'm teasing or not.'

'You'd better be. Murray, we had the play at school, and Ralph was there. I had a long talk with him afterward.'

'That's nice. How did the play go?'

'What difference does that make? I'm trying to tell you that I had a talk with Ralph, and he told me all about what happened. I mean, about you and Arnold, and about the partnership— Did you ever hear Ralph once he gets started? He goes on and on. I would have been here before this, if he hadn't taken so long about it.'

'Here for what?'

'Murray, listen to me. What happened that night between us – you right about me then, don't you know that? You were only wrong about one thing. What I felt then – it was the strangest feeling I ever had – was a sense of freedom. It was as if I had been chained to a shadow all those years, and then suddenly I knew it was a shadow, and I was free. That's why I came up here with you. Because I was free to do it, and I wanted to. Murray, do you understand what I'm saying? If you don't, I'll kill you.'

'That doesn't leave me much choice, does it?'

'No, and if you think that looking like a stag at bay means anything to me, you're mistaken. You can take that look off your face right now. Nobody with a sense of humour should try to look terribly hurt and noble. It doesn't become him.'

'All right,' he said gravely, 'then I'll try to be the perfect debonair host. Would you care to remove your clothing? I have a new bath towel that will—'

'And don't overdo the humour, either.' She placed a hand against his cheek and let it rest there, cold and wonderfully soothing. 'Feel that? It's from being scared. When I came up in the elevator I was scared silly. I knew what I was going to say, but I didn't know what you would say, and I was terrified. And now, even though you haven't really said anything yet, I'm not scared any more. What do you make of that?'

'Only that you're damn sure of yourself. And if you want to see why, look into that mirror there.'

He turned her so that he was standing behind her, both of them facing the mirror on the wall above the fireplace, and then, free of his own shadow at last, he put his arms tight around her, so that he could feel the warm, firm weight of her breasts on them.

Ruth let her head fall back against his shoulder and smiled at the reflection in the mirror.

'What a handsome couple,' she said.